THE DIVINE UNION

THE SECRETS OF THE SUN
BOOK 2

CLARE ARCHER

Paperback ISBN: 979-8-9871628-4-2

Hardback ISBN: 979-8-9871628-3-5

Edited by: Jade Church

Cover Art by: Hannah Sternjakob

✿ Created with Vellum

For those who feel that life on Earth just isn't enough.

Blood was supposed to be red, but everything was muted and dead on this planet—at least the little I'd seen so far. Theo's blood flowed like gleaming black paint, the darkness robbing him of the appearance of vitality. I counted each drop, the sound magnified in the painfully quiet space.

Kane had brought me to my new room as soon as we'd arrived, and Theo's was right next door. His snarky and intimidating cronies had followed closely behind him, making sure I didn't do anything to upset their future king.

Don't touch me!

I shivered thinking about how he had snapped at me, but we had all lost a lot that day.

Despite whatever he felt toward me, he still managed to make sure I was comfortable, instructing me to come down for food whenever I was ready and that he'd give me my space until then.

It was unclear how much time had passed, it felt as if it was at least twenty-four hours, but the sun had made no appearance, and it seemed unlikely to do so given the time that had passed. I sat in the same spot I'd occupied for hours and continued to follow the directions of a Varjun healer in bleeding Theo to rid any ill effects of dark magic the Guardians might have inflicted on him. Others had tried to relieve me of his caretaking, but I sent them away, desperate to be there in case he woke so I could tell him what happened. I especially wanted to know what he had done that had seemed to affect the Guardians.

But he still hadn't woken. I cleaned his sallow, pale skin and simply thanked the universe that he was still alive. I would do whatever I needed to ensure he stayed that way.

The absence of the sun made everything more unbearable. I always felt a connection to grandpa Amrel when the tickling warmth of the sun's emissions seeped through me. Now I felt chilled to the bone, lost and frightened. Sitting in the darkness, I had nothing but time to think and fester. Flashbacks of Adelram's death and Theo's attack, relentlessly on repeat.

My situation was even worse since I was stuck wearing my white Hvala dress, which was soiled and ruined. The dress that had once made me feel on top of the world and had made Theo swoon at the sight of me now felt like a cruel mockery of the hopes we'd had a day ago.

I was also worried about Meili and Vish's safety. There was no way for me to contact them, and I figured that Varjutus would be the last place they'd look for me, perhaps other than the Void—the wasteland planet of Eredet galaxy.

One unwelcome thought kept weaseling its way to the forefront of my mind, giving me sickening chills: Was Theo *actually* the king of the prophecy?

I had unthinkingly accepted my role as Theo's companion to save the galaxy, and he had charmed my affections. Despite his professed love for me, I knew deep down that I wasn't in love with him, but I admired and respected him. I was *resolved* to marry him because of my parents' hand in our union. *But was Kane the king I was destined to be with all along?* The strange connection I felt with him would make much more sense.

Looking down at Theo's peaceful, sleeping face filled me with conflicting emotions. Guilt. Anger. Betrayal. How could he not have told me that there were other kings in Eredet? Beyond all that, though, was the unrelenting fear that he would never wake. Closing my eyes, I could see the endearing smile that lit his face when he looked at me, and I'd do anything to see it again despite what he'd done. We would have a lot to talk about when he was well again.

I shuddered in the cold, my hand shaking as I reached to brush more dirt from Theo's face with the damp cloth I'd been given. Solis' pleasing, blistering heat had become a part of me—much like the comforting warmth of Arkansas. Varjutus was relentlessly cold so far, and it infiltrated every inch of the room I'd been trapped in, freezing me mentally and physically.

The heavy door creaked open, echoing in the empty room, stirring me out of my inner festering. Quick footsteps approached as a man cleared his throat with evident agitation.

"I'm sorry to bother you, Reina. My name is Brugan, and I'm the king's *marjordom*. I help him with whatever he needs. He asked me to bring you some clothes; this was all I could find in the castle, so it'll have to do for now. I'll make sure to get you more when I have the chance. Reina?"

The king.

It was overwhelming and unsettling that he was referring to Kane. The man I'd fought so hard to expel from my thoughts, whom I'd felt guilty for admiring so much and had such a bizarre, unexplained connection with. The aching deep in my muscles and bones cried when I finally turned around and sat up, every inch of my body screaming with defeat. I couldn't help but feel like I deserved the pain, my mounting failures unforgivable.

An impatient, slight, Varjun male with dark gray skin stood

before me, attempting but failing to appear subservient. I scoffed at the scraps of red and yellow fabric that couldn't possibly cover my body.

"Those are clothes?" I asked alarmingly, my voice strained and cracking from lack of use.

"Yes, Reina. They're the Varjun women's fashion. I'll leave them here for you. Breakfast is served in the dining hall if you'd like some sustenance."

"It's *morning*?" It was still pitch-black outside. I was holding out hope that it was just a long, never-ending day of hell or simply a nightmare I was stuck in. The nightmare possibility was still viable.

"Yes, Reina. I must be going unless you need anything else."

God forbid I keep him stuck any longer in my presence, so I silently shook my head.

As soon as he left, rushing as fast as his feet could carry him, I cleaned Theo's wound, which had already closed, and kissed his cheek, deciding it was finally time to return to the room they'd given me next to his. I stood from his simple bed, where he lay on an old linen sheet. The bed was the only furnishing in the room besides two torches with flickering flames on either side.

"I'll be back soon," I whispered, squeezing his hand in reassurance. It pained me to leave his side in case he woke alone in this unfamiliar darkness, but I had to make some plan of what to do next. Everything felt helpless at the moment, but giving up was not an option.

I entered my quarters which were as empty as I felt. Its gothic aesthetic was stunning, with dark textured and papered walls and intricate chrome molding, but it seemed as if it was stripped bare of all furniture and accents apart from the modest bed and a cushioned window bench. The room's beauty made it apparent that it was once lavishly furnished, and I could see indents on the dark carpeted floor that once housed essentials. It seemed everything in this galaxy was disappearing into nothingness, all stemming from the Guardians and their reign of terror.

Ignoring how unsettled I was, I walked to the bathroom to wash away my grime. The silver clawfoot tub had a nob, but no water poured from it when I turned it on. I also tried to magically release the water from the plumbing as I did on Solis but felt no presence of water at all.

With no other choice, I begrudgingly changed into the clothing Brugan provided without bathing and shivered. It was not at all suitable for the cold. The top was a bandeau with two straps, and the skirt was light and flowing, with a side slit that hiked to my upper thigh. The fabric was not extravagant, as if handmade and dyed, the yellow and red swirling together in a pleasant pattern. Despite its humble creation, it would be beautiful on other women. It left a gaping section of bare skin that I was *thoroughly* uncomfortable in, but this was all I had unless I wanted to stay in the wrecked white dress from the *Hvala* ball.

Brugan didn't leave me shoes, so I only had the golden heels Meili had given me for *Hvala*. The thought of her made my stomach twist into knots with worry, but I buried it deep to focus on the task at hand. I contemplated simply going barefoot, but I would only freeze even more.

The last thing I wanted to do was leave the room like this, so I sat on my bed and brooded despite knowing my small tantrum was useless. After a moment, I heard another knock on my door, and I braced myself, reluctantly opening it to the seething face of the Varjun with the dark amethyst-colored eyes who'd met us in front of the castle after we lost the *mikla.*

His eyes bulged as he bent over in laughter, any sign of irritation gone.

I was not at all amused.

"I'm sorry, seeing a Solian reduced to wearing a Varjun wardrobe is just too amazing. Let's stay like this for a moment, so I have the image etched into my brain forever." He put his hand to his chin as if in mock concentration. It annoyed me that he was striking and exquisitely dressed in a tailored midnight blue jacket over a button-down vest. His full, silken ebony hair fell to his shoulders and bounced as he taunted me.

"Is there something you *want*?" I was in no mood for any asshole sarcasm.

"Want from *you*? Absolutely not, just to enjoy this special little moment. The king sent me to ensure you wouldn't die of starvation under his watch. He told me to play nice, but we can't help who we are, can we? Get your ass up, quit your pity party, and go and eat something. We're not here to wait on you, no matter who you are, so I won't be coming back with another invitation." He started to walk away but stopped short, his black knee-high boots clacking on the stone floor as he turned back to face me. "Oh, by the way, my name is Merick, not that you asked. I'm the king's advisor, spy, and right-hand man. The *pleasure* has been all mine." His grating laugh continued down the stairs.

I earnestly hoped Kane didn't take any advice he had to give.

There seemed to be a trend with these Varjun—their nasty sarcasm matched my desire to punch most of them squarely in the face. Even the *majordom* had an air of disdain about him under his polished words. Even though I was Solian, I'd had no part of their tumultuous history, given that I'd grown up on Earth. But it was clear I would have to earn their trust if I wanted to survive here.

Taking a deep breath, I put on my glittering *Hvala* shoes and walked in the direction Merick had headed. He was already long gone, leaving me to find the hall alone.

It was eerily quiet, and my heels echoed with each step. Seeing much artwork decorating the hallway was surprising, making me realize there was little to no art in Eluroom. These people openly celebrated beauty and life, which gave me some hope for fitting in with them. Where Eluroom had magical lights illuminating their world, this castle was full of flaming torches appearing to need no magic, and the movement of the flickering shadows added some charm and life to the artwork.

Many paintings in the dark stone corridors featured lush forests and stunning foreign landscapes amongst the night sky. One that caught my eye was a painting of a glowing pond with curved trees and radiant lavender-colored leaves hanging over it. The pond appeared to have a magical quality to it, and it instantly drew me in. I stopped to admire the majesty of it, running my finger over the textured paint and wondered if it was a real place on Varjutus.

A shadow in my peripheral view disturbed my concentration, so I turned and was startled at the sight of the massive Varjun that had accompanied Merick the day I'd arrived. I had to look up to see his face, and he looked back down at me with a scowl like he wanted to crush my bones. Unlike Merick, he was dressed in leathers, as if ready for combat at any moment. I attempted to swallow, but no moisture was left in me to get down. Without a word, he pointed down the hallway, and I headed in the direction he'd suggested as he trailed silently behind me. The only sounds were my raging heartbeat thumping in my ears, our steps, and his breathing.

But after a few moments, my breath came easier, my heartbeat evened, and calm enveloped me when I began to feel the familiar buzz that I had associated with comfort and safety. It was as if Kane's presence was calling to me, welcoming me home at his side, and while I cherished that feeling, my hands continued to fidget. I wasn't scared, but nervous about this new world and dynamic. Was he still upset with me? Would things be different now that he was a king in his home world?

We went down a few flights of stone stairs, and the Varjun behind me finally took the lead into a quaint room with a mahogany wood dining room table that sat twelve people. I stopped short when I saw Kane at the head of it, looking stunning in a regally tailored and tightly fitted hunter-green blazer with a high neck. I had never seen him in anything other than the sleeveless fighting leathers he wore on Solis, and this polished king before me knocked the breath right out of me. Seeing him again after unknown hours apart knocked me out of the funk I had been in. I had the overwhelming desire to run into his arms, a place where everything always made sense…everything always felt *right*.

Merick sat to his right as Brugan served them, cementing that things were different now. I was now completely at Kane's mercy for an indefinite amount of time, and I wasn't sure how I felt about that. How long would I have to stay here? Theo and Vish told me that the Solians and Varjun were enemies for millennia, and I could only hope we could change that.

Kane's eyes slowly slid over my body, searing my flesh with heat as if I could feel his gaze as a physical thing. I was suddenly very aware of how I was dressed and how little skin was covered. I straightened my spine and quickly walked to a seat, leaving an empty one between me and Merick. The scary one sat across from him and sniggered as if he wasn't surprised by my choice to stay away from them.

"Afraid we're going to bite? Don't piss us off, and you'll be fine. By the way, *that* is Kalmali, and if you were wondering if he wants to eat you for breakfast, he does. His name, after all, means 'dispeller of darkness,' and he's not too fond of outsiders. Especially Solians." Merick started laughing after his introduction, and a rumble escaped from Kane's chest as he squinted his eyes at both of them with disapproval, making them fall quiet. I wanted to return to my room, bury my head in a dark hole, and pretend the past week hadn't happened. Make that the past year. I'd do anything to be back home in Arkansas with warm lazy days and not a care in the world in the comfort of grandpa Amrel's loving arms. But that wasn't my reality now.

Brugan set down some gruel-looking oatmeal before me. I took a bite and tried not to cringe at how horrible it was, but it didn't matter because sheer hunger compelled me to devour it. When I finished and drank my whole glass of water in a few gulps, Brugan refilled both.

"Good to know you're not above the gruel we have to eat," Merick said, his lip curled.

"I might be crazy, but I don't think I've done anything to provoke you into being an ass?" I folded my arms and glared at him. Perhaps they were testing my strength of will.

Merick tilted his head to the side and raised one brow. "We just don't trust outsiders. You'll have to earn that."

"Cyra will be treated with respect while she's with us, and my trust in her will be enough for everyone." Kane looked at Merick and Kalmali, but I could tell they weren't convinced, genuinely worried about Kane's welfare and safety. It's not something I could fault them for. In fact, it gave them a few brownie points.

Instead, Merick wiped his mouth with his napkin and changed the subject. "The ceremony is set for tomorrow in the courtyard. The people have been mourning Adelram's loss but are happy to finally have you home. It's been tense without you both here. They've been eagerly waiting for you. It's just not the same community without their king."

My brows raised in surprise. The people were *fond* of Adelram? He had grown on me a bit, and I had trusted him, but he was still an ass. I was so confused, but I noticed Kane watching me with interest, so I stopped my thoughts in case they gave me away. Kane would still be mourning his loss.

"Do we have candidates in case of an alternate outcome?" Kane's voice was calm authority, and I listened closely to figure out what they were discussing.

"Sir, that is unnecessary because it won't happen. You'll be sworn in in a week, so we must start thinking about the kingdom's future and current state."

"It's not final until tomorrow. We respect tradition. I'm still happy to talk about affairs until then. How are the food stores faring?" Kane leaned back in his chair, looking at ease.

"We got our last delivery the day you returned, so I doubt we'll receive more. We'll have to find a solution," Merick said, shaking his head, some of the gray paling in his face as if he was afraid. All three Varjun looked worried, but Merick quickly perked up and stood.

"First thing's first, however. You've been gone too long, and nothing can be done before a proper Hunt to win what I've kept safe for all these years." He petted his pocket as he wiggled his brows, and Kane's eyes came alive with genuine excitement.

"Yes!" Kalmali belted with agreement, slamming the table with his fist and making me nearly fall from my chair. They all stood readying to leave as I looked on in confusion.

"What's happening?" I finally spoke.

"What do we do with that one?" Merick pointed, not even looking in my direction.

Kane's voice was loud and even, as if he was tired of repeating himself. "Respect, Merick. And she comes with us. Always." Kane disappeared before I could get any more information out of him.

"What? Where are we going?" Being alone with my two biggest fans, I couldn't hide the panic that laced my voice.

"Nope. Not me." Kalmali shook his head before disappearing, leaving Merick, who grunted in annoyance. He wasted no time pulling me to him before driving me outside.

We appeared in a withering forest, only half of the trees still green and living. My panicked breath escaped in a cloud of white vapor, and I rubbed my arms in anxiety and an attempt to warm myself. It was frigid, and my pathetic lack of clothing didn't help.

I kept studying my surroundings to plan an escape if needed, but when I looked up, I noticed the stunning night sky, cloudless and clear with bright, colorful nebulae and stars peeking through the canopy of trees. My awe didn't last long as the need to clear my throat grew, attempting to fight off the unpleasant smell of the decaying plant life.

"Where are we? What the hell are we doing?"

"We are fighting for possession of the Lucky Pecker." Kane's hands were on his hips with pride, like his words somehow explained everything.

"I don't follow."

Merick whipped out a small wooden figurine about two inches in height, and I walked closer to inspect it.

"You've got to be joking." The Lucky Pecker looked just like its namesake. "You're playing for a small wooden penis?"

Kane put his hand to his heart and inhaled sharply. "Cyra, don't be ridiculous. It's one of the last leavings from our Night Shredder birds. They would trim the trees of our forests and keep watch over the creatures of the dark. The shavings of wood they left behind were called peckings—or peckers. This is one of the largest pieces we've ever found, bringing us immeasurable luck over the years. We fight for possession over it since the luck it gifts the bearer is immeasurable." Kane's eyes shone with an exuberance I had never seen before, and it truly hit me how out of place he was on Solis. He was clearly at home here, happy to be with his people again, causing him to glow despite his recent loss.

"None of us had possession of it since it would have been unfair with one of our brothers forced away from home for so long," Merick said, patting Kane on the back so hard I winced and rubbed away the sting, feeling the ghost of it myself.

"So you guys literally take turns carrying a small wooden penis with you at all times?"

"It's not a penis, Solian." The absurd seriousness in Kal's tone made me hold my tongue. I ran my hand over my face in disbelief. Fine, we could all blatantly pretend it wasn't a legit penis. The universe was falling apart, our enemy list was growing, and our worlds were dying, yet I was staring dumbfoundedly at the wooden pecker in these warriors' hands like it was a holy grail.

But the more I watched the three of them smile and huddle closely together, I saw they desperately needed this to reunite their friendship and work through their grief. They were so at ease with each other that they seemed more like brothers than anything else.

Kane began to unclip his fine blazer, and I choked on my spit when his chest was bare, showing off his toned strength and the slightly glowing moon and flying beast tattoo right over his heart. Kal and Merick followed his lead, and they weren't too shabby to look at either. What the hell was happening?

"It's freezing out here. Why are you guys taking your clothes off?" I bit my lip, allowing myself to live in denial that I wasn't beyond entertained right now.

"Are you insane?" Merick bit out, his forehead wrinkled in disbelief.

Yeah, sure, I was the crazy one. They stood almost naked in a freezing, decaying forest with a tiny wooden pecker.

"This is glorious weather." Kane's eyes fluttered closed, and he breathed deeply, savoring whatever he felt when he smelled his homeland. Where I smelled rot, decay, and frigid air, he smelled something dear to him. It was clear why he was always in a sleeveless vest. If this was ideal weather for him, he must have been sweltering on Solis.

"We blend in with the night. Why would we keep our tops on if we're on a stealth hunt?" Kane slowly walked closer to me, his head tilted down, looking into my depths. I had to put my hand over my heart since it felt like it was trying to jump from my chest. One side of his lips turned upward mischievously, and I nearly melted into the ground when he put his blazer over my shoulders. It was warm from his heat and smelled so much like pine and evergreens that I had to fight to keep myself from sniffing loudly.

He spoke softly and put his hands on my shoulders. "I'll make sure you're properly attired from now on so you're always as warm. I know you're not accustomed to the cold. After all, a blazing star would lose its light if it didn't have the heat of its fire."

If I weren't already shivering from the cold, I would have from his words. Without warning, they all ran away so fast that they were a blur of movement. Within seconds I couldn't see or hear any signs of life. After a few minutes, I wondered if they had driven away to another location or left me here as some cruel hazing prank until Kal zoomed into view and tackled what appeared to be nothing, but a loud grunt sounded before Merick appeared from thin air.

"Holy shit!" I jumped back in surprise at how violent and loud they were as they fisted at each other, punching, tumbling, and outmaneuvering each other until Kal finally bent Merick's elbow back and stole the freaking pecker plus a feather he was holding.

"Fuck!" Merick screamed into the sky, his muscles contorting in frustration. I assumed that meant he had lost.

"You've gone soft, Silver Tongue!" Kal's chest heaved with exertion, and he held out his hand to help Merick stand with a toothy smile.

"I just took pity on you losers since I was the last to have the pecker."

"Don't be sore because you lost, Silver Tongue."

Kane used Kal's distraction to rush out of nowhere and jump onto Kal's back, snatching the feather he had just won. Merick quickly pulled Kane off him, and they both went after Kane as a team.

"Hey! Unfair disadvantage! Stop ganging up on him!" I yelled through cupped hands. They looked back at me in shock, and Kane kicked them both off, allowing him to take Kal's feather for the win.

"Ah, victory is sweetest when it is aided by a woman!" Kane laughed, raising his hands to me in gratitude, and I couldn't help but laugh back at him.

"I call interference!" Merick whined, pinning me with a death glare and folding his arms.

Kane held out his hand, and Merick reluctantly smacked the tiny wiener into it. Kane quickly pocketed it and tapped it in triumph.

"I guess it's fitting the king gets the first stab at the Lucky Pecker," Kal reasoned with a shrug of his shoulder.

I was still smirking until Merick turned his attention to me. "If you're so smug and confident, it's your turn. I'd run fast if I were you because Kal and I don't take it easy on our prey." The maniacal look in his eye left me without a doubt of his intent.

My legs moved faster than my brain could comprehend because before I knew what was happening, I was sprinting, running into the unknown forest on this strange world of this still relatively foreign galaxy.

My stupid heels caused me to fall, skinning my hands and knees, so I quickly kicked them off and stood again to run like hell, barely feeling the dry, cracked debris covering the ground. My lungs quickly gave out, burning with defiance, so I had no choice but to stop. Why the hell hadn't I done more running in my training sessions?

I looked at the darkness surrounding me, terrified yet exhilarated by the unknown. I started to climb the nearest tree since I couldn't walk another step. The bark was rough, and I was sure my feet were bleeding, but I persevered until I was as high as I could manage. My hand brushed over the cracked bark, noticing old grooming, likely from the birds Kane mentioned before, but most of it was overgrown and unkempt since they were now extinct. My eyes fluttered shut as I breathed in the scent of the tree, which was so similar to Kane's, but there was an unmistakable hint of death in them, and I could imagine how lush and intoxicating it must have smelled when it was a thriving forest. Kane was the living embodiment of it like he was molded from his home world.

A violent shaking brought me out of my trance, and all I saw was Merick's two glowing violet eyes attached to an invisible body. I screamed at the foreign sight and tried to climb down quickly. It was clear Merick had some powers of invisibility, which made it impossible to win against, but he grabbed my hand, pulling me to him. He threw me off the tree with a maniacal laugh as I screamed in the air, attempting to drive unsuccessfully.

My fall was broken by a harsh thump, landing in the arms of a growling Kalmali, showing his slightly elongated canines in a feral smile. I screamed yet again and childishly pulled on his thin braids until he released me, and I used the opportunity to run like hell.

The forest seemed to go on forever, the massive silvery moon above providing enough light for me to maneuver the endless trees. Kal and Merick caught up and ran on either side of me as they slowly began closing the gap between us. I was so busy looking at both of them that I didn't see Kane standing firm with his arms crossed, causing me to ram into him. He picked me up and gently pinned me to the ground in one fluid movement until I was trapped. Merick and Kal's laughter faded, leaving Kane and me alone while I attempted to catch my breath and reign in the wild adrenaline.

"Checkmate," he drawled in my ear.

"I didn't take you for a chess player."

"Life is a chess match, and we're all players. We must plan our moves to survive long enough to defeat our enemy." His eyes flashed with trouble, and I slid my hands up his bare solid arms on either side of my face as he rested on his elbows.

"You have a lot more work to do if you're going to beat any of us."

I let out a mock gasp. "You mean I get to compete for the lucky penis?"

"Lucky Pecker. Get it right, or you'll be expelled from the club."

The club? It sounded as if he was immediately welcoming me

into his inner circle without question, making goosebumps erupt all over my skin. Or maybe that was the cold. Either way, I basked under the bulk of his weight, inspecting the moonlight that danced over each curve of his skin as if he was a radiant work of art.

Kalmali ruined the mood by reappearing, followed closely by Merick as his eyes widened, a vacant expression coming over him like he was seeing something far away.

"What is it, Kal?" Kane questioned. He helped me stand as my heart sank that the game was over. It may have been brutal and terrifying, but it made me feel exhilarated and alive.

"Outsiders have arrived at the castle entrance. I'll go investigate," Kal said before disappearing, and Merick wasted no time following him. Kane's mood had quickly changed, his playfulness and lightness gone. His arm was covering me as if ready to defend me against danger. I couldn't imagine being on the receiving end of that intensity, and I already missed the new, lighthearted version of him.

Kal reappeared, all signs of their previous fun gone. "Two strangers called Urien and Meili are here demanding to see the Solian."

CHAPTER TWO

"They're here?" My pulse quickened in delight and hope. Kane visibly relaxed and nodded to Kal before pulling me close and driving us back into the room we were in for breakfast. The first thing I saw was the familiar golden glow I had come to associate with friendship and loyalty.

I was unable to swallow since I was so choked with gratitude and relief. My shaking hand covered my mouth as I smiled and thanked the heavens for seeing Meili's angelic face again. Tears fell down my cheeks as I ran into her arms, and she squeezed me so tight I grunted. She was a lot stronger than she looked. It was the first time I realized that she smelled like sunlight, floral greenery, and—*life*. I desperately missed it. Yet another scent that I was starting to associate with the feeling of home.

"I was so worried about you!" Meili cried, her hands holding my wet cheeks.

"I was going out of my mind not knowing what happened to you," I echoed. My eyes scanned her whole body to check for injuries, but she was just as breathtakingly beautiful and perfect as always. I touched her golden hair and grabbed her hands, which

17

were filled with bags, and gasped when I realized who was behind her.

"I came across Mylo before I left and just couldn't leave him there. I didn't think you'd mind."

His head was down, and he shifted his weight from each foot as if he was a burden.

"I am beyond thrilled. I'm so happy you're here, Mylo." He brought his blood-pooled eyes up to meet mine, and a hint of a smile appeared on his lips.

"Urien, I'm glad to see you as well." I walked over and hugged him. "How did you two find me?"

"Meili, here, tracked me down and insisted I find you and take her with me. She is one persistent ally. I can tell you that. When Kane and Adelram didn't return to the castle, I assumed they went home and took you into hiding. Looks like I was right."

"Adelram was killed by the Guardians," Kane told Urien. I was surprised by his tone, which seemed devoid of emotion.

"I didn't know. I am sorry for your loss."

I searched Urien's face, but he seemed to say it genuinely. Maybe there was hope for an alliance between the Varjun and Solians after all.

Urien grabbed my hands. "Theo. Please, tell me he lives."

"Yes, he's alive but is still unconscious."

"Oh, thank heavens. Might I see him before I go?"

"Of course." I responded without thinking, earning a growl from Merick. My eyes slowly slid to Kane, whom I apparently now needed approval from, and he nodded.

"Do you know where Vish is?" I asked Urien and Meili.

"Eleri has given him sanctuary at the Temple of Our Creator. He's safe."

"Oh, thank goodness." I sighed with relief. "Meili, you must stay here with me. It isn't safe on Solis anymore."

"That is not your call to make, Reina." Merick's arms were folded in front of him, but at least his voice had less disdain.

Clearly, I was now in Kane's world, and I no longer made the rules. While Kane clearly wanted me at his side, his friends still needed to make sure I wouldn't betray them. I shrugged it off and half smirked at Meili, trying to put on a brave face for her. She didn't look at all convinced as she warily studied the unknown Varjun and our precarious situation.

"Meili may stay with Cyra if that is her wish. Urien, we will need to discuss matters further if you plan on staying here," Kane stepped in with authority.

"Don't worry. I'm not staying. I have too much to watch out for around Eredet, especially with Theo out for the count. I'll come to visit you often and report on my findings, Reina," Urien said, his voice cracking, trying to stay strong despite the danger of Theo and all our people.

"Does all of Solis know he's disappeared?" I asked quietly.

"The Guardians have practically been screaming it from the rooftops, calling him a traitor to Solis. They named themselves high rulers, claiming the monarchy doesn't work and cannot be trusted. The people are terrified."

Guilt was a festering acid rising within me. I was the Reina of Solis and had abandoned our people to a group of homicidal maniacs. "I can't stay here. I can't leave the people of Solis alone and frightened," I whispered. "I must go back."

"You can't!" Urien said incredulously. "They'll murder you on sight, and then how will we open the *mikla*?"

"At the risk of siding with a Solian—it's true, you must hide. The Guardians can't last long outside their own temple, so they probably wouldn't venture here themselves. Although I must hand it to you, wanting to return takes more guts than I would have given you credit for," Merick mused.

"Perhaps that's because you've prejudged me."

Merick pursed his lips together and shrugged. "I need to keep my eyes and ears around Eredet," Urien said, "and you need to stay here. The Guardians will be planning something now that the Solian rule is over." He sighed and ran his hand through his short, messy hair. "I will meet with the people and keep tabs on the Guardians' next moves. We need to be prepared. I will protect you and the hope you bring until my last breath. I won't let Solis disappear like it never existed."

"I'm so grateful for you, Urien. I'll need your reports of Solis when I can't be there myself, and trust me, I won't let that happen to Solis either. Please meet with Blaze and let me know what the commoners are up to. Will Vish be driving here anytime soon?"

He shook his head. "Not anybody can just drive between planets. Few actually can, and Vish is not one of them. I am able to, as well as the Varjun here."

I made a mental note to find a way to get to Vish and bring him to Varjutus.

"By the way, I thought Meili was insane for making me lug all this stuff with us, but thank goodness we did. What in the world are you wearing?" Urien asked in disbelief.

Meili nodded, her eyes wide with horror.

Merick and Kal crossed their arms and stepped toward Urien like they wanted to attack him.

"Will that be all, Solian?" Merick asked with mock sweetness.

"Uh, yes. I'd like to see Theo before I go?"

To Urien's chagrin, Kal trailed his arm out in invitation, his voice deep and menacing. "Follow me." Urien followed him, and I was just grateful nobody killed each other. Yet.

I turned my attention back to Meili. "Do you need something to eat?"

"No, I'm okay, Reina. Let's return to your room, and I'll fill you in on some things."

I began to stand and leave, then stopped sheepishly to look at Kane and make sure I was…dismissed.

"Merick, help them with their bags."

He rolled his eyes but didn't hesitate to pick up every item Meili had brought and winked at her as he led the way.

I stopped short and turned. "Wait, what about Mylo?"

Kane walked toward him, his eyes warming with kindness. "I will personally show him to a room that is his, and we will find something for him to do that will be entirely his choice."

My shoulders dropped in relief, my outpouring of gratitude so strong I knew Kane had felt it when he smiled at me. It hit me that Theo had looked the other way with the Voidlings while Kane easily made Mylo one of us. It should have been a red flag.

Merick began to leave, so we followed him to my room. He dropped the bags outside the door, not coming inside but nodded his head with the respect Kane kept drilling into him.

"Ladies." He left swiftly, causing the flames of two nearby wall torches to flicker, nearly snuffing them out entirely. When he was out of sight, Meili and I hugged each other tight again.

"Meili, I'm so scared, not knowing what the future holds. How are we supposed to find the *mikla* now? What if Theo never wakes?"

Water pooled in Meili's eyes as she took my hands. "When I heard what happened…" Meili shook her head, unable to finish. "Solis is suffering, Reina. We must find a way to go on together as things are."

And that was the truth of the matter. But, by no small miracle, I had Meili by my side to help me through our next steps.

We lugged the bags inside, and she began pointing to their contents. "I brought some necessities. I have my sewing machine and some fabrics. I also have some of your personal items, including your grandpa's box and *Coralin's Song* seashell. There's a bunch of other stuff in here you can look through later."

"Thank you so much, Meili. You are my guardian angel."

"And you are mine."

Our small moment of peace ended with the now-familiar, quick, pulsing knock of Brugan.

"I will show the *criada* to her room," he said haughtily, his nose firmly in the air. It seemed he didn't like someone impeding on his territory, and I covered my mouth to hide my amusement.

"I'll find you later," Meili promised, following him out with furrowed brows.

Once she left, it felt like the sunshine she beamed had been snuffed from the room. And in the constant darkness of Varjutus, I needed it more than ever.

Unsure of what to do with myself, I sat on the plush window bench to take in more of the backdrop of Varjutus. After a few moments, I realized it wasn't as dark as I'd thought, primarily because of the massive chrome-colored, glowing moon that illuminated the landscape.

Various floating specs drifted through the air like fireflies, while some of the living vegetation had some subtle glow. The mountains in the distance were dull rock formations with no plant life that I could see, and there was a vast amount of barren land that looked devoid of life and any vegetation that might have once existed there.

Dead land.

More death and emptiness. It wasn't just the people that were dying in Eredet. And yet sitting here and studying the land, I could see the beauty still there, buried beneath the surface.

"You still haven't learned to lock your door."

My body stilled at the overflowing magnetic pull I felt all over my body. I slowly turned and saw Kane standing before me in all his majestic, dark beauty.

"What's the point?" I let out a harsh breath. "Anything that wanted to get me wouldn't need a key."

"You'd be surprised," Kane replied. He straightened his back but looked down, unsure of how to deliver what he had to say. "We're having a *Valik* ceremony soon, and I'd like you to attend."

It didn't go unnoticed that he invited me, even though he could probably order me to do so.

"What is a *Valik* ceremony?"

"Right now, I am an interim king. The people must accept me as their ruler or vote for another they find more worthy."

"But you are the king's son. Wouldn't the crown pass to you automatically?"

Kane chuckled and put his hands behind his back. "We don't do crowns. And that's generally the result, yes, but not always. Our people choose the sovereign they feel best to lead them. If they disagree with me taking my father's place, another will be chosen by consensus."

"Wow," I said, thoroughly surprised.

"It prevents plagues in history such as Dokoran or the Guardians."

Heat flushed to my cheeks at his words and that Solis wasn't as diplomatic in their system. I was also ashamed that Dokoran was a relative of mine. That nagging whisper of doubt always made its way to my waking thoughts. With my strange and growing powers, could I be like Dokoran? Could I end up like Orphlam?

I didn't clue in Kane to my deepest inner fears. "Will you be disappointed if you're not accepted as king?"

"It is a serious burden to bear the weight of our people, and it's not one I would get pleasure from but will gladly do for their protection and in my father's memory. I trust they will make the right decision and do what's best for Varjutus. My feelings do not come into play in this matter."

Kane's selfless words somewhat took me aback. He seemed more relaxed and comfortable than I'd ever seen when we were on Solis. He exuded confidence, and it only made him more appealing.

I cleared my throat. "So, the people…chose Adelram?"

"The people loved him, and he was a selfless ruler." Kane sat next to me on the window bench. "Cyra, I want you to know you're not a prisoner here. I don't want you to feel like you are. I know what it's like to be stuck in a world that is very different from your own."

"As do I. This is the second time for me now." My eyes darted away from him as I rubbed my arm self-consciously.

Kane looked surprised by my answer but slowly nodded, realizing it was no picnic on Solis.

I shrugged. "I'm getting used to it now."

A tingling of sadness passed from Kane, and he went to grab my hand but then decided against it. He looked pained, wanting to say something, but he stood and walked toward the door.

"You will continue your training, it's more important than ever now, and Kal will take over as your instructor. He'll be by tomorrow morning to take you."

My body suddenly felt heavy. "Kal? You won't be training me anymore?" I freely admitted to myself that I was terrified to have any lingering interaction with the "dispeller of darkness."

"He's the greatest warrior in all of Eredet. He could best me in melee combat any day. I'll counsel you in magic when I can, but I've been away from my people for too long. They deserve my attention."

Of course, they did, and I'd be damned if I was the one to keep them from him. If the warrior Varjun was going to pommel me mercilessly for my supposed benefit, then so be it.

M eili returned to my room about thirty minutes later, flushed and frazzled. It was endearing to see her looking discombobulated, and it was clear I wasn't the only one lost on this planet.

"Brugan told me you'd be training tomorrow. I threw together what I could between Varjun stores and my own. It'll have to do since I didn't prepare for heavy combat with ruthless warriors," Meili said, rolling her eyes in disbelief. I loved her for it.

"I'm sure whatever you have is fine, Meili. Thank you." Her offerings included pants and a rich, brown leather corset vest with matching leather cuffs. They had intertwining knot designs that I've seen sporadically throughout Eredet, a small consistency tying the various worlds together. Underneath was a charcoal-colored short-sleeved tunic that looked almost knee-length with black pants and knee-high leather boots. It was unlike anything I'd worn before, and to my dread, I realized it meant that the Varjun meant business since I hadn't previously needed protective clothing.

I began circling the room, lost in thought. "Do you know anything about the Varjun, Meili?"

"No, I haven't had much interaction with them. They don't leave Varjutus often, and I haven't ventured far from the castle. So far, it seems that they're struggling to trust us."

I nodded in agreement and grabbed her hand. "We will just have to prove we're here to help."

Meili and I stayed together the rest of the day and fell asleep together. When I woke, I remembered that the sun wouldn't rise, and I hoped it was morning. Meili was gone, so I dressed in my training leathers and left to check on Theo. A nurse was sitting beside his bed, and I frowned when I saw him. He didn't look well, having grown dark circles under his eyes with black veins like he'd been poisoned.

"What's wrong with him? Is he getting worse?"

"I'm not sure, Reina. We can't be sure what Orphlam did to him, and even though we've tried to purify his blood and energy, it doesn't seem to be working."

The door opened without warning, my future tormentor taking up the entire space of the doorframe, waiting to lead me to hours of pain.

What the actual *fuck.* He was going to ruin me.

If he could relax his permanent scowl from his face, he might be considered beautiful even with his sharp features and dark glaring eyes. His long white silky hair had a few small braids that fell to his shoulder blades. He wore a sleeveless leather similar to Kane's, which complimented his light shadowy skin, displaying his sculpted muscles rippling beneath. He had visible scars like he'd seen his fair share of war, and his skin was adorned with multiple tattoos.

"Let's go," Kal boomed in a deep, dark voice. "I don't wait for anyone, so keep up, Solian."

My eyes rolled. It was my minuscule attempt to appear unaffected by him. I was scared to death by Kal and the kind of training he would give, but I wasn't opposed to getting out some of my aggression and anger. It was better than rotting away in my dark room alone with memories of my loved ones' deaths and counting the seconds waiting for Theo to wake. So I bucked up and felt the cold absence of my fire beneath my skin as I followed the *dispeller of darkness*.

We exited the castle and walked along a dirt path where the grass was permanently stomped away by continuous activity. It was clear more of an effort was made to keep the castle grounds groomed and properly managed, but this well-used path to my future torture was beyond help.

The irony of parallels between me and this sad path was not lost on me.

Tired. Worn. And possibly beaten beyond redeeming.

I abandoned my internal pity party and noticed we were near the edge of the land that fell off to a giant empty chasm, so I made a mental note not to end up at the ledge. There were others in the distance training, and they all stopped to gape at me.

"Kane filled me in on the measly training you received on Solis. You were given teachings to merely crawl away with your life and run away. I do not take on cowards as pupils. You will henceforth be trained to become a warrior. Kane is certain that you are vital to our survival, and I will do everything I can to protect the Varjun. So we will not waste a moment of our time. Our training will be hard and brutal because we have no other choice."

His words made my inside feel like bubbling liquid, even though they made sense.

Kal's powerful legs moved, his long stride carrying him to a makeshift table full of weapons. He picked up two swords and threw one at my feet.

"Pick it up and do your worst."

It was bad enough that it was cold and dark out, but I also felt entirely uncomfortable in my surroundings. Even though my eyes were now well-adjusted to the dark, fighting didn't feel ideal. Kane had helped me realize that my power flourished and thrived under the energetic emissions of the sun.

And now I would have to relearn everything.

The sword was tattered and unremarkable but *very* sharp. I picked it up as if lifting a newborn, which was the wrong move. It was so heavy I was sure I would drop it holding it with one hand. I also had no idea how to grip it properly since I had only used daggers in the past.

This wasn't going to end well.

With all the false confidence I could muster, I lifted my head and walked up to Kal with two hands on my sword, and he kicked it from me and pushed into me with his forearm with little effort. He had barely moved, yet it took a few moments before I could inhale again. The flashing lights in my eyes did nothing to ease my fear. Only a minute into training, I thought I was going to die.

"Get up." While he wasn't cruel, Kal seemed thoroughly unamused.

Unwilling to be defeated so quickly, I stood and grabbed the sword again.

"Bend your knees and square yourself. If you keep coming at me standing lazily, I will keep easily knocking you to your ass."

My self-doubt and distraction from Theo's welfare were getting the best of me. Yes, I had absolutely no skill with a long sword, but I had plenty of training under my belt now. Straightening my spine, I gripped my sword tightly with determination and circled him on bended knees. He faked an attack to my left, and even though I stumbled, I used my speed to get my bearings, tumble toward his other side, and stand with my sword pointed to his flank.

…Before it slightly drooped from my arm weakness.

Shit, that had almost looked badass.

His brows raised with surprise, and I damn near lost it when he raised his head and nodded as if in respect. "Very good. Now we can dance."

The fighting portion of the training lasted about an hour. My arms were mercilessly twitching and shaking, now feeling like limp noodles. The Varjun, who were previously training, had watched the entire time with amusement at the pathetic sight of Kal destroying me while not breaking a sweat. But that meant they were also there to witness my tiny victories by evading one or two of his advances and even unexpectedly driving once out of his way.

He spent another hour showing me other large weapons I hadn't used before, explaining their uses.

"That's enough for today. By the time I'm done with you, you'll be able to wield all the weapons in this camp, and you'll be able to hold that longsword for hours without dropping it in fatigue. I'll see you here tomorrow at the same time." When he was finally out of sight, I fell to the ground, broken and spent. The Varjun spectators finished laughing and went back to their business. There was one who lingered a moment longer, looking at me with reddish-brown eyes, slightly filled with pity before he turned to join his brethren.

After a few moments, I stood and limped back to my room. I didn't want to show it in front of Kal, but I had never been in such physical pain from head to toe in my life. When I looked in my mirror, I had a black eye, my lip was busted, and my hands were covered in painful blisters. A cut on my leg still hadn't stopped bleeding, so I was sure I left a trail of blood behind me. When I was at the side of my bed, Meili walked in and screeched at the sight of me.

She began circling me and shaking her head like a mother hen. "What did he *do* to you? This is unacceptable."

"Meili, it's okay. It wasn't that bad. I did it mostly to myself by falling and running into him by accident. He's as rock hard as he looks."

"No, it's not. Come, let me heal you."

I held up my hand. "No." Meili stopped short at my answer. "Thank you, but no. It'll heal soon enough."

"I don't understand. Are you sure you don't want me to heal you?" She thought I was out of my mind, probably from too many elbows to the head, but she didn't force the issue.

"I'm positive. Thank you."

"Okay, I'm one floor beneath you if you need me."

I nodded before she left my room.

My body shook as I slowly got into bed and laid down, the blood staining my sheets. Nobody would try to make my pain disappear like it wasn't real. I wanted to be able to learn to fight through anything, and that included pain. What if I was captured and had nobody to heal me? What if I was detained and tortured as Kane had been and couldn't mentally make it? I needed to be able to protect myself and the ones I loved.

Theo might never wake to be able to feel anything again. And Kal was right. I had so long to go before I was ready. So I welcomed this pain, let it sink into me, and just laid there for a while, becoming one with it.

I was interrupted from my trance-like state by knocking. They let themselves in and walked toward me.

"That bad, huh? Kal can be tough." It was Kane, and I knew the pain was terrible when I could barely feel his presence. "I brought some *choku* leaves that help alleviate body aches. I thought you could probably use some."

My back was turned to him, and when I didn't attempt to move, he walked around until he was face-to-face with me. He stopped short, his eyes bulging out of his head.

"What the hell did he do to you?" Kane growled and kneeled before me. "I will talk to him about this. This is…absolutely unacceptable."

I finally looked into his bright, forest-green eyes that were filled with concern.

"No, don't. I'm fine. Don't fight my battles for me. It wasn't as bad as I thought, and I need his trial-by-fire teachings."

Kane shook his head, unconvinced. "Let me get Meili to heal you."

"She already offered. I said I'm fine."

"Cyra, I'll say this one more time. You're not here as a prisoner or to be punished. I hope you will be comfortable here in time. I know you're grieving as I am. Just know I'm here if you need help."

He entered the bathroom and returned with wet and dry cloths. He slowly and carefully cleaned and bandaged the open wounds on my arm, followed by the one on my leg. He reached his hand to my face and moved away some hair caked to my face from blood. His touch on my skin sent shock waves through my whole body, startling me. I sat up quickly through the pain and found we were inches apart since he was bent down to my level. His lips being so close to mine fueled the intense friction within me.

"Wow," Kane said.

"What?" I wondered if he felt the same bizarre reactions.

"Your eyes emitting flame is a beautiful sight."

"I didn't feel anything. Well, not with my eyes."

"Then you felt something somewhere else?" One side of his lips turned up, making butterflies erupt in my core.

My fist covered my mouth, and I cleared my throat with a smile. "I'm just aching." He surprisingly looked disappointed by my answer. I tried to change the subject.

"What are your tattoos?" I asked, pointing to his arm. I remembered them glowing when we arrived.

"They're my call signs for Merick and Kal. I can summon them from anywhere by touching the marks, and they can find me. It's also how I got home. I have one for all the planets in Eredet. It's a different magic than driving, and traveling from such a great distance is easier."

"The one over your heart," I said, touching him there. Kane looked like he'd been shocked by jerking back, and he felt himself where my hand had been.

"You noticed?"

"Of course. I also saw that design on the emblem I bought for your blanket and the ship Adelram brought me in."

"Yes, that's my father's ship." At the mention of Adelram, the lighthearted humming from Kane turned dark, making me feel guilty for bringing it up.

"Tonight, we will meet and discuss a plan of attack against the Guardians. Tomorrow is the *Valik* Ceremony I mentioned to you before. Will you come?" he said, changing topics abruptly.

I didn't see why I wouldn't, as I had nowhere else to go. And if I was being honest with myself, I was curious.

"Yes."

He smiled at me, taking my breath away and easing my physical and emotional pain. My heart felt like it was pounding twice its normal rate.

"Dinner is in an hour."

"I'll be there.

W hen he was gone, I went to find Meili's room and told her about dinner and needing to bathe. She returned to my room with me, carrying a comfortable dress, and quickly battled the dreaded faucet on the bathtub. She explained that the reason I couldn't feel the water's presence was due to it being a scarce resource.

The dress she put me in was much more casual than I would have worn for a Solian dinner. It was a black, cap-sleeved dress with green beads on the scalloped trim falling modestly to my knees. The design of the beads made it appear to be a drop waist dress, and it was loose-fitting and comfortable. Meili braided my hair and kept it up, so I didn't have to bother with it. Not that I was ever a beauty queen, but it was no longer about fashion and soirees and impressing the public. I was here to become a seasoned warrior, defend my people and find our way back to possession of the *mikla*.

We went downstairs to the dining hall, and Kane, Merick, and Kal were already eating. Kane smiled at me in an even more stunning deep blue tunic with a rosy hue peeking through the skin of his cheeks, and I quickly looked away to control my stupid emotions. Instead, I focused on Merick's eyes bulging at my state.

"Well, it looks like Kal went easy on you." Merick stifled a laugh.

Kal never looked up, but Kane shot daggers at him, growling deep in his throat. I sensed Kane had already talked to Kal even though I'd asked him not to.

We sat down next to everyone while Brugan brought us soup. I couldn't tell what was in it but ate it anyway, utterly ravenous from the day's training.

I noticed Merick shamelessly staring at Meili, and he didn't stop throughout the entire dinner.

"Are you going to introduce me to the cherub properly?" he finally asked in his best impression of an innocent voice.

I rolled my eyes since he had now seen her plenty of times. "Merick—Meili." I ended it there. Merick smiled at her and nodded his head while Meili blushed profusely.

The soup was terrible, just like breakfast, making me wonder if culinary arts weren't important on Varjutus. Bad would be horrified by the cuisine, and I felt another ache clench on my heart at leaving Bad behind, a man who was like a father to me.

Kane ran his hands through his hair and addressed the table. "We will meet soon and discuss a plan of attack against the Guardians and the Bellum."

I blinked slowly and let out a long breath, not realizing how uneasy I constantly felt since we had no plan in place until Kane took charge.

Merick nodded. "I would like to spend some time on The Void myself to see if I can make any headway on where the Bellum King is."

"That will probably be best, but for now, I need you here to see to Varjutus' immediate needs. And Urien will keep us apprised of any advancement by the Guardians. So we can begin our next steps once we ensure Varjutus has a ruler and doesn't starve."

When Meili and I finished eating, we got up, causing Merick to nearly knock back his chair standing so fast.

"Shall I show you around the castle grounds? It's easy to get lost, especially for those not used to the dark," he said with his own dark smile.

I was keenly aware that he was seeking an excuse to be with Meili. It was easier to agree, especially since it would be to my benefit to know my surroundings. We followed him to a few common rooms and studies on the first floor that he said we could use at our leisure. The corridors were filled with stunning labradorite columns, and when you moved past them, the deep colors of gray, green, purple, and electric blue within the precious stones shimmered and changed. It was a magical setting and was beautiful, with dark wood interiors.

He then led us to the library, which appeared to take up the whole second floor. I was shocked by its massive size but was more dumbfounded by the number of empty shelves. There were very few books to fill up the amount of space available. I made a mental note to come back and search the stacks for any useful history of Eredet, even though something told me there wouldn't be any.

Merick took us outside to an ample open space with a small cobblestone ground.

"This is the courtyard. We'll be having the ceremony here tomorrow." Merick walked on ahead with Meili, but I was drawn to a large painting that was in the courtyard. I stayed behind to examine the rendering of the same castle behind me, but it was completely different. Beautiful waterfalls were running around the castle, with the spray and mists adding charm.

It looked like the area where I'd gone training today had the largest waterfall in the distance, filling the chasm. There were lovely, vibrant, crimson and violet flowers covering the castle and full trees with luminescent leaves of various colors before a backdrop of mountains. In the painting, the castle was stunning, Bavarian and Gothic, with a Byzantine-like design made of what was probably sandstone brick and white limestone. The roof scraping the sky appeared to be blue-black slate. I looked back at the castle as it was now and frowned. It was run down and dirty, much darker than the vivid stone in the painting. The people here were unable to maintain its upkeep. But from the picture covered in flowers and life...it was once romantically stunning.

"See anything you like?"

I yelped and jumped around at the deep penetrating voice. Why could he sneak up on me, even with our connection?

Kane laughed at my reaction. He constantly witnessed me falling over myself, screeching in shock, or making a spectacular fool of myself. It made me jealous of his constant composure.

"Sorry, I was curious where Merick was taking you, but it looks like he lost you."

"Uh, yeah. I was admiring the painting. It's beautiful."

Kane beamed at me. "Thank you. This was what my home looked like...long ago."

"What happened? Compared to this image, everything here looks...dead."

Kane shifted his weight on his feet before holding out his hand. "Come with me?"

A slight grin grew on my lips. I couldn't deny that I wanted to go anywhere he wanted to lead, so I interlaced my fingers with his. He pulled me close as we drove to a new location.

My jaw dropped when I took in the gravity of the landscape. Beautiful dark sands and a massive conclave of dirt with a missing ocean.

Kane winked at me before looking out to the vast emptiness. "I brought you here because I know your fondness for playing in the sand."

I laughed, recalling our little scuffle in the sand on Solis. Our relationship had truly changed that day. But that beach was full of sunshine, colorful vegetation, glistening waters, and life—a stark and painful contrast to what I saw before me.

Sitting down, I took off my shoes and dug my feet into the cold, chrome sands, and sifted some through my fingers as the moonglow caused the tiny crystals to sparkle. Kane sat at my side.

"You wonder why everything appears dead. That's because it is. You didn't think the curse affected only Solis and The Void, did you? We're one step away from becoming the next Void. A wasteland planet."

I was silent, clutching onto the sands left behind to mourn the life it was once a part of. The tiny rock crystals bit into my skin, realizing my folly, thinking that if I wished hard enough, I could return it for him.

"Varjutus and The Void are locked in place in the galaxy. They do not rotate. We don't have seasons or changing days. Our waters dried up long ago. The only way to keep the few remaining forests semi-alive and our people from starving to death was to stay at the mercy of Solis."

"That explains the missing waterfalls and bathtubs with no water."

"Correct. Crops needling sunlight and water don't grow here anymore. It doesn't rain, and the sun doesn't shine. The Guardians drain energy from our planet, and it dies a little more every day. Why do you think my father and I played nice with the Solians and Guardians? Because we liked it? We were reduced to groveling for the sake of our people on a planet of individuals that despised us. And now that we are serving no more purpose to the Guardians, and the fact that I took you away, means we'll probably receive no more water or food supplies. Varjutus is in serious trouble, and tomorrow the people will have a major decision to make when they place their trust in the next king. They will be choosing their last hope for survival."

My head drew back as I blinked away my shock. "I don't know what to say. I had no idea. I'm sorry your people are suffering so much." He looked deep into my eyes, and the loss and despair inside them nearly knocked the breath from me. "What will we do about the *mikla* and the Guardians?"

"We will make a plan of attack very soon. As I mentioned at dinner, I will likely send Merick to The Void to gather any intel he can, but I need him here for now. I need to address the immediate needs of my people since they've been neglected for far too long."

"I completely understand." Yes, we needed to continue on our journey to get the *mikla* back and figure out how to protect ourselves against Orphlam, but I would stand by Kane just as he stood by me.

"Orphlam isn't stupid. He will know that you're here. But we're lucky that he's mostly confined to his temple at Solis where his power sustains him, so we have some time. Driving here would weaken him, plus he hasn't done it for millennia. Of course, he could send some men here, but I think he'll be too busy planning his next move."

I nodded and changed the subject. "So the sun used to rise here?"

"Yes. It wasn't the incessant blazing of Solis but a gentle warm bath. Varjutus is further away from the sun than Solis and The Void, and our nights were longer than our days, but we do greatly miss seeing it crest over our lush waterfalls."

He pointed off into the distance. "A few miles in that direction used to house our cutting-edge scientific facilities. We were never one for overly intricate home technology since it distracted us from our community. Still, we excelled in scientific advances in medicine and finding ways to improve our quality of life. As you can imagine, that's all lost now. Jonsi has a few remedies from that time, but we rely on what resources we have left."

My head shook in disbelief, struggling to imagine such a profound loss of all that hard work and innovation. "Whatever happened to your father's ship?"

"It's hidden on a northern island on Varjutus. We used to manufacture some spacecraft, but it was a small affair, and now we prefer to stay where we are unless necessary."

"Imagining what this world used to be like, I can imagine why." I needed something else to get off my chest while we were alone, picking at my fingernail beds before speaking. "Did you ever think that you were the king of the prophecy?"

His head jerked to me in surprise, opening and closing his mouth a few times, struggling to respond. He took a deep breath and interlaced his fingers with mine.

"Honestly, no. There are too many reasons why I didn't think it possible, but there's no denying our extraordinary connection, and I'm willing to explore where that might take us."

His words made my heart beat out of my chest. I inched closer to him and rested my head on his shoulder until he wrapped his arm tightly around me. Watching the twinkle of the stars with Kane at my side relaxed a tension in me I hadn't even realized was there. In that moment, I was at peace.

He cleared his throat before speaking again. "I think it very likely that we're mates, and I wanted to prepare you for that possibility."

I jerked my head up and looked up at him.

"At first, I thought it was simply duty and perhaps some magic Amrel used to keep me tethered to you so I could keep you safe. But now I think it's much more than that."

My heart began racing, incredibly excited by the idea. "Is that a magical thing?"

"Yes, it's a magical romantic connection to another person of varying degrees. It used to be somewhat common, but it's been rare in recent years. I don't know for sure, but it's possible."

"Well, considering I didn't know mates even existed, things make much more sense."

"Indeed. It's been on my mind for the past few weeks."

"Thanks for telling me." I rested my head back on his shoulder, sitting silently, letting this information sink into our skins. Being with a king of Eredet I was supposedly fated to work with was one thing, but having a true soul mate that was perfect for me? That was another thing entirely. I allowed myself to bask in that knowledge, feeling warm and safe for the first time since arriving here.

After about ten minutes, a rapid succession of streaks in the sky caught my attention. "Woah, did you just see that? It looked like shooting stars, but they were really close."

"Ah, yes. You'll see a lot of that on Varjutus." He chuckled to himself as if sharing a private joke. "Come, I'll take you back to your room. It's late."

I nodded my head back in the direction of the castle. "Do I have to worry about those two?" I asked, referring to Meili and Merick.

"Only mildly."

CHAPTER FIVE

My sleep was disrupted by a strange vision that seemed way too vivid to be a dream. I was on Earth with my dog Xenos, and he transformed into a Sunya Rei, complete with wings, fiery heat, and intensely bright light.

His voice was deep and ethereal, causing me to shiver at its peculiarity. "When you're ready, just speak my name."

The words reverberated through me as if on repeat as I awoke and rubbed at my eyes, feeling the stark disparity of complete darkness.

My voice was a whisper, feeling slightly crazy. "Xenos?" When nothing happened, I dismissed it as a bizarre dream.

Meili's absence was out of character, but maybe she also needed some extra sleep. I went to my closet and found a casual dress waiting for me. Knowing I had training, I put on my fighting leathers and headed to breakfast. I was surprised when I only found Kane and Kal, and I looked to Kane with confusion. He shrugged, appearing just as astonished as I was. How late was Meili out with Merick?

When I sat, Brugan served the same gruel-looking oats I had

yesterday. Now with the realization of Varjutus's starving people, it made a lot more sense, and I would never again be mentally complaining about the food. Nor would I take seconds when it was so scarce.

When I finished eating what was in front of me, Kal rose.

"Ten minutes."

Kane looked at me apologetically, but I didn't want his pity. I awkwardly sprang from my chair and ran toward the training field at lightning speed while I felt Kane laughing in the distance.

Kal was already there with one sword in his hands and one on the ground, waiting for me.

"Let's dance."

Here we go again.

I crouched, bending my knees, and walked toward him with faltering confidence. He faked me out immediately, knocking the sword from my hands. But this time, right before he struck me in the face, I dropped and rolled away. I ran to the weapons table and grabbed a smaller sword.

"Excellent, some action. Come at me again."

I had never been more eager to fight. With a rush of adrenaline and resolve, I charged at Kal repeatedly with every ounce of strength and energy I had to take him down. I'd never had more ammunition fueling me before, either. I wasn't fighting for brag-ging rights or neat tricks. I wasn't even fighting just for my life. I was fighting for the entire Eredet galaxy and felt that crushing weight on my shoulders. I didn't want to let these people down—or grandpa Amrel.

After about two hours, Kal finished with me.

"Today was better, and I felt the growing fight within you. You're still very weak, but it will improve with time." Kal stormed back to the castle, and for the second day in a row, I limped back to my room in severe pain while the Varjun training in the camps laughed mercilessly, blood trailing behind me.

Meili was waiting for me in my room when I returned.

"Cyra, you must let me heal you. At least for the ceremony today."

"No. I don't want to be healed, just cleaned and bandaged."

"I'm so sorry I missed this morning, Reina. Please forgive me. It won't happen again."

"Meili, you don't have to apologize. I'm not at all upset. What happened? Oh, and can you turn on the bathtub? I want to soak for a while before I change."

Meili turned on the water, but there was barely any available. She warmed up what little there was, and it still felt lovely on my aching body.

"So, what happened to you and Merick last night?"

She pursed her lips and fidgeted with her plain cream-colored dress. "Uh, we just walked around the castle grounds for a few hours. In fact, he said we did until morning. But I didn't know—it's so hard to tell when there's no sunlight!"

"You were with him all night? If you were with him that long, you must have had a lot to talk about."

Meili blushed a deep shade of crimson.

"I won't ask you anymore about it. But you have every right to have a life or take a walk with whomever you'd like. You're not bound to me, Meili."

"I *am* bound to you! I always will be. I was just interested in seeing the grounds and hearing about a different way of life."

I had mercy on her and didn't press the matter, trying to make my evident smirk disappear. I just hoped Merick knew I would kick his ass to the Void if he hurt Meili. The thought made me laugh internally. They were both blindingly beautiful specimens. That much beauty in one couple would be hard to look at head-on.

Theo's endearing smile flashed into my head, and all light-hearted thoughts ended there. The burning pit in my core returned, and it was difficult to breathe again.

I dried off, dressed, and remembered why I was here. I bandaged up my minor wounds and steeled myself.

Meili put me in a one-shoulder, iridescent seafoam, and amethyst-colored silk chiffon maxi dress with a train that started at the waist and flowed out behind me. My back was primarily bare, making me feel exposed, but not nearly as much as a Varjun outfit. It wasn't like Meili's usual fashion, but times were different now. It was beautiful, more powerful than any attempt to doll up a pretty face.

We stopped by Theo's room before heading to the courtyard, but he looked worse. The poisonous infection under his eyes was now on his hands and fingernails.

"This doesn't look good," Meili said softly.

"Any idea what it is?"

Meili held her hand over the sickness as her eyes widened. "It feels like he's holding onto the dark magic within him. He should be waking up any time now. I'm not sure why he's stuck like this."

I grabbed Theo's hand and squeezed. "You can let go. We're here waiting for you."

Meili sighed and tucked her bouncy golden hair behind her ear. "Come, we're going to be late."

When we exited the castle, I was floored by the amount of people already there. Meili held my hand in support as they stared with a mix of mistrust and curiosity. It was the first time I'd seen so many Varjun together, and I took the opportunity to take them in as well. They were a stunning group of people, tall and sleek with varying degrees of gray skin—some deep as charcoal gray while others were so light it looked as if they merely stood in the shade.

I was impressed by how colorful and vibrant they were able to make their fabrics with their scarce resources, and it was clear they didn't feel the cold the same way I did. Some of their arms were covered with long sleeves, but many women were sleeveless, showing a good amount of skin. The men's tunics, vests, and blazers appeared stiff, clean, and tailored, but I could tell the fabric was light and airy on closer inspection.

These were people that took pride in themselves.

Kane's voice boomed through the crowd like it was blasted through a megaphone. "Friends." He stood on a platform with Merick, Kal, and a man I didn't recognize. "I must make one thing clear before the ceremony begins. I have two guests staying with me, Cyra Fenix and Meili of Solis. Cyra is the one of the prophecy, here to help us restore our world to what it once was. Not only that, but she saved my life once before. I expect everyone to treat her respectfully while she is my guest."

There were hushed voices and shocked gossiping in response to Kane's statement. Frankly, I was surprised as well. When did I save Kane? He certainly didn't need any saving, especially from me. I looked down at the bruises all over me as proof.

In an uncanny action, the entire Varjun group nodded slightly in my direction in some kind of solute. It was unlikely that I could have flushed a deeper shade of red, probably matching my hair.

Their expressions had evened after Kane's speech, but they certainly wouldn't be throwing any parties in my honor.

Everyone in the crowd held something in their hands, each item different, unsure what they were for.

Many Varjun had slight luminescent flecks, like glowing birthmarks, on their faces and bodies. Some had tattoos that shone, just like Kane and his men.

Merick walked to the center of the platform and addressed the crowd.

"If everyone would settle down, please, Jonsi will now begin."

The Varjun male I didn't recognize stepped forward, and I was surprised that he appeared to be aged. Jonsi looked like he might be in his fifties.

"First, I must thank Amrel for Varjutus's son returned home. Prince Kaanan Distira, now interim king."

I looked up in surprise at the mention of Grandpa's name. My grandfather's reach kept growing before my very eyes. The crowd cheered their gratitude with great respect for Kane and Amrel. Kane was stoic as ever, not smiling or joining in the cheering.

"We are joined here for Valik and the *Huvasti* of Adelram Distira, our beloved king who ruled us for three thousand years."

My jaw dropped to the floor. Three...thousand...years? I knew time moved differently in Eredet, and I wasn't sure how Varjutus operated versus Earth, but it was still an incredible number.

The Varjun started chanting *Huvasti* as I stood dumbfounded at how much I didn't know Adelram.

Meili inched closer to me and whispered, "Merick told me it's their ceremony of respect for the loss of important members of their society. It's their final goodbye, like a funeral service."

"Let us regale remembrances of Adelram's goodness," Jonsi said.

Almost every Varjun raised their hands. Someone in the crowd glowed and walked to the platform with Jonsi and Kane. I didn't know where the magic was coming from, but the Varjun's voice projected throughout the crowd.

"One thousand years ago, my son was one of the abducted. Adelram searched for days, found him, and returned him to me. He was one of the very few ever seen again after they went missing. He never told me where he found him, nor can my son remember. King Adelram was brutalized by the Guardians for months afterward, insisting they were merely barfights, but we all knew the truth. My son was only five-years-old at the time. Now he's here in the crowd mourning King Adelram's loss."

A Varjun that must have been his son glowed in the crowd causing everyone to cheer. The father stepped down from the platform and returned. Hands raised again, and another Varjun glowed and made his way up to speak.

The cycle continued for countless Varjun in the crowd, which took a great deal of time to get through. There were stories of Adelram absorbing mortal injuries to his own detriment, saving people. He kept multiple families from starving by bringing them food and even giving them his personal meals. People recalled him avenging lost loved ones and providing shelter for families attacked by Bellum raiders. He rebuilt two entire villages that were sacked during the Great War and again during Bellum attacks with his own two hands. He ransacked most of the castle, giving what property he could to his people, which explained its lack of extravagance. Adelram had personally slept out in the villages to protect the people when threats were imminent, and he found extra stores of food and water to smuggle in from Solis. I was blown away by the selfless acts Adelram had committed during his time as king.

When everyone seemed to be done, Jonsi walked back up to the front of the platform.

"I knew Adelram for eight thousand years. I was there beside Amrel, The Creator when he was born. Amrel took one look at him and declared they would be friends, and he was right. Adelram was a Chosen One of Amrel's, and they were inseparable for Adelram's long life."

I was captivated listening to history unfold of people I had known and loved. Details that could possibly help me in the future.

"Amrel once told him that he had a great destiny with one of the biggest roles to play in the fate of our worlds, with one of the heaviest burdens of all. Adelram's burdens were tremendous, but he persevered for his family and his people. He died protecting Amrel's prodigy and absorbed his son's injuries to save his life. Adelram died a hero to us all so that we all might live. Tonight, we honor Adelram's extraordinary life and service." Jonsi held out his hands. "Present the item of remembrance."

The people moved as one and held up a cherished item. Jonsi raised his hands like he was lifting something into the sky, and the objects floated above us and glowed until they disappeared into pure light. It swirled together into a vortex until they were all united into one, and the light was released in a burst through the sky like a small, controlled firework. We all gazed at the sky and watched the light trickle back down to us in pieces, beloved memories of Adelram falling evenly amongst his people.

I tried to hide my sniffles from my crying. This was the most beautiful service I'd ever witnessed, and I hated myself for not getting to know Adelram better. To try to understand what made him so miserable. These people didn't just support him. They didn't follow him in fear. They *loved* him thoroughly. And now they would pick a new ruler to lead them with as much ferocity as Adelram did for three thousand years.

"Adelram, we bid you farewell and thank you for your unwavering service. Now we pick your successor. May they be as fearless and protective as you were. Kane is the interim king of Varjutus. Anyone who would like to see this challenged by someone greater, raise your hand."

"There is no one greater!" one Varjun yelled. Many responses mimicked that sentiment.

"This is the last chance to voice a rejection!" Jonsi spoke.

"Kaanan! Kaanan! Kaanan!" The crowd started chanting his name.

"So be it!" Jonsi took Kane's hand and walked him to the front by his side. "Kane, do you accept this unanimous voting for your ruling as our King of Varjutus?"

"I do," Kane responded thoughtfully.

"Then, it is my pleasure to announce Kaanan Distira, son of Adelram Distira, future King of Varjutus. The oath will be taken one week from this day."

I felt a warm tingling running from my head to my toes. I looked up to Kane's penetrating gaze, watching me—the king's gaze.

The crowd cheered while Jonsi bowed to Kane, followed by Kal and Merick. The people followed suit, bowing as one. Meili and I did as well, but I felt that magnetic force pulling me to stand straight as if Kane didn't want me bowing to him, but I didn't dare move until everyone else did. I wasn't going to disrespect this precious ceremony.

When Jonsi announced the proceedings over, everyone dispersed to mingle and talk with each other like they were all the dearest of friends. Meili and I stood awkwardly in utter shock, tears still in our eyes. We were both equally emotionally overwhelmed by what just happened.

A few curious Varjun started to crowd around Meili and me. Some laughed at my beat-up appearance, joking that I had pissed off some big, angry Varjun. I guess they weren't wrong there.

"There you are." I turned to the source of the voice. The Varjun who were laughing, quieted immediately and nodded their heads at Jonsi.

"I have been waiting a very long time to meet you, my dear. I've heard nothing but good things."

I wondered who he could have been talking to because I could count the number of people who liked me on one hand—and half of them were dead or unconscious. It felt like I was still earning my place everywhere.

"Jonsi, this is Cyra. Cyra—Jonsi," Kane introduced.

"Amrel showed me a vision of this lovely child before your father was even born. I know very well who she is."

My jaw dropped in surprise and a small amount of jealousy. My time with Amrel, no matter how precious, was painfully short. "I hope you'll tell me everything you know about my grandpa." I smiled at him with hope.

"My dear, I think you and I will be *great* friends."

Adelram was a Chosen One of Amrel's. Oh yes, I had many questions for Jonsi, but I yawned, suddenly feeling like I had hit a wall.

"Yes, it is very late. It was a long service, understandably, since

Adelram was so beloved. And you will be *time-shocked* for quite a while with the constant darkness here and the world not moving. Does time pass if the world does not move? I beg to argue that it does not. My complexion is suffering these days, so I will contend in my favor." Jonsi winked at me and warmly touched my shoulder as he said goodnight.

I was immediately fond of him.

Merick began dodging and weaving quickly through the crowd as if he knew we were about to leave. He fought to catch his breath between his words, and I covered my mouth, hiding a laugh. He was infatuated with her. "Meili, it would be my pleasure to escort you back to your room." Even in the darkness, I could see her cheeks deepen with embarrassment.

"I couldn't. I must escort Reina back."

"Meili, if you would like to go, please do. Don't you worry about me." I smiled encouragingly at her.

"You heard the Solian." Merick nudged me away to get to Meili, wrapping his arm around hers. Before whisking her away, she turned to me and mouthed, "I'm sorry."

I shook my head at the pair of them. Meili's purity and Merick's dubious mannerisms…I would need to talk with him.

Dragging my feet and fighting to stay awake, I groaned, beginning my walk back, when I heard a voice behind me.

"Are you sure you can find your way back alone?"

It was Kane, looking striking in the moonlight like it was made to glow on him.

"I can manage. I'm the *Chosen One*, remember? I'm sure I can find a room."

Kane laughed so loud that some remaining onlookers peered in our direction at the one who could make the stoic Kane erupt in laughter.

"Even Chosen Ones can get lost. I'll walk you back."

"Don't you have some incredibly important kingly thing to do?"

He pursed his lips and shrugged. "I couldn't imagine anything kinglier than making sure a woman alone gets to her room safely." He bent down and whispered so that only I could hear, his voice full of mischief and excitement, "Especially one that could be a potential mate."

My body surged with warmth, fully appreciating how attentive he always was. Kane was always at my side whenever I was in danger on Solis. While Theo was... strangely absent. Theo was full of lovely words and intentions, but Kane had proven time and time again that he was a man to be trusted and respected. Someone who deeply cared even if his face didn't show it. And despite Adelram's cutting words, he had been at his son's side, keeping me safe.

"Well... who am I to refuse a king?"

I felt a lighthearted buzzing of delight the whole way back to my room, making me grin and swoon like an idiot. When we arrived, he turned to me with a look I'd never seen before. He appeared vulnerable.

"I just wanted to thank you for tonight," he said.

"I didn't do anything." My head tilted in confusion. "In fact, I felt like I intruded on something sacred for your people."

"I... felt your respect and grief for my father during the ceremony. It meant a lot to me, and I invited you personally. You were not intruding."

"I might have wanted to punch Adelram in the face on more than one occasion, but I did respect him. And I trusted him. I had visions of him and Grandpa together, and they were very close. But in the end, I knew he was a force of good. I regret not trying to get to know him as well as Grandpa did. Now I'll never have the chance."

I raised my finger, remembering something Kane said in his speech. "Oh, by the way. Why did you lie to your people? I never saved you, as if anyone like you would ever need saving." I laughed, but Kane didn't. He looked serious.

51

"You did. On *Mikla* Island, you blasted about fifteen guards to dust. You fought to save us."

"I..." I couldn't think of an argument. I just thought of it as fighting, not necessarily saving their lives.

"See, you did. And now my people won't bother you. A life debt is very serious with the Varjun people—especially a royal life debt."

"In that case, I could use some chocolates and a serious full-body massage." I laughed, stretching my neck until it cracked.

"I can't help with the chocolates, but I give excellent body rubs."

It took effort to swallow. This Varjun god-king wanted to pamper me, and goddamnit, I wanted to let him.

"I'll leave you to get some rest," Kane said.

My heart sank a bit, but I was too tired to function anyway. "Yeah, good idea. I can barely stand up straight."

I opened the door and was halfway in when Kane spoke again.

"Oh, and Cyra?"

"Hmm?"

"You looked beautiful tonight."

Heat rose all over my body, and I could do nothing but watch him leave. Content and exhausted, I plopped onto my bed, ready to sleep, but a thump at the window bench made me groan and turn to see what it was.

"Oh my god! Tulah!" How could I forget the incredibly magical birds who could drive within the galaxy and find people? Bad's bird flew over to me and nuzzled my face. She dropped a note into my hand and sat on my shoulder as I ripped it open as quickly as possible, eager for word from Bad.

My dear Cyra,

I pray that you're safe and protected. If anyone can find you, it's Tulah, so I know this note will make it to your hands. Solis is in turmoil. Workers and shoppe owners are talking about banding together and fighting the Guardians. They're desperate and terrified with no leader. The nobles only come out to get food and hide in their mansions. Nobody has seen the Guardians, so we have no idea what they're up to, which only increases the fear.

I hope to hear from you soon. I love you, girl wonder.
Bad

I ran for a pen and paper to send a response.

Dear Bad,

I am safe on Varjutus with Kane's protection. We are trying to come up with a plan to overthrow the Guardians. You MUST NOT allow the workers to make any attempts against the Guardians. We fought them on Solis and saw firsthand that they are impervious to all our attacks—water, fire, electricity, and other magicks. They cannot be fought by traditional means. Please, do everything you can to talk them down. Believe me when I say I will not rest until I find a way to end this.

Bad, I have something serious and dangerous to ask of you. The Varjun people are starving and will no longer be getting any food supplies now that the Guardians are looking for us. Is there any way you can send food and water from Solian farms? I'm sorry to ask, but the Guardians affect everyone in this galaxy. If we don't help each other, nobody will be left to fight them.

I love you too,

Cyra

Attaching the note to Tulah's claw, she vanished. Maagaline birds were incredibly intelligent, so if there was danger of interception, she would return the message to me, and if not, it would be safely delivered. It was only about five minutes later when Tulah returned with Bad's response. I took the letter with eager anticipation.

Cyra,

I will help you get food to Varjutus, especially if you're one of the ones starving. That won't happen under my watch. But I need you to find a way to get the food from Solis to Varjutus—I don't have that kind of power, and Tulah can only transfer so much. Let me know what you find out and the food is as good as theirs.

I will speak to the workers immediately with your information and keep you posted on their response. Be careful, be safe.

Bad

Oh, Bad. I was so grateful to him. He'd never stopped looking after me since I was born. I crawled into bed, happy I had the food figured out but worried about getting it here. I stilled as I grew dizzy, and a vision overcame me.

Grandpa Amrel was in a place I'd seen before. He walked to the stone archway and wrote into the stone with his finger, symbols magically appearing. When he was done with the runes, he touched his right palm to the stone closest to him, and the inside of the arch changed into what looked like a portal to a different place. He walked into the gate and appeared in a castle that looked much like the one I was in now.

The memory vanished, and a warmness rushed through my body as if Amrel was still watching over me even through death. He must have been able to use these gates to travel between worlds —*this* must be why he had ensured I had the knowledge of the *Sild Gates*. Bad could transfer the food to the Fenix lands then we could send it through the gate. Not only that, but I could also bring Vish back with me.

But how could I get to Solis without being detected immediately by the Guardians?

Laine. If Kane could get us to the Temple of the Creator, which was shrouded land, Laine could get us both to the private lands without using magic. I resolved myself to tell Kane of my plan tomorrow.

The following day Meili wasn't around again, and I wondered what was happening between her and Merick. Concerned for her safety, I'd have to talk to her about it when I saw her again.

I went to breakfast to tell Kane about the food delivery plan but stopped short at what I saw. In addition to Kane, Merick, and Kal, there was another Varjun male with a female I'd never seen before.

They all stopped talking and looked at me.

"Tarian, you know, Cyra," Merick said, bored and not looking in my direction.

"Ah, yes. The Solian who saved the Varjun King. And who is apparently staying in the castle," Tarian said with disdain. "This is my daughter, Caelan. She and the king grew up together, so they have a long, long history."

I nodded and sat down quietly. "Nice to meet you." To avoid this awkwardness, I shoveled my food as quickly as possible while they continued talking as if I hadn't dared to interrupt them.

"We look forward to your oath next week. I always knew you'd follow in your father's noble footsteps," Tarian said, beaming at Kane.

"I appreciate your confidence, Tarian. I'll do my best to live up to his memory."

"I know you will. And you must save the first dance for Caelan. It's been too long since I've seen the two of you dance."

Caelan's voice was soft and gentle, with a playfulness that made nausea boil in my gut. "Only if the king promises not to trample my feet to death. The last time was a disaster with his two left feet."

Kane's face lit up, and he laughed while Caelan shot me a devious grin. *Oh, that's how we're going to play this, huh?* I choked down the bile threatening to make me puke from how Kane's eyes danced when he looked at Caelan. *Bitch. Instant dislike.* There were only two words on repeat in my mind.

Mate.

Mine.

"That was millennia ago, and you know it." Kane leaned back in his chair, all ease and comfort with this person he obviously cared for. And that made my teeth grate while scarfing down bland food.

Merick chimed in. "Kane is the most desired eligible man in Varjutus now. How clever are you, securing the first breakfast since his acceptance as king and the first dance at the oath?

"I have no idea what you're talking about," Tarian laughed, his arms stretched out beside him in a shrug. "We're merely having breakfast with a very old friend of my daughter's."

Unable to stomach anymore, I stood up quickly and turned to leave.

"Ten minutes," Kal boomed after me.

I heard Tarian ask from a distance, "Ten minutes until what?"

"Until her pommeling," Merick answered. They laughed, none louder than Caelan. I ignored the strong tug trying to pull me back to the hall, having to push hard to break free from it, and marched back to my room.

Meili was already there waiting for me and saw I was in no mood for chit-chat, so she helped me dress into my leathers before I stormed to the training camps. I grabbed the sword waiting for me on the ground before running toward Kal.

"Is there a reason you're so angry?" he asked with boredom.

"I'm not angry."

"Yes, you're full of rage."

"No, I'm just motivated."

"You need to control your emotions. Heightened emotions lead to rash decisions which lead to death."

"I said I'm not angry!" My hands ignited in flames as I swung at Kal.

He knocked the sword out of my hand without effort, snuffed out my flame, and landed a blow that had me spitting blood. He put his sword to my throat.

"See, you're dead. You can lie to yourself, but you cannot lie to me."

To my utter horror and embarrassment, I started crying on the ground. My reaction repulsed me, but it felt as if my bubble of warmth and safety of a world where only Kane and I existed had burst, and all my hopes and dreams came spewing out of it.

"Get up," Kal said, seething with disgust. But I couldn't move.

"*Get up!*" Kal boomed, his voice echoing through the grounds, so the other fighters stopped to watch us. It made me cower with my hands over my head.

"Are you really throwing a tantrum because the king is noticing another woman?"

"That's ridiculous," I said, fuming.

"I see the way you look at him. If folks shut up long enough to pay attention, they'd notice all kinds of things."

"I'm not angry," I said defiantly, unsure why I even bothered to deny it.

"Again, you can lie to yourself but don't bother trying with me. Do you think your tears matter to the Guardians? Do you think they will save my people from extinction? Do you think they'll bring back the ones we lost? Now get the fuck up, and *fight* for what you want."

His words were exactly what I needed to hear. I rose slowly, wanting to beat Kal to a pulp. But while I successfully parried with him, I realized—I *did* want to fight. I want more than scraping by with my life. I *wanted* to be a warrior. The rest of the training was brutal and tiring, but I relished every moment.

"In the future, leave your petty troubles outside of my training camp."

CHAPTER SIX

The next few days passed in the same pattern, doing nothing but focusing on my training. Theo was unchanged, and Mylo had found a task that he was very much enjoying—tending to the care of the land and some special animals on an island up north. I had spoken to him a few times, and even though it physically pained him, he smiled, enjoying his new life. Kane had given him his home with resources so he could spend his days in peace. I hadn't gotten the chance to visit him there yet, but I would as soon as I could.

Kane was also incredibly busy visiting every home of his people, so I didn't get to see him even though I requested to tell him about my plan to obtain more food. But I didn't push, waiting for him to come to me because I knew he needed this time to reconnect with them and see to their needs.

It was the day before the oath, and while my body was aching and tired, I was starting to feel stronger in my resolve. Fighting helped get me out of my head and offered something to focus on other than my constant fear.

Kal had just tried a new move which sent me falling to the ground, but, for the first time, he bent down his arm to help me up.

"I'm pleased with your progress. You've stepped up your game, and you're not as pathetic as I thought you'd be. You could turn out to be a passable warrior."

My hand went to my heart, and I gasped with mock enthusiasm. "That's the nicest thing you've ever said to me." There was an infinitesimal upturn on the side of his lips. Was that a smile? Did the *dispeller of darkness* who ate Solians for breakfast just half-smile at me?

"Tomorrow, we will break in training for the oath. It is an all-day affair, so we won't have time to train. Don't go soft on me now in the downtime."

My brain sputtered, finally seeing Kane outside, off in the distance with Merick. I didn't realize how the long separation had profoundly affected me.

"Never," I responded.

"Good. Get some rest."

"Yeah, I just need to speak to Kane first."

I could get used to Kal's good side. I followed closely behind him, and as luck would have it, they were discussing the food crisis.

"We need a plan now. The people are panicking, and we haven't faced mass hysteria in eons. I'd hate to see it now," Merick said.

"How much do we have left?" Kal asked.

"Enough for two weeks' stores. Then it's gone."

"Fighting the Guardians, the Bellum, and their meige isn't enough. Now we have to deal with our impending starvation?" Kane's arms were folded, and his eyes squinted, deep in thought.

"I think I have a solution for this."

The three of them jerked their heads to me in various states of doubt and surprise. Merick's eyebrows raised. "Do tell."

"What is it, Cyra?" Kane smiled and sent a signal of gratitude through me, making me shiver.

"I've contacted Bad, the Solian chef in the castle. He coordinates the transfer of food throughout the galaxy. He agreed to smuggle food and water if we could transport it from Solis to Varjutus. I had a vision of Grandpa involving the *Sild Gate* in the Fenix private lands. He opened it, and it turned into a door to Varjutus. Kane, if you can get us to the shrouded island, the Temple of the Creator, I believe Laine could get us to the rear entrance to the private lands without being detected. If I find out how to give Bad access, we could make it a weekly replenishment."

I waited for them to respond, but they simply stared.

"That very well could work." Kane stepped toward me, his thumb reaching to circle my chin. I felt joy and excitement radiating from him, and a light glowed between us where he touched me. "There's my bright star."

"Uh, what is that?" Merick asked. Kal's lips were parted in confusion.

"Don't worry about it," Kane replied. "The day after the oath, we will go to Solis and try to open the gate."

Merick and Kal both nodded their appreciation and walked away, leaving me alone with Kane.

"Why are you nervous around me?" he asked in a deep, sultry voice.

"I'm not nervous."

"No? I feel it pulsating off you." He walked toward me, put his hand on my face, and the place of contact glowed again

"And now?" he asked quietly.

"I…" God, why did my body react like this? I thought my heart would burst out of my chest from beating so fast.

"Yes, Cyra?" His voice was low and gravelly, like a dark song. I got lost in his forest green eyes, stunning against his shadowy skin that blended beautifully into the night. I wanted to touch his raven hair that fell to his eye on one side. To feel the skin on his face. To hold his arms and feel him against me. Kane's very essence called to me like a beacon guiding me home.

"Sire, Caelan is here and requests your presence," Brugan said, startling us both.

Of course, she did. She'd better not get any ideas of requesting anything more than that from him.

Kane sighed. "Okay, I'll be right there." He faced me and let go. "We'll discuss this later." He turned and walked away, leaving me utterly confused. I saw Caelan from a distance, and even in the dark, I could see the details of her stunning yet revealing, flowing dress that showed off every supple curve she possessed. Her striking periwinkle eyes glowed in delight at Kane's approach.

I realized what I must have looked like compared to her, covered in sweat, dust, old dirty leathers, bruises, blood everywhere, and a broken spirit. How could I ever live up to the pristine beauty of Caelan? I limped back to my room, regretting I would have a whole day off from my training.

M eili and I spent time together the rest of the afternoon in my bed since I could barely walk. We laid around and talked about the state of things and how scared we were for the Solian people, and I finally decided to ask her more about what was happening with Merick.

"Do you like him?" I asked.

"Like him? Uh, he's been nice to me. And he is handsome."

"Oh, impossibly handsome," I agreed, smiling.

Meili blushed. "But…"

"What is it, Meili? Has he been rude to you?"

"No, nothing like that. I've been blown away by how sweet he is with me. I think I *do* kind of…like him."

"Well, Meili, that's wonderful! What's the problem?"

"There's too much going on. There's too much suffering in this galaxy. I can't allow myself to have feelings like this when so many are dying. I just…don't deserve to be happy. It doesn't feel right."

"I know exactly how you feel." It's what I struggled with daily. There was no room for romantic ties in such a world. Although…

"I've been thinking about this since I came to Eredet. There is a great deal of suffering here—more than I can handle. But love is the reason we're fighting. If we fail, we must grab as much of it as possible. If you've found something real, don't let go of it for anything. We might not get another chance."

Meili started sobbing, and I held her close.

"How could my people ever forgive me when they're rotting away? How can I be happy when they are in constant agony? It's not fair to them. I'm tormented by it every single day. The guilt…"

"They would be more upset if you wasted a chance at a full life. We will do everything in our power to save your people. To save all of Eredet. But in the meantime, don't delay a single minute for a chance at happiness."

She nodded and wiped her tears. "Thank you, Cyra."

I realized the hypocrisy of my words since I found it hard to apply them to myself, but Meili wasn't the prophesized one, and she didn't have to live up to Our Creator's last will and testament.

We went to dinner that night, and Kane wasn't there, making my heart sink. No doubt he was still prancing around with Caelan and her perfect loveliness. Meili went off with Merick hand-in-hand, and Kal watched me like he knew some secret he wouldn't say aloud. He nodded his goodbyes to me as I walked back to my room alone.

T he day of the King's oath arrived, and I had no idea what to expect. It took much longer than I liked to admit getting out of bed because of my body aches. Once in the bathroom, I cursed loudly at the fact that a grown woman couldn't start her own bath. I was slightly ashamed of my petty tantrum, but then the bathtub began to fill out of nowhere. I turned around to see if it was Meili helping me, but there was nobody there.

The water never stopped and eventually threatened to spill over the tub, so in a panic, I yelled, "Stop!" The water obeyed my command. The strangest part was that the water wasn't coming from the faucet. It was filling from nothing. *From me? Did I seriously fill the tub?*

There was no water on Varjutus…where was I getting it from? I ran to the empty cup by my bedside table, gripping it tight with slightly shaking fingers and imagining it full of water. It filled to the rim at my mere thought. A slight prickling of lightheadedness hit me but disappeared just as quickly. This was so simple to me—as easy as breathing, even though it took more energy than usual. How had I had such a difficult time lighting a small flame yet could make this water appear with a mere thought? I was so confused about my powers. I would do anything for Grandpa's guidance right now, especially because Kane——the man who taught magic and knew a great deal about it—had no idea how to help me. What were my actual gifts?

It then hit me that Meili said my power wasn't fire. Did she know what my power actually was? She'd never admitted to me one way or another.

I returned to the bathtub and decided not to waste perfectly good water, a precious commodity on this planet. The water was room temperature, and I wondered if I could heat it with my fire. Igniting my hands, I tried to shoot flames into the tub. It made the water warm, but I knew there must be a more effective way to do that. Water didn't really work well with fire. I got in and bathed quickly, but sitting in a full tub was a treat, covering every inch of my aching muscles.

There was only one dress in my closet, so I figured that was what Meili intended for me to wear today. It was a deep green, long-sleeved dress with beads and sequins throughout. The skirt was knee-length and fringed on the bottom, making it feel like a flapper dress from Earth. I absolutely loved it.

There was a knock on the door, and I went to open it with a smile expecting to see Meili. But Kane stood there instead, looking resplendent, causing my brain to short-circuit. He wore an emerald high-necked tunic with brocade knot detailing of the same color, fastened in the front by clips in the shape of gold leaves. His black pants and knee-high black leather boots were pristine and form-fitting—and I might have unintentionally gaped at his beauty. My mother from Earth would have told me I was "catching flies," standing with my mouth open for so long.

"I uh...I'm sorry, I'm in the same color. I can change. It's the only dress I had in my closet," I fumbled. It was a wonder that he could still cause me to act like a fumbling idiot when I had known him long enough. But the dominance and intensity of his mere presence engulfed me to the point of bewilderment. Even at rest, his power thrummed in thick pulses, which my body thoroughly responded to.

"You look beautiful. I don't want you to change. It's perfect," he replied gently and with an endearing smile.

Suddenly I couldn't swallow. Despite all that overwhelming potency, he was sweet and tender with me.

"Why are you here? Surely you have someone to escort me to the courtyard."

"We're not going to the courtyard. We'll be in the forest, which you've never visited before. Meili left with Merick, and I assured her I'd escort you myself."

"Oh. I'm sorry to be a burden."

Kane's eyes closed tightly for a moment as if slightly frustrated. "If you were a burden, I wouldn't be here. I volunteered."

My heart skipped a beat at his deep, soothing voice as his gaze moved from the floor slowly up to my eyes. He did things to me that I didn't understand. And he was right. I needed to stop myself from being in the default position of defensiveness as if I didn't merit his attention. We were most likely mates and deserved the chance to explore that.

"Do you mind if I come in?" Kane asked.

"Of course, sorry." I stood aside, letting him in. "Are you nervous?" I asked. "About today, I mean."

His face was grave and reserved, looking like the king he was about to be. "No. I'm only concerned about how my life will change with this great responsibility. I hope to live up to it and be a fair leader to my people."

"I think if anyone can do it, it's you. You will be exceptional."

"Thank you, that means a lot."

Kane walked toward me until we were toe to toe, wrapping his arms around me slowly so I felt his touch from my shoulders down my back. He held me tight and put his head down on top of mine. I leaned into him and rested my head on his shoulder, taking in his soothing smell of pine, wood, and cool, crisp air.

The world around me disappeared, and I only existed in the warmth of his large, comforting body. I didn't even realize we had left my room until I heard an audible collective gasp. Kane raised his head in surprise, lost in our embrace as much as I was.

We were in the forest, and the Varjun community was gaping at us, mostly confused. When I locked eyes with Meili, she slowly smiled before pursing her lips to stop laughter. I quietly walked in her direction and willed away the overwhelming heat in my cheeks.

Kane joined Jonsi in front of a radiant, multi-colored pond with glowing lavender leaves draping over it from large trees. I'd seen that pond before—in the painting in the castle. It was stunning and like nothing I'd ever seen on Earth or Solis. Kane locked eyes with Merick and Kal and patted his pocket, and they nodded back in recognition.

My hand immediately rubbed down my face in disbelief. They'd just had a silent moment about the Lucky Pecker.

"Welcome, everyone, to this sacred event. Today we gain a new leader. Someone who has volunteered to put the people beyond his own needs, and we have accepted him in return. Now we will make it official. Kaanan, if you would please step forward and kneel before your people. Take off your tunic."

Kane did as he was told. When he took off his top, I had to stifle an intake of breath at his perfect body. His tattoos glowed slightly in the night as he bent his head and knelt before the people he was swearing to serve, bare and open.

"Kaanan will now recite the song of our people."

Kane started singing, and his entrancing voice blew me away as goosebumps erupted over every inch of my body.

The words were in an old language I didn't understand, but

when he finished singing, the people replied instantly, as if they had heard it many times before.

"We are one!"

"Now, everyone will bring an offering for the king to bear." The Varjun lit up one by one, and when it was their turn, they placed the offering on the ground before Kane. I noticed knitted stuffed animals, clothing, trinkets, paintings, letters, plants, and books. There was an endless array of offerings, most of them appearing handmade. Once the individual placed the item on the ground before Kane, they put their hand on his left shoulder and returned to the crowd. Even the very few children of Varjutus placed an item before the king, and Kane winked at them as they did, keeping his head bowed. The children were in awe of him, giggling at the attention the new king gave them.

It took a few hours for everyone to get a chance, and I was blown away that every single citizen contributed without question. They seemed honored and connected in a way I'd never seen in a society before. The respect from these people was touching, and it could be felt in the air all around them. They truly did seem like one. I also couldn't believe Kane's resolve. He did not fidget or move once during all that time on his knees on the ground. It must have been excruciating.

When they were finally finished, Jonsi spoke. "The offerings have been presented." He lifted them all in the air, and they merged, becoming light, as I'd seen in the last ceremony, but this time it transformed into a thick golden chain. Jonsi lowered it until it magically clasped around Kane's neck. He walked to Kane and placed his hand on his shoulder where the people had touched him.

"Kaanan Distira, you now carry the weight of our people on your shoulders and bear the mark of the Varjun King. The chain shall remain until death or until a new ruler is chosen." A black, interconnected-knot tattoo appeared on Kane's shoulder when Jonsi removed his hand.

"Rise and Rejoice! For our king, Kaanan Distira!"

Cheers erupted from all the Varjun as Kane stood in all his fierce, majestic beauty. A tear escaped down my cheek from the magnificence of the ceremony, and Kane looked right at me, putting his hand to his heart. I smiled at him genuinely, and he returned it, making me weak at the knees.

When the applause ended, music erupted, and my world seemed to stop. Sound began to muffle and mute around me until I could hear nothing but a piercing ringing in my ear. My heart raced as I looked all around in shock and immediate fear of retribution from the Guardians. As my breathing intensified, stars erupted before my eyes from lightheadedness. Kane ran over to me and grabbed my hand.

"We're not on Solis. You don't have to worry. Nobody will punish you here for your love of music."

His words sunk in slowly as my brain caught up, letting out a massive breath, realizing I was overreacting. Seeing those poor dead musicians after the symphony still haunted me daily.

"My king! Congratulations. As promised, I present my daughter, Caelan, for the first dance." Tarian practically nudged me out of Kane's hands and replaced them with his daughter's. I rolled my eyes and skulked away as Kane bowed to her and offered his hand. Grumbling curses to myself, I sauntered off until I found a tree stump that looked sturdy enough to hold my dark mood. I caught sight of Meili and watched as Merick tossed her around in a fast dance, her head tilting back in laughter.

Meili's happiness meant the world to me, and my mood lifted watching how light and free she looked. Nobody deserved it more than she did, and Merick seemed to treat her respectfully despite my previous doubts.

"Amrel would be very upset to see his girl brooding in a dark corner alone while there is music and dancing to enjoy. He would say *music is the language of our souls...*"

"*While dancing is the embarrassment of them.*" I finished Jonsi's sentence.

"Ha! You knew him well. But what did he know? He was a wretched dancer. There is much beauty to be had in a graceful dance," Jonsi said while he wiggled his hips comically, forcing a smile to my lips. I loved the warm familial ease and lack of pomp and circumstance from such an authority figure.

A tingling pull caught my attention, and I looked up to find Kane watching me as he slow-danced, holding Caelan closely.

"Sure, there is," I answered shortly. Jonsi looked to where I had been staring and then nodded knowingly.

"How do you like Varjutus so far?" Jonsi flattened his lovely teal tunic as if he took pride in his appearance.

"I haven't seen much of it yet, but I like your customs and traditions. The planet feels awfully...dead. After seeing some of the portraits in the castle, it breaks my heart." Jonsi smiled sadly at me. "You seem very important to your people. What is your role?"

"Ah, my only claim to fame is that I'm a bazillion years old. I'm known as the Varjun Elder. I'm a magical vault," he said, pointing to his head. "I have knowledge of our magic, customs, and way of life from our ancestors. I help preserve it and keep it alive in our people. When my predecessor died, he transferred thousands of years of memories to me so I could access them as if I experienced them all myself. I have lived a hundred lives through the minds of our ancestors."

"That's incredible. I wish more worlds treasured their history the way you do."

"My dear, you hold too much sadness in your heart. I feel it threatening to ruin my night and snuff out my joy."

"Are you an empath?" I asked, surprised, thinking of Theo. What would Theo think of Varjutus?

"No, I'm not, but I'm very in tune with my surroundings and can feel things others can't. One so lovely as you should not be so sad—even if you're covered in bruises from head to toe," he said, putting his forefinger and thumb to his chin.

"What does beauty have to do with it? There are ugly and terrible things happening all around us. Sometimes it's hard to hold onto joy."

"It's true. There are more terrible things than we can fathom right now. But look before you." I followed his hand to the hundreds of celebrating people, laughing, singing, and dancing. Their planet was dying, they were starving, and they didn't know if they'd live to see tomorrow. But they celebrated life regardless, and I wanted to emulate that.

"I wasn't lying when I said I've been waiting a long time to meet you, Cyra. I live in Baum Village. Come find me when you can, and I will share some memories and portraits with you."

"Okay, I will. Are you here alone, or do you have a special lady out there dancing?"

Jonsi laughed. "The ladies aren't really my thing, Cyra. My partner died long ago, and I've never been able to get past his loss, but I'm happy to serve my people. I'm never alone."

"I'm so sorry for your loss. I hope to find a love that great one day."

"You will, Cyra. You'll find an epic one."

Two males approached Jonsi in haste, and worry instantly bloomed within me by their troubled demeanors. "Elder, we've run out of water. The night has just begun, and we have no more in the community store here."

"That is sooner than we thought." Jonsi stood up, frowning with concern, worry marks on his brows that were now permanently etched into his wrinkles. He walked toward the refreshments table, and I followed him. People were standing near it, explaining quietly that all the stores were depleted, not just at the party, but for their daily life.

Jonsi released a reluctant sigh and turned to face Brugan, standing off to the side of the table in case needed. "Brugan, get the king."

"Wait." I touched his arm to stop him and walked to the large water container, which was the size of a medium-sized aquarium tank. My hand touched the cold glass, and I prayed for it to fill for these people who needed a little help. They didn't deserve their beautiful planet to decay like this because of another man's greed. I was worried I had imagined the whole bathtub incident earlier. Still, I felt the energy releasing from within me, and the container began filling with precious water that I would never take for granted again. I had to steady myself when it was full since the world was spinning, but I did my best not to let it show. This defi-nitely took more energy than I was used to.

Jonsi looked at me with pride, and I blushed, looking down at my feet. Luckily the large crowd was in the throes of joy, unaware of what had just happened.

I felt a warm tingling from right behind me, and I turned to see Kane looking at me with wonder. We stood for a moment, so close but untouching, unable to break our connection, and it was as if we were the only two people in existence. I swore I could hear nothing but our breaths, magnified and slowly increasing as our airs combined and mixed like we made our own form of magic. But as was the case recently, it was as brief and delicate as a dandelion bursting apart and the seeds being carried away in the wind.

Another Varjun woman took Kane's hand and dragged him off, causing all sound to come rushing back with a deafening effect. After about an hour of watching the festivities, I found Kal, who was also isolated in a dark corner.

I decided I could like him a little bit more at that moment.

"Kal..." Already having tried to drive myself unsuccessfully, I admitted defeat.

"Yes, Cyra?" His voice was gentle but slightly amused as if he already knew what I wanted.

"Can you...drive me back to the castle?"

His features softened for the first time since I'd met him, a nice change since they were usually stuck in a permanent hateful sneer.

"Yes, I will take you." He pulled me in close and we were outside my bedroom without a second thought.

"Thanks, Kal."

CHAPTER
EIGHT

My leg pulsed up and down in a nervous twitch as I sat on the window cushion ledge, looking out at the very distant light of the celebration. The magical pond, the glowing lavender drooping leaves, the floating tea lights, and Varjun with bright tattoos and flecks on their dark skin were breathtaking, even with the decaying landscape around them. I knew that something was wrong with me that I couldn't enjoy it like I wanted to, but I was feeling off, my skin burning and itching as if my energy was its own living entity begging to burst free. Now that I was sitting alone and not spending hours getting beaten to a bloody pulp and using every ounce of my body's energy to focus on fighting like hell, I was utterly restless.

To stop my leg from incessantly bouncing, I stood and went to check on Theo, who was still unchanged, so I went back to my grandfather's box and took out the contents to be close to him again, re-reading his letter.

I hoped I could be the answer Grandpa sought, but I felt like I was spiraling out of control. In fact, the room was spinning while the fire within me bubbled like lava, ready to burst to the heavens.

The anger and fear all spiraled into the same black hole surrounding my heart, and I held my head, trying to block out the swirling vision until I burst into flames.

Letting go, I became one with the fire. My hair and eyes were flaming, and I saw through a fiery chasm like a dream. My entire body, head to toe, was engulfed with embers and smoke, and I stayed still, letting the fire consume me, and I felt…relief, succumbing to the blaze—sweet, sweet release.

Kane appeared before me with Jonsi, but I could only see them as wispy visions beneath my flaming eyes. Their words were muffled since I could only hear the soothing, crackling inferno within me, but I could tell they were screaming at each other and toward me.

Kane ran to me and put his hands on my face.

"Cyra, you need to calm down." His words were muffled. He squinted at the light like he could barely see me, bent his head to one side, and kissed me. His lips started to glow on mine, and the brighter it blazed, the more my flame started to die out.

"Kane? What are you doing here?" My words slurred together before I collapsed and started shaking.

"Lie her on the bed," Jonsi instructed. He put his hands on me, and a warm, peaceful feeling rushed through me, quelling the shakes.

"Her power is multiplying, and she's unable to contain it. Amrel warned me she has immeasurable ability that she won't know what to do with. She will need help to manage it, or it could consume her before she's ready to wield it. This was probably from her water ability. She might have opened something she wasn't ready to handle. He advised that her ability would grow over time and manifest randomly, and it might never stop growing. You must keep an eye on her. Our future depends on it."

"What is she that she can wield that much power?" Kane asked, astonishment lacing his voice. "I don't know anyone who can *make* water. Wield it, sure. Create it? It's unheard of. Her powers are so varied and random that it makes no sense."

"Kane, she is unlike anyone you will ever meet. Don't forget, Amrel protected her and counted on us to continue after his death."

"You *know* what she is," Kane said with disbelief.

"My dear boy, I am older than dirt. I know a great many things. She's the prophesied one."

Kane scratched the back of his head before clapping Jonsi on the shoulder. "I will go back and be with our people."

"I'm not going back tonight," Kane said, folding his arms.

"Your first decision as king, is a sound one. I'm proud of you, and your father would be too."

Jonsi disappeared, and I opened my eyes to find Kane huddled in anguish.

"I'm fine. You should go back."

Kane lifted his head quickly with no sign of his previous troubles.

"Because a certain Solian tried to burn down my family's home. I'm going to have to start fireproofing the furnishings."

I let out a small laugh.

"I'd like to show you something if you're up for it. Will you join me?" Kane held out his large, calloused hand to me.

There was no denying how tired I was, but I couldn't say no to Kane when he was reaching out to me like that. I took his hand, glowing yet again when we made contact. He intertwined his fingers with mine, and it sent sparks through me.

"Your eyes are glowing," Kane said softly through an endearing smile.

I shook my head and blinked rapidly as if trying to wipe away the glow. He laughed at my pathetic attempts.

"It's not something you can control. And it becomes you. They're lovely, like little nebula emissions."

He managed to make me feel beautiful despite how rough I looked. He helped me out of bed and looked down at my state of dress.

"You'll probably want to change into pants."

The fact that he wanted me to change had me mildly concerned. This had better not be another wicked chase through the dark forest.

Or...did I want that?

There was only one pair of pants in my closet, reserved for fighting, so I took those and found a long-sleeved cotton dress that I suspected was meant to be a night dress. I carried them to the bathroom and changed, putting on my knee-high leather boots. Even though I probably looked disheveled, Kane grinned at me like he'd never seen anything so extraordinary.

He pulled me close, and I tried not to breathe in his intoxicating pine scent. Within one blink, we were somewhere else, full of animals I'd never seen before. Actually, it appeared to be only one type of animal. They looked similar to deer, with large tree-like antlers, but were the size of large horses. I was shocked to find they had massive white wings that emitted a soft glow like their antlers. Freckled spots decorated their hide and snouts, more elongated than a deer's. Their eyes were all varying colors, bright amongst the dark.

"Oh my gosh, they're so beautiful."

"Remember all those shooting stars you saw in the sky the other night? They weren't stars, but these guys flying around at incredible speed. They're the Kometa, which translates to comet. As you saw, they look like comets shooting through the night sky."

I had a quick flashback of a horse Grandpa took me to ride after my tenth birthday. His name was Comet—I wondered if he did it on purpose. Knowing him, he did.

"They're stunning."

"These are the creatures that Mylo now cares for. His dwelling is here if you'd like to see him."

"Yes, of course!"

We walked for a few minutes to a small hut, and relief washed over me when I saw Mylo dispersing some seeds on the ground that some Kometa were eating. When he saw me, he stopped and attempted a smile. He looked at peace, and I could have kissed Kane then and there for doing this for him.

"I'm so happy to see you. Do you like your new situation here?"

He bunched his hands together as if grateful and nodded to us silently. There was no possibility of long conversations with him, but I saw his home and how happy he was. Jonsi had given him some pain tonics, which also seemed to be helping. I watched as he continued to work, dispersing seed with a twinkle in his eye as if he could finally feel some relief.

We said our goodbyes to him, and Kane touched his right forearm, which had a tattoo of a creature with its wings spread open. I had wondered what it was, but now I had my answer. The tattoo glowed bright, and a massive Kometa appeared before us with dark hair similar to Kane's skin. His eyes were bright violet, and he had many luminescent freckles that radiated before us.

"This is Vindur. It means wind." Kane laughed as the beast nudged at his hand. He has been with me for many years, and I missed him terribly when I was away on Solis for so long."

Vindur nudged him again, begging to be petted. Kane put his arms around him and rubbed his back.

"He's affectionate." The beast raised its head, enjoying Kane's attention.

"What's that?" I asked, pointing to a small stone on Vindur's forehead, connected to a small chain that wrapped around the base of his antlers.

"It's a *syn*. I have the other half that I wear when I ride him." Kane pulled out a headband with a matching stone in the center, which he put on his forehead. I couldn't stop staring at him. Some force kept telling every fiber in my being to grab onto him and never let him go, but I yanked myself back to reality.

A Kometa came over and nudged my hand.

"Oh, hello, beauty!" I said with delight.

"I was just going to say that when they become more comfortable around you, one might warm up and let you ride them. But it appears this one already trusts you. They're generally shy and mistrusting creatures. It takes some people millennia to make a connection with a Kometa. Although somehow I'm not surprised you were able to find favor with–"

Kane was interrupted because nearly every Kometa in the vicinity suddenly approached me in interest. My lips parted, overwhelmed with the majestic moment of these stunning, magical creatures acting as if they heard some silent call.

"Literally all of them," Kane finished his sentence in utter astonishment, his hand rubbing the back of his head, making a mess of his thick hair. "I have *never* seen this before."

It was like I had stepped out of a fog I had been lost and stumbling through, and I felt restored. I studied every creature before me and touched my fingers to their fine hair, warm, glowing antlers, and pillowy wings, just as eager to connect to them as they were to me. They all nudged or nuzzled me, begging me to pet them and give them attention as if they had longed for this moment forever. I laughed and began slowly turning in circles, feeling a vibration of something similar to a contented purr surrounding me. There were so many of them that their luminescence provided enough light that my vicinity was bright with an ethereal glow, and Kane's green eyes were filled with charming bewilderment.

My chuckles continued as I studied an inexplicable understanding in their eyes. A secret that I would probably never be privy to. They eventually started to disperse and the original

Kometa who approached me stayed by my side, nudging her head against my side.

Kane was still gaping at me.

"What?" I laughed, petting my new friend.

"Who are you?" I couldn't decide whether to be alarmed or amused by that question. The longer I spent in this foreign land, the more I felt like a freak, even among two galaxies worth of people.

"Just Cyra." The same old clumsy nerd I'd always been, even if the beginning of my life had been a lie. I shrugged my shoulders and decided to bury those pesky thoughts away.

Kane shook his head with a smile and folded arms, clearly not convinced. "Uh-huh. Anyway, I did bring you here for a reason." He reached into his pocket, dug out two more syn, and gently secured one to my forehead, fastening it behind my ears. My face burned with intensity where he touched me, and he seemed to notice. His responding smile was so attractive that it made my knees weak, and I longed to feel the tiny lines at the edges of his eyes caused by the unbridled happiness expressed on his face.

"This belonged to my mother," he said softly, now avoiding my gaze.

My heart skipped a beat recalling his memories of his mother and sister's death and how much it broke his father. It must mean a great deal to him to share this personal item with me.

He quickly put the other *syn* on the Kometa's head and waved his hand, causing a saddle to appear on its back.

"Now, just because she chose you doesn't mean you'll be able to ride her. Some Varjun can never master the ability because it requires complete control of your emotions. We can't communicate with the Kometa like you can with a Paela. It's pure emotion and instinct. The orbs on the saddle will help you control direction. Most folk find it more comfortable with controls in their hands than pure mental connection."

"Well, that's my forte! It sounds a lot like a video game minus the mind control." I laughed.

Kane's blank stare was comical. "I don't have any idea what you just said."

"Don't worry about it. So, what do I have to do?"

"First, you watch how it's done from an expert." Kane smirked and jumped onto Vindur. Without a word, they went shooting into the night sky, and I saw that familiar sight of a shooting star disappear. It was so fast you'd never know it was a Kometa and a Varjun man flying above. After a minute or so, they came back toward me, and I was mesmerized by more than a magical flying creature. Kane's happiness and sense of freedom being back home and doing what he loved was addicting for me, and I couldn't help the smile that grew on my face in response. I was so used to his somber attitude—always a hint of sadness in his demeanor, which I now knew was from his servitude and being forced away from his people. His features lit from within with bliss and excitement, were among the most beautiful things I'd ever witnessed.

They descended, and Vindur's wings created a big gust of wind, causing my burgundy hair to run wild around me. I shivered at the tremendous chill but was too fascinated to care about it. "That was incredible." I couldn't wait to try it, and I started hopping on my feet like a child about to play with a new toy.

Kane jumped off, took my hand, and led me toward the center of the Kometa, who hadn't left my side. His large, strong hands gripped my hips, and I faltered momentarily at the shock of his touch. He lingered as I felt him inch closer, breathing deeply as my heart raced so quickly it was all I could hear. Instinctively, I put my hands over his and felt disappointed when he lifted me onto the saddle. I settled my face quickly so I didn't give away the wild desire running through me, but I wasn't sure I was successful. He looked up at me with penetrating eyes like nothing else existed except me.

"Now, let's do some breathing exercises to calm your mind. It must be empty and open for a Kometa to react to your lead." My brain was a horrible, dirty place because all I could think was *Yes, I'm already empty and open! Want to help me with that?*

Bad, Cyra!

But given recent events, even if I wasn't thinking of Kane's intoxicating presence, I was still in a bad mind space.

"Uh, that's a little difficult to do right now with everything that's happened."

"Exactly. You have to do it anyway if you want to be successful."

Great. I had absolutely zero shot of getting off the freaking ground.

"Kane, what if someone was afraid to fly?"

He laughed, nodding his head and petting my Kometa. "That is another reason some people will never be able to ride one. They can't get over their fear of flying. Imagine you were a simple beast, and someone was invading your mind. Your natural instinct is flight; you're never freer or more in your natural element than in the air. Suddenly that invading voice is screaming in your head in terror. The Kometa can't help but react to that emotion like it's their own, possibly falling to their deaths."

It made sense. I could *totally* control my thoughts and emotions.

"Now take a deep breath in and breathe out through your mouth." He demonstrated by performing it himself then had me repeat that ten times. It surprisingly helped empty some of the background noise so that I felt calmer than I had in a long time.

"Empty your mind. It is just you, the beautiful nature around you, and your Kometa, allowing you to fly with her. Hold onto the controls on the saddle, speak to your Kometa, telling her where you want to go."

I took another deep breath and said, "Walk forward."

She jerked forward, walking awkwardly like she was drunk.

"Really? I can't even get her to walk?" The Kometa started freaking out by my outburst until we both fell over. She immediately got up, but I was planted on the floor in shame. Kane bent down over me, smiling, his hair falling toward me.

"That didn't go very well," I mumbled.

His white teeth showed since his smile was so big, while his Adam's apple bobbed with a quiet laugh. "Don't take this the wrong way, but I didn't think it would. Your emotions dictate your actions way too frequently. We are all at the mercy of them, but they don't have to control us. You need a lesson in learning to master it, or you'll keep turning into an unwieldy inferno. You could even end up hurting someone inadvertently. I think mastering flight with a Kometa will help you get there while providing me with some entertainment."

The nerve of him.

I tried a few more times but miserably failed. Kane was patient as he watched me fall on my ass repeatedly. It's all I seemed to do on Varjutus—constantly get knocked down on my ass in a painful recurring loop. I was ready to give up for tonight and Kane saw it too.

"Can I see you fly again before we return?" I asked.

"Sure." He hopped onto Vindur in one fluid motion, and they were up in the sky before his bottom hit the saddle.

Show off.

He made it look so easy, but I supposed I didn't have thousands of years of experience like he did. They turned and descended to the ground, and Kane reached out his hand to me. I latched onto it without question, and he picked me up and put me in front of him on the saddle. I screeched at the shock of his deftness and strength.

As soon as I felt his warmth behind me, I thought I would lose it as he cradled me so protectively against him. I relaxed while still on the ground and slowly turned back to gaze at him. He looked down on me intensely, with no hint of a smile. I was worried he could look right through me with the intensity of his stare. Did he know what was happening to me while he was near? Did he feel it too?

It took everything in me not to melt into his arms and give in to him. A piece of his hair fluttered to his eyes, and this time I could not resist brushing it away as he closed his lids and breathed in deeply. I couldn't take my hand away and didn't want to anyway. He put his hand over mine and held it there as if in agreement, and my heart seemed to run at double speed, causing heat to rise within me. I was utterly breathless at his gentle touch, a soft admission that maybe this wasn't one-sided.

Without warning, the Kometa hurled into the air, and we were propelled backward as we raced through the sky. I screeched yet again in utter fear while Kane laughed with abandon, squeezing his arms around my core. A silent assurance that I was safe in his embrace. He leaned forward and put his cheek to mine as we sailed above the trees, and my eyes fluttered shut, taking in his evergreen scent.

"This is my home," Kane said with undiluted pride into my ear, causing me to shiver and melt. He spoke as though he'd been waiting to share this special part of him and who he was with me for a long time.

"It's absolutely beautiful," I replied honestly. Even though it was dying and much of the suffering land was barren, I could see beyond that to the beauty still there—the luminosity of the silver moon and bioluminescent plant life. The trees that fought the drought and malnutrition refusing to decay without a fight. The mountains and craters of land that were once waterfalls and fresh running waters or lakes. Stunning flying beasts that had a beautiful bond with a species apart from their own. Fierce passion, love, and community of the Varjun people that lived as one. Even though I'd despised the darkness when I first arrived, I quickly recognized the beauty here, understanding Kane's adoration.

We flew for about thirty minutes until I was stunned by a new sight.

"What's that!" I intertwined my fingers with his, which were still tight on my waist, and he squeezed them in acceptance.

"Varjutus has two moons. That's the second one. It's stuck in place since we don't rotate because of the curse. You can't see this one from the castle." This moon was slightly smaller than the other one but with a bright cerulean color and a brilliant light with a magical quality.

I leaned back to his shoulder as his King's Chain glistened in the bright moonlight. Every bit of him seemed to embody Varjutus, and I was charmed by his loyalty to his people and world. He lowered his head and touched his forehead with mine, careful not to hit me with his *syn*. Who knows what that would have done to the Kometa?

I couldn't say how long we stayed in the air with him holding me close against him, but I would have been happy to stay there forever—soaring with him through the twilight skies. Vindur finally brought us to the ground, and I realized with some disappointment that we were back at the castle. I didn't want the night to end. Kane jumped off and helped me down. The Kometa pushed him aside and put his head on my shoulder like he was hugging me. Kane's eyes bulged with surprise, then laughed self-consciously, rubbing the back of his head.

"Uh, that's enough of that." When he removed his *syn*, the Kometa appeared confused and quickly backed off me. "Good night, Vindur," Kane said, patting him twice on the rear. Vindur blasted into the air and out of sight within seconds.

Kane removed my *syn*, pulled me close, and drove into my bedchamber.

"That was unbelievable. Thank you for taking me."

"Thank you for joining me. Here, keep this." Kane opened his hand to offer me the *syn* I was wearing. His mother's *syn*.

"Oh, I couldn't take that. It's too special."

"She'd be honored if you took it, and so would I."

Kane's previous confession about how Varjun felt about gifts was forefront in my mind. Giving a gift was a sign of great respect, and the more precious the item, the more treasured the recipient. This was an extraordinary gift. The butterflies wreaking havoc in my stomach agreed.

"Okay...thank you. I'll try to put it to good use, but I won't lie, I'll probably clock more time lying on my back or bum than actually in the sky."

Kane burst out laughing, and I relished the wondrous sound. He hugged me, lifting me off the floor and spinning in a full circle. When he gently placed me on the ground, his forefinger grazed against my chin. His voice turned deep and gravelly, full of emotion. "You're special, Cyra."

"So are you." The small amount of rosy color peeking out through his shadow-kissed cheeks made breathing difficult.

"Thank you for what you did for my people, providing them with water. And for creating a plan to get them more food. It means everything to me."

"You're welcome, but I'd do it again. I'd do anything for you." It just slipped out of my mouth, but it was the truth.

Kane's eyes widened slightly before his lips turned upward into a smile. I was still unsure what was happening with Theo and the prophecy, but these past few hours with Kane had left me in a protected cocoon of a world where only he and I existed, and I was loath to leave it.

Kane straightened and folded his arms before him, becoming the king of duty and responsibility again. "Well, after your training tomorrow, I'd like to try your plan and make a trip to Solis. Are you up for it?"

"Absolutely."

"Great. I'll see you tomorrow, beautiful Cyra."

I gaped for a second but then stopped him from leaving.

"Kane?"

"Yes?"

"Were you angry with me when we arrived on Varjutus? You almost pushed me to the ground and told me not to touch you like I made you ill. What has changed?"

His brows raised in surprise.

"Nothing has changed. I could never even come close to hating you, Cyra. I was out of my mind from grief at the loss of my father and what he did to save me. My emotions were out of control, and I was terrified that if you touched me, I would erupt in magic and hurt you. I have great power, and when I'm not in control, people can get hurt. They *have* gotten hurt. I didn't react that way because I didn't want you to touch me, Cyra. I reacted that way because I *wanted* you to. I have to try harder to control myself when I'm around you. It might have something to do with this."

Kane reached out and took both of my hands in his, and they glowed before us. Before I knew it, he had disappeared, leaving my hands in front of me like I was still holding him and desperate for more.

CHAPTER
NINE

Sleep overcame me quickly that night, exhausted from the emotional rollercoaster of the day. I tossed and turned until a dream invaded my mind, and, to my surprise, it was a letter from Adelram, but it played in my head as if he were speaking the words.

"If you are seeing this message, it means I am gone, and you are King. Don't even ask yourself if you would have seen this message if you were not chosen—Amrel assured me you'd be the next king. You were always too hard on yourself, but I suppose you got that from me. There are some things I have to tell you that I'm not proud of. They've been my constant torment for the past few thousand years.

"You don't remember this, but your mother was murdered in our home protecting your sister. The Guardians were keenly interested in both my children, but you were away with me. They ended up taking your sister. I never got to say goodbye. I couldn't leave Ilus's side when we returned to the castle. I held her for hours in a stupor of grief, and the Guardians took you in my weakness. You were gone for five years, and I searched the galaxy for you tirelessly. Finally, the Guardians approached me and told

me that they would spare my son and my rapidly dying planet if I did their bidding. What they wanted me to do was deplorable, but they assured me that they would annihilate the Varjun race and keep me alive to face the horror of my choice. I agreed to be their puppet. I couldn't bear the thought of losing you and my people. They forced me to erase the memories of every person in Eredet galaxy so they couldn't remember our histories. They wanted us to forget who we were so we were easier to control. Please forgive me for taking some of your memories. I promised I would never touch your mind but betrayed your trust. Everyone's memories are safe, saved in an orb.

They forced me to wear the Solian bracelet so they could keep tabs on me. It made me physically sick even to this day, and through the bracelet, they could drain my power and torture me when I was 'out of line'.

I'm plagued with flashes of millions of horrific memories of Eredet's suffering people, and I've often been on the brink of madness. Even with the memories stored, I can't wholly erase them all from my mind. It's an endless cycle of flashes of gruesome memories. It's the worst form of torture I've ever experienced, and I've experienced more than my fair share.

Taking our people's memories of our cherished traditions and loved ones nearly broke me. I was their king, and I betrayed them most of all. I will never be able to forgive myself. I am a stain on the list of honorable Varjun Kings.

The Guardians had me destroy hundreds of thousands of books filled with history and knowledge of Eredet's past. I've lost a part of myself over the years in order to survive and watch over our people.

I leave you another orb that contains some of your lost memories. It is entirely up to you if you choose to return them—some things are better left unknown. Take it from an overburdened soul. I understand if you hate me, I don't blame you at all. I'm sorry I was a disappointment to you and our beloved people. Just know I would go to the ends of the galaxy and beyond for you, and my limits were tested for over a thousand years. I'm not sad my agony is over, only that I won't see my extraordinary son again. You will be the king I never could be, leading our people to salvation to witness a new, bright age. I couldn't be prouder. I would suffer this all again and endure the madness.... for you."

I shot up in bed, sweating and crying. That hadn't felt like a memory. It was different—like it was happening right now.

"Kane!" I shouted as I jumped out of bed and ran to the hallway in my night dress. An immense amount of static was reaching out for me from upstairs, riddled with sorrow. My legs instinctively barreled toward it as fast as I could, dodging around the guard and following the overwhelming tug—it was stronger than I'd ever felt.

"Hey, you can't be here!" The guard yelled behind me. I ignored him and started banging on a door I'd never seen before.

"Kane! Are you okay? Kane? It's Cyra!" The air started to ripple and contort like it was forming a vortex. Not wanting to waste any more time, I tried the door, and it mercifully opened. Kane was kneeling on the ground with an orb beside him, the room unnaturally dark, like he had sucked all the light from it. There was indeed a vortex of icy wind swirling around him with objects flying in all directions. It almost looked like Kane was emitting darkness from his body, and his eyes were so bright that green light was projecting around him in the dark.

"Kane!" I yelled, but the sound of the wind muffled my voice. I walked toward him and put my hand into the vortex to push my way through to him. I expected to be cut, windburned, or even worse, but it was as if the wind was repelled from my hand. I stepped closer, and the vortex engulfed me but didn't touch me. Able to enter the bubble unharmed, I ran to Kane and knelt with him, taking him in my arms and holding him. He finally showed the first signs of life, moving his head to look at me with a hint of a tear in his eye.

"Kane, I'm so sorry." I pulled him in close and wrapped my

arms around him. All the magic stopped instantly when he lifted his arms to embrace me.

He blinked and took a deep breath as if coming out of a trance. "Cyra, what are you doing here? You could have been seriously hurt."

"Your magic bounced right off me. I'm fine. I don't know how, but I know what you saw. I dreamt the whole thing about Adelram."

He backed away from the hug to look at me with his penetrating green eyes. "That's unusual, even for mates."

"I'm sorry if I intruded, but I felt you...I couldn't leave you alone."

Kane looked off into the distance as if lost in his thoughts, and his Adam's apple bobbed as he swallowed, preparing to speak.

"I remember my mother's broken body in a dark underground tunnel. They were trying to hide beneath the castle. My mother was brutalized trying to save her children, and I never saw my sister again. They took her body, so there wasn't a proper funeral."

He stilled for a moment as if gaining the strength to continue. I squeezed his hand in reassurance.

"My father was a broken man after their deaths, in both mind and spirit, and it was only made worse when he had to endure my disappearance for five years. Little did I know it only got worse from there. He sacrificed his freedom and mental sanity to save me and my people. And he did it utterly alone since he couldn't talk to me about it. He's the reason I walked away from the Guardian's torture dungeon. My father had sold himself to set me free. He called himself a disappointment to me which is the worst part. I can never tell him that I'd die happy and proud if I could ever be half the man he was. I can't fathom the amount of anguish he suffered to keep everyone but himself safe. I want to rip Orphlam limb from limb and send him into a pit of torment from which there is no escape. I will have no mercy when I figure out how to end them."

Dark shadows surrounded Kane, creating even more of a chill than usual.

"I will do everything in my power to help make that happen," I promised.

He gently brushed a thumb across my cheek as pain and fury left his eyes. "I know you will. I appreciate how bloodthirsty you've become."

"I suppose that tends to happen when people keep trying to kill you."

He let out a small chuckle then rubbed his hand over his forehead. "Sleep is pretty much unattainable now."

"Come." I took his hand and helped him stand, leading him to his large, canopied bed. His look of vulnerability in his wide eyes made my heart skip a beat. I forced myself not to notice his bare torso and low-hanging lounge pants as he climbed into bed. I sat beside him and tugged him down, so he lay on my chest. I held him in silence, stroking his lush hair and holding his calloused hand, the soft sounds of his breath growing heavy as he slowly fell asleep.

I lay there for a while, the overwhelming desire to protect this man blazing through me. The fact that this amount of pain pierced through his unwavering strength to the point where he seemed helpless made me cling to him even tighter until sleep overtook me.

The following day I woke before Kane and returned to my room to dress and prepare for the big day ahead. As if he were attuned to my actions, Kane knocked on my bedroom door the second I was ready.

He leaned against the frame and folded his arms with a refreshed look, no hint of his turmoil from last night. "Are we ready?"

"That I am. But, Kane, I've been thinking that I also want to work on bringing as many Solians to Varjutus as we can to ensure they're protected. I think it's the best course of action if you're open to it."

Kane nodded. "Agreed. If they will come, I will welcome them, but don't be discouraged if they don't agree to it. Our feuding history won't be easily forgotten. Let's discuss a plan of action for our next trip." He touched his arm to the intersecting circles, Merick's call sign, which glowed in response. "I need to tell Merick where I'm going. He's at the castle entrance."

Kane held me close, and I ignored the shudder of excitement that ran through me at his nearness. We drove to Merick's location and found him with Meili, running his hand through her hair. After Kane explained his plan, Kal showed up in the middle of Merick's lecture about the dangers of their king going to Solis without his team.

"We're going with you," Kal agreed. "It's non-negotiable. You're King now, and it's our job to ensure your safety. Going to Solis is extremely dangerous."

Kane finally gave in. "Fine, you can all join. We're traveling to the shrouded Island of the Creator. You've been there before, so you can drive with us."

"I'm coming too," Meili demanded. We all looked at her with surprise, it was the first time I'd heard her take a firm stance, and I was beyond proud of her. Kane nodded in agreement without hesitation, and I couldn't help but swell with pride at that as well. It occurred to me that Theo probably wouldn't have reacted the same way. The distinction of rank and duty was always important to him. Small things I'd never noticed with Theo now seemed like red flags that should have been glaringly obvious. But my overwhelming fear of failure, my violent change in circumstances, and my grief had skewed my perception of reality.

Thinking of him made me remember something. "How do you all know where the island is? Theo told me no outsiders had ever been allowed inside."

"You think some Solians could keep us from anywhere we want to go?" Merick responded with a sarcastic laugh, folding his arms in front of him defensively.

"But how did you get in? I doubt they invited you. Eleri barely even let me stay."

Merick disappeared before my eyes, and I felt something touching my hair. I jerked back in alarm and heard a laugh, but it wasn't from Kane or Kal. Merick reappeared right behind me.

"Boo!"

I screeched and moved away from him, and he burst out laughing as Kane and Kal joined in. Meili came to my aid and gave Merick a displeased look before he put his hands up in defense.

"Sorry, couldn't resist. I'm the King's spy. I have the power of invisibility, and Kane can see hidden magicks. He only had to point the way."

"Right, how could I forget our special little hunt and the glowing eyes with no body."

Kane folded his arms in front of himself and glared at Merick with a look that even had the blood draining from my face.

"Okay, okay, I feel like I'm being attacked here. I'll take Meili. Let's get going. You have the Lucky Pecker, Sir?"

Kane whipped out the ridiculous wooden penis, and the men sighed in relief. Meili looked at me with horror, and I shook my head, silently telling her I'd explain later. I was happy she had the good sense to be as dumbfounded as I was.

Kane approached me and tucked me into him. He touched a

spot on his right rib cage, under his arm, which must have been his call sign for Solis.

"Kane—did you put your call sign for Solis…in your armpit?"

"It's where they belong, Cyra," Merick said with a saccharine smile. Kal and Merick raised their arms and revealed matching tattoos under their pits. I rolled my eyes in disbelief but silently laughed.

CHAPTER
TEN

Moments later, we were back in the land of sunlight. The three Varjun were temporarily blinded, their hands over their eyes, doubling over in pain. Meili and I took a moment to adjust, but we weren't affected like they were. We basked in the rays and took it in with a desperate hunger like we hadn't eaten in a week. It was glorious, and I relished it as long as possible. Meili held out her arms and turned, head raised to the sun, mimicking my delight. I felt like I was absorbing rays into my cells and regenerating life within me. I didn't realize how much I loved it or how powerful it made me feel.

"Blasted planet! I always forget how much I hate it here," Merick shouted, rubbing his red, running eyes.

"I never forget." Kal's monotone disapproval made me put a hand to my mouth to stop myself from laughing at them. His own eyes were just as bloodshot and runny.

"You won't hear any arguments from me." Kane's reply held much more hurt and trauma, making a knot twist in my gut. He had too many bad memories of this place that kept him and his father as unwelcome hired help.

The door to the temple burst open, causing us all to flinch and turn to witness Eleri running toward us, screaming. I sighed, bracing for impact. Whenever I saw that woman, it grated against my nerves in a way that even Adelram couldn't achieve. At least he was honest and upfront with how much of a dick he was. The fake front and the fact that she betrayed our trusting people with lies bothered me.

"I knew you couldn't be trusted! Where is Theo? Did you get him killed?"

I raised an eyebrow at her, refusing to acknowledge her antics. *I* was the untrustworthy one?

"As if I needed *more* reminders of why I hate this planet. One minute of merely standing and minding our own business, and we're hit with theatrics." Merick spat.

"Eleri, that's enough. We're merely in need of temporary shelter, and we will be gone quickly. We have no quarrels with you, and Theo is not dead. He's just unconscious and healing." I kept my voice even as possible, trying to be the bigger person.

She stopped directly before me, her head high, as if she'd get a message from Amrel at any moment. "Why do I find it so hard to believe that?" A small, nagging part of me knew that if he passed away, she would be correct, and I stood still as she came at me, about to slap my face, but Kane held out his hand, and a force made her fall back to the ground as a feral growl erupted from him.

"You will not touch any of my people, including Cyra." Kane's voice boomed through the island, causing the onlookers from the temple to cower. I felt him look down at me to make sure I was okay, and as our eyes locked, my breath hitched at the wild concern and possessiveness there. He called me one of his people, and those simple words damn near made me cry. I belonged with him and didn't know why it had taken me so long to realize it.

"Cyra!" I heard a yell from behind the people in the doorway, and they parted to reveal Vish.

"Vish! I ran to him and jumped into his arms, thankful he was safe and in one piece. He twirled me around and kissed me on the cheek multiple times. Eleri stood and brushed herself off, clearly seething but unable to do anything about it.

"I'm so glad you're protected. I'm so sorry for leaving you behind," I said with tears.

"It wasn't your fault. I'm just glad you're safe. How is he?"

I knew he was talking about the only family he had—Theo. "He's alive and stable. We're looking after him."

Vish sighed in relief then looked at Kane. There was no love lost between them.

But Kal was the one to speak. "Hands off the lady." The grit in his voice would have made anyone cower. He closed in on Vish, causing him to put me down, and I could see the color drain from his face while Kane beamed at Kal with his arms folded. A small part of me was giddy by Kal's desire to protect me as one of them.

"Okay, everyone, relax," I said. "Vish is my friend, and I'd like him to return with us to Varjutus since the Guardians will be looking for him. It'll be safer for everyone, including the Solians hiding at the temple. We will work on a plan to bring more Solians over safely."

"Is that necessary?" Merick asked, rubbing at his temple.

Kane looked at me, and I sent him a plea through our connection. He softened immediately and pursed his lips.

"The Solian will come with us."

Kal was about to speak, but Kane cut him off.

"It will be my responsibility to watch him. One tiny step out of line, he returns to this hell hole where the Guardians can feast on his flesh."

Vish's eyes bulged, but he didn't say anything. He just looked at me and smiled, holding my hands.

"Well, you're not coming in here," Eleri said before turning her back and leaving us. Her long, flowing dress billowed behind her as she took the Solians back inside and closed the door. The temple disappeared once again.

"Finally," I said, rolling my eyes. Everyone looked at me, surprised I'd talk that way about a fellow Solian. "What? I've never liked her. She's a fraud. Now let's go while we don't have an audience."

Kane's lips turned up at one corner, and he winked as I silently chided my racing heart for acting like a love-struck schoolgirl.

I inched closer to the ocean and cupped my hands to my mouth, yelling into the skies. "Laine!"

"Has she lost it? Is she summoning someone from Eluroom? Because I don't think they'll be able to hear," Merick jokingly asked.

"Just wait," Kane assured him.

A delicate pulsating voice entered my mind as if she spoke through caverns in the ocean. "I'm almost there." Laine's echoes increased as she got closer, and I could feel the rushing velocity of her speed. Moments later, she flew from the ocean, diving into the air as we all witnessed her full glory, a serpent-like sea dragon that commanded attention. She fell to the shore and stood before us, massive and intimidating. Kal stumbled back, and Merick fell over, his eyes bulging and mouth parted in utter shock.

I took the opportunity to boast since most of my hours were spent in the company of others with more talent, power, and knowledge than me. "Don't worry, Merick. I won't laugh if you pee yourself. Laine can have that effect on people." Vish choked through a laugh, and Merick hissed at him.

My hand went to Laine's lowered head as she spoke again. "I've missed you. I'd hoped you hadn't forgotten me."

"I missed you too. I wish I could take you with me. I could *never* forget you. Plus, you wouldn't be pleased with the lack of water."

"You must be on Varjutus."

"Yes, how did you know?"

"The Paela are in tune with the balance of the galaxy. We can feel the suffering planet barren of water and have visions of some things fated to pass. Amrel also told us what would happen to our worlds."

"Is she talking to herself? What the hell is happening?" Merick asked.

"Just shut up, will you?" Vish retorted.

They began quietly arguing, but I tuned them out as I focused on Laine. "You are here for the gate in your family's land," Laine surmised.

"Yes. Again, you surprise me. Laine, can you take Kane and my friends with you, or am I the only one who can ride you?"

"I can if I must, but there is no need for the one called Kane."

"What do you mean?" I quickly glanced at Kane, and he tilted his head, wondering why.

"There is another living *Paeladon* waiting for acceptance."

Suddenly a midnight blue, lavender, and cerulean-colored Paela flew into the sky and landed before us next to Laine. The two Paela side by side was enough to humble anyone, and we were lucky enough to witness this rare and incredible sight that would be ingrained into my memory forever.

"Oh my god," I said, turning to Kane. "This is Josko, and he is *your* Paela."

"Mine?" he asked, his hand to his chest and his mouth parted. "I'm not even from Solis."

"Laine says you are a King of Eredet and are worthy of the bond."

Hearing those words was like experiencing wondrous silence after harsh, anxiety-inducing noise like my body could release and be at peace after worrying for so long. I closed my eyes and felt every inch of my body heat up with awe and relief.

He is my king.

"Cyra?" Kane asked desperately, jarring me from my internal thoughts.

"Sorry. All you need to do is touch him to accept the bond. He will wait for your lead. You'll be able to breathe underwater through the *Paeladon*. As Laine told me, he will be your breath, and you will be his voice."

Kane looked at Kal and Merick with disbelief. "I don't know what to say."

"Are you sure you can trust this?" Merick asked.

"This is unbelievable," Vish grumbled, shaking his head and running a hand down his face.

But Kal was in total awe, causing us to stare at his uncharacteristic enthusiasm. "It is the highest honor. My father told me of the *Paeladoned* Warriors. They are extremely rare and thought to be the greatest protectors of our lands. It would be a mistake to refuse."

"Extremely rare, yet *she* was able to bond with one," Merick said, pointing at me.

Laine let out a piercing shriek, her eyes glowing red with rage. Liquid lava shot out of her mouth toward Merick, and he ducked onto the ground, barely escaping the molten heat. She stalked closer, causing the earth to quiver, until she stood over him, nearly touching her face to his.

"Oh, holy fuck!" he yelled, trying to inch away on his back. She raised and spread her massive wings to look even more threatening.

"Cyra?" Kane called to me, worried for his friend.

I walked up to her with no expression, running my hand along her muscled body, and looked down at Merick with a smugness I wasn't used to. But I certainly didn't hate the feeling. "Don't worry. She won't kill without my permission. I didn't even know she could do that. Pretty cool, huh? Oh, by the way, she said never to disrespect me in her presence again. Or she won't wait for my permission. Guess I lied." I shrugged with indifference, my lips pursing to the side.

"It was just a joke, I swear, but yeah, no worries," Merick responded, his eyes still wide. Any trace of his usual sarcasm and arrogance was gone. Laine tucked her wings into her sides again and slowly stalked back toward the water, arching her long neck backward to look at him again as if daring him to speak again. He didn't move an iota except to widen his eyes even further, making the scene comical.

It was an effort to keep my fierce no-nonsense persona intact as Meili rushed to his side to help him. Kane looked as confused as ever while Josko moved his head down closer to Kane so he could touch him. I grabbed his hand and nodded with a reassuring smile.

"Go ahead. You won't regret it. It's unlike anything you've ever experienced. Or at least I think so. You are much older than me, after all." Kane let out a laugh but nodded his head. He reached out his hand, and light shot from the point of contact down the Paela to Kane's feet. He gasped loudly.

"He's talking to me. I feel him within me." Kane slid his hand down the Paela's long neck while Josko nuzzled him. "This is incredible."

A wave of exhilaration shot through our own unknown bond. Two little secrets only we knew—the bond of a Paela and the one with each other.

"We should get moving," I said. "Meili comes with me."

"Merick, go with Kane. I'll stay behind until you return for me, and I'll kill anyone who comes outside of the temple," Kal promised, tucking his arms behind his back.

I raised my eyebrow at him, but he smirked in response and winked at me.

Oh lord. *Let there be no dead bodies when I return.* Vish had the same thought, nervously shifting his weight back and forth. He was no green warrior, and I had seen his awe-inspiring skills and unparalleled strength, but there was something about Kalmali that commanded fear.

"Vish, I'll be right back for you." He nodded to me but side-eyed Kal in a silent request to hurry back for him.

CHAPTER
ELEVEN

With all four of us on the backs of Laine and Josko, we went diving into the ocean's depths at lightning speed. Laine and Josko played with each other as we swam, crossing paths with each other, racing to see who could arrive first.

"Josko is slow. He is no match for me," Laine said in my mind. Josko must have said something in return because Kane smiled at me. By some magical force, our eyes didn't seem to be affected by the velocity of our travel. I couldn't feel the water hitting my eyes or drenching me.

It was like a rollercoaster with a drop that never ended, my stomach doing somersaults in my core, and I loved every freaking second of it. The speed, the agile movement, and the brief glimpses of exotic Solian sea life had me brimming with exhilaration. And it only grew when some of the little seahorse creatures I had played with long ago found me and tried to race alongside us for a few moments before they ate Laine's and Josko's dust.

We reached the private lands in no time, and the Paela emerged from the water like magnificent soaring beasts. Dismounting Laine was always fun, like a fifteen feet long wet and wild slide. My sweet Paela was like an adventurous day at a theme park.

"Will you be able to get us inside?" Kane asked, bringing me out of my silly daydreams. We walked toward the invisible barrier and watched the energy from it shimmer like heat evaporating in the summer.

"I've been praying that I can. I was able to escape by willing myself out of the invisible barrier, so I hope I'll be able to do the same to get in with guests."

My hand reached out to the barrier and mercifully went through without trouble. It began to close around my hand, sealing itself up again, but I willed it to open further, creating a small doorway.

"Kane, try to walk through."

He stepped inside successfully, so I motioned for Meili and Merick to join. Kane came back out since we had to bring Vish and Kal.

I turned my attention to Merick and pointed a finger at him. "Don't touch *anything*!"

He folded his arms, shifting his weight to one leg. "Why am I always the bad guy?"

"I trust Meili. Don't touch anything."

"Fine!" He held his hands up defensively, eyeing Laine uncertainly, still sore about their tiff. She let out a loud huff through her nostrils as if reminding him what she could do if he didn't behave.

Kane and I mounted our Paela again and headed back to the Island of the Creator. Laine could feel my unease leaving people there without me, so we made our trip quick and undistracted.

Vish and Kal stood far away from each other, facing opposite directions as if it pained them to be in each other's presence. I rolled my eyes and motioned for Vish.

He jumped up, sat behind me, and put his hands on my waist. A swelling, fierce static emitted from Kane, causing me to jump in surprise. Vish and I looked in his direction, and when he saw Kane's threatening look, he wrapped his arms around me completely. We dove into the water before Kane could jump off Josko and attack Vish.

"Kane does not like another male touching you," Laine observed. The corner of my lip turned upward of its own accord. "And you quite enjoy the fact." The smile was wiped from my face as I looked up in shock. "Don't forget your mind is an open book to me, and whether you can process your thoughts accurately or not, I see things for what they are."

"What do you mean?"

"I know what you and Kane are." She spoke as if she was reporting the news and not dropping life-altering information.

"Mates? Kane already told me he thought we were." She went silent since we were approaching the shore, and Laine emerged from the water, stepping onto the sand as the sun caused the dripping water to look like she was sparkling. Vish jumped off and helped me down, waiting for me to let him in, but I turned back to Laine as Kane surfaced with Kal.

"It is much more than that. Seek the Varjun Elder, and he will be able to guide you." She turned and returned to the ocean, Josko following, leaving me with my jaw to the ground.

"Wait! What do you mean!"

"Cyra, what happened?"

Crap. Did I say that out loud? It was confusing at times to go between the two methods of communication. And why was a sea dragon always outsmarting me?

I put my hand on his arm, which glowed at the touch. "I'll tell you later." He placed his hand on the small of my back and led me toward the invisible barrier. It parted at my command, and as we entered, it didn't escape my notice that Vish watched us suspiciously.

"I didn't let him move an inch, Cyra!" Meili said, puffing her chest with pride. I laughed at Merick, sighing in annoyance. Not that I thought I had to worry much about Merick anymore since he got a taste of Laine's wrath, and she was a tad scarier than Meili and her sweetness.

"Thanks, Meili. Welcome to the Fenix private lands." The warm air infiltrated my lungs as I breathed deeply, missing my birth-place's familiar, clean, energetic smell. The lush varieties of oak trees and other unknown species swayed slightly, creating that calming symphony of clashing leaves that I loved so much. Outside of these barriers, the air was still and tainted, but here, the evil influence of Orphlam could not be felt.

What an astounding contrast to the decay of Varjutus.

The grasses were vivid green and fresh as if they were tended to daily, even though nobody stepped inside. It was a small paradise maintained by magic and the beautiful hope of our future.

The small cottages that appeared to be handmade from the same wood of the lands were off in the distance, housing some of the most vital documents we had left. "Vish, that cottage is where I found all the history books. You're welcome to take a look."

"Truly?" For the first time since seeing him again, genuine excitement and joy emanated from him.

"Yep! We need an official historian to recover our lost knowl-edge. I'd be happy if you studied everything you can in this place."

"Cyra, thank you so much."

Meili knelt to her knees. "These are fertile lands." She dug her fingers into the dirt and inspected it closely. Vish joined her, assessing the soil.

"Yes, they're ideal for growing," he agreed, utilizing his family's long farming history.

"Vish, can you get seeds from your farm?" Meili turned to him with a fresh excitement in her eyes.

"What are you thinking, cherub?" Merick ran his finger through one of her curls. His sweetness toward her was touching, even if I sometimes thought he was a pain in the ass.

"Come, I'll show you." Meili led us to a single smaller tree, slightly contorted with thinner bark. "This is an apple tree, but it's not in bloom. It could be how these maagaline birds survived here since they don't need to eat often." She touched her hand on the tree, and her hands glowed. It slowly started to bud flowers that transformed into vibrant, ripe apples. She picked one and held it up.

"Can someone cut this in half?" The apple was immediately sliced in two, and I had no idea who had done it. She took a few seeds from it and buried them in the soil. Putting her hands back into the earth, they glowed, causing a small plant to sprout.

"I can encourage and accelerate growth but can't create it from nothing. If I have seeds, I can create a whole garden in these lands. There is lots of space for it."

"Meili, that is perfect. It'll help supplement food from the stores we can get from Bad," I replied.

"Excellent, Meili, you have my utmost thanks." Kane lowered his head to her in a nod while Merick took her hands and kissed them.

"Thank you, my treasure."

Kane tilted his head at Merick with raised eyebrows, perhaps unaware of how quickly their relationship had progressed. It's certainly how I felt about it since I hadn't seen much of Meili recently, but it was clear they were becoming infatuated with each other, and it lightened my heart that Meili had that comfort.

"Speaking of the stores, I will use one of these maagaline to send a message to Bad to meet us here." I encouraged one of the birds to come to my arm before entering the cottage and writing a note. They were magically gifted creatures who could understand speech, so I instructed the bird that it was for the chef in the Eluroom castle kitchens. I folded the note and put it in the bird's claw, and it took flight, disappearing outside the barrier. Perhaps they were living here for protection from the outside which made me feel guilty for sending it into a land they were trying to avoid.

Everyone joined me inside the cottage and started looking around.

"Kane, look, these are books about Varjutus," Merick shared with excitement.

"And Looma!" Meili said, mirroring his enthusiasm. "But I can't open it."

"Nor I," Merick agreed.

"Kane, this is the book I took the sketch of that Adelram said was the symbol for Amrel. I'm not able to open this either."

"I wonder if it's a biography." Kane took it with interest, inspecting the cover and running his finger over the solar flare design with galactic rings surrounding it.

"Those were my thoughts as well."

"Imagine how invaluable that would be?" Merick hesitated for a moment, his brows lowering as he blinked quickly. "Or dangerous that would be in the wrong hands." He looked at Kane, then all of us. We nodded, agreeing that we would keep it safe here.

"I might be able to copy these books so we can take them back with us." Meili picked up the Looma history book and bowed her head with closed eyes. "Something is blocking me. I can't copy it. We're probably better off leaving all of them here anyway."

The maagaline bird reappeared, its long, colorful wings flapping powerfully as it hovered before me to deliver Bad's note into my hand.

I'm here at the gates. Hurry.

"He's here!" I raised the note, flapping the paper. "Let's go get him."

We went to the front gate, where Bad was waiting with massive amounts of produce, meats, and water containers.

"Bad you've outdone yourself. This is incredible." My eyes ran over the bountiful supply of food as the crushing weight of dread and worry of Varjutus starving dissipated, letting me breathe with ease. He grabbed me tight in an embrace.

"I'm so happy to see you, my sweet one. I'm glad you're not on Solis so we can ensure your safety. Thank you for watching her," he said to Kane, who looked surprised but nodded back.

"What word do you have of the Guardians?" I asked.

"Not a thing. They've been eerily quiet and non-existent, which has everyone on edge."

"Well, at least there's no bad news. We need to get this inside quickly."

"I can shroud this area so the food is invisible to outsiders," Merick offered. A thin translucent veil shot from his outstretched hands. It wrapped around the massive pile of food until the veil disappeared while the food was still in place.

"We will be the only ones who can see, smell or sense it. It'll be like it doesn't exist," Merick promised. Meili smiled at him with pride, interlacing her fingers with his as he pulled her tightly.

"That's perfect. Then this can be the drop-off spot. Will the invisibility hold?" I asked.

"It'll hold until I make it disappear so we can use this in the future."

"Well, let's get it inside then." Bad threw out his hands as he stumbled a little bit.

"What is it? Are you okay?" He appeared to have some vertigo, so I helped steady him.

"Yes, my energy stores are running low. This transfer takes a lot of power," Bad admitted, rubbing the back of his head.

Power and energy are the real currencies of Solis.

"How do I transfer energy to you?" I asked.

"Cyra, that's not a good idea," Kane advised, straightening with kingly authority. "You're still learning about your ability, and your powers are uncertain. You'll need every ounce of energy if you're in danger."

"I don't care. Bad is risking his life and energy for us. I will return some of it if I can."

"Cyra, it's okay, really. I don't need much power. I'm only a cook, after all." Bad gave a dismissive shrug, diminishing his importance which stung me. He was like a member of my family and an essential part of Solis's community, always selfless and empathetic.

Grabbing his hand, I closed my eyes and felt that matrix of energy all around me. The more I attempted it, the quicker it was to respond. And while it still wasn't second nature to me, it was becoming less difficult. I absorbed what little I could and pushed it out of me into Bad's essence. His hands began to glow as he successfully absorbed it.

It was only a moment or two before Bad cried out. "Woah, Cyra, that's enough!" He held his head, looking woozy again.

"But I barely sent you any energy. It was next to nothing." I was confused by the minuscule drop I shared that he almost seemed sickened by. It scared me more than I liked to admit because all I could think of was Orphlam and his unnatural energy–and it always made me sick.

Was there something wrong with me?

Bad's brows hit his hairline in shock. "If that's what you consider a little energy, then you have the most power I've ever felt." There was a flash of fear behind his eyes, making me shiver with dread. With my Solian grandfather, known as the Demon Reina, and the Guardians so interested in my power, I prayed with everything I had that I wasn't more like them than I feared.

I thought back to when I recklessly put on the power bracelet. It had felt *so good*, and I gave in without a second thought. I'd been trying to keep that horror buried deep in my mind since it happened, but it kept resurfacing—a constant nightmare that followed every step I took, waiting for me to give up on this fight. Or for me to fail, which was still a high possibility.

Kane looked as if he was studying me again, and I recalled his conversation with Jonsi, trying to figure me out like I was some rare, dangerous creature. Shaking those destructive thoughts away, I began picking up food to bring it in, but Kane stopped me.

"I can transport all of this inside and to the gate." He held out his hands, and the food was lifted into the air as if it were all connected, and it floated with ease to the *Sild Gate* as he promised, not even breaking a sweat.

"Bad, why don't you come in? I'll show you my parents' private lands."

"Me? In the royal secret, enchanted lands?"

I laughed and nodded. "Yep."

"Are you sure?"

"Just come in, silly." I grabbed his arm and pulled him in.

"Can this Solian be trusted?" Merick asked, holding his hand out to block Bad.

My eyes fluttered in annoyance. "You don't trust anyone, do you?"

"Absolutely not, and you shouldn't either if you know what's good for you."

"I let you in, didn't I? But Kane and Meili trust you, so that's good enough for me. Just believe that I would never risk my parent's land."

Kane smiled at our interaction as Merick loudly huffed in response, backing away with his hands raised. I took that as his resignation.

"Come, Bad. I have something to show you." I took his hand and quickly walked back to the cottage.

"Everything is not lost. We have tons of history books my parents kept hidden here that document who we are. Most of them are locked but look. I was able to open this one."

I handed him the last book in the Solian series. He opened it and turned the pages, his eyes slowly growing wide as his hands shook. Tears lined his cheeks as he took a deep, cleansing breath.

"Cyra, this place gives me so much hope. I will spread the word to the people that you are doing everything possible to defeat the Guardians. They need some hope too."

"Just don't tell them of this place or anything in it," Kane said.

"No, of course. I won't. Your parents would be so proud of you," Bad said through tears.

I gently took the book from him and grabbed a picture I had seen the last time I visited. "Here, look at this. It's a memory of my parents when I was a baby. You'll appreciate seeing them again." It came to life once he took the photo and repeated the scene I saw months ago.

"Is that Amrel the Creator?" Kal's jaw mimicked his eyes, wide and astonished as he moved toward the life-like holographic images as if hoping to touch them. The projection from the photo made it seem like Grandpa was standing right beside us, if only a little grainy and less vibrant.

Merick and Kane mirrored Kal's reaction, nearly falling to their knees with deference. Kal and Merick looked at me like they'd just seen me for the first time, and I might have even seen some fear in there somewhere. I could handle many things but couldn't handle being a monster, and I felt more and more like one by the minute.

"He's absolutely beautiful," Meili said breathlessly, tears falling down her cheeks.

I was confused. Did Grandpa really *never* appear to anybody in the galaxy but just a select few? Is that why they called Adelram a Chosen One of Amrel's? Suddenly I heard a part of the memory that made me cringe. How did I not remember it was in there?

"No! Do not use that asshole Adelram to take my daughter's memories of us. I beg you, please don't take them from her," Rhythen pleaded.

"We must, Rhythen. I'm so very sorry, but we must. And never speak of Adelram in that way again."

"Kane...I'm so sorry. I didn't remember that. They didn't know or understand Adelram as we do. I'm sorry." I panicked, mortified of what these Varjun would think of my parents talking ill of such a misunderstood but beloved man.

"Kal, Merick, I apologize for my parent's comments." They both stared at me, unsure of how to react but distraught by what they heard.

"It's okay, Cyra. You're not your parents. I know how you felt about my father. Also, you have no idea how happy it makes me to hear Amrel the Creator defend him from his own mouth. I..." Kane put his hand to his heart and cleared his throat, unable to speak.

I instinctively went to him, burrowing into his body as he put his arm around me.

"Kane, I know I told you before, but Grandpa shared some of his memories of Adelram with me. He loved him dearly."

Kal stepped forward. "Why do you refer to him as Grandpa?"

"He cared for me on Earth, as you saw in the memory. They were planning to take me there if anything happened to my parents. Amrel The Creator, as you call him, raised me himself with my adoptive parents. To me, he was just Grandpa. There's another memory here where the Oracle tells Grandpa that I have his closest genetic makeup since the beginning of time, so I am basically his daughter."

"What? You didn't tell me this," Kane blurted with disbelief.

Kal straightened and scratched the back of his neck. Meili came over and hugged me. "I could feel it in you, you know?" Meili said, smiling.

"What do you mean, Meili?" I asked, astounded.

"Remember when I told you your power wasn't fire?"

The blood drained from my face, and my pulse quickened. "Yes, it's about time you explained yourself. I assumed in the meantime my power wasn't fire since my abilities have been random and unexplainable."

"I felt it from you since the moment you came. You have Sunya in you. You're not just Solian. Amrel The Creator's power comes from the sun and the universe." My breath stopped waiting for her to finish. "And so does yours."

CHAPTER TWELVE

"Wait, what? What are you talking about?" Why was the rug pulled from under me whenever I thought I was starting to understand who I was?

Kane said nothing, rubbing his hand over his face in disbelief. His shock unsettled me the most.

"That's incredible," Bad whispered.

"Well, you're Sunya, Meili. Does your power come from the sun?"

"No! Well, technically, the sun provides energy to everything around us, but we absorb our energy from small sources like fire, water, earth, etc. It's generally concentrated in an area, so we're only tapping into a few resources while the sun replenishes our energy. You can access energy directly from the source and the world around you."

"That's why my fire didn't ignite by trying to connect with it. My power was easier to wield outside, connecting with the sun and nature."

Meili nodded. "It was told to me by the Immortal Counsel that Amrel the Creator was a piece of our sun that broke free and took form. He *was* pure energy, which meant he could create life."

I sat on the closest sofa, needing to steady myself as Meili continued her explanation.

"His first creations were the Sunya Rei, higher beings of Looma. They were a step below Amrel the Creator and unable to procreate as regular beings do. His next creations were the Sunya, who got their power from nature. It's why we have similar characteristics to The Creator but on a much smaller scale. Next, he created the Varjun, who could draw power from their moons and surroundings in various ways. His last creations in Eredet were the Solians, thus completing the beings of Eredet, the first galaxy with life. If your genetic makeup is close to Amrel, it makes sense that you would have some similarities in power."

"Well, I didn't expect that," Merick said.

"Yeah, what he said," Kane muttered.

"It's no wonder you're in the prophecy," Vish said. "But now, what of the King of Eredet?"

Everyone went silent and awkwardly turned toward Kane.

"It's obviously Kane. Theo's laying on a slab, unable to wake," Merick said. "You are the only functioning King in Eredet right now, and it's glaringly obvious to everyone here that you have some connection with her. It's you, Kane."

Vish crossed his arms so tightly that his biceps were bursting. "No. No, that can't be right."

Merick and Kal growled simultaneously.

"Look, if Kane is the King the prophecy refers to, that is nobody's business but his and mine, and we don't need your comments. I would be so lucky if a fiercely loyal, protective, and loving Varjun would ever consider me." When I realized what I'd just said, heat rushed to my cheeks with embarrassment. "Not that I'm asking any of them to."

Kane looked down and bobbed on his feet with a smirk while

Merick and Kal gave me genuine smiles. Merick walked up and patted my back.

"You're making it really hard for me to continue hating you, and I had so much fun doing it."

"I told you I'd never hang out with you again if you did," Meili said.

"And what of Theo? How quickly you forget him?" Vish rubbed at his arm, shaking his head as if trying to erase his pain.

Vish was clearly speaking out of loyalty and love for his friend, but it felt like a punch to the gut. Guilt still plagued me, with him lying close to death as I pined after another man. I know I had never formally committed or given him a firm answer, but it was all implied. He would be blindsided when he woke.

Shame and dread came crashing down on me. I couldn't control the shaking of my hands or my erratic breathing, so I ran outside, attempting to calm myself down. Meili began to follow me, but Kane rushed to my side faster.

"I can't breathe." It was frustrating how I had been struggling lately with my wild emotions, as if they had a life of their own and I was no longer in the driver's seat.

Kane scooped me up in his arms and walked away with me toward the apple tree with the maagaline birds cuddling on a twisted branch. As we approached, they both whistled a soothing song as if they knew what I was going through.

"Take slow breaths in and out. Theo's injury was not your fault. It was a tragic accident. Try to calm yourself. You cannot burst into magic here. The Guardians could sense it."

His soothing scent enveloped me, his pheromones bonding with mine, slowly easing my panic. Kane was right. The last thing I wanted was for the Guardians to find us.

"I miss him. I do feel guilty. He was a joy to be around and cared about people. I loved him..." Kane flinched. "...but I don't think I was ever *in* love with him."

I pictured my Earth parents, and at that moment, I understood why grandpa Amrel had chosen them. They had given me a clear and wonderful example of true love, and deep down, I knew I didn't have that with Theo, no matter how much I buried the truth and lived in denial.

"I know, Cyra."

"And I feel guilty for that too."

"You can't help who you love." He gently touched my chin, and raised my head to look at him. "All you can do is accept it when it's right."

"How do you know when it's right?" My heart was pounding out of my chest for an entirely different reason now. I had been so convinced that choosing Theo was the right thing to do, and I was beginning to feel like an idiot for not looking at things more clearly. Kane answered as if he could see right into my thoughts.

"I don't think it's a rational choice you make, but an all-consuming need that lights a fire within you and makes you feel the most delicious yearning that only one person in all the universe can fulfill. It's existing for a thousand years only to learn what it means to be alive, and the senses you've lived with all your life are awakened with a new dawn so that every precious moment tastes that much sweeter in a way you never knew possible. It's some-thing that lives forever here," he said, putting his palm on my heart between my breasts.

I stifled a moan, leaning my head back onto his bicep as he held me with one arm. Nobody existed except him and me at this moment, and I was filled with every emotion he had just listed. "You sound as if you've been in love."

Kane was quiet momentarily, and his lids lowered slightly as I melted at the softness I only saw when he was with me. But he didn't answer my question.

"Your heart is beating pretty fast. Anything the matter?" Kane's piercing green eyes sucked me in, and I wanted to get lost in them forever. He touched my face causing my whole body to light up in a soft white glow.

"Well, that's new. It seems like you like that." His deep chuckling was hypnotic, and his smile was a new joy I never knew I needed. My crimson cheeks were just one more piece of evidence of my body so easily giving me away. It wasn't fair. But I held his hand, which was on my face, and I turned into it, breathing him in.

"Cyra, you should probably come in here!" Meili yelled.

Kane rolled his eyes and growled, the rumbling in his chest solid and loud. He put me down reluctantly, and I took a moment to return to reality, slightly annoyed that we were interrupted. But I ran back to the cottage anyway. Everyone was standing there like their hand was caught in the cookie jar, not moving an inch. And Vish had a black eye.

"What's going on here?" I put my hands on my hips, questioning my life since I felt like a mother hen disciplining a group of men older than dirt.

"We're just bonding," Merick said, an exaggerated smile on his face.

"Vish has nothing more to say to you today," Kal said in a monotone, his eyes dead and cold.

"I'm just trying to stay far out of the way," Bad whimpered, shrinking as small as possible to remain unseen.

Kane bellowed in laughter, folding his arms before him, clearly pleased with his friends.

I pinched the bridge of my nose. "Look, we're spending too much time here. Let's try to open the gate and get the food in. The Varjun people are the priority. We can come back another time and look through the rest of the stuff that's here."

Kal held up a hand. "Wait! Before we go, can we see the memory where the Oracle says you're Amrel's daughter?" I did a double-take at him to see if he was serious.

"Uh, sure. It's a really quick one. Here." It began playing when I picked it up. Everyone watched with wonder seeing the beautiful High Oracle Siare and awe-inspiring Amrel before us. When it finished, Merick spoke first.

"I feel like there was something between the lines they didn't mention when they spoke about you."

"I don't know," I said honestly.

"The Eredet King…" Kal said, looking at Kane, raising his head and his chest with pride.

"Cyra, I better get going. Send a bird when you need more stores of food. I will try to provide it once a week if that works," Bad said.

"Yes, it works perfectly. I can't thank you enough, Bad. Also, speak to Blaze. We will start arranging for Solians to come to Varjutus for refuge. Tell him to create a schedule of people that will come over in the order he thinks best."

"Great idea."

"Bad, you have my utmost thanks, and I am forever in your debt for helping my people. You may call on me when you are in need of help." Kane shook his hand with a firm grip making Bad wince a little in pain.

"I..uh…wow, thanks." Bad kissed me on the cheek and left the grounds.

"Maybe not *all* Solians are scum, huh?" Merick's timing on insults was impeccable. My nostrils flared as Kane gave him an incredulous look. Vish sneered but kept his distance, not wanting to start another 'discussion.'

I rubbed my temples, realizing that having a large amount of Solians and Varjun together would be significantly more compli-cated than I thought.

"Now, let's open this gate," I said, trying to put that out of my mind. When I was directly before it, I tried to recall Grandpa's symbols. The vision reappeared again quickly when I shut my eyes and concentrated. I wrote the runes onto the stones with my hands, and I felt something happening, connecting to my power. When I copied the vision exactly, I put my hand on the stone as Grandpa did, and the gate started to transform before our eyes.

"That's the basement of the Varjun castle." The tone of Merick's disbelief was music to my ears, albeit a little insulting—even if I wasn't even confident in my own skills.

"I will go in first and test it," Kal insisted.

"No, Kal, I should do it." Kane touched his shoulder, but Kal quickly shrugged it off.

"With all due respect, my king…fuck no." Kal walked through without a moment's hesitation. We all held our breath, wondering if he'd actually make it to Varjutus, but we were reassured when Kal turned back to us with a comical smile plastered on his face.

"I can't believe it worked. Sire, try to move the food through the gate."

Kane magically grabbed all the newly acquired precious resources and slowly pushed them through the gate, and Kal moved aside to let them in. He successfully placed it on the ground on the other side, causing excitement in everyone except Vish, who was still skulking around. I was doing cartwheels in my mind. We had just outwitted the Guardians, and the Varjun people would benefit. There were so many horrible things happening in Eredet that I couldn't help but celebrate this one victory.

Merick and Meili were the next ones to go through the gate. I looked back at Vish, who just stood there.

"Vish? Are you coming?"

"Are you sure you want me there?" He couldn't make eye contact with me, and I knew he felt guilty for his previous comment. All of us were feeling the stresses of the state of our worlds, and I didn't hold it against him.

"Yes, or I wouldn't have asked. Come on," I said, motioning toward the gate. Vish hesitantly walked through, leaving his beloved home behind and stepping into the unknown. Kane took my hand, so we walked through together, a small parallel to how our journey was progressing.

When we were all on the other side, I touched the gate at the same spot, and it closed again like there was nothing but a wall.

Kane bent down, picked up a shiny red apple, threw it in the air, and caught it. "Let's go celebrate with our people and share the wealth, shall we?"

Merick was the first to respond. "Fuck yes." Kal clapped Kane on the shoulder with relief and excitement on his face.

After placing the apple back in a basket, Kane raised his hands, causing all the food and water to disappear.

"To Baum Village." Kane took me in his arms, and we appeared in a new location I'd never seen before. I gasped at the condition of the shacks falling apart.

"I know, it's terrible. We haven't had new resources in over a thousand years to be able to rebuild. We can't afford to cut down any of our trees, although now, with even less water, many more will die. I know my father has tried in the past to get resources from Solis but was usually unsuccessful."

"I'm so sorry, Kane." Meili, Merick, and Kal appeared, and it took me a minute to realize Vish wouldn't be able to find his way here on his own.

"Can someone please bring Vish here? This is a new planet to him; I don't want him to be left out."

"You still want to look at his ugly face after how he spoke to you?" Merick asked incredulously, running a hand through his thick, lush hair.

While I appreciated Merick's growing respect for me, he was still a bit of a jerk. "He's still grieving. Give him a break. He is a good person. He's just hurting because his best friend, and the man who saved his life, might not live. He's lost."

Merick shook his head and grunted, taking a step away from me. "Ugh, I have to be careful that her goodness doesn't rub off and infect me. She and Meili both. Fine! I will go get the idiot." Merick disappeared, and I giggled at Meili.

Kane touched his King's Mark and took my hand in his. He folded his fingers into mine, light emitting at the point of contact. He had a blindingly beautiful smile, and I was afraid I'd swoon and pass out in front of the incredible number of Varjun that just appeared before us.

"I can call on my people in emergencies or important announcements. I'd say this is one of them," he said quietly. My lips turned upward at his swell of pride, able to provide for his people.

I noticed Merick and Vish appear behind us, and when I turned around, Vish was pursing his lips at the sight of Kane and me holding hands.

The people erupted in noise at the sight of the bountiful food before them.

"My friends!" Kane's voice boomed through the crowd as if he had a megaphone so everyone could hear.

"I have some incredible news. We have been blessed by finding a way to bring food now that the Guardians have cut us off. Cyra has contacted some of her loyal friends on Solis, who have agreed to help us in our time of need. They are risking their lives to smuggle food that only Cyra can transport here undetected. We thank The Creator for this blessing, and I will divide the food evenly by village."

The Varjun erupted into cheers again, some chanting out praises as many people ran up to start drinking the water. The supply was already half depleted when they were done with it, and worry was etched into the creases of Kane's forehead. Thankfully, I knew how to fix it and approached it, filling it again with ease. Gasps and muffled sounds of surprise sounded.

"We are also blessed that Cyra can replenish some of our water stores with her power."

Many of them started coming up to me with interest, causing

me to be embarrassed and elated in equal measure. I was glad I could finally do some good, having felt useless on Solis. Here, I was finally making a difference in Eredet, taking a step toward doing something to make my grandpa proud.

"I am happy to come to your homes and refill your water if needed. We'll try to make as many trips to Solis as possible."

Kane was beaming at me, welling with pride, making me unsteady on my feet. I wanted to run into his arms when he looked at me that way, but I didn't want to make a fool of myself. He was the king of Varjutus, and I was in his world as a guest. And as if to rub it in, Caelan burst my glowing bubble by greeting Kane with as little clothing on as possible.

"Welcome home, stranger," she said in her best sultry voice.

"Thank you." His reply was short, but he gave her his undivided attention.

I quickly escaped that nightmare and went over to Vish, wrapping my arm around his.

"Walk with me?" He nodded in response. When we were out of earshot, Vish apologized.

"Cyra, I'm so sorry I spoke to you the way I did. I'm sorry I'm such an ass. I just… fuck, I just miss him so much. I don't know what I'd do without him—he is my only family. I have no other purpose in life but to be at his side. I'm a nobody with nowhere to go. I can't believe I took it out on you."

I smiled at him, satisfied with his apology, and squeezed his arm.

"I know, Vish. Trust me, I know. I will take you to him as soon as possible. But Vish, you will always have me, and I'll always have a place for you. You're welcome by my side as long as you wish it. If you want to go back to Solis, that is your choice too, but I think you'll be safer here away from the Guardians. Plus, I miss you terribly, so I also want you here for my own selfish desire."

"Do you, really?" he asked, unbelieving.

"I wouldn't say it if it weren't true. I'm not cruel."

"No, you're not."

I felt a strong pull that caused me to fall over Vish, but thankfully he caught me.

"Sorry about that, clumsy as always!" I forced a fake laugh, but I turned around, glaring at Kane, and he returned a devilish grin. I wrapped my arm even tighter around Vish, held his hand, and gave Kane a sarcastic smile before turning back around.

"I've never been to Varjutus. How have you liked it?" Vish asked earnestly.

"I think it'll take you a bit to adjust. There is no daylight, so to a Solian, it's as unnatural as it gets. I'm still suffering from *time-shock*, but it's rapidly growing on me. Some things here are just magical, and the people work together as one. I teared up a few times, watching their traditions. They're truly beautiful people."

"I have a tough time imagining that after knowing Adelram, Merick, and Kal. Even Kane gets under my skin."

"I know what you're saying, but I think everyone is suffering from a history of bad blood that is no longer relevant. I don't think Grandpa ever intended for his people to be at such great odds. In fact, I know it would break his heart. I hope we can all change that."

"Excuse me, but I need Cyra." Kane grabbed me unceremoniously toward him, ignoring Vish.

"Watch yourself," Vish spat. Kane glared at him and started emitting black shadows, the air around us becoming unnaturally windy.

"Okay, chill, everyone! Vish, remember what we literally just talked about? Kane, what is it?"

"The Elder would like a word." Damnit, he knew I would go with him.

"Uh, yeah, I've been wanting to talk to him. I'll see you later, Vish." He nodded, and I left begrudgingly with Kane.

"Y ou must have *really* missed him. You were hanging all over him." Kane's voice was light and playful, even if full of sarcasm.

"Well, I had no choice when invisible forces began throwing me around. But don't worry. He caught me." I fluttered my lashes at him.

"He'll catch something else if he touches you again."

"That sounds an awful lot like jealousy."

Kane squinted at me as I flashed him a huge toothy smile, and when I heard the deep rumbling of a growl in his chest, it made me feel somewhat triumphant.

"Here's the lady of the hour!" Jonsi exclaimed.

"Hi, Jonsi." I went in for a hug. "I've been meaning to speak with you."

"Oh yes? What about?"

"Well, my Paela informed me that you would know what Kane and I are." I grabbed Kane's hand, folding his fingers into mine, and right on cue, they glowed.

Jonsi was silent for a moment, gaping at us.

"Damned, devilish creatures, those Paela. Charmers, but always getting into mischief, butting into other people's business. Why don't you come in?" Jonsi led us a few shacks down and walked inside. It was disheartening that this valued member of Varjun society and my grandpa's friend were reduced to living in this squalor. But I wasn't surprised that he lived the same way as his people instead of in the castle with Kane.

Four large wooden chests were open and overflowing with a vast array of items. Jonsi saw me examining them and explained.

"Those are cherished gifts from people of past times. I have even more chests out back." He blinked slowly, a sadness overcoming him.

"Elders used to be charged with the spiritual welfare of hundreds of cities and villages. We would travel to every one of them over the years." He looked down at the chests. "I can still hear the whispers of my people through these offerings."

His eyes went blank, staring at nothing, appearing haunted by thousands of years of history and people that are no more. "Now that the numbers are so small, all Varjun live in relative vicinity to the castle, so I have a unique situation that is both a blessing and a curse that no elders have had since the beginning of time. I can be intimately connected with every soul alive on Varjutus. While it's heartbreaking facing the dwindling number of civilians, the close attention I can give my family is unparalleled."

I couldn't fathom the loss he must feel at the drastic change in their circumstances and way of life. A painting on the wall caught my eye, and I stopped to inspect it. It was of Jonsi looking younger with his arms wrapped around a laughing man.

"Is this your partner you spoke of before?"

Jonsi's eyes creased as he smiled with heart-felt infatuation, joy returning to him. "Ah, yes. That's the love of my life, Lydon."

"He looks like a warrior." I squinted at the painting, admiring his long black ponytail with the sides of his head shaved. His dark chrome armor was intimidating yet beautiful.

"He was. That was how he died. In battle, protecting his people. He died with honor, a hero saving an entire planet, but it doesn't hurt any less."

"You seem so peaceful and gentle. Was it odd being with a fighter?"

"Not at all. I loved all of him the way he was. We were the perfect match, and he gave me the best years of my life. He was in charge of the welfare of our people and me, the spiritual." I smiled at the love on their faces.

Kane moved us from the conversation, more interested in our love connection. "You've been holding out on me again, Jonsi. You know something that you're not telling me. What are we, if not mates?"

"It's true. You two have a physical and magical connection. I suspected it the moment I saw you together, being more sensitive to the spiritual connections of my people. But I was convinced after a day or two. The term in the old tongue is called, *Imana*, now more colloquially called Star Mates."

Kane jerked his head back in surprise. "I didn't expect it to be that rare." His brows were raised to his hairline, and his lips were parted in disbelief.

"Star Mates." I side-eyed Kane. "How is that different from what you thought we were?"

"Would you like to explain to Cyra what a Star Mate is? Or would you like me to?"

Kane shook his head, still in shock.

"What is it?" I asked impatiently

"It is a special bond that is incredibly rare. In fact, I've only known of one pair of Star Mates my whole existence, but the signs are easy to spot if you know what you're looking for. You two can feel each other's presence and emotions. When you touch each other in acceptance, you emit an energy. *Imana,* meaning magnet in the old tongue, can choose to accept each other and become one. Or they can reject each other, and you'd likely be permanently repelled, unable to stand in each other's presence. If you ever argue, your anger is probably heightened and uncontrollable since it's the *repulsion* taking over. The more you accept each other, the stronger the bond will become, and the more you can accomplish together. Star Mates are able to access each other's powers to double their effectiveness or even create a new power. I can train you two to access it and control it."

"Goodness, I can barely control my own power. How would I be able to handle Kane's as well?"

"Well, the good news is you could leverage his controlled state. Tapping into his power might allow you to see into a mind different from your own and help you control your own energy."

"I don't even know what to say right now," I admitted. "How did nobody on Solis know we were Star Mates?"

"As I mentioned, it's exceptionally rare. Most people don't know it even exists," Jonsi offered, his lips pursed to the side. "But to me, it's incredibly obvious who the king of the prophecy is," he said, nodding at Kane.

"I don't know what to say either," Kane replied. "First, I become *Paeladoned.* Now I'm a mythical Star Mate? I feel like I've accidentally stepped into someone else's life."

"How fantastic! I always knew you were a special boy, and so did Amrel. He was right, as usual."

Kane did a double take at Jonsi, shaking his head. "What do you mean? Amrel knew me? I have never met him before."

"You did when you were a baby. I saw the memory of it. Adelram was very proud," I said, looking down and uncomfortably fidgeting with my hands.

"Well, what did he say?"

"He said you were quite the special one. And he thanked you for being extraordinary–for him."

"For him?" He asked, running his hand through his thick black hair.

"That's what he said. He had a way of…seeing things—I didn't know what he was talking about," I admitted.

We sat silently, absorbing this new information and unsure of what to say next. I knew I had a million questions, but my thoughts were too jumbled to form them into words.

Kane was the first to break the silence. "This day has been exhausting. I think I just need some sleep to process everything that's happened."

"I agree with you there." I locked eyes with him and was relieved that he was just as confused as I was for once. But there was also hope and excitement within his gaze, which melted my heart.

"Then it's settled. Go to bed. Come back when you want training. Good? Okay, goodnight, you crazy kids," Jonsi said as he pushed us out of the door and closed it, leaving us utterly confused.

"Did he just kick us out?" I laughed.

"Yes, he absolutely did."

We stood for a moment, unsure what to say or do. For all his steadfast confidence and wisdom, I could see he was struggling with words. We would have time to talk about this news once we'd let it marinate a bit, so I took his hand, deciding not to address it for the present.

"Come, let's go watch the celebration before we head back," I said, smiling with excitement.

Kane squeezed my hand in response, shoulders lowering in relief, and we joined the crowd. I caught sight of Meili and Merick dancing slowly and intimately under the moonlight, and Meili's soft, natural glow was lighting them up from a distance. Merick held her face, leaning down to kiss her gently. I was happy to see that even though I thought he was a jerk, he was sweet to my Meili.

"It looks like our best friends have officially become a couple," Kane said, looking at me with amusement lighting his eyes.

"I guess so. I'm just glad she's happy. She's been alone, trapped in Eluroom castle for so long. She deserves this."

"I've never seen Merick serious about anything, so she has him infatuated. It's great to see someone able to tame him. He's desperately needed a woman's influence for millennia."

I laughed, not at all surprised.

"Ah, speaking of young love..." Kane said as a couple approached. "Tess, Niko—it's great to see you two still going strong."

"King, it is great to have you home, and yes, we are still together. We've been waiting for the King's return to receive a blessing for our marriage," Niko said.

"I'm sorry you had to wait so long, my friends. Name the day, and it will be done," Kane said joyously.

"Thank you, Sire!" Tess beamed. "We're eager for children, so we'd like it to be soon."

I looked on in shock at the exchange. Why were they asking permission from Kane?

"I am eager for you as well, we've had far too few births, and I've been told our population is the smallest it's been since our beginning."

"Thank you, King!" Niko exclaimed before they ran off.

"Your people need permission from the king to marry?" I could only imagine what kind of mayhem that would cause on Earth or Solis.

"Our people are a very close-knit community. I consider them all my family. It's more of a sign of respect that by asking permission, no union will be a detriment to the people. The king or queen is no exception. I must seek the approval of my people when I decide to marry, and they must accept her as future queen, just as they accepted me as king. We would both be carrying the weight of our people together."

That made my heart drop. The people must accept his wife? I imagined Caelan would be the perfect *Varjun* fit to be accepted as queen.

But I was his mate. My blood boiled in my veins with all the power of my magic.

Suddenly all the excitement of the day and the triumph of the food delivery was drained from me, and I was left with a burning pit in my gut.

"Are you okay? Your aura just dimmed by half," Kane asked, concerned.

While still looking at my feet, I nodded. "Can you take me back?"

"Sure."

Kane brought me to my room, and I sat at the windowsill and looked at the glow of celebration off in the distance.

In a move that took my breath away, he knelt down before me and put his hands on my knees. "What is it, *imana*?"

I still didn't know what it meant to be his Star Mate, but my heart fluttered with his new pet name. The acknowledgment and complete understanding of our connection were long overdue, and to hear him talk of it so freely felt incredibly intimate and binding.

"Do your people expect you to find a wife?"

"Wife?" he asked, confused.

"Oh, that's what we call it on Earth. A *vordne*—do they expect you to marry now that you're King?"

"The Varjun definitely like when their king or queen are coupled, they're very family-oriented, and rulers are usually chosen through the family since they're well-groomed to lead, but I'm not required to."

"Oh, well, that's good, at least." My voice was as small and insecure as I felt.

"Why would you say that?" Kane asked, surprised and somewhat disappointed.

"I assume your people would prefer to...accept...a Varjun woman."

A look of understanding came over Kane's face. "Ah, I see."

"But if you're not required to marry, then your people don't need to choose..."

Kane slid his arms up my legs, which were regrettably in pants, and around to my back so he was holding me. I had to widen my legs to let him inch closer to hold me, and I shivered at his nearness. My whole body was alert to his proximity, and I tried not to let it show.

"Cyra, when I find a woman who loves and accepts me, I will take her as my wife, not just my lover. She will rule by my side as my equal and my queen. There is no negotiation for anything else."

My nod was a little too enthusiastic, betraying my worry. Kane stood, picked me up in his arms, and sat on the windowsill with me on his lap.

"You know how my father was lighter skinned than most of us?"

"Yes, I had noticed," I said through tears.

"His mother, my grandmother, was Sunya. My grandparents had a short reign, but our people accepted her as Queen. They were quite beloved by the people."

"But the Varjun seem to like Sunya. They flock to Meili when they see her."

"It's true that most people, Varjun and Solian alike, were drawn to the Sunya race before the curse. Many of them are pure souls, like Meili. I don't know how I remember that, but I know it was always true."

"I imagine it would be a much harder decision if it were a Solian."

Kane held me tighter, and the glow returned between us. "I trust my people to make a fair and honest decision, my Star."

I studied Kane, whom I had once looked at with distrust, but now felt entirely different. I doubted that I could ever live without him or survive him choosing a Varjun wife. Our *imana* bond was growing by the day, and when he wasn't around, I felt like a part of myself was missing. It took a long time for me to admit it to myself, but I think I felt it on Solis as well. But when I looked at him now, I saw a future with him in it, by his side. He made me feel things I'd never felt in my life and experience physical and mental responses I didn't understand. All I knew was that I felt whole and safe when he was with me. Something I hadn't felt since Grandpa died.

He lifted my face to look at him again while he caressed my cheek with his finger. I wanted to ask him if he felt the same for me, but I was too scared to do it. I was terrified of losing what we had now because I couldn't bear being without him anymore. I rested my head on his shoulder, and his soothing pine scent and warm, comforting presence eventually made me drift to sleep in his arms.

CHAPTER
FOURTEEN

The next morning I had no memory of how I got into bed. Kane must have tucked me in after I fell asleep. I smiled at the recollection of spending so long in his arms, alone together, before realizing that he was my first thought when I opened my eyes. I wondered if that meant I was bordering on obsession, but I wouldn't know. I'd never felt this way before.

I jumped out of bed and put on my leathers, excited to return to training. When I rushed to breakfast, I was disappointed not to see Kane in his usual place.

"Just me today, I'm afraid," Kal said, shrugging his shoulders.

A gasp sounded from me when I sat down to find there were eggs for breakfast. It was the first time since I'd been here that it wasn't gruel-looking oatmeal.

"We have you to thank for this meal. I freely give it. Thank you," Kal said, nodding toward me.

The eggs were bland but a world above tasteless oats.

"Where is Kane?" I asked, looking intently at my food.

"He received a suitor call. He's with a Varjun male and his daughter."

I immediately choked on the eggs I was chewing and glared at him. "Excuse me? A suitor's call?"

"It's pretty commonplace for women to pursue men. Kane will likely receive dozens of suitor calls now that he is king."

My fork dropped to my plate as I suddenly felt ill.

"I'm ready to train."

"I figured you'd say that."

Did we not just find out we were some mystical Star Mates? What the hell was he doing still accepting suitor calls?

Kal and I walked together to the camps as I silently seethed. Picturing Caelan's face as my opponent proved to be a truly effective training method, and we parried for thirty hard and fruitful minutes before we were interrupted.

"Are you ever going to introduce us or give us a shot at the girl?"

My head swiveled from the ground to the new voice, and saw one of the Varjun regulars who trained at the camp giving us a devilish smile.

"Not a chance in hell, Migor," Kal sneered.

"Do you think training with just one person is a good idea? You only learn one fighting style," the man next to Migor said.

Kal looked hesitant and glanced at me.

"I don't mind, Kal. It's probably a good idea."

"Fine, but Garwein, you go first."

"Ah, you're going easy on her. He's only five hundred years old and couldn't hurt a pecker bird even if he wanted to," Migor said.

"Nice to officially meet you, Cyra. I thank you for my fine meal this morning and the large water supply. It is an honor to help you hone your skills." Garwein nodded his head.

There was something in his friendly demeanor that made me instantly like him. "Thank you for the help, Garwein. You'll see that I desperately need it."

He may have seemed sweet, but it was clear he wouldn't go

easy on me. He approached me without notice, but I astonished myself by blocking his attack. We sparred for about ten minutes before Kal called an end to it. By some large miracle, I didn't fall to the ground once and only received one small bruise.

"Cyra, you actually did very well. I think the problem is that you're fighting with the greatest warrior ever known. Most of us can't fight that well. You should be proud of yourself," Garwein said, his eyes lit with approval.

I could do nothing but gape at him in shock. Was that true? Was I not a complete failure at fighting? If that were the case, I could owe my life to Kal and Kane by their dedicated training.

"Thank you, Garwein. That means a lot." I couldn't stop my cocky, dopey smile.

"Don't let it go to your head, Cyra. I don't consider you a true warrior until you've bested me at least once," Kal advised.

I scoffed at that thought, having serious doubts that I'd ever be able to do that in my lifetime.

"Understood, Kal."

"She should be tested in the *Warrior's Sanna*," Migor said, looking between me and Kal.

"Don't be a fool, she might have shown a tiny fraction of improvement, but she's nowhere near ready," Kal frowned.

"Don't be an ass, Migor," Garwein said.

"What's the *Warrior's Sanna*?" I was immediately intrigued.

"It's the ultimate test of fighting. You cannot be called a true warrior until you've passed. It's held before the whole Varjun community to witness, and you must best the *Curadh* warriors to pass—then you can become one of them." Garwein looked up in awe as if imagining himself as one of them in that position.

"Who are the *Curadh*?"

"They're Varjutus's elite warriors. The best fighters in all of the Eredet galaxy, there are currently only five," Garwein answered.

"They're something all Varjun boys dream of when they're little—being part of the *Curadh* is the highest honor of the Varjun.

"Who are the five *Curadh*?"

"Kalmali, Kaanan, Ondour, Erek and Migor," Garwein replied. "In that order."

"Well, I've already bested one of them and fought another. Migor, I suppose you should be next," I said with faulty pride.

"And who do you think you could have possibly bested on that list?" The genuine disbelief and annoyance on Kal's face was comical.

"Why, the king himself." My tone and smile were dripping with arrogance. "I pinned him during a training session on Solis."

"You have to come by it honestly, not with distraction," Kal said fiercely, protecting his king.

"I'm not surprised you have little faith in me, Kal, but I assure you I did. You can ask him yourself."

Kal nodded and folded his arms, a silent promise to do exactly that, then motioned for Migor to fight me next. I did end up on the ground three times with more bruises than with Garwein, but they were right. The three of them had different fighting styles, and I learned something from all of them.

"I'd like to include fights with others in our training," I told Kal.

"Very well."

We ended the session a few hours later, and as usual, I was limping and bruised but excited for what was to come. I also noticed how greatly my stamina had improved.

"If I still have to pulverize you mercilessly, at least I can escort you back to the castle." Kal offered his arm, and at that moment, I wasn't above taking it.

I smiled at him. "That would be wonderful, thank you."

With Kal's help, my hobble was almost imperceptible. My eyes darted to his face, and even though he was at peace, there was a line of concentration deep between his brows as if he were always primed for attack. It made me wonder if he ever simply relaxed and had fun–other than competing for the Lucky Pecker.

"I was told once that the Varjun used to be peaceful healers and scientists. Why do you have these intense fighting traditions?"

"It's true. We used to be a very peaceful people that valued family, life, and health. We were healers, scientists, and scholars. We still value those things, but we've had to adapt to survive. We were forced to become greater warriors than even the Solians, which is probably why we started to become enemies long ago. Now the Solians are weak and defenseless, and we have the greatest fighters in the galaxy. The only problem is our people barely have any magic anymore, and the great fighters we do have barely stand a chance if there was another Great War."

"Do you know why Kane has so much power if the rest of the Varjun do not?"

"Most of our power was tied to our planet and our surroundings. I can only guess that since our planet is dying, so is our people's power. For myself, I know I cannot use any power because I can influence the weather. Since there is none, there is nothing for me to wield. Those with greater power keep it longer. Jonsi, for instance, had immense power in his day. There were Varjun younger than he who perished from old age faster than he is. I truly fear for how long he has left with the state of our world. He is starting to age faster, and it scares us all. I don't know why Kane is so powerful. I'm only grateful that he is."

We stopped our conversation when we crossed paths with Kane and a woman I'd never seen before. He looked surprised by the sight of Kal and me locking arms but not more surprised than I was by him, his secret woman, and a flower in his hand. Was this the same suitor that came to him this morning? Was he with her for hours? Was this a second or a third suitor? Kal stopped for Kane, but I nudged him on. Not looking Kane in the eye, I nodded quickly, and we continued our walk back to the castle.

"Thank you, Kal. I'll make my way upstairs."

"Okay, I'll see you later."

CHAPTER FIFTEEN

Halfway up the stairs, I heard, "Cyra—wait!" It was my treacherous mate. I kept walking even though I knew I wouldn't outrun him. When I reached my door, Kane caught up with me.

"That was a cold greeting outside," he said lightheartedly and slightly out of breath.

"I didn't want to bother you." I opened my door, walked inside, took off my leathers, and sat down clutching my shoulder. I didn't want to admit just how bad it still hurt to hold that sword for so long.

"I can help with that."

"Help with what?"

Kane walked closer to me, and I went rigid.

"Just relax."

He loosened my tunic, making my pulse begin to rise out of control.

"What are you doing…?"

"I said, just relax."

"I can't."

"Just humor me, Star."

Ugh, he knew what to say to get me to comply—even though I wanted to be pissed at him right now. I wanted him to go away so I could attempt to diminish some of this connection between us. If he accepted one of these Varjun suitors, I wanted an iron-clad shell around my heart to protect me so I didn't fall apart.

His constant presence made it nearly impossible for that to happen. I also didn't think I had it in me to kick him out. He burrowed his hands beneath my tunic so they were directly against my bare skin, and goosebumps erupted over my whole body. He started to massage my shoulders until I thought I had died and gone to heaven. His pine and wood smell like my version of aromatherapy.

"Ooooh," I groaned in delight. With my body having been in shreds since I arrived on Varjutus, this felt like a dose of morphine. Not only that, but his touch on my bare skin was also making my whole body react in a serious way, and right on cue, my skin exuded a luminous glow.

I moaned again, causing Kane to bend toward my ear and murmur. I relished his hot breath on my skin, evident by my goose-bumps. "If you keep moaning and glowing like that, I will have to rip this tunic off of you, and we'll be doing something very different than a shoulder massage."

I immediately went rigid, overcome with desire, but it was dampened by confusion. I stood up and pulled my shirt back tight to cover myself. If I didn't stop him now, I would let him do anything he wanted to me, but I had to speak my mind first.

"I don't get what's happening here."

"What do you mean?" Kane's head was slightly tilted to the side, looking all innocent and fucking delicious. Damn him. I was trying to be angry here.

"You just spent all morning with suitors, or even worse—one suitor, and Kal assured me there'd be countless more. You were holding a *flower*—did you give it to one of them?" Flames ignited from my hands to my shoulders, and I could tell my eyes were also on fire.

Kane grabbed my hands, unaffected by my flame. I could see my flaming eyes in his reflection, and it was sort of terrifying. When did I become this menacing being of power? I used to be a nobody who worked in an arcade.

"Cyra, it is my fault that you don't understand our customs. It would be considered extremely rude and even irrational if I refused these Varjun suitors. This is a custom that helps ensure I've considered all my options and that I make the right decision. I did not give anyone a flower. It was given to me—which, by the way, is a very special flower to us that no longer grows on Varjutus since the curse. It must have been very difficult to come by. If I refuse these suitors, it will be much harder to make my case if I decide to wed a non-Varjun woman. I'm not interested in any of these women, Cyra. I meant what I said. Nothing would give me greater pleasure than ripping off every piece of your clothing and not leaving this room for at least a month."

Holy hell. My body burned with heat at his admission, and he'd find that if he *did* rip my clothes off, I would be more than ready for him. He lowered his forehead against mine, and I felt his breath coming more rapidly. It took everything in me not to lunge at him. He made me feel things I'd never felt before, and my yearning was more like an ever-growing *need*.

"Does that answer please you, *imana*? Because I feel a change in you through our bond. Something that was always there, but now it's lit on fire—and I love it."

I turned my head. He was always able to read me like an open book.

He took my face in his hand and turned it back to look into his intense, green eyes. "Don't ever be embarrassed by it," he said seriously.

Merick's call sign began to glow on Kane's arm, and I sighed. Just when I was starting to like Merick, now I wanted to kill him for interrupting us.

"I am to meet Merick and Kal in my study. I would like for you to come if you are willing." Kane pulled me close so I was right against him, and I was astonished to realize that he was stiff beneath me. I looked up at him biting my lip, debating whether we should skip this meeting and I should rip his pants off here and now.

He gave a lustful smile. "To be continued at a later date, Star Mate."

"I...I will come with you," I said through rapid breaths.

"Excellent." He took my hand and kissed it. "Although, I can't touch you again, or I'll never be able to return to my previous state," he said, looking down.

Oh lord, help me.

We walked to another part of the castle I'd never seen before and we did it at a safe distance, at opposite sides of the hall. Before he let me into the room, I did a quick shameless glance at his pants, and they were thankfully normal.

"Would you like a closer look, Cyra?"

My eyes bulged, and I bit my lip again. Yes, in fact, I would. But I wasn't going to say it out loud. He raised his nose into the air, closed his eyes, and took a long breath before a deep rumble in his chest echoed through the halls.

He stalked closer to me as his pupils dilated with a predatory hunger. "You do, don't you, my Star? Your desire for me is saturating these halls, and it's the most intoxicating scent I've ever experienced. My mouth is watering, knowing you will taste just as divine."

I grabbed his arm to brace myself, ready to screw this meeting and test Kane's theory, but all I could manage was to stand gaping at him. Kane bellowed in laughter as he opened the door and led my stupefied and painfully horny self into the room. Merick and Kal were already sitting at a round, dark wooden table.

Merick nodded at me and said, "Welcome."

Kane sat first and I took the seat beside him, which was probably a mistake. The electric static buzzing between us was practically deafening. I could barely hear or feel anything else. Kane looked at me like he had the same problem.

"Uh..." Kane started, then looked back at me in confusion. I just shrugged. I didn't know what was happening either.

"We...we're meeting because..." Kane couldn't finish his sentence, and I knew why. He couldn't even hear himself think or speak. It was like having a bad cell phone connection, and the static and echo made it impossible to have a discussion. He cleared his throat and swallowed with difficulty.

"Oh, hell. I have to start by saying Cyra and I are Star Mates."

"Oh shit," Merick blurted, putting his hand over his mouth.

"I did not see that coming," Kal said, his eyes widening.

"That is *real*?" Merick asked, perplexed.

"I'm only telling you because we have some personal things to figure out, and we might be acting weird. Right now, I can't hear myself think through an incessant buzzing between me and Cyra. Jonsi said he would help control our powers."

"I can tell you can't hear us. You're shouting!" Merick replied.

"Sorry."

"What does that mean for you two?" Merick leaned closer with interest.

"I don't know. We just found out. We have a lot to work through. Anyway, now that our people are taken care of for the present, we're here because we need a plan to get the *mikla* and what to do about the Guardians."

"Well, I've been to that blasted wasteland countless times and have found nothing. It's beyond infuriating. Vjera is on that hell hole now in her tireless pursuit of revenge. She hasn't gotten any peace either."

"Vjera is my cousin, Cyra. Her family was killed by the Bellum long ago, and she hasn't stopped trying to avenge them. Her parents were highly respected by our people, and she hasn't been the same since their deaths. She's the only family I have left now. Merick, maybe it's time for you to bring her home and take her place for a bit. You don't have to stay there. Just make a few trips a week for reconnaissance. Maybe now that they have the *mikla,* they'll get sloppy and make a mistake leading us to their location." Merick nodded at him without an argument—his unquestioning loyalty nice to see.

"What about the Guardians?" Kane asked.

"I can write to Urien to get a report on what's been happening on Solis. Does anyone have a pen and paper?"

Kal got up, retrieved them from the desk, and handed them to me. I wrote Urien's name on the paper, said his name aloud, and ignited my hand until it burned away. Not a moment later, Kal looked up in alarm.

"The spider is already here at the castle door."

"Well, that was easy," I said, with raised brows.

Kal retrieved him and brought him to the study.

"Cyra, are you okay?" Urien rushed to me, his cloak billowing behind him as the strange glittering jewel around his neck sparkled with brilliance despite the dim lighting.

"I'm fine. I'm sorry to summon you like this, but we were discussing a plan against the Guardians. We were hoping to hear any recent intel you had."

He visibly relaxed, taking in a deep breath. "Now we're talking."

"They've been immune to every attack we've thrown at them, but every being has a weakness. Every single one. We need only find theirs." Kane looked off into the distance, scratching the bare hint of stubble on his face.

"True." Urien was holding a dagger and began fidgeting with it. "They're so powerful it's likely they can only be killed by the Sunya Rei, and as far as we know…they are extinct."

"There hasn't been a Rei sighting in millennia, so I think he's right. We have to find another way," Merick said.

"Even if we obtained the *mikla* and discovered how to unlock it, the Guardians would likely drain the energy from the box immediately," Kane said.

The conversation sparked something within me as if I had a vital piece of information. "I'm not so convinced they're extinct," I said slowly. Everyone stopped talking and turned to me, holding their breaths. It had plagued me since Orphlam interrogated me, asking about Xenos. Then I'd had the extremely vivid vision of Xenos telling me to call for him. It could have just been a strange dream, but it felt too similar to my other visions to be a coincidence. It was a long shot, but what did I have to lose?

"Xenos!" My hands were cupped to my mouth as if that would help somebody we couldn't see. Everyone looked at me with confusion, to no surprise. I really hoped I was right about this. I started begging in my mind, reaching out to him. *Xenos, please tell me you're more than what you seemed.*

"Cyra, what are you doing?" Urien asked, clutching the jewel around his neck.

It was silent and still for quite a few moments, and my cheeks began to burn in embarrassment. But when everyone looked away from me and began to discuss business again, the ground started to rumble a bit as a light began glowing next to me. I stood, with anticipation, bewildered that I was right. An outline of massive wings appeared first, followed by a man. The Varjun in the room yelled and shielded their eyes from the light. I was able to see him without issue, but he dimmed his light anyway.

"It's you, isn't it? Xenos, my dog from Earth! You're a...Sunya Rei?" I ran to him and fell into his arms, but he yelled, "No, Cyra, don't!"

I stepped back. My ego bruised a little.

"That's never happened before," he said in a deep ethereal voice.

"What?"

"Nobody has ever been able to touch The High Creator or a Sunya Rei and not die or burn away to ash," Kane said, unable to look away from Xenos.

Xenos laughed with his hands over his mouth in utter joy, and he picked me up in his arms and hugged me, my legs dangling in the air. "Cyra, I am so happy to finally let you see me in my true form."

My brain misfired as I attempted to formulate words. It was an unreal moment that I had to keep second-guessing if I was imagining. "Your wings— they're beautiful." I burrowed my face into his neck, which smelled like crackling embers and soot—just my kind of scent. It was bizarre that I only knew him as a dog, but the connection and familiarity were the same. It was him. We had always had a strong bond, one that I couldn't explain, and now it all made more sense.

"Are you serious? She can call upon a Sunya Rei at will." Kal stood quickly, causing his few braids to jingle, his back straight as a board, unsure what to do with himself.

"Xenos, I've missed you so much. Why did you never reveal yourself before? Why the cryptic message in a dream?"

"Not as much as I've missed you, I can guarantee you that. And I can't stay in this form for very long since my power is almost completely gone." His voice was almost other-worldly, a boom that echoed through the room.

Everyone at the table stood up and bowed at him, and he merely dipped his head to them in acknowledgment.

"Am I supposed to be doing that?" I asked incredulously.

"Don't be ridiculous." There was a playfulness to him that made me feel like I was home with my family in Arkansas again.

"Where have you been? What other form do you take? Do you know anything about my parents?"

"Your parents are well. They asked me to apologize that they kept this secret from you but felt it was best for you to have a normal life, and they want you to know that your room will always be yours. It will always be your home whenever you need to return."

Tears welled in my eyes, and I squeezed his blazingly hot hand in gratitude. Just having the first word of my parents and knowing they were okay was a huge vise lifted from my heart.

"You are very close to walking the path necessary to break the curse. I cannot tell you more than that, but Amrel would be so proud of you, my dear."

The tears kept coming at his mention of Grandpa. He took me in his arms and held me, wrapping his wings around me in a cocoon. I felt instantly at peace like Xenos returned a missing part of me. There was utter silence from everyone in the room, in a stupor at what must be a rare event. But to me, even in a form I wasn't accustomed to, he felt like home.

"How is she able to touch him when nobody can touch the Sunya Rei or The Creator," Merick whispered. Nobody bothered to answer.

"Xenos, is it true the Guardians can only be killed by a Sunya Rei?"

"With someone of their power level, I'm afraid so."

"Why couldn't Grandpa destroy them?"

"He had the power to destroy them, but it could not be him to do it. They could have corrupted Amrel's energy, destroying something we desperately needed. I no longer have the power required to carry out such a task."

That admission made my heart sink. I could feel the strength of energy emanating from him, and he still wasn't powerful enough to kill Orphlam? "Are there more of you?"

"Right now? No. I am alone at this point in time."

I felt like he was speaking in riddles—hiding something he didn't want me to know.

"Will you help us destroy the Guardians?"

"The Guardians cannot be destroyed until the *mikla* is opened and all missing energies released. There is a small piece of Orphlam's essence in it, and he will keep coming back if he's not whole when killed."

"A piece of their magic is trapped in the *mikla* along with our sun's energy?" Kane asked.

"You can say that, yes." Xenos's wings ruffled, tightening behind him as if he were uncomfortable.

"Okay, then, when we open the *mikla,* will you help us destroy the Guardians?" He still hadn't answered my question.

"I would do what I could, but my part in this journey is over."

"What does that mean, Xenos?"

"When I agreed to come and protect you on Earth, I gave up a portion of my energies to become a lower life form. When I made that choice, I knew I could never again be who I was. I am Sunya Rei in appearance only. My powers and abilities are nearly gone."

It broke my heart that yet another person ended who they were just for me. My hands shook, unable to fathom why so many people believed in me. "Is there anything you need? Do you want to stay with us? You're not alone, are you? You must be careful. The Guardians are looking for you too."

He smiled at my rambling and touched my face, his hand burning so intensely that I wasn't surprised his touch was lethal to most. "Do not fret, dear one. It is not your job to watch over me. I must disappear again. I cannot stay in this form for more than a few moments."

"One last thing, Xenos. This is Kane...he's my Star Mate." I was compelled to introduce Kane to one of my few remaining family members. He might not be related, but I will always consider him family.

Xenos beamed at him and nodded his head in a show of respect, impressing everyone in the room. "King of Eredet, it is an honor. Take care of my girl."

Wonder filled Kane's eyes, and he straightened as if he didn't take anything more seriously. "Always."

Xenos disappeared, and the room went dark and cold again, making me immediately miss his blistering warmth.

"What the fuck just happened?" Urien asked.

"Agreed." Merick's eyes were comically stuck wide in shock.

Everyone seemed unable to get past the presence of a Sunya Rei, so I tried to continue our meeting. "Urien, have you heard any news on what the Guardians are doing now?"

He cleared his throat, attempting to get past his shock. "It's been completely silent. Eerily so. They're up to something. I just don't know what. I'll keep my head in the game and try to find out, but I'm worried."

"Okay, when we return to the private lands, I'll bring a maaga-line bird back to Varjutus to stay in contact with Bad. I'll check in with him periodically to see what the word is with the workers of Solis."

Everyone nodded in agreement.

"Well, I guess we have some sort of a plan now. Merick will try to get intel on the Void. Urien and Bad will get us intel on Solis and what the Guardians are planning, and hopefully, Xenos will figure out some way to help us kill the Guardians when the *mikla* is opened," I concluded.

"I couldn't have said it better myself," Kane said, beaming at me.

"Oh, sorry, I didn't mean to take over your whole meeting." Heat rose in my face.

"Don't you apologize. You're doing exactly what you're meant to."

The large, heavy wooden door creaked open as Meili and Vish entered the room.

"What did I miss?" she asked with a sweet smile.

Merick shook his head with his hand to his brow. "Cherub, literally *the* worst timing ever."

I walked Meili and Vish back to my room to fill them in on what happened and our plan for dealing with the Bellum and Guardians. Meili was beside herself that she missed a Sunya Rei sighting.

"It pains me that Theo is missing this. We have a Sunya Rei on our side—someone to help defeat the Guardians, but he still hasn't woken."

A knot twisted in my gut, sure that Xenos would be little help to us in the fight against Orphlam, but I didn't express that to my friends. It was fortifying enough for others to know he still existed, and I didn't want to ruin it. "I know. Theo worked so hard to see this through, and now he's missing crucial events. Xenos said we were close, but it still feels like we're lightyears away. I've been told many times that it's been impossible to find where the Bellum are hiding, and we have no idea what the Guardians are up to. It all just makes me uneasy."

"Well, I'm going to check on Theo, then return to my room. I'll catch you guys later," Vish said, nodding to us before leaving. I looked over to the windowsill and saw the beautiful Varjun flower

Kane received, claiming it was their cherished flower. The petals were a deep crimson color, while the stem and leaves were an enchanting violet. The flower looked like a full ranunculus of Earth except for the vibrant other-worldly color.

"Hey, Meili? Can you grow more of these flowers in the private lands from this?" I handed her the flower.

"Oh, this is beautiful, and it smells divine. Yes, I can! I can't create life, but I can nurture and encourage roots to grow from this stem."

I looked at her mischievously. "Care to make a spontaneous trip?"

Her face lit up at the idea.

We reached the basement and opened the *sild gate*, walking easily into my parent's private lands. It was wonderful to feel the sunlight touching our skin again, and I could tell Meili felt the same.

"We shouldn't use any areas we'll be utilizing to farm. How about we grow them around the cottages? It would look lovely."

"That's a great idea, Meili." She cupped her hands around the flower, closed her eyes, and concentrated.

"Yes, these flowers require some shade, so they'll do better under the protection of the cottages and around trees that provide enough coverage." She walked to the small house I had now been in twice, kneeling on the ground and beginning to dig into the dirt with her hands. Meili was in her element, not at all afraid to get dirt all over her. She placed the flower in the ground, returning it to the soil so it stood on its own. She wrapped her hands around it, concentrating as light emitted from her hands. I watched, unsure of what was happening.

"It is now rooted into the earth."

I beamed at Meili's wonderful gift, looking around me at this extraordinary place and imagining the private lands covered in this beautiful flower that meant so much to Kane and his people until the flowers started appearing all around the cottages and beneath most of the trees. A gasp escaped my lips at the magnificent sight, providing even more color and beauty to this protected piece of Solis. Unlike the small, barely open flower Kane had received, these flowers had whole, vibrant blossoms. I could instantly smell a plentiful freesia-like scent wafting toward me.

"Meili, it's fantastic. Thank you so much."

"Uh, I didn't do that."

"What?"

Meili laughed and put her hands over her mouth in shock. "Cyra, that was you!"

My brows furrowed in confusion. "Are you sure?"

"Of course I am. Your powers are growing!"

I didn't know what any of it meant. How did I go from struggling with fire to suddenly summoning water and growing an entire field of foreign flowers? I wondered if my growing *Imana* connection could have anything to do with my quickly escalating powers. "Meili....do you know what a Star Mate is?"

She stopped moving, and her brows lifted in surprise. "A thing of fantasy, I think. A *wonderful* thing of fantasy...I grew up dreaming that a Star Mate would sweep me away from my isolated life so I'd never be alone again. It's something any woman would die to have." She had a dreamy far-off look, biting her bottom lip. "Why do you ask?"

"You make it sound like an epic love story. Perhaps it's just a magical connection?" It was apparent that I was afraid to lose what I was so eager for. A growing, unbreakable relationship with Kane.

"Oh no, it's so much more than that. It's true that powers can be amplified through the connection, but it's the strongest bond two people can have. I've read in fairytales that *imana* can feel each other from great distances, know each other's emotions and even communicate telepathically. A deep love connection is usually so strong that the bond is unbreakable if the partners accept each other. By the same token, if the couple rejects each other, they can't stand to be in each other's presence. I don't know everything they're capable of, but they're the greatest love stories of all time in the cosmos. There are many different forms of mates, like Moon Mates, which are right under the level of Star Mates, and standard mates with a basic bond. But Star Mates are like a divine fated love so strong that destiny is altered because of their connection."

"Interesting…Kane and Jonsi didn't mention that part."

"Why would they be talking of Star Mates?"

I sighed, about to drop the bomb. "Kane and I are Star Mates. Jonsi confirmed it."

The blood drained from her face, and her jaw dropped. "Oh, my goodness, Cyra, that is incredible. Congratulations! What is it like? Do you love him?"

"I don't know anything right now. I just found out myself. But I do feel an intense connection to him. I have since the first time I saw him on Solis. I feel his emotions and even felt his abuse from the Guardians last year. I am happier and stronger when he is around. This is just all so unbelievable."

"Cyra, that's amazing. Have you…kissed?"

I blushed and smiled, recalling his small kiss when I was overcome with fire, but I couldn't really count that. Nor could I count the delicious taunting that made me want to jump him and do dirty things to him that I would never have considered before. To rip his clothes off and see just how beautiful he was beneath the fabric and trace each line of his skin until every inch of him was permanently etched into my soul. I could picture his lips on mine, and I wanted to try it again but have the chance to savor it. To feel his breath on my skin and taste him until nothing else would ever satiate me. My body shivered, and I shook my head and bit my lip, trying to dissipate the heat blazing all over me at the mere thought of Kane. He was always with me, a thought, a feeling, an aching desire, even when I was on another planet. My denial was no longer an option, and now that I've admitted it to myself, my yearning was uncontrollable.

He *consumed* me. And I burned for him.

"No, we haven't done anything. We just agreed to start training to utilize each other's powers. Meili—he's a Varjun king, and I'm a Solian. It makes things a little complicated."

"Star Mate relationships trump everything. It's so powerful and beautiful that it's impossible to ignore. It'd be a shame to reject the bond because of that."

"What if we're not right for each other?" After Theo's betrayal, I wanted to be careful about my options, even though as soon as the words crossed my lips, I knew it wasn't true.

"Impossible. There will be no person better suited to you if you searched for the rest of time in the vastness of the universe. You've won the greatest gift life has to offer, Cyra."

My mouth was suddenly dry as I struggled to swallow. "Wow, I don't know what to say." But her words weren't exactly a shock anymore. The more I listened to my urges for him, the more sense it made.

"Say you'll make the most of it. I can't imagine anything in life more precious."

"I promise I'll take it seriously."

"Hasn't the king been entertaining suitors?" Her right brow arched in question.

"Yes. Don't get me started." My fists clenched at my sides, and while seeing him in the vicinity of a woman trying to win his affection never gave me the warm and fuzzies, now I was ready to burn the goddamn world down to cinders for the next woman to look at him with a smile.

"Well, the fact that it bothers you is a good sign." She tried to hide the sideways smirk growing on her face, and I decided to change the subject. It was too overwhelming, and I needed to calm down.

"I'd like to check out the other cottage. Want to see what's inside?"

"I'd love to."

As we made our way over, I marveled at the breathtaking flowers everywhere and the incredible fragrance that saturated the air around us. The maagaline birds flapped their wings as if in greeting, and I beckoned for one to join me.

"Remind me not to leave without taking one back so I can communicate with Bad and Urien. I'm going to write to Bad now to see if he could get those seeds from Vish's farm and ask him for his first list of Solians who will escape to Varjutus."

We entered the cottage, and I wrote a note and sent the bird off to Bad. There didn't seem to be too much in the cottage that was useful. I inspected the various photos, most of them me and my parents, and it seemed like a place they frequently visited. I searched every inch of the cottage and was disappointed that I couldn't find any valuable information. The maagaline bird reappeared, alerting us that Bad was at the gate with the seeds.

"Let's go, Meili—Bad's here."

We opened the gate to his smiling face, and I ran into his arms.

"I'm relieved you're still safe," Bad said. He smiled and nodded at Meili in gratitude.

"I'm glad you are too. Anything new happening on Solis?" I asked.

"They've never been more banded together than they are now. I've told them about you and the prophecy, and it's given them hope. It's also keeping them from losing their minds and rioting in a panic. Blaze has been creating shelters and emergency hideaways in case of attack and providing secret training for anyone who wants to learn to defend themselves."

"Excellent, I knew Blaze would help lead. I hate this, but we're doing everything we can. Please continue trying to keep them calm. Thank you for everything, Bad."

He handed Meili the seeds, and she inspected them. "These are perfect! I'll get started now."

"I'm sorry I had to throw them all together. How will you know which seeds are what plant?"

"Not to worry, I'll know." Meili immediately walked off and got to work.

"How are they treating you there on Varjutus?" Bad's brows pinched with genuine concern.

"Very well, I have no complaints."

"That's not saying much. You're not one to complain."

"Then you've been living under a rock! Or tucked away in a kitchen," I said, laughing with him. "Are you doing okay? Are you safe?"

"I'm hanging in there best I can. The thought of you keeps me going. It could be the *only* thing. I'm still cooking for the nobles, so that keeps me busy, and I have Tulah to keep me connected with you on short notice. I just pray every day that this hell will end."

"I do, too, Bad."

"I better get back, Cyra. I won't have another delivery for a few days yet, keep a bird with ya, and I'll let ya know when I can make the drop."

"Thanks again, Bad. You're literally a lifesaver. Thousands of lives."

I returned to Meili and helped her plant the rest of the seeds. When they were all secured in the ground, she focused on making them grow to sprouts.

"I can only cover a small portion of ground at a time, and I'll have to return a few times to keep nurturing their speedy growth. I can't do it all at once…but you might be able to."

"Me? I highly doubt that."

"Look what you did with the flowers."

I shrugged, figuring it was worth a shot. Closing my eyes, I concentrated on growing the sprouts further, and they might have raised a few centimeters, but it ended there.

"My power is so inconsistent. I just don't get it."

"You'll get there. Your abilities are unlike ours, so it'll take some time to understand. I'll come back tomorrow to grow them further."

"Okay. Let's get back. I think we did a lot of good for today."

When we exited the *sild gate*, I closed it on the other side with the maagaline bird on my shoulder. We quietly left the basement and ascended to the main floor. On the way back to my room, I caught sight of Kal, and his eyes bulged at me with his white hair unkempt like he'd been rubbing at it.

"What?" I asked.

"Holy hell, do you know how long the king has been looking for you? He's out of his mind with panic." Kal shook his head at my apparent foolishness and touched the call sign on his arm for Kane. Half a second later, Kane appeared, and I was punched back by a wave of rage and fear that slammed into me, causing my heart to race and my brow to glisten with beads of sweat immediately.

Wow, that was overwhelming.

The bird disappeared in agreeance. Traitor.

"Cyra, where the *hell* have you been?" He stormed up to me and shook my shoulders. "Don't ever do that to me again!"

I caught Meili smirking at Kal before disappearing. Kal looked astonished by Kane's extreme reaction, and I agreed with him. Between one blink and another, we had changed locations, now outside at the highest point in the castle, where it was absolutely freezing. It was cold everywhere on Varjutus, but this was painfully frigid, causing me to shiver.

"Where were you?" Kane bellowed, growls echoing in his throat.

"Calm down. I went to the private lands with Meili. I got the maagaline bird so I could communicate with Bad. He met us there and gave us the seeds from Vish's farm, so Meili and I planted them for an additional food source."

"So, you're telling me you went to another *planet* where the Guardians are looking to kill you without telling me?"

The hairs all over my body stood on end from the intense thrumming of his power, desperate to be released. "Why are you freaking out? It's fine. The lands are protected. Nothing happened."

"You were gone for hours. I thought you were abducted! Do you realize what it would have done to me if I lost you? What it would mean to all of Eredet if you were killed? That was reckless and stupid."

My arms folded in defensiveness. "Kane, maybe I wanted to have a few quiet minutes without worrying about my enormous responsibility! I am breaking under this unbearable pressure, and the worst part is that I can't talk to anybody about it! Bad is like family, and I could always tell him anything. But I realized today, for the first time, our relationship has changed. He is no longer just a crazy uncle, but a desperate man, terrified and defenseless, depending on me to help him and his people. He told me today that the only thing keeping him going is the thought of me breaking this curse. I can't tell him how utterly terrified I am myself. I can't show him my weakness—it would *break* him and the people of Solis."

I was covered in flame, so emotionally unstable that I was afraid of blasting fire into the sky. Kane stepped closer and wrapped his arms around me, the fire unaffecting him.

"Calm your mind, Star. I'm sorry about my fierce reaction. I just couldn't bear it if something happened to you. There is no longer a me without you. So just know that you are wrong. You are my *imana*—the other half of my magnet. You will always be able to share every one of your burdens with me or tell me anything without repercussions or consequences of my disappointment. The weight on your shoulders will always be ours, and you will *never* again be alone while I live. If you disappear into the abyss, I will always find you. We are connected, and nothing in this universe can tear it apart."

I considered his words and the ones Meili spoke earlier, and they both told me one thing I needed to hear. Something that was a trauma rooted deep within me after losing everyone I held dear. The part that appealed to me most about this Star Mate bond.

I will never be alone again.

CHAPTER SEVENTEEN

The next day after another grueling training which included survival skills in various terrains, running endurance, and even a little melee combat, Kane spent some time with me where we practiced all my known magical abilities and tried to push the barriers of my limits. When he noticed my mind wandering and me growing slightly bored, he held me close, and we appeared on the island full of Kometa we had visited before. My familiar friend quickly frolicked in my direction, seemingly happy to see me.

"Hey, girl! You remembered me." My mood instantly began to lift as I grinned like a fool, eager to be near her again.

"Her coming to you again instantly probably means she's yours forever. Focus on emptying your mind and relaxing."

"Oh, sure, no problem. I feel super relaxed."

"All the more reason you need this training." His eyes and brows were fierce and sharp, leaving no room for jokes. "You need to be able to drop all your worries, fears, and desires immediately if you're attacked or find yourself in a dangerous situation. I'd feel better knowing you could master it. Especially if you feel like planet-hopping, leaving me behind."

"Man, you're not going to forget that one, huh?"

"As I said, it's no longer just you or me. It's us, and you made a choice to go into danger without at least telling me. It hurt."

I hurt him? The thought hadn't occurred to me. It was clear that it would be challenging for me to acclimate to this level of intimacy. I've always been independent, unaccustomed to this kind of relationship. But I realized I wanted to be.

"I'm sorry. I will have to get used to being this…connected to someone else."

"It's okay, it's a learning curve for both of us, and we'll master it together. But first, clear your mind, and ride the Kometa."

After a few moments of clearing my thoughts and when I thought my mind couldn't possibly be *any emptier,* I mounted the Kometa and gloriously only fell to my face five times. The last fall, I merely kept my face to the ground and asked if we were done for the day. Kane agreed we could continue another time.

"I think tomorrow we should visit Jonsi and learn more about power sharing. It could be an invaluable tool against the Bellum."

"Sounds good."

One of the call signs on his arm flashed. "Merick's calling me. Come." Kane pulled me close, and we appeared within his study. There was a Varjun villager with Merick and Kal, who was clearly distraught with watery eyes and fidgety hands.

"Sire," the Varjun bowed. "Many of the villagers are running low on water. There is much concern with the public water coolers —some need more water than others. Many are afraid to take the full amount of their needs, and they're going thirsty."

"Cyra, do we know when the next supply run is?" Kane asked me. I could feel his unspoken gratitude that I had ventured to Solis, after all.

"Not for a few days. The cook told me he'd alert us when he was ready."

"I don't think we have a few days," the villager said, shuffling on his feet.

"But...I'd be more than happy to make house calls and refill the villagers' water, so nobody needs to be the wiser on how much they're receiving." I felt Kane swell with pride beside me, causing butterflies to erupt in my core.

"That's excellent, Cyra. Thank you. Will that work?" Kane asked the villager.

"It will indeed! Thank you, King."

"We'll come first thing in the morning."

"Amrel, bless you," he said as he ran out of the room.

"And you thought you weren't popular with the Varjun," Kane said with a wink.

"Well, I wouldn't go *that* far," Merick said, one brow raised. "but they certainly aren't banging down her door with pitchforks either. Which really, for a Solian, is unfathomable."

Merick and Kal started talking among themselves as Kane took my hand in his, making me tingle at his touch, but a voice behind me made me jump out of my skin.

"I found youuuuuu!"

I screeched and turned around. "Oliver? What in the world are you doing here!"

"Hey! How did you drive in here?" Merick yelled and ran over, his dagger drawn.

"No! Don't harm him. We know him, and he didn't drive here. He...projected a version of himself."

"Excuse me?" Merick asked in bewilderment.

Kane ignored him and bent down to Oliver. "Are you in danger?"

"I think so. The bad guys took my adoptive parents. I ran away so they didn't get me. I think they want me too. Do you know what I should do now?" Oliver looked at us. "Do you guys know that you're supposed to be together now?"

Kane laughed at him, "Don't worry about us. Do you think you can drive to Varjutus?"

"I think so...but...I'm scared to do it, plus Blaze said they're ready for the first group of Solians to escape."

"You know Blaze?" I asked.

"Yes, he gives me food sometimes, and I told him I can find you."

"My parent's land," I said to Kane. "We can get them there."

"Oliver, do you know where Cyra's family's protected land is?"

"Yes. The Guardians want to get in there, but they can't."

"That's right. We will meet you and the others at the front gate and let you in. Look for a maagaline bird that we'll send your way when it's time to drive to the front. You and the others will come live with us."

"Yay! Does that mean you're ready to be my mom and dad now?"

Kane and I looked at each other uncomfortably at the strange things this boy said. "Let's focus on getting you here first, okay?" Kane asked him. Oliver nodded, satisfied by his answer.

"Okay, we'll leave now. Wait for our bird and be careful." Oliver disappeared slowly like a phantom in the wind.

"Cyra and I will be back shortly. I don't want to bring too many people and cause any problems with our...new guests." Kane scratched the back of his head and huffed, clearly not happy about Solians moving into his precious world, but it made me swell with pride even more that he didn't complain once about it.

"Are you sure that's wise?" Merick snapped. "This boy has enormous power if he can project part of himself between worlds, and who knows what tricks the Solians will have up their sleeve? Are you sure this isn't some sort of trap? Any one of them could be working with the Guardians or, even worse, forced into servitude."

"Those are all valid points, and I will be counting on you and Kal to keep an eye on everyone and give me daily reports. I'll want at least a few Varjun living amongst them to ensure we're safe, but we'd be remiss if we didn't try to save everyone we could. We will need as many allies as possible in our final fight." Kane's voice was sharp and succinct, making it clear that the discussion was over and that he had decided, but Merick seemed pleased by his answer.

Kane took my hand, and we made our way to the basement sild gate, leaving everyone behind. I easily opened it, and when we stepped through, Kane stopped short and put his hand to his mouth. He stood silently for quite a while, and a small layer of water formed in his eye. I felt a multitude of emotions run through him. Exhilaration, shock, and awe, but the one that concerned me was heartbreak.

"Kane, are you okay? I'm sorry if this upset you, maybe I should have checked with you first, but I thought you were fond of these." Man, did I feel stupid. "I can get rid of them if they make you unhappy."

"No," Kane whispered, his voice cracking. He wiped the water from his eye before it had the chance to fall. "This is the most beautiful thing anyone's ever done for me. What you're feeling is my grief over my mother. She used to cover our castle with these flowers. They weren't just a treasure to the Varjun—they were a staple in our household. They're Noctis flowers. The sight and smell of them in abundance like this reminds me of a time when we were happy and whole. My family and the Varjun people. Seeing so many of them in full bloom…I'm just overwhelmed. It's completely extinct on Varjutus now, it's like seeing a ghost from a time when love bloomed free and plentiful, and my mother and sister's smiles were always there when I needed them. You did this all yourself?"

"Well, not all myself. You left the flower in my room, so I asked Meili if she could plant it on fertile lands. She said they liked some shade, so she planted the first over there by the cottage under the shade of the roof. When it was rooted, I grew the rest from that one flower by thinking it might please you. Your suitor might have been able to get you one, but I can give you thousands."

Kane beamed at me and pulled me in close. "Is this your official request to be considered as a suitor?" He playfully knocked into my side, and I looked down at my feet so he couldn't see the color in my cheeks, but my dopey smile gave me away. I shrugged and looked up at him, nearly losing my breath at the thought of us truly being together. I had thought Theo was sexy and sweet, but I was never this overcome that I couldn't think straight. Kane was like gravity. No matter my trajectory, a force pulled me back to him. And the connection was always there, shining within us, reminding each other that no matter how dark our worlds fell, the light of our tether could always be seen.

"Thank you so much. I will never forget this. I can't believe you were able to grow all these from one flower." He kissed my hand softly, his eyes penetrating mine, as he put our combined hands to his heart in gratitude.

"I wish we could stay here all day and admire them, but we should hurry and get Oliver and the others." He never let go of my hand, and I squeezed it tight, not wanting this magic to end. A moment of admissions spoken aloud in a sea of stunning, extinct flowers that I had cultivated purely from my feelings for Kane. Soil of Solis nurturing the beauty of Varjutus, a coming together of worlds that had been at odds for thousands of years. Perhaps it was the first step in a new era that we would see to fruition together.

"Yes, you're right." We walked to the apple tree where the maagaline bird liked to rest, and I reached for it, instructing him to find Oliver. When the bird disappeared, we walked to the gate and waited only a few moments before Oliver appeared with a crowd of about twenty dubious-looking Solians.

"Cyra! Kane!" Oliver immediately ran to us and embraced us in a big hug.

"Come, hurry, let's get inside," I said to him and everyone behind him. I had to keep motioning the Solians to move since they were so hesitant to come, but after a minute or two, everyone was inside, and I quickly locked the gate behind us.

I didn't want anyone to wander in my parent's private lands, so I motioned for the group to keep moving. "I'm glad you all decided to join us. You'll be safer away from the Guardians."

Everyone was carrying provisions of food and clothing which was good since there wasn't anything to offer where we were heading. A woman nudged through the crowd, and my eyes bulged in shock.

"Celestine, I'm glad to see you're okay." But her hair was ragged and out of place, which was extremely out of character for her. She looked utterly terrified.

"Reina, thank Amrel, it's you. Are you sure this is a good idea? Living in a world we're unfamiliar with?" Her eyes motioned toward Kane, who was good enough not to retaliate at her.

"Celestine, it's completely up to you, but would you rather be the next target of Orphlam?" She pursed her lips, cleared her throat then kept walking. "Excellent," I mumbled under my breath.

"Wow, it's pretty in here! Thanks for letting me come with you," Oliver said, grabbing mine and Kane's hands and swinging them enthusiastically.

Kane smiled down at him. "You're quite welcome, little man. I think you'll like my home, but the planet is suffering a little."

"I can help with that." Oliver's eyes were wide with an unfathomable intelligence behind them, making us both curious.

Kane and I looked at each other with a frown because, knowing him, he might actually be able to. He was unlike anything either of us had seen, and I guess we'd soon find out what else he was capable of.

The Solians walked slowly, heads down, like they were on a funeral march. They were indeed about to embark on a different way of life with much more struggle ahead. They'd likely miss their accustomed comforts, but it was better than the alternative.

It was a mix of nobles and commoners. And other than Celestine, I recognized Giorgima and Derek.

"Hey, Derek, no Blaze on this trip?"

"Jolly nice to see you again, Reina. Glad no harm has come to ya. No, he wanted me to go in first and be his eyes and ears, ya know, get the lay of the land and report to him. He wanted to stay behind and continue to organize the escapees."

My hand went to his shoulder and squeezed in gratitude. "Understood."

We entered the gate, and I closed it from Varjutus, earning a lot of bewildered looks since I imagined nobody had ever seen a *Sild Gate* before. Kal and Merick were waiting for us with fierce eyes and hands behind their back, ready to intimidate the newcomers. I remembered that spiel from my own recent arrival, and I pitied them. But Jonsi was also there with a comforting smile and a welcome which made me physically relax, knowing he would keep the peace.

"Welcome to Varjutus, Solians. There has been a painful history between our peoples, and as the Varjun Elder, I remember all events of our past as fresh as if they happened yesterday. My mind is a magical vault of our memories passed down from Elder to

Elder, so none know the heartbreak more than I. But that being said, all who seek refuge here are welcome as long as they come in peace and respect. If you will follow me, I will show you to your new villages."

Jonsi nodded to me as I motioned a silent thank you with my hands. I now had an equal love for all of these races of Eredet, and for the sake of Grandpa Amrel's legacy, I hoped we could successfully coexist.

I kept hold of Oliver's hand, fully intending on keeping him with me in the castle so I could keep a close eye on him, and when I looked to Kane for a silent approval, he smiled and nodded as I knew he would. We brought him right outside the dining room since it was time for dinner. Merick and Kal glared unblinkingly at Oliver, bewildered by having an insanely gifted Solian boy in the same vicinity as them and their king. Luckily Brugan interrupted us, announcing that it was dinner time. Meili arrived and gave Oliver a big hug hello.

"Perfect timing. Hungry Oliver?" Kane asked.

"I'm so starving, you have no idea."

When we walked into the dining room, it appeared that Oliver wasn't the only new face in the castle. Already sitting at the table was a fierce-looking Varjun woman sprawled out with her leg over the armrest, picking her nails with a dagger. She had long white hair, piercing moon-glow eyes, and a sneer reminiscent of Adelram. My heart sank, assuming this was another damned suitor trying to win Kane's heart.

"Vjera! You've finally come home," Kane yelled with his arms out. She didn't even attempt to get up, so Kane walked over to her and wrapped his arms around her from her chair. She flinched at his touch, slightly disgusted.

"Whatever. Who's the squirt," she asked, nodding toward Oliver.

"He's an orphan I tutored on Solis. He's going to be staying with us."

Vjera rolled her eyes and pocketed her dagger. "Why does it seem like your bleeding heart is constantly trying to pick up strays," she said, looking directly at Meili and me.

Well, it seemed like we were going to be fast friends.

"Vjera, play nice. This is Cyra and Meili." Kane pointed at us each in introduction.

"Yeah, yeah, I know who they are. I saw them at the oath, remember?"

"You were at the oath?" I asked innocently, not recalling her face.

She flicked her hair to one side, and her nose crinkled in disgust. "It figures you'd think I wouldn't return to present an offering to the new king. Especially one that is my cousin."

I decided I was just going to keep my mouth shut.

"Just ignore her," Merick said. "Her womanly cycle is all year long—there's never any relief for any of us."

Brugan put a plate down in front of her, and she stabbed it with her fork, causing us to all flinch at the sound.

"See what I mean?" Merick said.

We all found our seats, and Kane pulled mine out for me and touched my hair before sitting beside me. Vjera had taken his spot at the head of the table, and he didn't seem to mind at all. He just looked at me sweetly. I couldn't help but blush.

"What the hell are you doing?" Vjera's eyes were locked onto Kane.

"What do you mean?"

"Why are you gushing like an infatuated boy all over the Solian?"

Merick and Kal groaned and put down their utensils, preparing to break up a battle. Merick put his head on his hand and sighed, looking longingly at his food.

"Cyra and I are Star Mates," Kane said simply, taking a bite of his food and ignoring her growing rage.

Vjera shot out of her chair, her knuckles turning white as she gripped the table. "Are you fucking kidding me?"

Oliver gasped and giggled into his hand at her language, watching with great interest, his head shooting back and forth between Kane and Vjera. I don't think he'd seen this much entertainment in a long time, and was clearly enjoying himself.

Kane let out an exhausted sigh. "What's the problem now, Vjera?"

"She's a damned Solian. You're telling me I'm going to be stuck dealing with her *forever*?"

"First of all, watch your language. There's a child present. Secondly, why can't you just be happy for me?" Kane was emotionally drained, and I could feel it from him. It was evident Kane loved her dearly, but they had spent many years butting heads. Talking to Kane that way made me want to slap her in the face. I gripped the fork in my hand so tight I knew there was an imprint of it on my palm.

"What is there to be happy about? And he'll have to grow up fast anyway. In case nobody could tell, our galaxy is a dead piece of shit controlled by bigger, dead pieces of shit. The quicker he learns that, the better. And here you are, playing fairytale with a fucking Solian. How could you even consider accepting anyone other than a Varjun woman after what those scum did to your father and our planet? It makes me sick." She spat in my direction, luckily hitting the floor and not the food.

I think she likes me.

I started to feel a rage so intense that I began shaking, afraid of bursting into flame. But to my surprise, I realized it was Kane's anger, not mine.

"Vjera, no matter how misguided you've been over the years, you have always had a home here. I endure everything you throw at me without a second thought because you are my cousin. But if you ever speak that way about my *imana* in future, you will never step foot on this land again." Kane was dangerously quiet, and somehow that was the scariest I'd ever seen him.

"You would seriously threaten me and choose her?"

"I don't want to choose, but I will."

Vjera threw her dish with the food on it off the table, so it went flying to the other side of the room, crashing into pieces. She stormed out of the door and slammed it behind her, causing it to break off of the hinges.

"Well, that went way better than I thought it would," Merick said seriously. Kal looked at him and nodded in agreement. Kane pretended nothing had even happened and took another bite of his food.

"Wow! You were right, Kane. I love your planet!" Oliver exclaimed in excitement.

Most of the dinner went by in silence, and Meili and I exchanged a few looks of quiet shock. I finally broke the silence.

"Has anyone seen Vish?" I asked.

"Pretty sure he's been sulking in his room. He knows where the dining room is," Merick said, unconcerned.

Right, I remembered. They didn't cater to anyone here, but I recalled how hard it was leaving my room in a new place when I had lost everything.

"Brugan, can I have another plate?" I asked. He bowed and brought another one full of food without hesitation. I said my excuses and left with the meal on my way to Vish's bedchamber. When I knocked, he didn't answer.

"Vish? It's Cyra. Can I come in?"

Footsteps slowly approached the door, and I gasped at his state when he opened it. Vish had always been exquisitely polished, and now he was unshaven, hair disheveled, lounge clothes wrinkled and unkempt, and the dark circles under his eyes made it look like he hadn't slept in days. I was too wrapped up in my own life to realize he was suffering this much.

"I brought you some dinner. I thought you might be hungry."

He moved aside to let me pass. "Thanks, come in." He looked down at the food and winced. "That looks disgusting."

"It is. But it's food. The Varjun don't complain since they have no other choice. So please eat and don't make me regret wasting their precious food."

Vish nodded and took the plate.

"We're heading to the villages tomorrow morning right after breakfast. Will you join us?"

"You don't need me there," Vish responded.

"No, I don't. But I'd like you to be involved." It was time for Vish to come to terms with our situation.

"Okay, I'll come. I'm sorry, I'm just…having a hard time."

"I understand, believe me. I'll be here if you need me and I'm glad you'll come with us. I find if you hold your breath when you chew, it's not so bad," I said, nodding toward the food. He finally smiled and laughed, rubbing some of the gruff on his face. Touching his shoulder, I kissed him on his forehead and wished him a good night.

CHAPTER
EIGHTEEN

When I returned to my room, Kane was there, leaning against my door with his arms folded in front of him. My shoulders slumped as guilt crept up inside me from the tenseness at dinner. "I'm sorry I was the source of the argument between you and your cousin."

"Don't apologize. It's not your fault. Vjera hasn't been the same since her family died many years ago. Everyone grieves differently, and she chooses to be angry at everything and everyone. She's also spent too much time alone on the wasteland planet, unable to be around others for long. Don't think for one second it has anything to do with you, my Star."

I opened the door to my room, and he followed me inside, the static between us intensifying the further we ventured. It was doubtful we'd be able to continue meeting in bedrooms if we ever wanted to have a successful conversation. Suddenly my throat was so dry I couldn't swallow while my heart pounded like a drum being so close to him alone. My hand went to my neck to pull at my collar since the heat singing my body was nearly unbearable. My thighs clenched together of their own accord, overcome with *need*. This limbo we were in was torture, and I considered making the first move and throwing caution to the wind.

"Everything okay, suitor?" he asked mischievously.

"Hey, I never officially said I was a suitor."

"Oh, my mistake. I guess I'll have to revisit my other options."

"Stop it!" I said, playfully pushing him and having no effect on his toned chest. "Why must you tease me?"

His voice was dark sin, and it rumbled with savage dominance. "If I were teasing you, you'd be squirming far more than you are now. And you wouldn't beg me to stop. You'd beg for more."

Good *lord*. "Do you speak to all your suitors this way?" I moved closer to him, unwilling to be the first to break or clue him in on how feral a few of his words could make me. But breathing him in threatened to do me in. Pine, wood, and fresh air…*divine*.

His small, teasing chuckle made me astonishingly wet, and I clenched even tighter. "Only the ones I want to keep."

"Will I have to step it up a notch from the flowers?"

"I don't know how you possibly could, but you're more than welcome to. I'm *really* starting to enjoy this suitor competition," Kane said, raising his eyebrows at me.

And his mention of other suitors was enough to douse my unimaginable itch. "Well, I despise it. I can't be held accountable for what happens to the competition."

"Now, now…play fair, or you'll be disqualified."

I flashed him a look with fire emitting from my eyes.

"I'd like to see what else that fire in you could do," he said against my ear, and I shivered, leaning my head back so I was open to him. I was ready for him to make a move, for this flirtation and yearning to become more until that constant ache was sated. I wanted him to use every one of his domineering qualities and finally claim me. My heart raced with anticipation, and his hot breath tickled my skin as I shivered.

But I was shocked out of my fantasy as he took me and threw me over his shoulder.

"Hey!" I yelled, trying to wiggle free unsuccessfully. We disappeared and ended up by the Kometa.

"Time to give it another go. Clear your mind and direct the Kometa to fly."

What the hell? Was this some kind of punishment or test?

"Ugh. Why do you always take me here after you've riled me up?"

"And what has you riled, *imana*?"

I rolled my eyes then closed them, trying to concentrate. How did he expect me to be able to go from the bedroom to this island and take flight within mere moments? Hearing his quiet laughter in the background did nothing to help my case. He came up behind me and slid his fingers down my arms which were luckily covered. Otherwise, it would have sent electric shocks through me. He bent down to my ear again from behind.

"Try not to think about me ripping your clothes to shreds and tasting you inch by inch until I've discovered the secrets of your entire body. Try not to think about moaning my name from the mind-bending pleasure I can offer. And definitely don't think about how wet you will be for me every day from here on out with a lust that no other man will ever be able to satisfy. Because you are mine." The last word burst from him in a growl, making these panties unwearable.

Goddamn. It was obviously all I could think about. And his words couldn't have been more accurate. His hot breath in my ear and his quiet, deep, melodic voice whispering only for me made my body burn, and I was so enchanted I wanted to forget the Kometa and attack him until he delivered on all his promises.

"Kane! Am I supposed to be training or not?"

"A true warrior cannot be distracted from the task at hand. Pay no mind to me and clear your thoughts. And try not to think of me naked and hard, rubbing myself from the sheer need of you." He brushed up close against me so I could feel his impressive, rock-hard erection, and I had absolutely no choice but to think of riding that beautiful length and putting that stiffness in his pants to better use than simply mocking me. I wanted to feel his soft lips and touch, caressing every inch of me in ways I'd never explored before. I didn't want an *imana* connection that was just about power enhancement…I wanted *more*. I wanted all of it. I wanted Kane, and right now, I fucking wanted his body.

I didn't take flight.

Kane lifted me from my Kometa and brought me down so slowly and closely that our lips grazed, and as my feet touched the ground, my head tilted back, welcoming Kane's embrace as his nose tickled my neck.

"Cyra?"

We both stilled and straightened. Every hint of blood in my face disappeared as I was overcome with debilitating nausea. I slowly turned to see what had also made Kane lose color, but I already knew exactly who it was. That voice had whispered its own words in my ear countless times, making promises of a future united forever to protect our world. Time moved in slow motion as I turned and met those turquoise eyes, soft lips, and cheeks that showed no signs of their usual dimples or bright smile. His brows were slanted, and my heart broke into a thousand pieces at the tears freely falling down his sweet face. His poise, his confidence, and his…love were gone. Only pain and betrayal were etched onto a face that was still full of dark veins of poison. A face that I often looked at with reverence, respect, and gratitude.

Theo. My Theo.

I took a step toward him, but he backed away. "No." The venom and disgust that laced his voice gutted me.

I cleared my throat, attempting to ease the vice that was clamped there. "Theo, please listen. A lot has happened since you were injured." Kane stepped beside me in a show of strength and grabbed my hand, intertwining his fingers with mine. And normally, I welcomed that, but right now, it was the exact wrong move.

Theo's eyes burned with rage at our joined hands. "Disgusting." His voice was a whisper, but it packed such a punch that I felt it deep in my gut.

"Theo, we're...Star Mates."

His head whipped to the side in abhorrence, like he couldn't hear any words coming from my mouth anymore. One more tear fell before they started to dry up, and his pain turned to rage. His body shook, and his beautiful eyes turned wild as the strange darkness infecting the skin under his eyelids intensified.

It took everything in me to keep my own tears at bay so I could speak to him coherently. "Theo, I swear to you, I didn't plan this. But it's true that we're Star Mates. For Kane and me, it's destiny."

He couldn't even look me in the eyes as he spoke. "And you never loved me. Not even a little."

"Theo, I did love you."

"Don't you fucking lie to me!" All I could think of was when he told me how he could feel the lack of love from his family, and he could feel it from me.

It was as if I could see all our special moments together running through his head one by one. Our dance on a wave over the ocean, the moment he said he loved me, our small touches and caresses, our beer together at Blaze's, the tour of Solis West, when I met his surrogate mother, Onna. All of it came crashing down before him into a pile of rubble of faulty memories like it had never really occurred.

I saw the exact moment it happened. The darkness under his eyes grew and melded into his skin as swirling red infiltrated the blue of his irises like poison. Theo was changing...into something else. My legs began to move to help him, to stop whatever poison was overtaking him, but Kane grabbed me and held me close.

"Demon," Kane whispered, his eyes wide with genuine fear.

Theo raised his hands, and an unnatural wind began to swirl. Light poured from his Solian power bracelet, and it was clear that he was absorbing all the dark magic from it until the bracelet shattered from his wrist, completely spent. We had hidden that bracelet in my room. He must have deliberately gone back and stolen it for power.

Lightning splintered overhead, and the ground shook, cracking the earth as a black poison spread throughout. Over the wind, the slowly decaying trees snapped and fell, and I could faintly hear Varjun citizens joining with screams. Kane was knocked backward with the wind, and time seemed to slow as I could barely move. My head was only able to turn an inch to make out that Kane was holding onto a tree that was scarcely in the ground, the only thing keeping him from flying hundreds of feet in the distance. I could feel Kane's tremendous power from where I was stuck in place, and he was using every inch of it to steady himself to the ground and fight against Theo's storm. It was unfathomable how powerful he was that he was inching so slowly toward me, unwilling to leave me at Theo's mercy. Through our bond, I could feel it causing him severe pain that he utterly ignored. A tear escaped me as he proved himself with actions over and over again. *There is nothing in this universe, mortal or divine, that could keep me from you if you are in need.* Kane was always action, while Theo was nothing but sweet words.

Theo's infected voice crept into my brain, causing me to shudder at the unusual invasion. I had practiced keeping people out of my mind, but Theo's skill was beyond comparison, and I could do nothing to fight him. "The Guardians were right about you. They said you'd betray me. It was just as well that I kept giving them intel on you."

All hope crashed down to my feet, the breath stolen from my

lungs. *No. Please tell me that isn't true.* "You...you were working for them this whole time?"

The wind festered and grew so that my dark berry hair billowed all around me, and branches slit my skin as they blew past.

"I was working for *me!*" He spoke with a desperation that broke my heart. "Something nobody else had ever done. What choice did I have but to try to keep the peace when you were gone? They could have annihilated any one of us at any time, including myself. I told them about what you were up to and what you said about them to keep them appeased. What theories you'd concocted. The only reason you're still alive is because I kept them privy to your actions." His eyes were wide as if trying to convince me of his goodness. He really believed he had done me a kindness.

"I trusted you. How could you do that? To me? To your people who counted on you? You can't work *with* Orphlam and come out of it unscathed."

"It was only meant to be until our marriage. Then we would have found a way to get rid of them together. But you ruined it all, didn't you? Now I will go back home and find out how to get the power I need to control all of Solis on my own. It could have been you and me."

"You're insane! You're just like your parents, selling me out to help yourself like they did to you. Did you know they're working for him? Orphlam? I thought you wanted to be better than them!"

Theo held out his hand, and I could no longer speak. "Enough. Come to me."

I didn't know what was happening, but I couldn't ignore his command. He was forcing me to obey him, and I slowly walked toward him, now unaffected by his maelstrom of magic as Kane screamed for me in the distance, still making his way to me but only capable of moving inches at a time.

"Cyra! Stay away from him!"

Words could not escape my lips. I could do nothing but obey

this command Theo had given me. I was sure Theo used this power on the Guardians on Solis before they attacked him. If he had this ability, he could have worked with us to take them down, but he had chosen something else. I fought like hell to expel his hold on me, but I was overwhelmed with sickness, his dark magic weakening me to the point where I felt faint like it was my own personal poison.

When I reached him, his maniacal smile and blood-red eyes were now so similar to Orphlam's that a tear fell down my cheek, heartbroken that he had allowed himself to break. We were all suffering. We all wanted a reprieve, but he had given up and allowed his last goodness to die until he was something reborn. Something terrifying.

He squeezed my shoulders to the point of pain and leaned down to kiss me. My eyes closed, not wanting to witness any of it. I had never been so repulsed, and Theo laughed against the kiss.

"There is nowhere you will be able to hide, Theo! I will fucking kill you for laying your hands on her." Kane's screams were a muffled cry under feet of water, my thoughts and actions no longer my own.

He continued to chuckle. "Repulsion. Really nice, Cyra. How quickly you forget the lust you had for me. How quickly you forget how badly you wanted to feel my cock inside you. You can't deny it since my empathic abilities are tenfold now. Not only that, but I can make you feel whatever I want. All this time, I simply had to give in."

Lust bloomed within me, strong and insatiable.

"That's more like it, my treasure. We can still rule Solis together as you promised." His red eyes penetrated me, and I moaned, desperate for his touch all over my body while horrified at the same time. A whimper escaped me, unable to live without him holding me, touching me, kissing me, filling me. I could still hear the muffled screams of Kane in the distance, but I couldn't feel the connection to him anymore. It was dead and gone as if I never knew him.

There was only Theo.

But a massive shaking in the ground knocked Theo backward, and his spell against me was broken. I immediately stood and ran to Kane, who could now move freely, twigs and branches slicing my skin now that I wasn't immune to the storm.

When I reached Kane, he pulled me tight to him, and I looked up to see a fiercely glowing Meili who appeared to be made of lava and fire. I gasped as I saw a sputtering vision of an outline of wings coming from her back, but it only lasted for a moment before it was gone again. She touched Theo's arm, and he screamed in agony as she burned him. His insides were glowing with whatever fire Meili had in her, causing him immense pain as if burning from the inside out. I was stunned beyond belief. Was Meili a Sunya Rei? Was her grace suppressed all this time by the dwindling energy of the galaxy?

My heart nearly stopped as I watched the tremendous glimpse of power she wielded for a moment before it started to subside. But it was enough. Theo locked eyes with me once more before he completely disappeared, and the night was quiet once more.

CHAPTER
NINETEEN

Kane called an emergency meeting in his study with Kal, Merick, Vish, Meili, Vjera, and Jonsi. I couldn't stop pacing the room before everyone arrived, so Kane embraced me, holding my head and running his hand down my hair. The embarrassment from how Theo had made me act and feel was overwhelming. It didn't matter that he'd made me do it. It felt like I had dishonored my Star Mate and needed to bathe the memory off me. I felt utterly violated and scratched at my skin, willing it away.

How could Meili almost incinerate him while I felt so ill that I couldn't fight him off?

"It's not your fault, Cyra." Kane knew the emotional turmoil that was warring within me.

I was fucking furious about what he did to me, but there was still a small seed of remorse knowing how he was raised and how he felt betrayed. "Yes, it is. He shouldn't have found out that way."

"Look at me." He held my head and tilted it up until I locked eyes with him, and I was relieved that there was absolutely no accusation or disappointment there, only acceptance. "I saw every-

186

thing with my own eyes. I felt him dampen your bond and mess with your mind. This. Was. Not. Your. Fault."

I couldn't speak, so I simply nodded, rubbing my arms. I didn't force Theo to give the Guardians intel or give into the darkness. He made those decisions on his own and would have to answer for them. Once everyone had arrived, Kane led me to a seat and took the one next to me.

Kal was the first to speak, his sword drawn and ready for battle. "What the hell is going on? There were screaming villagers and some dark blight near Leht Village." He looked to Merick, who nodded his agreement, his hands invisible, clearly warring to keep his power at bay.

"I feel the sickening dark magic all around me," Jonsi said, coming behind me and putting a hand on my shoulder in comfort, like he knew I was still suffering from the effect of it as well. My nausea level was at an all-time high from the dark magic and the other events of the night.

"Theo has woken. And he has betrayed us." Kane's power was simmering at the surface, causing the flames from the torches to keep flickering.

"Well, there's a fucking surprise. A Solian betraying us." Vjera's arms were folded. Her eyes dead and cold, clearly not moved.

Vish withdrew a dagger, glaring at Vjera but didn't move when he saw the threatening stance of Merick and Kal. "You're lying. Theo has been fighting for our freedom for *years*. He would never." But I could see the tiny seed of doubt in his eyes.

"It's true, Vish." I relayed every detail of the incident, and he turned away and crossed his arms. I would have to check on his welfare later because now I needed more information. I looked to Meili, who had been utterly silent, fidgeting with her hands.

"Meili, what was that? I had no idea you had offensive power, especially fire."

"I have no idea what that was. It was as if I could feel your cries for help, and I instinctively knew where you were. And that power is...new. I don't think I could replicate it if I wanted to. It was also something instinctive that I had no control over." It was clear that she had no idea that she was likely a Sunya Rei, and I wasn't sure I should tell her without knowing one hundred percent that it was true.

Jonsi put his hand to his chin. His lips pursed in thought. "Interesting."

"Do you know what that could be?" Merick asked, holding Meili tight.

"I do not, I'm afraid. This is a mystery we'll have to discover on our own." Jonsi had looked more careworn beneath his luminous smile than anyone else on Varjutus since I met him, but at this moment, it looked like he had aged even more, and I worried for his health with the serious trials we faced.

Kane spoke again, his deep and commanding tone leaving no room for argument or doubt. "Kal, Merick. Summon the Curadh and scour the planet. I want a guarantee that Theo has gone back to Solis."

Vjera walked closer to the group, the leather of her pants faintly squeaking. Unlike many of the other females of Varjutus, she was always dressed for a fight, not simply for beauty. "I'm going with them. If I find him, I'd like to kill him with my own hands."

Jonsi spoke again. "Well, if he was injured in the manner you explain, at least he will not be a threat while he recovers."

Kane nodded his agreement. "We're at a serious disadvantage now. I had more hope for our safety, only having to worry about the Bellum since the Guardians can't leave their temple for long, but Theo can come and go as he pleases once he's recovered, and our power is no match for what he's become." Kane turned to face me. "We used to have the power to block certain people from driving onto our planet, but we no longer have that kind of energy. It's hard enough to protect the citadel. We'll have to be on our guard now more than ever because that is not the last time we'll see him."

I ran a hand over my face and let out a frustrated sigh. "What did you mean when you called him a demon?"

Jonsi shook his head and spoke first. "Demons are made, an unnatural corruption of one's essence. It's usually irreversible once the shift happens, and it requires a tremendous amount of energy. Theo had taken on more power than he could handle and gave in fully to the dark energy, altering himself on a cellular level. It takes *a lot* to endure that change, and many don't survive. But he was likely already on the cusp, having worn that bracelet for so long and using it as frequently as he did."

"It's likely what Orphlam is as well," Kane said.

Theo had been dealt an unfair hand, and my choosing Kane over him was his final breaking point. His final hope was crushed before his eyes. I couldn't excuse his choices, but I was still heartbroken over the pain and loss he had endured causing him to succumb to the darkness. He wasn't born evil but a sweet boy who lacked love and guidance, thrown away by those who should have nurtured and protected him. No, I didn't excuse him, but I was somewhat horrified that I understood.

After we finished debriefing the group, the first thing I did was jump into the bath to wash away the events of the night. I sat in the tub, naked before my Star Mate, and it was so raw and intimate that I knew we had crossed another line in our relationship.

We had crossed an ocean.

An ocean with waters commanded by Theo, who had laid his goodness to rest and erased the final piece of doubt that was still unwittingly there before.

There was only Kane.

"I just can't help but feel bad for him. He had an emotional gift, and he was emotionally abused. It was torture for him growing up, and then his parents offered him up to die so they could save their own asses. What parents do that to a child? And his last hope…was me. He was holding on by a thread, holding onto that last hope that I would return to receive the unconditional love he was so desperate for. And he lost it all. I saw the moment it broke him beyond repair. The final straw."

Kane took the sponge and began to clean my back as I closed my eyes, hoping I could will away the memories. "You're too good, Cyra. He blatantly betrayed you. He'd been working with the Guardians that whole time, and you still grieve for him." He turned my head to look him in the eye. "You truly are the light that will guide our way to salvation and a new beginning." I laid my head against him as he finished bathing me. He brought me a towel to dry myself off, and he modestly turned around as I dressed for bed, even though he'd already seen me completely naked. I started to wonder, with all our teasing and confessions, why hadn't he made a move? He began to leave but I stopped him.

"Stay. For tonight. Please, stay."

I awoke the next morning with a vast range of emotions for what the day would bring. Theo was now another enemy we had to contend with. Meili was a powerful Sunya Rei and I wasn't sure if I should tell her or not. The new prickly Varjun woman who was also related to Kane was disgusted by me, and I would be spending the day with the Varjun people who might have been affected by the blight of Theo's attack. And we were now responsible for the six-year-old, highly-magical Oliver, who was staying on the same floor as Meili and Vish.

Kane had already left for the morning, and I had been in such a deep sleep I wasn't even sure when he slipped out. With his warmth and security at my side, I fell asleep immediately.

Dread overcame me by what I saw when I went to my closet to dress. I had gotten used to wearing fighting leathers and warmer clothing that covered me nicely since it was cold on Varjutus, and the only dress in my closet looked like the top comprised of two straps covering the whole top of my torso. I figured maybe it looked different on the hanger than what I feared, but no—it was worse.

It was gorgeous, but I felt incredibly *naked*. The two straps only covered my breasts in a crisscross pattern, so I had a substantial gaping diamond shape of bare skin to my waist. The skirt was flowy with a multitude of ombre colors—orange, green, blue, and mauve. The halter straps were a dark teal, and my back was bare as well.

I was supposed to be supplying water for the people of Varjutus, a pair of sweats would do just fine. I wondered if this had anything to do with the fact that I had *just* told Meili about Kane and me being Star Mates. She had also left a note with a contraceptive tonic explaining that it was effective for a month at a time. I rolled my eyes, downed it, and marched to the door to find Meili and discuss her new passive-aggressive innuendos, but *of course*, Kane was there, about to knock on the door.

We stood there for quite a while in silence.

"Wow. You should have more dresses like this," he said, his voice filled with desire.

"A little impractical for what we're doing today, no?" Perhaps it was impractical, but I couldn't deny that I relished how he looked at me like he wanted a taste. Maybe Meili knew what she was doing.

"You look breathtaking, and it wouldn't be unusual for the people of Varjutus. They tend to expose much more skin. If anything, you'd look like you were trying to fit in. And use your fire magic. It can keep you warm."

Great. Now I couldn't change the dress without Kane thinking I was disrespecting his people.

"I only came up to ensure you were awake since it's an important morning, and it'll take a while to get through all the villagers. May I escort you to breakfast?"

I loved it when he got all formal and chivalrous. It was adorable. So I did my best to relax, telling myself it would be okay, and decided to rock it confidently.

"Sure."

We went down to the dining hall arm and arm and walked into the sight of Oliver telling a story that made Meili, Merick, Vish, and Kal laugh with joy. The only one who wasn't amused was Vjera.

I locked eyes with Meili and raised my brows at her, my eyes darting down to my dress. She put a hand over her mouth and laughed, giving me a thumbs-up and a wink. I would kill her later.

"Good morning, Cyra! You look so pretty!" Oliver exclaimed at me with a look of enthusiasm. Bless his soul.

"Why, thank you, Oliver. Did you sleep okay?"

"I slept so well! It's so nice and dark here. I really like Varjutus. Can I come with you and Kane today? I want to show you how I can help."

The answer almost escaped me, but I stopped myself. I slowly looked at Kane and waited for his response. He was the King of this planet. He called the shots on what was appropriate for his people. But he squeezed my hand and encouraged me to answer.

"Of course, Oliver. I would be very grateful for your help, and I think it would be great for you to meet the Varjun people."

"Yes, the Varjun will be so excited for more Solians invading their villages," Vjera said, finally breaking the silence. She appeared drunk, having missed putting food in her mouth and dropping her utensil. It was unfortunate that she resembled Adelram so much. Tortured every moment of every day by too many tragedies unknown to me, and it was evident in their outbursts. They were masked cries for help from an existence they couldn't escape. Maybe that was why Kane tolerated her so easily. He was used to it.

"I think you'll find that they are desperately excited for it," Merick answered, unamused by her comments.

"Really? Merick, *of all people,* is siding with this imposter?" she asked with acute sarcasm.

"Yes. I am."

Meili grabbed his hand and held it in hers.

"And Kal? You despise them just as much as me and Merick. Where do you stand?" She asked with a devilish grin on her face.

Kal shifted in his seat, rubbing the back of his head, and looked to me for my reaction to her harsh comment. I offered him a small smile to let him know I wasn't upset.

"I would die in the service of Cyra Fenix without question," Kal answered, dipping his head to Kane and then myself. Kane returned the gesture.

Undoubtedly, they despised me when I arrived, but I supposed their opinions had softened, and I was grateful. I wouldn't be able to handle this whole table of Varjun hating me.

"This is unbelievable." Vjera had not expected his answer.

Vish threw his utensil onto the table and breathed heavily, causing Vjera to grow a wicked smile, happy to finally have the opportunity to fight.

"Anything to say, Solian?" she said in a sickly-sweet voice.

"Vish," Kane said sternly, trying to reason with him, but despite his warning, Vish stood up slowly, and Merick and Kal wiped their faces and put down their utensils again like they did last night, readying themselves for intervention.

"You don't fool me, bitch. You have some major chip on your shoulder and a massive hole in your heart that no manner of treasure could fill to make you happy. So, you shit on everyone else, threatening to spread sunlight in your direction. Cyra is the purest, kindest soul you could ever meet, and that's exactly whom you gravitate toward, trying to punish her for your own faults. Maybe you should just shut the fuck up and keep to yourself, and everyone would be much better off for it."

The second Vish finished his speech, Kal and Merick stood up, emotionless, preparing for what was coming, and right on cue, Vjera lunged at Vish.

Kal and Merick made it in time to hold her back, and Kane held Vish, struggling beneath his wild rage. Oliver looked like he had front-row tickets to a WWE match, but Meili looked horrified, unsure how to intervene.

I'd finally had enough. "Everyone *stop*." I screamed, so it bellowed through the room at an amplified volume. A new trick I'd have to ponder later. They stopped and looked up at me.

"I'm going to assist the people on this planet who asked for help. You can all stay here and waste the precious little time you have left."

I walked away, fuming at the stupidity of these inconsequential arguments. Kane followed behind me until we were outside. A grunt escaped me when I realized I couldn't get to the villages by myself.

"Don't worry, my Star. I have you." He stepped in closer and held me tight, and we appeared in a village I hadn't seen yet.

The houses were no more than huts, pieces of decaying wood

thrown together to create shelter. Many of the roofs were conclave and next to falling down as if

"This is Riva village. It's in the worst shape of Varjutus, and we just don't have the means to renovate it. I've already taken much from what was left within the castle to give to them, and it isn't much after my father's attempts. Varjuns take immense pride in our architecture and homes, and once they were works of art—mastery of craftsmanship displaying our talent, technological advances, and unparalleled skill. The interior of many homes was filled with lush greenery and stone giving one the feeling of actually living in the forest and mountains, and at night our ceilings were instilled with advanced technology that let you see the splendor of the night sky in real-time."

I was horrified by the people's conditions and the drastic change in their circumstances.

"The majority of our homes were destroyed during the war when Orphlam was still able to travel within the galaxy. We had to salvage what was remaining to provide for the remaining citizens. Now we are simply fortunate to still have shelter for everyone."

Rage rushed through me at what these incredible people had lost, but I was distracted by a little boy crying outside the first shack we came across.

I knelt beside him. "What's wrong, little one?"

"It's my name day. Father usually makes me a wooden toy, and this year he couldn't because we can't use any more wood."

I turned to the house, and his parents were staring out the window, privy to exactly what he was doing.

"Do you like warriors?"' I asked.

"Yeah! I have other soldiers my dad made me, they're all *Curadh,* and they go on lots of adventures saving the galaxy!"

"Well, you're in luck. I might have something for you. Will you wait here a moment while I get it?"

His sadness quickly turned to excitement, and he jumped up and down, his little fingers bunched into fists. "Yeah!"

I walked to Kane. "I know we just got here, but will you take me back to my room for a few seconds?" He smiled at me but didn't say a word, not needing an explanation, and his trust just made me care for him even more.

He took me back to my room, and I found exactly what I was looking for. Thank heavens for Meili bringing everything I needed from Solis. We reappeared at the boy's house, his parents now beside him.

I knelt back down beside him. "What's your name?"

"Joven." His little body swirled side to side in anticipation.

"Well, Joven. This is Fela." I revealed my Dungeons and Dragons dark elf character my friends had given me for my birthday.

"Have you ever seen a female warrior before?" I asked seriously.

"No," he said with wonder.

"Well...I will tell you about her. She was not very popular. Most people didn't like her at all. She cried about it for a while, but when she worked hard and became a *Curadh* warrior, she learned how to be brave even when everything in her life was scary. She went on countless adventures, killing many demons and saving thousands of people. In the end, she was the greatest fighter that ever lived, and now she wants to spend her time with you. Would you like to keep her as your birthday present?"

"Wow! Yes! I can keep her?"

"She's all yours, but you have to watch out for her. Even brave warriors need to be taken care of sometimes."

"I promise I will take care of her."

"Okay then. Happy Birthday, Joven."

"Thank you...uh.." The boy realized he didn't know my name.

"Cyra. And you're very welcome." I looked at his parents, who were crying. "Where should I leave your water?"

They led me inside, and from my side view, I noticed the rest of the crowd from breakfast had arrived, and they were staring at me in silence. I ignored them, entering the shack and delivering another week's worth of water with Kane by my side.

"Thank you, Cyra. You've just made our boy's day."

"It's my pleasure. I'll come back anytime you need more water." Their beautiful clothing caught my eye, and I could almost imagine them in the splendid homes Kane had described. And although the fabric was likely cheaper quality, the style wasn't. And it was the last piece of culture from the past that the Guardians hadn't stolen from them other than their memories and traditions.

We left the hut and headed for the next one. It took hours, but we hit every home in Riva village, the last home was in the worst condition of all.

"This is Ondour's dwelling," Kane said. "He will probably not want to be disturbed."

"Ondour...wait—isn't he a *Curadh*?" I whispered in horror at his living conditions.

"Yes..." Kane responded, surprised I knew he was part of the *Curadh*, much less what the term meant.

I knocked anyway and was unprepared for the face that answered the door. His features were sharp and fierce, angular cheekbones, hooded eyes, and brows pointed down so severely they could cut. What surprised me the most was that I could feel some power thrumming from him—a first in Varjutus. He was utterly terrifying, and his sneer made it seem like he wanted to crush my skull for daring to be in his presence.

"Ah, Ondour. We're here to supply water," Kane said, unfazed by this man's apparent desire to kill us all.

I caught a glimpse inside, and there wasn't even a bed. He had a sheet on the floor where he must have slept. I started to walk inside to help him, but he held out his hand, and I painfully ran into it.

His fierce growl made me flinch more than the bruise to my head. "I don't need assistance from anyone."

He slammed the door, and I looked at Kane in confusion.

"I expected as much. He's very proud. He won't accept help, Cyra."

I looked around, disparaged that I couldn't help the man who obviously needed it. Oliver brought me out of my internal thoughts.

"King Kane, sir?" Oliver said.

"Yes?"

"Your trees are starting to die over there." Theo's blight had caused even more damage to the trees, leaving me with little hope of them recovering.

By now, we had attracted a vast audience, and villagers followed us as we made our way through the huts to deliver water. They watched us now in curiosity.

"I know. There's not much we can do now. We can only hope we can break the curse before they all die out," Kane said, plagued with grief.

"No, sir. You're wrong. That is why I came. Here is where I can help," Oliver said in his sweet boyish voice.

"Come, Cyra and Meili. This is our job now." He took Meili and me by the hands and led us closer to the dying trees, and the Varjun onlookers came closer in curiosity.

"Oliver, what are you doing? Cyra is tired and needs a break from using her energy." Kane was stern but kind.

"I would never hurt her. We can do this. Cyra, you can make the water appear for the trees to drink."

"Oliver, I would need to create an immense amount of water, and I just don't think I could do it. There's a lot of trees in this part of Varjutus."

He completely ignored my statement. "Cyra will provide the water. I can grow the amount of water you give by a lot. Then Meili can spread the water within the dirt to make sure it reaches all the roots of all the trees. The three of us together can save *all* the last trees of Varjutus."

My eyes widened at the idea, and I looked to Kane as he took my hand and squeezed in hopeful anticipation. I wouldn't let him and these people down, so I took the last bit of energy within me and created as much water as I could muster, and it rushed out of my hands to the ground. Oliver raised his hands toward the spray, and it turned my trickle of running water into a massive waterfall gushing outward.

Unprepared for what was happening, Meili stood in shock for a moment before rushing to action. She dove to her knees in the wet dirt and dug her hands into the earth, connecting with the roots beneath her. She started distributing the abundance of water throughout the land.

"Meili!" Oliver shouted over the sound of gushing water. "Let us know when the water is spread as far as it'll go, and we can stop. We can't reach all the forests from here." She nodded in our direction and closed her eyes to concentrate, feeling the connection to the roots beneath us. We probably stood there for fifteen minutes before Meili informed us we were done. I stopped my water and fell toward the ground. Kane scooped me up before I made contact, and we immediately disappeared.

When I opened my eyes, Jonsi was looking over me, and I appeared to be in his home.

"Well, you had a very busy morning," he said with a twinkle in his eye. I looked down, and Kane was seated with his legs folded on the ground and me on his lap.

"Did we get enough water to the trees?" My voice was dry and sore.

"Yes, but don't worry about that." Kane rested his head against mine, causing me to smirk.

"Here, take this. You'll feel as good as new," Jonsi said.

"What is it?" I asked, uncontrollably shaking all over my body.

"Think of it as a 'mana potion.'"

"Did...did you just make an Earth video game reference?"

Jonsi laughed. "I did, indeed. You don't think Adelram was the only one getting an extensive education of Earth, did you?"

I shook my head, thoroughly confused, but downed the "potion" because I was still out of it and incredibly thirsty. The second I drank it, I felt my energy returning fully as if I had never used any of my energy stores. I sat up in Kane's lap, never feeling more restored in my entire life.

"Did you put something else in that mysterious tonic of yours? I feel wonderful. Better than I have since I can remember." Wow, why had I felt so shitty for so long when I could feel this free?

"Jonsi...did you drug her?" Kane asked quietly, his jaw clenching tightly.

"There are various properties in there. But she's fine. Now, would you mind showing me that lovely power of yours? Fill this cup with water, please."

I filled it without moving at all.

"Excellent."

"This pot has a seed in it, and I desperately need it to help someone with a tonic. Can you help it grow for me?"

Again, I didn't move, and the plant grew into a full small bush.

Jonsi kept rattling off tasks for me in quick succession that took me no time at all to complete. I had no idea what this exercise was for, but I was having fun. "Great. This pot here has a dead plant. Can you bring it back? It's invaluable."

My eyes locked onto the dead plant, still dumbfounded that I felt utterly unburdened and light, and the feeling only kept increasing. I knew it was only because of what Jonsi gave me, but I didn't care. It was euphoric.

I went back to concentrating on the plant and willed it to return to its previous state of life, and it responded to my command, revealing one of the most beautiful orange flowers I'd ever seen.

Jonsi brought out another pot of dirt. "This was once our beloved Noctis flower. Can you revive it? I think you know that it is a favorite of Kane's."

He knew my weakness, all right. With great concentration, I realized this time it was much more complex than the other requests Jonsi had just made. My weight shifted on my bottom as I straightened my back and put every ounce of my attention into the pot before me. To my utter relief, the familiar crimson flower with violet stems began to bloom, and Jonsi stood in a sudden fascination.

"Excellent..."

"What? What is happening?" Kane asked, suddenly concerned.

"Cyra, come with me," Jonsi requested. I obliged, got out of Kane's lap, and followed him outside, damn near skipping with joy. *Fuck I felt good!*

He pointed to a spot in the ground right next to his window.

"This spot had a beautiful pomegranate tree, and I miss it terribly. It has an essential vitamin I need that I can't get anywhere else."

Geez, how did he survive so long without it then? I shrugged it off and stared at where he pointed. This one was even harder to feel than the Noctis flower. I reached into every part of my being and borrowed the available energies surrounding me. This time I had to pull from many sources for this request in a way I hadn't attempted before. To be honest, I didn't even know I had the ability to reach as far as I did.

I knelt on the ground, touched the dirt, and felt the earth beneath me. My fingers laced into the dirt and felt roots starting to burrow into the soil to take hold. I felt a rush coursing through me, and I was filled with a warm, welcoming essence I had never felt before, but it felt pure and right. It was a feeling of ultimate freedom and abundant life force energy. I fed the feeling and allowed it to grow, which helped me nurture the plant to full height.

I embraced the power within me, felt each branch of the tree form, and expanded and encouraged it to flower and bloom until I could smell ripened fruit in the surrounding air. It took great effort to detach myself from the tree's energy, but I finally yanked my hands away, slowly coming to the scene before me. It took me a moment to realize I had transcended to a different place, and I had to remember where I was. Sound, color, and sight slowly returned to me as I reacclimated to my body as if my mind had completely traveled elsewhere. Jonsi had his hands on his mouth, and Kane was beside himself in shock.

"What?" I asked. "Did your tree look different?"

"It's absolute perfection, Cyra," Jonsi said, beaming. "I've never witnessed anything more beautiful."

But Kane was stuck in place. His mouth parted for a while before he spoke. "Jonsi—what the *fuck* is a pomegranate? And what is going on?"

My legs were like jello as I stood, and I had to steady myself. "You've never had a pomegranate? They're delicious. You should try one." I went and picked a fruit and handed it to Kane, who still looked like a deer in headlights. "Do you need a knife?"

"Cyra...there are no pomegranates in Eredet galaxy. Jonsi never had a thing in front of his window, and I'm fairly certain he didn't have a Noctis seed in his pot."

"No, I did not. But I would *love* to try this fruit. Once-in-a-lifetime opportunity before it withers away. And that's coming from a man who's had an exceptionally long lifetime."

"Oh great, I'll pick one for you." I practically sang with exuberance, picking another lovely fruit and handing it to Jonsi.

"Thank you, my darling."

"Oh, anytime. They're to die for. There are so many things you can do with them."

A growl erupted from Kane's chest, ending our pleasant conversation. "Jonsi, what did you give her?" Kane demanded, folding his arms. Damn, he was scrumptious in that position, his muscles bursting as if intentionally tempting me.

"Hey, calm down there, Mr. Grumpy. You need to cool it with all the...*rawr* stuff." I curled my fingers at him like I was mimicking a lion roaring, but I think it sounded more fearsome in my head for some reason. He rudely ignored me completely.

"I told you I gave her an energy tonic."

"And?"

"And...something to make her inhibitions and worries disappear. I needed to see what she was capable of, and she'll never be able to realize her potential if she's burdened by her own self."

"Jonsi! That is dangerous and reckless! It is taking everything in me to remember you are our Elder, so I cannot berate you!"

"Relax, it only lasts...thirty hours, give or take."

"Are you kidding me?" Kane's chest rumbled again, and I rolled my eyes at his theatrics.

"What's wrong? I feel freaking fantastic. Lighten up, Kane," I said through giggles.

Kane was unamused, arms still crossed and nostrils flaring like he was a big bad. Please, that act didn't fool me. We all knew he had a soft gooey center like a tootsie roll pop. Just as lickable too...

"Now that I got my answers, are you ready to start some *imana* training?" Jonsi asked with a grin on his face.

Kane was livid, but we followed Jonsi to his backyard, which looked like a Zen Garden. It was lovely and tranquil, which I usually would have been grateful for, but I didn't need it right now.

"Now, we will test what you can produce with your connection as *imana*. Stand together and hold hands," Jonsi directed.

When we were next to each other, I burrowed my nose into Kane and took a deep, *loud* sniff, taking in his addictive scent.

"Ah, he smells like pine. Did you know that? Do you have pine here? It reminds me of Christmas, glistening snow, presents, and evergreen trees. Santa and ecstatic children waiting for the happiest time of the year. My parents decorating our home to celebrate their faith and the holidays. I smell hot, crackling fireplaces and marshmallows toasting to make s'mores. Our fresh Christmas tree twinkling with lights and ornaments every night before going to bed, counting down the nights before Santa arrived to prove to us that magic was *real*. That's Kane. He's winter magic." I gasped so loud that Kane and Jonsi jumped in shock. "Oh my god! You're my Candy Kane!"

I stood there smiling like an idiot, proud of my clever new nickname for him. Kane burst out laughing but then shot an angry look at Jonsi, who sheepishly laughed.

"She could be reacting strongly to the dose, but she'll be fine. And why are you upset? That was a lovely story. I'll make sure to take a good whiff of Kane sometime."

Kane groaned and put his hand to the bridge of his nose. "You smell me, old man, and you'll pay for it."

"Jonsi! Is that a banjo!" I squealed in excitement, thoroughly missing the sound of music.

"Yes, it is something very similar."

"I love music. Would you play for me?"

"I'll tell you what, that young couple is getting married in a few days, and I will be playing up a storm in celebration. You will get to hear me then." Jonsi spoke to me as if speaking to a small child. Weird.

"Oh, a wedding. How exciting. It's so nice that we can celebrate a little bit of love amid the complete shit show that is Eredet. That's why we're fighting, right? Isn't love the only thing that matters? Love of people, life, and our planet and culture. I'm sick of the petty hate."

"Now you sound exactly like your grandfather," Jonsi said.

"I miss him *so much*. Most of the time, I'm just positive I won't make it through the day without him. And apparently, he is The Creator, and everyone worships him. I'm supposed to make him proud. Imagine those ginormous shoes to fill."

"You're doing a fantastic job, Cyra. Now let's try some magic."

I went to Kane, slowly wrapped my fingers into his, and looked into his eyes. Gosh, he was *so* gorgeous...I didn't give a damn about magic. I just wanted to ravish him. Kane gave a nervous laugh, feeling my all-encompassing lustful energy.

"Jonsi, this is impossible. We're not going to get anywhere while she's in this state. We should wait until tomorrow."

"*A true warrior cannot be distracted from the task at hand.*" I repeated Kane's words seductively, laughing at his shock.

"Touché," Kane said.

"Scared?"

"Fine, let's give this a shot."

"Maybe you two should sit. I think it'll be safer," Jonsi said.

We sat with our legs crossed, facing each holding hands. I stared at Kane's exposed, toned arms and bit my lip, trying to contain myself since I wanted to throw myself at him.

"Oh, lord," Kane mumbled.

"Okay. Close your eyes. Reach within and open yourselves to each other. Allow your Star Mate access to your well of energy and powers unique to you. They will now be available to both of you if you accept each other. The more you accept the bond, the more you will be able to get from the *imana* relationship."

I felt a tickling sensation causing me to laugh and open my eyes. Kane was smiling at me, aware of what he was doing. We closed our eyes again, and the tickling returned. It was Kane trying to probe my energy.

"Will you let me in, *imana*?"

"You can have anything you like of me, mate." My voice was heady and low, full of need. Kane opened his eyes and looked at me in shock, and I bit my lip again. I opened myself to his request to enter my essence and felt Kane's soothing presence penetrate my soul. The pit in my core was gone entirely. With Kane connecting to me, I felt utterly and completely whole.

"Holy hell!" Kane gasped and released my hands.

"What?" I asked, suddenly self-conscious, pulled from my trance.

"What is it?" Jonsi asked with fascination.

"I…I've never seen anything like it. I don't know what to say. Who *are* you, Cyra Fenix?"

That was not exactly what I wanted to hear.

"What did you see, Kane?" Jonsi was desperate for information.

"I saw a matrix of energy coming from every single thing around me like it was interconnected. It felt like I could see the very essence of all life and matter in its simplest form, and I think if I tried, I could access the energy of literally anything. Jonsi, it was like I could see and feel the structure of the universe, and it was at my disposal. I think Cyra does have almost limitless power if she knew how to use it. It was beautiful and yet the most terrifying thing I've ever witnessed. That much power… it could destroy worlds."

A heavy knot twisted deep in my gut. "Is that…not what you see when you use your magic?" My worry was growing, even through my fog of bliss.

"Not a chance. Nobody has that ability," Kane responded.

I didn't want to be the freak that could destroy worlds. I just wanted to return to Earth and be the nobody Cyra Fela I used to be. Looking at Kane again, I'd give anything to disappear and go back to my room in the Varjun castle and hide in my bed.

A random pressure surrounded me, followed by a sensation like I was being sucked away. I blinked and was back at the castle door as I had wished.

What the…did I just drive? I found myself more frequently performing magic by accident by merely thinking of the action, and to be honest, I found it much easier to perform with this tonic Jonsi gave me. Despite having just felt like a freak show, I was invigorated by the possibility of going anywhere on my own.

The feeling didn't last long because I doubled over in panic and burning fear. It took me a moment to realize they weren't my emotions. It was Kane looking for me.

I began walking to my room and remembered Theo's story

about his emphatic ability and the times he couldn't discern what were his emotions versus that of another. I finally knew how difficult it was to differentiate. My *imana* connection made me an intimate empath to one person, Kaanan Distira, King of Varjutus. I heard him calling my name, which sounded like a whisper in my head.

"I'm here, mate," I whispered back out loud, letting him feel my location in my bedroom.

Kane appeared before me, darkness surrounding him from his emotional turmoil. He looked like a dark god, brimming with power and strength. I was overcome again with lust, the sight of him alone making me weak at the knees. My legs reacted before my brain could catch up, lunged at him, jumped into his arms, and started kissing him all over. I went for his neck, tasting him with my tongue—feeling him with my lips.

"Uh, Cyra...what are you do—" Kane gave up his argument and tilted his head back in an open invitation, and I ravished him with my growing hunger.

"I want you, *now*," I said, panting. "No more waiting."

Kane rushed me to my bed and pinned me down with him on top of me with strength and grace that took my breath away. I lifted my arms above me and invited him to take me completely, but he stopped, looked down at me, and groaned.

"Dammit to *hell*."

"Kane, take me...now. I want you more than I've ever wanted anything." I leaned up and pulled him back down to me so I could kiss him, aching for him in a way I never could have fathomed possible.

"You have no idea how much I've wanted to hear those words. But not now. Not when Jonsi has you drugged out of your mind."

"I'm not drugged. I'm just in desperate need of you. You are my drug."

"No, Cyra."

"Don't do this to me…please. I need you," I whined. "I'll prove it to you," I whispered into his ear, teasing him as I did. I grabbed his hand and guided it under my dress to my underwear, which was saturated. "That is no drug. That is all just for you, my Star Mate."

Kane roared in response, conflicted on whether to give in or side with reason. He bent down and kissed me, finally matching my fervor, and I melted into the bed beneath me in euphoric bliss. I craved him, body and soul. And I wanted him in me, giving me everything he had. He jumped back off the bed quickly, breathing quickly with his eyes in shock and confusion, burning a bright green. He was hard as a rock beneath his pants, and I couldn't understand his hesitation.

"Don't you want me? It looks like you do…." My mouth damn near watered in delight at his massive erection.

"I've never wanted anything so bad in my life…but not like this. I'm sorry. I can't."

Kane disappeared, leaving me confused, angry, and never so turned on in my fucking life. I yelled out in anger, screaming so loud I could feel his emotional response, disparaged to hear my frustrated cry. Was I not good enough for him? Would he be running to another suitor now to see to his physical needs? I erupted in flames and jumped out of bed, but a knock on the door took me out of my tunnel vision of anger.

"It's Jonsi, Cyra. May I come in?"

I stomped to the door and threw it open, still flaming. I looked at Jonsi, daring him to say something that would make me blow up even further.

"Oh, dear," he said, looking at my state. He walked in and sat cross-legged on the floor. "Come, sit, love." He patted the ground at the space beside him. "We didn't finish our training for the day."

I rolled my eyes but complied.

"It's clear you're going to need more work to master your abilities than most people. Let's try some meditation. Amrel did it daily. He said that with his burdensome gifts, it could be overwhelming just existing in a calm state. He needed to work daily on centering himself to function within the chaos of the cosmos. I think you and he are very similar, and meditating will help you as it did him. Would you like to try it with me?"

Jonsi had a knack for making me shut up and listen, and yes, I desperately wanted to try anything that would help me command my power the way I wanted to.

"Fine," I murmured grumpily.

"Great. Close your eyes and take a deep breath in through your nose and out through your mouth."

I did so but was still doubtful and defensive. A sound flowed through the room—rustling leaves swaying in a breeze, and my eyes shot open. They instinctively darted around the room, looking for Kane.

"Relax, Cyra. I know you are connected to sound, so I am projecting the sounds of a windy forest for you to concentrate on."

How the hell did he know?

"I want you to lie down and close your eyes."

I complied, already relaxed by the sound of the leaves.

"Lie quietly for a moment listening to the leaves rustling in the wind. Take a deep breath in and let it out through your mouth. Do it again, absorbing the cool, refreshing air and letting out hot, negative air. All your troubles and fears are carried out through the hot air. When you breathe in, warm glowing light will fill every inch of you and every cell in your body until you radiate healing energy. Breathe in that calming light and exhale the hot air containing your negative energy. Listen to the leaves blowing in the wind. Calm the thoughts within your mind and only focus on the wind. You are pure light energy and calm relaxation. I will count down from five, and you will feel more relaxed as I get to zero."

The soothing sound of Jonsi's voice was entrancing, and I had never felt so unburdened before, just from a few minutes of this guided meditation. I listened to Jonsi count down and let the sound of the leaves swaying put me in the most restful and peaceful state I'd ever experienced. I couldn't tell how long I stayed like that after he was finished guiding me, but he finally spoke again.

"Now, slowly open your eyes."

The sound of the leaves stopped, and I returned to wakefulness when I opened my eyes. But I was also in shock because I was glowing and floating off the ground, causing me to yelp and fall to the floor.

Jonsi laughed. "Except for just falling, how do you feel?"

"I feel…amazing. Thank you, Jonsi."

"You should get into the habit of doing that every day. It will help you control yourself and your power."

Knowing exactly where I wanted to go, I closed my eyes and concentrated, appearing on the island where the Kometa lived. I looked around for my familiar Kometa, and it didn't take long for her to prance toward me.

"Hey, girl. I guess you need a name." I was overwhelmed by her glowing beauty in the darkness. She was like a beacon of life on a dying land. I recalled my Spanish lessons in school, and one of my favorite verbs was *brillar*. To glow, shine or sparkle. For some reason, it always made me think of Grandpa when I was young, and that's exactly what I thought of when looking at this Kometa.

"Hmm, how about Brillan? Do you like that name?"

She nuzzled my face, so I took that as a sign of agreement.

"Okay! Brillan it is. Will you sit with me, girl?" To my amazement, when I sat down, she followed suit. My hand ran down her short, fine fur, and she rested her head in my lap. There was no way I couldn't have fathomed a creature as beautiful as her when I was on Earth.

She still had her saddle on, waiting for a time I would be able to use it. A smile formed on my lips since I always had my *syn* on me now, as Kane suggested. Meili made it standard practice to sew pockets into almost every one of my dresses, although I've been told I could summon it if I needed it when my power was great enough.

That was another thing…how great was my power, really? Kane said he was the most powerful being in Eredet besides Orphlam, yet he was scared by my abilities. What did that mean? Was I a monster? Did I seriously have it in me to destroy worlds? The idea horrified me. If it was true…was I really that different from Orphlam? I recalled Grandpa's opinions on absolute good and evil —he believed people suffered and were coerced into making evil choices until it consumed them. If that was true—was I the early product of an evil being? Did Grandpa spend his time on Earth watching me because *I* was the real threat to others?

I shivered at the horrific thought. Kane saw the truth of what was within me, yet still wanted me. But he also wouldn't fuck me. I didn't know what any of it meant, and I threatened to explode again…so I repeated Jonsi's meditation practice and emptied my mind. I told myself I was allowed to feel those thoughts but would do it later. With the help of Jonsi's tonic, becoming relaxed again was easy. I emptied my thoughts and found myself in a state of calm, still petting Brillan, who was nuzzled in my lap.

"Come, Brillan." I stood and put on my *syn*. She waited while I mounted her, and I sat with her for a moment gazing at the foreign stars. The same constellations I'd been seeing all day every day, since the planet did not rotate. "Let us explore the dark sky," I whispered, and she took off into the air.

There was no fear or doubt. In fact, I was exhilarated. I let my head fall back, took in the freezing cold wind, and felt alive and powerful. I laughed and yelled through the night air as Brillan, and I flew over quiet lands. A buzzing sensation ran through me, and I looked down to the source, finding Kane, Oliver, Kal, Merick, Meili, and someone else I couldn't identify from here.

"Let's go investigate, Brillan." She dove to the ground at incredible speed, causing the ground to quake upon our landing.

"Cyra!" Kane gasped. "You're riding?"

"I am. I see you've recovered just fine from our previous encounter," I said, seething. Caelan was the woman I couldn't identify, and her arm was around Oliver. At least to his credit, he looked adequately miserable. Kane nervously laughed.

"I'm sorry...but is that the late Queen's *syn*?" Caelan was mortified, and I wanted to slap the look clear off her face.

"Do you have a problem, *Caelan*?" I asked with a wicked grin.

She straightened up and grinned at herself. "Not at all, Cyra. I just volunteered my services to the King to watch over Oliver when he's out on business. I'll be in the castle a lot more helping out."

I jumped off Brillan and walked up to her so we were face to face. My eyes flashed with fire, causing her to gasp and step backward. "I so look forward to it." Her fear was utterly priceless. I turned to Kal next. "Can you spare some time to train with me?"

He actually bellowed with laughter. "It would be a pleasure, Reina. Let me escort you to the training grounds."

"Oh, there's no need. I'm capable of taking care of myself." I winked at Kane before disappearing to the training grounds.

It was utterly silent and dark since it was after hours. The usual lit torches were out, so my eyes took a moment to adjust. I perused the weapons table, sick of the heavy sword I had been using, so I grabbed two small swords I could more easily wield, and they felt comfortable in my hands.

Kal appeared, and I struck at him without hesitation, but he blocked my attack. Damn, his reflexes were *so sharp*. I came at him with everything I had, feeling confident and capable, and I faked an attack, finally knocking him to the ground for the first time with my knife at his throat.

"Well, your powers are growing at an incredible rate. I'm impressed."

"It could also have something to do with her being drugged by Jonsi. Don't let her fool you, Kal." Kane appeared with his arms folded while I was still straddling Kal.

"You're just jealous," I said. "Care to take his place?"

Kal nervously wiggled away from me quickly. "What the hell did he give her?" Kal asked fearfully.

"Something to lower her inhibitions…isn't that nice?" Kane said in mock enthusiasm.

"Oh, good heavens."

"My thoughts exactly."

I sauntered over to Kane with my knives still in my hands. "You still didn't answer my question. Would you like me to pin you down as well?"

"Oh shit," Kal blurted from behind me, choking on his shock. "I'm uh…. just…going to go." Kal disappeared.

"Now you ruined my training lesson, and it was just getting good," I said in mock disappointment.

"Amrel, help me."

The world began to swirl, and I held my hand to my head. "Ugh, I don't feel so good." My legs gave out, but Kane caught me before I could hit the ground, bringing me back to my room.

"What's happening?" I asked.

"I think the tonic might be wearing off, although it's way sooner than thirty hours."

"I'm just going to lay down for a sec—" I didn't even finish my sentence before I passed out.

CHAPTER
TWENTY-ONE

The room was a bit blurry when I awoke the next day, and it took longer than usual for my sight to come into focus. I first noticed the smell of pine and a sweet, familiar hum of energy behind me. I turned in the bed and smiled at Kane lying beside me, asleep, vulnerable, and utterly stunning.

My eyes followed the curving divots his heavy body made into the bed, his smooth skin speckled with black hair, and his tattoo of Varjutus's symbol etched over his heart. I couldn't pull my gaze from his bare, muscled chest as it rose and fell slowly. His typical fierce gaze and demeanor were gone, and only quiet grace remained. He was beautiful in this state, with no worries, no responsibilities, and simply at peace by my side. Having him alone to myself was overwhelming with this bond between us begging for more, yet it was the most incredible feeling in the world to simply exist quietly in the same space with the man I couldn't get out of my thoughts. The trembling energy between us grew the longer I watched him.

I moved his hair from his closed eye and held his stubbled cheek.

"Uh oh, are you at it again?" Kane asked with a smile, his eyes still closed.

It took me a moment to recall yesterday's events, and heat bloomed all over my body in utter embarrassment at what I had done. I put my hands over my eyes as if that would hide me, causing Kane to chuckle.

Unfortunately, I now remembered every detail. "Oh god. What the *hell* came over me?"

"Don't worry, Star. You were drugged. Although I can't say I disliked any of it." He took my hands away from my eyes, and I looked at him. Even though the drug had worn off, it didn't lessen my desire for him. I burrowed closer to him, and he wrapped his arm around me.

"I'm sorry I embarrassed you like that," I said sheepishly.

"Embarrassed me? Cyra, I have never been so proud of anyone in my life. You spent all your energies nourishing my people, going door to door into their homes when I know you're uncomfortable about what they think of you. You tossed aside your own worries to help people in need. You shamed my petty cousin for her ridiculous actions and stopped a fight from escalating, and you gave a young boy a great gift on his name day. All day, I had to keep my emotions in check that I am the luckiest man in the cosmos to call you my mate. You could never embarrass me if you tried."

Water swelled in my eyelids. The truth was, I felt the same for him. How did I get so impossibly lucky that I was connected to such a selfless, caring man? It almost didn't seem fair that the rest of the world couldn't experience this magnificent person the way I could. He wiped a tear that escaped and held my face. I had to confess to him. I owed it to him to know the truth, whether he accepted it or not. And last night had opened up the floodgates, revealing what should have been evident all along, and I wanted us to take the next step.

"Kane, I know I was ridiculous yesterday, but it was all real. The way I feel around you...it's unlike anything I've experienced before. Looking into your eyes, I see hope, possibility, and a future. When I'm near you, I instantly feel comforted and at home. When I touch you, my whole body burns with an electric firework sensation. I am not myself anymore if you are not near me. You feel like a part of me, and I'm lost without you. I'm embarrassed by taking your hand under my dress, but it wasn't a lie. I..." I stopped. The words were so hard for me to admit.

"Go on, my *imana*. Say what's in your heart." Kane's voice was gravelly and low, both soothing and full of yearning.

"I want you, body and soul. I think of you every minute of every day, and I desire you even more. I don't understand this *imana* connection between us, but I don't need to. Kane, I don't want you to keep accepting suitor proposals. I want to destroy any of those women I see you with, and I'm not the jealous type. I feel like they're trying to scratch at a piece of my soul, and I can't allow a part of me to be taken. It took me way longer than I'd care to admit, but...I know you are my soulmate."

Kane's throat bobbed as he struggled to swallow, and his eyes slowly closed as if he had just heard the most beautiful sound.

"I've waited many lifetimes to hear those words. Back on Solis, I felt you before I ever saw you. I was fighting with my father about escaping and returning to Varjutus to be with our people, who desperately needed us. He wouldn't hear of it, insisting I had to wait—that Amrel the Creator had a purpose for us and that it would be even more dangerous for our people to return when it was not time. I thought he was a fool, and I cursed him almost every day we were there. Now I curse myself every day because *I* was the fool."

My hand reached for his and squeezed as he continued to speak.

"I was feeling low in my room on the third floor when I felt an intense prickling and pulling sensation I'd never felt before. I followed it all the way to your music room, and there you were, glowing with an aura so bright I couldn't make out your face. I thought I had seen a Sunya Rei, or even The Creator, himself. But when I dimmed my sight, I saw the most heavenly creature I'd ever laid eyes on. For me, the bond took instantly, and I knew in that moment that my life would never be the same. But it was clear you didn't feel as I did. I watched as Theo let you wallow in sadness and didn't lift a finger to offer you proper training. I was ready to blow up the planet in a rage for those assholes who attacked you and tried to take your blood, and what did Theo do? He apologized."

Kane chuckled, anger rising through him enough that I could feel it.

"Sometimes apologies aren't enough. I was ready to kill every Solian male who'd ever look at you sideways again, but you weren't mine, and I didn't want to influence your choices in any way. There were many nights where I trained alone until my hands were bloody and my body was spent just to get my mind right. I stood by and watched as your manner changed. You became more accepting to the Karalis, thinking he was what you needed. The day I saw you on *Hvala*, I thought I would never recover knowing that you were not mine and with someone entirely unworthy of you."

My heart began racing, remembering Kane's strange behavior the day of *Hvala*, and now it all made sense.

"When I brought you here, I thought you hated me for it, but at least I was finally in a position to keep you safe under my watch and my terms. I could try to contribute to your comfort and well-being and keep you safe by training you and having control of what happens to you. When it was suggested that perhaps I was the King in the prophecy, I only dared to hope and pray that it was true because I couldn't bear the thought of it being someone else. I want to be everything for you, Cyra and I've been trying to keep my mouth shut so you would have the choice. I have been waiting my whole life to be here, with you saying those exact words to me."

His confessions shook me to the core. Sure, we had some occasional flirting, but I had always blown it off, thinking he couldn't possibly feel that deeply for me. I also hadn't realized how badly I needed to hear those words, and it felt like I could finally breathe again.

"I had no idea you felt that way. Didn't you have other loves throughout your life?"

He hesitated for a moment, looking down and pursing his lips. "I've been with women, but I've never been in love. I had entirely given up on the idea."

Something else from yesterday bothered me still. "Why did you walk away when I was offering myself to you?"

Kane's eyes darted to the sight for the briefest of moments. "Would you really have wanted our first time together to be when you were high out of your mind?"

I laughed quietly, accepting his answer even though I got the feeling there was something a little more to it. Deciding to leave it alone, I burrowed into Kane again, and we laid cheek to cheek. I couldn't get enough of this man. In fact, I only wanted more with every day that passed, and at this moment, it felt like something had solidified. I knew without a doubt that he was the man that would be by my side until the end of this journey Grandpa had me on.

His thoughts also returned to our task at hand. "Tomorrow, we will visit Leht village, followed by Baum the day after. We will pick up the next food delivery on the day we visit Baum, and the wedding is the following day. We have a busy week ahead, so you should rest up while you can. Perhaps you should even cease your training with Kal."

"Not a chance. We don't know what's coming, and Merick still hasn't found anything about where the Bellum are hiding. I'm getting better, but I'm still not a master fighter. I can't stop training now."

"I don't know. I haven't seen many people on top of Kal able to get a knife to his throat." Kane's eyebrows rose with delight, and I could feel pride emanating through our bond. "Your power and skills are growing exponentially, and soon I think you'll be unstoppable."

"I think he's been taking it easy on me since our trip to the Fenix private lands," I said, shrugging him off.

"Or, you are just getting that much better."

I knew I wasn't even close to being able to fight in a war, but did I really improve that much? It didn't matter either way. I wouldn't quit until the Guardians were dead. Even if I were the best warrior in the galaxy, I wouldn't stop training or trying to better myself.

A knock on the door surprised me, so I regretfully left Kane's embrace and opened the door to find Oliver looking upset.

"Oliver, is everything okay?" I asked.

"No, I've been stuck hanging out with Caelan and don't like her. She wants to take Kane from you. She doesn't realize that's wrong."

Rage rushed through me at that bitch, thinking she could take what was mine, but I calmed quickly when I heard Kane sigh behind me.

"Oh, hi, Kane! I didn't know you were here. It makes sense. You should be with Cyra. I'm bored, and I wanted to visit," Oliver finished. His little body swiveled side to side with his hands behind his back as if he was shy to ask something. "Is it time to play hide and seek yet?"

I laughed at the horror of finding a boy who could easily hop through galaxies. "How about we play some cards instead?"

"Yeah!" Oliver exclaimed excitedly, running into the room. Kane, Oliver, and I played together for a few hours like none of us were plagued by endless burdens. It felt like I was home again on Earth, with my parents and Brendon playing video games on a quiet Sunday morning. It was freeing, and for a moment, I remembered that life could be uncomplicated and simple.

After a few hours of blissful peace, we visited the Solians, situated on the outskirts of Baum village, and ensured they were settled nicely.

Back at the castle, we ate dinner together, just the three of us in my room, and Kane and I enjoyed the intimacy with a youth to share it with. I pictured a life where this could be possible for Kane and me, but I didn't dare allow myself to think it could be that way forever. I couldn't bear the heartache of what would happen if we were unsuccessful in restoring the energy of the *mikla*.

We sent Oliver off to bed when he looked like he was fading. I couldn't help but be disappointed by a life that might never be.

"What is it, Star?" Kane asked.

"I miss home. I miss my Earth parents, and I miss my friends. Things were so simple and easy, and I was blessed with a good life. I'd give anything to have a taste of that life again, unknown and unimportant."

Kane considered me for a moment. "Come, follow me." The innocent smile and excitement in his voice instantly had me intrigued. I'd follow that grin anywhere it wanted to take me.

We appeared somewhere he'd taken me before, but this time it was with a much different attitude. We were in the highest tower of the castle, outside.

"I made this long ago when I was interested in the world around me. Now I wish I never had to leave Varjutus." Kane revealed what looked to be a telescope. I was astonished for a moment at his knowledge and skills but then remembered his people were once technologically advanced. This was probably standard education for them.

The telescope was huge with mismatched pieces like it was made with available scraps, and I was intrigued by what I could see in it. He smiled and motioned for me to come closer. I walked up beside him as he looked into the eyepiece and moved it into the position he wanted.

"Look, see if you can recognize this," he said. My face moved to the eyepiece, and I gasped at the magnificent sight. Stars, nebulae, and colorful gaseous emissions were amplified to create a tapestry of wonder. Even though I had been in a spaceship, there was something magical about seeing it through a telescope.

The most prominent object was a bright planet with blue seas and two land continents. "Is that Solis?"

"It is, indeed. It's strange to think that the source of our end could lie within the depths of its surface. So small and insignificant, yet the most threatening thing to the universe."

Kane was right. The cosmos were so vast and complex, and yet one man held so much power in his small, insignificant body that he threatened the existence of us all. He and his accomplices were responsible for the deaths of millions of people, and he wasn't nearly finished. He likely felt his own triviality, and it consumed him.

Kane moved the telescope and looked into it again. "Here, look at this." When I bent over to the eyepiece, he positioned himself right against me. It took everything in me not to abandon what I was doing and grab hold of him.

"It's another planet. It looks...dead." I gasped in horror. "And what is that next to it?"

"That is The Void...or Looma, as it was once known. It's the Voidlings' and Meili's home planet. The mass in the distance is a black hole. It threatens to swallow The Void along with our galaxy every day. My father told me Amrel had his ways of keeping it at bay, but now that he's gone, I wish I knew what those ways were."

Oh my God. Just when I thought I finally understood the full gravity of our situation, another terror presented itself.

"This is right outside of The Void? How are the Bellum and Voidlings surviving?"

"As I said, Amrel did something to keep the forces of the black hole from destroying us, but I don't know how long that will hold. That planet is in grave jeopardy, and it is no surprise that the Bellum have reacted the way they have. If it was Varjutus in danger of being wiped out, and my people were dying and starving to their extent, I would probably seek out the *mikla* too," Kane admitted. "Looking at that black hole off in the distance daily must be the ultimate morbid reminder of their predicament."

I stood back from the telescope, lost in inner turmoil. My grandfather left me in a world of gray. Nothing was black and white, and I knew I had some difficult decisions ahead of me. The Bellum stole our chance of saving the galaxy by taking what they believed could help a desperate, suffering race. Were they wrong in trying?

The Council on the Void facilitated the Sunya children in reproducing to keep the race going, only to live in a perpetual state of death until they succumbed. Were they wrong in not wanting to die out?

The Solian nobles lived in complete denial, devoid of substance in self-preservation. Were they wrong to give up their fight so they weren't murdered? The workers were starting to take a stance, but it would mean their death—I asked them myself to lay low and not get involved in fighting back. Did I make a mistake in not letting them fend for themselves? Kane spoke again, interrupting my thoughts.

"Here's what I brought you up for." He adjusted some of the mechanics on the telescope, likely changing the magnitude.

Through the lens, I only saw black space with a plethora of stars, and in the center was a tiny galaxy the size of a needle head on the lens.

"That is your home. That's the Milky Way galaxy." Kane gently put his hand on my shoulder, waiting for my reaction. As soon as he spoke the words, they didn't feel right. Whenever someone spoke about home to me, I pictured Earth, but this time...I didn't. It would always be a special place in my heart that I couldn't forget, but I realized I finally knew what my true home was for the first time in my life.

I rose from the telescope and turned to face Kane.

"What is it? Do you miss it terribly?"

"I do miss it, but that's not what I'm reacting to. I've never been anywhere where I felt like I belonged. I loved Earth and my family there but in the back of my mind...I *knew* I was different. Something always made me feel out of place, just like I did on Solis. But for the first time, I have that feeling I've longed for all my life—belonging, security, and total comfort. I've found it by finding you. Wherever you are, I will have that feeling no matter where it takes me. It's you, Kane...I've just been waiting for you."

He took my hands and kissed them under the moonlight. I could see multiple shooting stars, which I now knew to be the Kometa taking flight, and Kane and I did nothing but hold each other under the glow that the universe provided for us. We didn't need the sun to light our way. We had each other. And in his arms in a strange land, one hundred million light years away from the world I'd known, I found my true home.

The next morning I awoke reaching for Kane only to realize he wasn't there. We hadn't gone to bed together, but for some reason, I expected him to be there when I opened my eyes. I didn't know if it was just the *imana* bond or my genuine attachment for him, but I didn't like being apart. I wondered if I was just obsessive or crazy. It wasn't like me to be dependent on other people, but my need for Kane grew by the day.

It was time to get dressed and join breakfast before our next outing to provide water for another Varjun village. I went to my closet and grunted at another skimpy dress that would leave me half-naked, testing me to master my fire power to keep me warm. I would have to talk to Meili about this, but I rolled my eyes, put it on anyway, and quickly made my way to the dining hall. I took a seat next to Kane, who was grinning like a horny schoolboy, making butterflies erupt within me.

He leaned toward me and whispered in my ear. "If you keep dressing like that, I'll be forced to carry you over my shoulder to my bed and lock us in until I've had my fill of you. And that could be a few years. Then where would Eredet be?"

225

I bounced back into my seat, blushing profusely but rose to his challenge. Bending to his ear, I whispered back, "Don't tempt me because I'm willing and ready." His eyes flashed with light, and he smiled, holding my chin with his forefinger and thumb.

"Now, what could my cousin have said to put you in such a bother?" Vjera's voice was full of venom, quickly killing the mood. "Did he remind you that you'll still be an outsider no matter how many cups you fill with water? You don't fool me. I can see the desperate attempts of a suitor trying to win the spot of royalty."

I'd had enough of her rude remarks. "You are much mistaken. Perhaps you hadn't heard, but I already hold a spot of royalty and don't need another."

Vjera flashed her teeth, and her response cut me deeply. "So, you're a ruler without any people? You've left most of them alone to fend for themselves so the Guardians can pluck them off one by one while you give googly eyes to my cousin."

I stood with rage, but most of it was directed toward myself. I couldn't help but agree with her. There were only a few Solians who had refuge on Varjutus, meaning most of them were still suffering alone. Why was I not with them?

Kane felt my emotions through our connection, and he stood beside me. "I think you'll recall, Vjera, that Adelram and I had to leave our own people alone for their benefit. Sometimes we must make decisions we're unhappy with for the greater good. But you wouldn't understand that, would you? You're too lost in childish selfishness and never-ending tantrums to see beyond your own wishes."

She stood up, and the hairs on the back of my neck rose as if electricity was brimming right beneath the surface of her skin. "If you weren't my cousin, I would kill you." She ran out of the dining hall and slammed the door. Why did she keep showing up if every-thing set her off so easily?

It was also clear to me that just because someone was hundreds of years old did not mean they had life figured out. The long years only seemed to instill a touch of madness, fucking them up even more.

Vish made eye contact with me and rolled his eyes. Oliver was grinning from ear to ear and looking around for more exciting remarks. I sat down and held my head in shame.

"She is right. I hate myself for leaving them alone."

"You can do nothing for them from Solis, Cyra," Kal responded instantly. "Our best move is to watch, wait, and stay alive. You dying on Solis helps nobody. The Solians here have been quiet and respectful, so we will soon be able to bring more to safety."

"Pay no mind to Vjera," Merick said. "Kane is right when he says she's too consumed by her tantrums."

I looked down at my food and was too repulsed to eat, but I forced down every bite, unwilling to waste a single morsel of the Varjun's precious resources.

As soon as breakfast was over, the whole crew made their way to Leht village. Kane mentioned that Riva was in the worst conditions on Varjutus, but I started to doubt him, especially after what he did next.

"There have been some reports of sickness in this village. Everyone wear a mask to protect yourself." He handed us all a clear mask, and I held it in confusion.

"Is this the same sickness that afflicted the Solians?' I asked.

"I don't think so. This village has had repeated illness, but Jonsi informed me that it has mutated and become more severe overnight, likely from the blight Theo had released. The Varjun are especially vulnerable now because most of our magic is gone. I don't know if you've noticed, but most people no longer have power. Their only magic lies in the extension of their long lives. But even that is unsure to us now. Jonsi has been aging quicker recently, and we're all scared he might die of old age before we break the curse." The muscles in Kane's face and arms bunched with tension as if he was trying to keep himself from bursting with magic.

The village didn't just look worse. I could smell and sense the unnatural decay here as well. Me and dark magic had some kind of lethal connection which only made the fear and dread rise within me, always nurturing that seed of doubt to grow within me. Why was I so in tune with it?

Vjera appeared before us with her arms crossed, and Vish stepped away from her. Kane silently handed her a mask without looking in her direction, but she just laughed at him and refused to take it. To her credit, a mask probably would do nothing if dark magic was to blame for the illnesses.

Kane knocked at the first door, and a man answered, coughing. He was a sickly pale color. The lovely gray of the Varjun skin was now lighter with a sickly green hue. His wife was lying on a cushion on the floor in a pool of sweat. I ran inside and filled their water supply before filling a cup and running it to the woman on the ground.

"Can you take some water?" She was unresponsive, so I looked to Meili. "Is there anything you can do for them?"

"I can try. Physical wounds are easy to fix and heal, but magical forces interacting with the body chemistry are hard to influence, especially if they are too far gone."

"She is near death," Oliver said quietly, his brows furrowed. "She is too far gone." How that little boy innately knew such things blew my mind.

"I can still try," Meili said, determined. She knelt before the woman and gasped when she touched her. "This woman is pregnant!"

"Amrel help us," Merick whispered, bowing his head as if silently praying.

"Can anything be done?" Kal asked.

"I will do everything I can," Meili responded. She held the

woman with sweat dripping down her face for thirty minutes. The rest of us stood utterly silent, and I could see prayers and wishes written on everyone's faces.

"Please tell me something is happening," the vordne pleaded. "How could Amrel let a pregnant woman die from illness?"

It was becoming a festering wound, witnessing the people of Eredet praying for Amrel, especially when they thought he was ignoring their suffering. There was only us, and we were failing his wife and child. I went over and held his hand.

"What's her name?"

"Annia. We've been together three thousand years and tried to conceive the entire time we'd been together. Considering the state of our galaxy, we thought ourselves blessed by the growing life within her. There are so few children on Varjutus, and we would finally be among the few to experience the joy." He was overcome with another coughing fit, and I rubbed his back in a lame attempt to ease his suffering.

"Meili, you've done enough," Merick said gently, kneeling beside her.

She shrugged him off forcefully with a defiance I was surprised and proud to see. Meili was going through her own journey of growth and transformation, and the strength it took to come out of her shell gave me courage. "I have done enough when she is awake and safe from death."

"No, my love. If something could be done, it would have been done by now."

Meili's lip trembled, unable to stop her tears.

"Sir?" Oliver asked the grieving vordne.

"Yes, son?"

"Meili is not able to help her, but I can. What makes her happy?" Oliver said in his sweet childish voice.

"Uh…well. The happiest I've ever seen her is for something that hasn't happened yet. Annia pictured showing our little boy a land that wasn't plagued by sickness. She wanted to show the glory of our magical forests before they were threatened to extinction and our waterfalls and seas that glowed florescent blue on the shorelines. Most of all, she wanted to show him a life without the fear of extinction. She had many happy memories, but she shined the brightest when she thought of a beautiful future for our son."

I had never fought so hard to keep tears at bay, attempting to be a show of strength for a family about to lose everything. How would this man survive the death of his wife and child? How would he overcome his sickness when he felt he had nothing left to fight for?

"That's a beautiful thing to show them, and I can do it. Would you like me to?" Oliver asked innocently.

The man looked at Oliver in confusion, then to Kane for guidance. Kane nodded at him with encouragement, so he agreed.

"Yes, please don't let her suffer. Let her leave this world believing she showed our son the life we will never have."

"I will show him too. The baby. They will both see it together."

My fist covered my mouth, and my eyes burned as Oliver knelt before the woman, and everyone stepped away to give him room.

He gently held her hand and put another on the tiny swell of her belly. When his hands began to glow, he closed his eyes to concentrate. Everyone gasped when we saw what Oliver showed the woman and her baby, like a projector emitting short videos. I watched as Annia gave birth to a beautiful boy, and the happy parents glowed in love as if it were a real event. The moving images morphed and changed as the boy grew older and learned to walk outside underneath the glowing Varjun moons I had never seen so close together. Next, the three of them were in the thick forest, gazing at the stars through the cracks of the various colorful trees and extensive plants that were bursting with life that was new and exciting to me.

The scene changed to a shoreline, and where the water touched the sand, it glowed bright blue. The boy played in the water, and his family joyfully chased him. After another scene change, the Varjun people were dancing in the forest by the sacred pond, practicing some of their traditions with no sign of worry. Oliver showed her a rising sun over the large waterfalls near the castle covered with bright Noctis flowers, and the three of them were holding hands, watching Varjutus glitter in the light.

Annia, previously unresponsive, now smiled as a tear fell down her face. Her vordne rushed to her side, touching her as the visions kept coming. Kane held me, and I looked to Kal and Merick, who were shockingly emotional with thin, tight lips and furrowed brows. But what surprised me the most was Vjera, whose eyes were wide with wonder at the sight of her world in its previous glory.

We were all captivated by the beauty before us and the wondrous things this small boy was doing to ease the suffering of a dying woman and her baby. I had no idea how Oliver knew what Varjutus used to look like, but it was spot-on by the Varjun's reactions. But what crushed me so greatly that it became difficult to breathe was the awe and debilitating grief I felt from my mate.

Oliver opened his eyes and stopped the projection. "I'm sorry, sir. She is gone now, but she was happy. They both were."

The man broke down beside her in loud, uncontrollable sobs. We all stepped away to give him space to mourn the overwhelming loss of his family. I came here to help these people, yet I'd never felt so useless.

My hand went to my heart, watching Kane kneel before this grieving man. "Jaike, I'm so sorry for your loss. Please come to me if there is anything I can do for you."

"Thank you, my King. And thank you, Oliver. You have given my family a gift that can never be repaid. I will never forget how you eased my love's passing or the smile on her face as she left this world with our son."

"We should all help each other, sir. Cyra tells us we need to help each other every day since we're all we have left. We are stronger together than apart, and it is how we will win and break the curse."

"Then she is a wise ruler, indeed," Jaike said, bowing his head to me and Kane. He picked up a rattle that he explained was a gift from his neighbors, and now it was all he had left of the memory of the son he almost had. He handed it to me and closed my hands around it.

"Take this as a reminder of why you're fighting. Think of my family, always."

My hand shook as I took the rattle. "You have my word that I will never forget."

Meili healed Jaike with no issues and assured us that he'd make a full recovery, to which he didn't look particularly pleased.

We gave our final goodbyes, and I was scared to go to the next house. We had only visited one shack, and I was already an emotional wreck.

There ended up being a lot of diseased people in Leht village. Meili was able to help more than we'd thought, which was a true blessing, but there were some she could not. Oliver helped one more villager in their passing, and it was no easier than the first one.

We spent the entire day replenishing water, healing the sick, and comforting the suffering villagers. I was not at all prepared for the devastation I saw that day. By the end of it, all of us were quiet and empty as we made our way to the last house.

"Iason?" Kane asked, knocking on the door. "Iason, It's Kane."

We waited, but there was no answer.

"I'm coming in with my council. We're supplying water and healing aid."

When Kane opened the door, we all walked inside to a disheveled home and a boy kneeling by a man in a bed.

"Lorcan, what is it? Is your father ill?" Kane rushed to his side, putting his hand to his shoulder.

The boy didn't even look up. We walked closer, and it was clear that Iason had been dead for at least a day.

"Come, Lorcan. There's nothing we can do for him now," Kane said, kneeling beside him.

"I can't leave him. We only had each other. He promised me we'd always be there for each other. I have no one now. Father always thought he'd die in a great battle protecting his people, but his end was a pathetic sickness brought on by our dying world. I'm waiting for him to wake and tell me it's not real, that nothing so small would ever take him from me. But he hasn't moved...in a long time," Lorcan said quietly.

"Your parents were both great warriors. Your father wouldn't want you to dwell this long on his death. Why don't you stay with us for a week while we figure out where to place you? Do you mind if Meili takes a look at you to see if you need healing?" Kane asked.

"I don't care what you do to me."

Meili helped him stand, and I finally saw his breathtaking face. I estimated him to be about fifteen years old, with beautiful chrome-colored hair and matching glowing eyes filled with silent tears.

"He had the start of sickness in him. I was able to eradicate it," Meili said.

"Just leave me here. I can live on my own," Lorcan said.

"You're only eleven years old. I'd like to place you in a home for a few years," Kane responded with a tone that wasn't to be argued with. Lorcan shrugged as if he was simply too drained to speak.

I could not believe the boy was only eleven years old since he looked like a teenager to me.

Kane talked with some of the villagers and made plans for the dead. Kane led us away from earshot while a few neighbors were consoling Lorcan.

"Why was I not taken here in the middle of the night?" Kane asked as an audible hum of his power pulsed from his body.

"We didn't know it was this bad. I think they didn't want to burden you," Merick said, looking embarrassed.

"I serve these people! *Not* the other way around! I bow before them in service, and I carry their weight on my shoulders," Kane yelled, grabbing his King's Chain. "I am utterly ashamed they have been suffering alone, with no aid before now. What if we could have healed every one of them? When my people suffer in silence, it is *my* failure for not acting. I want daily reports on their status henceforth, and someone will come in person to see to their well-being, and if I find they are suffering in silence again, there will be consequences. I count on my advisor and general to gather intelligence like this."

His men couldn't help but shrink at his command and the truth of his words.

"Yes, Sire," they both said in unison and bowed. This was my first time seeing their relationship change from lifetime friends to king and subordinates. None of them were prepared for today, and it was their first test in leadership.

I looked at Kane in awe at his powerful presence and fierce, protective love for his people. He was unyielding in his loyalty to them, and the fact that the formidable Varjun king lived in service to his people was the most beautiful of all.

"I'm so sorry," Vish said quietly. "I only knew how bad Solis was. I didn't think about how badly Varjutus was affected by the curse. It's so much worse. I'm sorry for your people," he finished, looking at Kane.

Kane looked astonished, but he nodded his head to Vish. "Thank you, Vish. I welcome any help you are willing to provide."

"I will help Meili grow the crops in the private lands on Solis. I'll help in any other way I can. Just ask it of me. I'll be happy to have use again."

My heart swelled at his offer, relieved to finally see some life in him.

When we returned to the castle, Meili and Vish asked for access to the private lands to cultivate the plants. I opened the gate, and afterward, we brought Lorcan to Oliver's quarters so they could room together.

Kane escorted me back to my room for some much-needed quiet, even though I felt restless after seeing the increasing suffering of the Varjun. "Have we made any progress in finding the Bellum hideout?"

His head lowered as if the weight on his shoulders was truly becoming heavy. "I wish I had better news, but no. We've made no progress. I'm starting to truly fear what will become of us all."

I looked at Kane in shock. It wasn't like him to show weakness and doubt, but he was opening up to me, showing what was hidden beneath the surface of the king. I ran my hands down his toned, exposed arms and held him tight.

"I'm scared," I admitted.

"Me too, Star."

There was a vast darkness emitting from this galaxy, threatening to swallow us all whole. And it had nothing to do with the black hole outside of The Void. I wondered if we had enough time to keep outrunning it before it consumed us all.

CHAPTER
TWENTY-THREE

I woke up the next day in a sweat after a nightmare about Varjutus being disintegrated into dust. There was no doubt I was feeling the pressure to find a way to end the curse plaguing us all, and I still had no idea how to do it. In this galaxy of magic, I still felt powerless.

Kal met me at the training camp, and I fought with an intensity I had never experienced before. My skills and determination were lightyears away from when I first arrived in Eredet, and even Kal agreed. My body was still covered in sores, bruises, and cuts, but I welcomed the badges of honor that mapped my successful sessions.

When training was over, I was happy to find that Meili had left me a coat for today's excursions, but the price was a dress even more revealing than the previous two. That was fine—I just wouldn't take off the long coat. It was tight fitting and flared out at the bottom and the wrists with feather-like fur around the collar, cuffs, and hem. The swirling midnight blue and silver designs were shimmery and stunning, the most beautiful coat I'd ever seen.

Breakfast went by quietly and without incident. Everyone was still too traumatized by yesterday's events. Even Vjera kept to herself with her head down. Lorcan still hadn't said a word to anyone since arriving at the castle, which didn't surprise me. Kane and I decided to give him a little space to grieve in peace.

A bird appeared out of nowhere, startling everyone out of their funk. It landed before me and nuzzled my hand.

"Tulah!" I straightened in my seat and eagerly took the letter out of her claw and read it.

"It's Bad. He's ready for another delivery of food this afternoon. He said he would leave it behind the shroud for us, so it'll be undetected."

"Excellent! Not a moment too soon since tomorrow is the wedding," Kane said, and there was a noticeable change in the air from everyone, thankful to have something positive to focus on.

"He did note here that he added some extras where he could because I told him we had an event coming up." I smiled at the letter. Bad always came through on his promises.

"I'll go retrieve it and ensure it's safely stowed in the private lands," Vish offered.

"I will go too," Meili responded. "Unless you think there are more infected Varjun in Baum village.

"No, I've had no reports of illness and had Merick check it out last night. You may go with Vish, and I'll be grateful for your help while we replenish the water in the village. Thank you for your assistance," Kane said, beaming at them.

"It's no problem. We'll also be able to cultivate the crops further today while we're there. A few more days, and we'll be able to harvest extra food." Meili's eyes were bright with excitement, happy to be able to help with something that she was genuinely passionate about.

Kane nodded at them. "The door is still open. You will go to Solis, and we'll be on our way to Baum."

I stood and joined Kane, automatically drawn to him. Vjera looked at us with disgust but didn't say a word.

"Why don't you two join us in helping the villagers?" Kane asked Oliver and Lorcan.

"I'd love to!" Oliver exclaimed. "Lorcan, you can tell me more about the Varjun. I can drive you there with me."

Lorcan shrugged but seemed to accept Oliver's terms.

We drove to Baum, our last destination for water replenishment, and it was in the best conditions of all the villages. The trees had more life and variety, with vivid green leaves and hearty mahogany bark. The huts, which I had initially thought were poor specimens, were well-kept and preserved compared to the other areas. Baum also had the largest population of Varjun interspersed within the forest.

Luckily the refilling went on without incident. We even saw the happy couple who were to be wed tomorrow, busy with preparations, some of the women helping the bride with some stitching and sewing.

We hit Jonsi's house last, only to find he was completely without water.

"Why did you not tell us sooner that you were in need?" Kane folded his arms and shook his head.

"The people come first. Besides, I use a lot of water in my tonics and medicines. I can survive a few thirsty days. You don't think it's that easy to kill me, do you?" he asked nonchalantly. I filled his supply, and he smiled with gratitude.

"Can I interest you both in more *imana* training while you're already here?"

I looked at Vjera, Merick, Kal, Oliver, and Lorcan standing around, looking at Jonsi's possessions.

"Don't worry, they can't come to the backyard," Jonsi promised.

"Well…okay, but I'm a little freaked out from last time," I admitted.

Kane looked down at me, his brows raised in surprise. "Why is that?"

"You really have to ask? Because you basically thought I was a freak capable of destroying the universe. I'd rather you not see that again."

"Is that what you thought? You couldn't be more wrong. I was in awe. I suppose I'm just not good at expressing my surprise. But I can't wait to see more of your beautiful mind and spirit."

I wasn't convinced, but I agreed to more training. It could only help in an emergency.

Before we even sat down in Jonsi's backyard, I felt Kane tickling my mind, trying to get in, and I smiled.

"You waste no time."

"You better believe it. I'm starving for more of you."

I wasn't sure if he was talking about power sharing or something else entirely, but I lowered my defenses and opened to him, feeling his presence meld with mine.

"Wow, this is absolutely incredible. I don't even know where to begin," Kane said breathlessly.

"Why don't we start with the pomegranate trees?" Jonsi asked. "Kane, you've never seen a pomegranate before Cyra grew one. That'll be a good test of your connection. Grow me a pomegranate, and Cyra will lend you some of her power to do it."

I felt a few tugs at my energy before he huffed. "I...nothing's happening. I don't know why. I'm not able to do anything."

"It's okay, Cyra has a very different ability than you do, and honestly, you might never be able to tap into it. That's why we're here. We want to test the boundaries of your abilities as a couple."

I blushed at his mention of us being a couple. It certainly felt like we were, even though he hadn't tried anything yet. *What the hell was he waiting for?*

"Cyra, how do you access your power?" Jonsi asked.

"Well...to be honest, I don't know. When I'm trying, I close my eyes and see the energy matrix surrounding me. I zero in on the most bountiful resources that can lend their energy and borrow it. I know this sounds silly...but I kind of...ask permission before taking it. I look at all the life and matter before me and know what can be utilized. Usually, I'm the most effective when the sun is out, and I soak up the rays into my body. It's harder for me on Varjutus since there is obviously only darkness, but I can still feel the sun out there. Can you, Kane?"

His eyebrows creased in concentration as he searched for quite a while until his face lit up.

"Yes...Yes! I do feel it. It's faint, but I feel it...through you, Cyra. Wow, this is incredible. I'm connected to the universe in a way that just *shouldn't* be possible. Cyra, I'm going to try to grow the plant, but I need your mind because I don't know what this plant is."

"Okay, I'm ready."

Kane probed me, and I gave him an image of the plant. I let him see the ruby-red kernels filled with sweet and tart juice. To taste its incredible flavor, I imagined the liquid on my tastebuds and felt him smile in pleasure, experiencing it himself.

I showed him how they felt in his hand and how to remove the kernels. He saw from me how inviting and beautiful the fruit looked on the contorted and twisted tree and the similar branches full of green leaves. From there, he could feel the seed needed to grow it.

With our energies together, he tried to take control, forming the seed in the ground and encouraging it to grow. He had sweat on his brow, and I'd never seen him struggle with magic before. I joined his efforts in encouraging the plant to grow, and life started booming all around us. About fifteen pomegranate trees took form in Jonsi's backyard.

"Well, I think there will be nothing you two can't do together, and in the meantime, we have dessert for tomorrow's wedding," Jonsi said with a twinkle in his eyes.

Kane looked at me in wide-eyed disbelief at what we had just done. I was no expert in Eredet magic, but I was pretty sure growing a plant not native to the galaxy with no seed was unheard of. Especially growing so many of them to full bloom. It made me wonder what else we could accomplish together.

Kane spoke, scratching the back of his head. "I still wasn't able to do it without Cyra joining in. But our powers together made it incredibly easy."

"Well, like I said, it's still her power—you just might be able to channel through her when she allows you. Now, Cyra, you haven't tried to use Kane's power yet. Access his energies and use one of his gifts," Jonsi said.

I didn't know where to start, but I closed my eyes and felt for that familiar buzzing connection. It was easy to enter. Kane was completely open, allowing me access.

But I was stunned into stillness, unsure what I saw or how to proceed. Magical energies usually looked bright in as many shades and colors as there were stars, but through Kane's eyes, it looked shockingly dark.

There was a darkness to Kane I didn't expect since he felt so warm and loving to me. His access to power was very different from mine. Where I could see vibrant life and connectivity to all things, there was darkness in him, and the available energies were the only bright beacons. When I searched for them, I could feel cold and ice, but it wasn't the frigid feeling I was used to. It was cool and refreshing.

A dark violet glow surrounded us, and I wasn't sure what it was. I started absorbing it to see what it could do, but Kane spoke in warning.

"Be careful with that, Cyra. I only use it when there's an enemy or a threat. It's incredibly dangerous. It's dark energy and can cause things to rip apart or explode."

I immediately stopped absorbing it. "What do I do now?"

"Just let it go back into the space around us," Kane said.

I released it haphazardly, causing one of the pomegranate trees to split and fell to the ground.

"Oh my God. Thank goodness that wasn't a person. Now I'm even more terrified that you think my power is the dangerous one," I said apprehensively.

I looked back into Kane's magic and saw another eerie-looking energy. It was dark and velvet-like, moving like thick smoke, but it was difficult to see even though I knew it was there. I realized it was a constant energy within Kane and always abundant, although I had never felt him use this power before. I soaked some up, and it felt sharp and cold—uncomfortably so.

Kane's demeanor immediately shifted, and I felt panic and fear from him. "I wasn't sure you could see that. No! Cyra, don't …."

Before Kane could finish, I attempted to repair the fallen pomegranate tree, but to my horror, it started to wither away and die until it was eventually dust. I jumped up off the ground, repulsed by what I had done. I had just totally drained the life of a living thing.

That dark and vastly abundant energy of his…was death.

"Cyra…are you okay?" Kane immediately jumped up and inched closer to me, his mouth slightly parted and his eyes wide. He was strangely nervous and self-conscious, and I felt his apprehension about me getting insight into his dark gifts. He had never spoken about that side of him before, and I could tell it was an insecurity of his.

I realized then that I had the power to grow, and he had the power to destroy. We were our own version of balance, and it scared the shit out of me—mates, millennia in the making, foretold by seers and brought together by unbreakable destiny.

We were life and death.

Kane's lips were in a thin line as he looked to the ground. "I feel your fear and abhorrence. You're disgusted by me, as you should be."

A flash of a vision entered my mind without warning. A Varjun woman, dead on a bed, and Kane, naked, standing over her with wide, fiercely glowing eyes.

He looked up at me in shock, realizing what I had seen straight from his mind, and he stumbled backward in a panic. His absolute dread made me think the impossible.

Did he kill that woman?

"I..." I didn't get to finish my sentence before Kane disappeared.

My eyes darted to Jonsi in confusion. These sessions were not going well so far.

Jonsi was unaware of the vision we had just shared, and I didn't want to explain it to him. "He's always been very sensitive about his gifts. He has immense power and a multitude of abilities, but many of them are considered dark. But you cannot think of death and decay as something shameful. With light, there is darkness. With life, there is nonexistence, and where there is birth, there is death. The balance of creation is sacred. If you know how to use Kane's powers properly, they can be used for good. He refuses to utilize most of his gifts because of his self-imposed shame, but there may come a time when they are desperately needed. You must master them through the *imana* bond and not fear them. You must also help him accept himself."

I had no idea Kane had such a profound weakness, but I had inadvertently found it through the bond. Why did he think I wouldn't notice the nearly invisible energy running through him that was so strong it was like he was made of it?

I considered Jonsi's words, and they made a lot of sense. Nobody wanted to admit it, but the price of our gift of life was death. Nothing could live forever, even so-called immortals. The death of my grandpa, Amrel The Creator, was proof enough of that.

The universe had a balance, including the good and the bad. If there were gifts for nurturing life, it only made sense that there would be beings who could extinguish it.

I understood Kane's sensitivity, but he was one of the most loving and compassionate people I'd come to know. He had no reason to fear his gift since I knew he'd never misuse it.

His strange reaction of him not wanting me to touch him when we first arrived on Varjutus now made more sense. He genuinely feared hurting other people when his emotions were out of control. I saw firsthand how effortless it was to use that power and kill accidentally.

Probing internally for our connection, I felt him back in the castle, toward the top, likely in his room. I closed my eyes and concentrated on driving right outside his bedroom, but was bounced far away from it and to the castle's front entrance. The repelled drive was so intense I was knocked back onto the ground, rolling in pain. Kal appeared before me, frowning.

"What are you doing?"

"I tried to drive outside Kane's room, but I got kicked here."

"Ah, yes, you're not given access to do that. I'll talk to Kane about your access levels now that you can drive."

"Okay, thanks," I whimpered. He helped me stand, and I hobbled up to his bedroom, knocking on his door.

"Kane, it's me. Please let me in."

I heard a noise coming closer, and when Kane opened the door, my heart sank at the sight of him. His brows and lips were tilted downward, and his green eyes were dull and full of pain.

He was ashamed. This was not the Kane I knew. He had no reason to feel this way.

"What is it?" I reached for him, but he jerked away, completely shocking me.

"Don't touch me…I don't want to hurt you."

"Kane. You have never hurt me, and you never will. You are my heart." His head turned back to me sharply, a raging growl escaping him.

"Don't say that."

"Why! I know you care for me too. You can't tell me otherwise after everything we've been through and this force that binds us." My hand motioned between us.

Kane hesitated for a moment, and darkness started to surround him. "No…you couldn't understand." He turned away from me and stormed to his window. I followed him to comfort him, but I felt him emitting *repulsion*, willing me to stay away.

The force caused me to stumble a little, and realizing what he was doing hurt so deeply that it took everything for me not to fall to my knees in desperation. I nodded my head without him seeing and quietly left his room. Kal was guarding the end of the hall near the stairs, and I ran past him.

"Cyra, what is it? Are you okay? Is Kane okay?" he asked nervously.

"Your king is just fine. I think he prefers to be alone," I said and ran at lightning speed to my room.

CHAPTER
TWENTY-FOUR

I didn't understand him at all. One moment he called me his soul mate, someone he looked for all his life, then used *repulsion* on me, which was a threat to deny the *imana* bond. I was livid, especially after completely opening myself up to him when I found it hard to trust. And after I admitted how I felt about him? How dare he shut himself off.

After endlessly pacing, I decided to attempt Jonsi's meditation breaths to calm myself to avoid blowing up the castle, but I heard a voice whispering in my head that tore me from my focus.

"Cyyyyyyyra." My eyes darted around the room to see if I was losing it.

"Cyyyyyyyra."

What the…

My first thought was that Kane was calling me back, but it wasn't his voice. It was one I'd never heard before—eerie and high-pitched, echoing in my mind.

"Cyra, come."

A vision entered my mind of a location on Varjutus, but it was somewhere I'd never seen.

An entrance to a deserted cave.

It appeared this voice was sending me a location of where to meet, which was the most obvious possible trap ever. I hesitated and considered my options, but I knew curiosity would win out. I didn't know who was summoning me, and the last time I disappeared somewhere dangerous without Kane, he wasn't pleased.

Well, too bad. He had pushed me away, literally. I was going to see what this person wanted. Making sure to put my coat and hood on first, I exited the castle with my Varjun dagger ready.

Luckily, I was able to drive to Brillan's island with no issues, and she immediately found me, prancing happily to my side.

"Good girl. I have to go somewhere that I'm unfamiliar with. I only have an image to give you. I hope that's enough."

I mounted the saddle before adjusting my *syn* into place, giving her the vision of the cave I wanted to visit, and she jumped into the air. But her flight was chopped and unsteady like she was drunk before she fell back to the ground.

"It's me, isn't it? Goddammit!" I yelled and jumped off, bracing myself against her and feeling my boiling rage still present from Kane. I knew I had to make it disappear if I wanted to get to the cave. It took me a good hour before I felt my head was clear enough to fly Brillan.

I hopped back on, showed her the image again, and she jumped into the sky and blazed into the night.

It took about an hour and a half of flying at immeasurable speed for Brillan to find the location. The enchanting cerulean second moon shone in the sky, so I knew we were far from the castle.

The amount of barren land we flew over was heartbreaking. Craters where bodies of water might have been and rubble and debris from what were once larger cities now abandoned. It was mind-blowing how few people were left living on this planet.

Brillan began to descend when we saw the cavern from above,

and I almost couldn't believe we had found the exact spot I had given her through vision.

What a good girl.

"Wait here for me, okay, girl?" I wasn't sure she would, but I pocketed my syn and made my way to the dark cave entrance.

Doubt overcame me, causing me to pause and rethink my choices, but I had come too far to turn back now. "Hello?" My voice was quiet but still echoed through the cave, and my weight nervously shifted back and forth on both feet. It was pitch black, and I was a little scared if I was honest, so I lit my hands in flame and went inside.

"Cyyyyyyraa."

I was breathing rapidly now and looking all around me but seeing nothing. There was no movement of air, indicating there was probably no escape on the other end of the darkness, and I wasn't sure if the increasing heat was from my fear or from what was waiting for me.

The voice was definitely in this cave, echoing in the darkness and no longer in my head.

"Who are you!" I yelled as my hands shook at my side.

Something grabbed me from behind, and I screamed and turned, grabbing my dagger.

But when I saw who it was, I spouted the first five curses I could think of.

Goddamn *Vjera* had followed me here.

Her voice was sweet and fake, grating on my last freaking nerve. "Well, well, well. I'm just *dying* to see what you might be up to. What, are you working with the Guardians or something? Are you trying to get close to my cousin so you can take us all down? Is that it?"

"Vjera—shut the fuck up and go home."

"Like hell, bitch."

"Hello?" I yelled back into the cave.

The responding voice had us both instantly stop breathing. "Cyra Fenix, we have been waiting for you, but we will only reveal ourselves if you douse that light."

"Who the fuck is that!" Vjera's voice shook as she haphazardly drew her sword. "Cyra, don't you put out that flame."

Vjera's exasperating demand gave me all the motivation I needed to snuff it out, so we were in complete darkness.

"You fucking idiot. You don't know what's in there!"

"I thought Varjun could see well in the dark." I made no attempt to hide the annoyance and sarcasm in my voice.

"There are limits to even what our eyes can see." Her whispers were laughable since she couldn't hide the anger that oozed like staccato notes through her teeth.

A soft glow appeared in the distance, and I readied myself for anything. Two figures approached us with slow and graceful movements, but I couldn't determine what they were. All I knew was they weren't a race from Eredet I'd seen before.

"What are they?" Vjera asked, mimicking my thought.

I gave her an incredulous sideways glare even though she couldn't see me. "If you don't know, I surely don't."

They had midnight dark skin with iridescent specs of light all over their body, making them look like glowing constellations. Their minimal clothing meant we could see most of their luminous bodies. As the two beings approached, I noticed that their skin was a blue so dark it was almost black, with a stunning silvery shimmer to it. Their eyes were bright with no pupils, and they both adorned beautiful bluish-purple gemstone necklaces that sparkled in the darkness. They were on the short side, her being around five feet tall while he was maybe five feet four inches. The female's voice was melodic and soft. It felt as if she had the power to put me in some kind of trance, especially with her being able to speak into my mind from a thousand miles away. How did she even know who I was?

"You brought an uninvited guest, Cyra." The female spoke, and while her voice was even and kind, she was displeased.

"I didn't invite her. She secretly followed me." I glared at Vjera once again, who completely ignored me. The illumination from the beings provided enough light that I could now see clearly.

"What are you?" Vjera demanded, still gripping her sword so tightly that her knuckles were light in color.

"We are the Buruj and have lived on Varjutus longer than the Varjun have existed."

Vjera straightened and shook her head with her mouth parted. "What? That's impossible. Someone would have known about that in all our history."

The woman slightly tilted her head to the side, causing the light within her and the gems around her neck to sparkle with incredible beauty. "And how sure are you that you have all your memories? Only a few in your lifetime have seen us, and most have had the memory wiped from their minds."

"Why don't you make yourselves known to the Varjun?" They seemed like powerful beings. I could feel a substantial collection of energy vibrating within them, a stark contrast to most of the Varjun who had lost their magic. Maybe they would be able to help us.

"There are only five of us left. We desire to be left in peace for our remaining days."

"I don't understand. You can increase your numbers," I said, looking at the male beside her.

"We know what dangers the future holds and the threat of extinction of the galaxy. We would never bring children into that. You alone will decide if we will go extinct or someday thrive."

Great. More to add to my ever-growing list of responsibilities.

"Any information would be appreciated if you're referring to the prophecy. I'm doing everything I can, but I know it's not enough."

"No, it is not enough. You are still fighting it. After all this time, you still are not accepting who you are, and if you work without the King, all is lost."

"What are you talking about? I'm not fighting against anything. I've accepted this destiny."

The woman looked down with a slight grin as if she didn't believe a word I said, and it lit a small amount of anger within me. What did she know that she wasn't telling me?

"If you insist, but your soul is riddled with denial and doubt. But we've also called you for another reason. There is a sword forged by Amrel The Creator himself, that has multiple magical abilities. He wanted you to find it when the time was right, as it could come in handy for you in the near future. You can find it hidden in the Schools of the Seas on Solis. But beware, it is extremely dangerous and can only be wielded as a weapon by you or one with the mark of the Sunya Reina. Anyone who uses it to fight could be drained of their magic or killed outright. You should keep it hidden and safe if you decide to retrieve it."

"How do you know all this?" It seemed as if these Buruj meant us no harm, but I was still highly suspicious. "We can see many things, even though we prefer to stay in the dark."

"You knew Grandpa," I said simply.

"Yes. Amrel knew and loved all his creations. Even the ones he had to destroy."

"Destroy? What do you mean destroy?" Those words greatly unsettled me. There was nobody kinder or gentler than Grandpa Amrel. And now, knowing he was The Creator, I could never fathom him willingly destroying... or killing.

"You don't imagine that creation comes without failure, do you?" She took a step closer to me, and the walls of the caves twinkled like stars with her movement. She looked deep into my eyes and spoke softly. "Sometimes the kindest thing you can do is end a life."

Her ability to be so intense yet so gentle made me shiver. "Why are you speaking so vaguely? What are you trying to tell me?"

But she completely ignored my question only to speak more riddles.

"We have been waiting a long time to meet you, Cyra. The Creator loved you before he even saw you. We have a gift for you that we've been keeping safe for millennia." She reached out her hand, which was previously empty, but now held a necklace with a shining, multi-faceted crystal.

"This is called a Nebula Diamond. You will find it immensely valuable. Heed my words and remember what I have said. You hold the power."

They faded into nothing before our eyes, and the cave was pitch black again. Fire immediately ignited my hands, but I protected the Nebula Diamond.

"What the fuck just happened?" Vjera asked.

I sighed dramatically. "Grandpa finds a lot of creative ways to speak to me beyond the grave."

"Why do you keep calling him that?" Her annoyance was apparent, but she was trying hard to mask her fear.

"Hasn't anyone told you by now? He cared for me on Earth for fifteen years and was involved in my life even before then." I told her about my genetic makeup, the prophecy, and other recent events she had missed.

"I still don't trust you," she finally said after a moment of shocked silence.

"That's fine. I don't trust you, either. How about we get out of here?"

"Yeah, fine."

We left the cave, and to my relief, Brillan was still there waiting for me.

"Hey, girl! You waited! Where's your Kometa?" I asked Vjera.

"I don't fly those dreadful things. I drive wherever I need to go. It's faster and safer. I'm just excellent at tracking targets."

And I bet she couldn't control her emotions for over five seconds. When she disappeared, I easily took off with Brillan for the first time, even though I was greatly disturbed by what the Buruj said about Grandpa killing his creations. When I returned to the castle, Vjera surprised me by waiting for me at the front door.

"What, are you still keeping tabs on me? I have no evil plans up my sleeves," I said, rolling my eyes and brushing past her to enter the castle.

"What I just don't get is…why you? Why is everyone's fate in your hands? What the fuck is so goddamn special about you?"

She couldn't make me feel worse about the fact that I *wasn't* special than I already did. "I wish I knew. So, what's your deal? Why do you hate the Bellum so much, and why are you so angry?" I just wanted to redirect the attention away from me, but to my shock, she wanted to answer.

"Because they murdered the most beloved couple in Varjutus. They were king and queen before Adelram ruled. They gave up the throne to be together and to be with me. My parents were one of the few Moon Mates known in history, just a level below Star Mates. The Bellum were looking for something my parents had, and I still don't know what that was. I won't stop until I find out. They tortured them in front of each other and had to watch their mate suffer terribly. I suppose you can understand what that might be like. Their pain would be felt twofold since they could feel their mate's pain through the bond. The Varjun loved them, and they were the best parents I could have imagined. I feel like I relive watching their torture and death every single day of my life."

"You saw it happen?" I asked, horrified.

"Yes. Well, I heard it happen but was shielded from the sight. I hid like a fucking coward, and they never found me. Reliving their agony for thousands of years is the punishment I deserve."

My body slacked, and I softened to Vjera for the first time. "I obviously don't know you or them, but from what you've told me —I doubt they'd want you to feel like this. It wasn't your fault, and you shouldn't be punishing yourself."

"Oh, what the hell do you know," Vjera responded as we reached my bedroom.

"More than you'd think. I've lost too many people dear to me."

She opened her mouth but immediately closed it. Her head nodded quickly in response. "Sorry," she blurted before storming off.

I knew she liked me.

CHAPTER
TWENTY-FIVE

S leep was immediate for me when I went to bed that night, but it was fitful when a dream plagued me.

Adelram was at the Pog again, face down at the bar. A cloaked man approached him and put his glowing hand near his back, and his voice was strong but benevolent, one I'd know anywhere. "Come, my friend. Let me take you home."

He lifted the unconscious Adelram, careful not to touch him lest he burn him, and they reappeared in a large, dark room with a comfortable, ornate bed and black silk sheets. I recognized the dark, gothic décor as the Varjun castle. The man lowered his hood, and my heart broke to vividly see grandpa Amrel's loving face. There was no evidence of wings under the cloak, likely so he wouldn't be recognized.

"Let's get you to bed."

Adelram hissed before a deep rumble erupted in his chest. "Why are you doing this? Don't you have more important things to do than fuss over a wasted existence?"

"This has been every night for a year and most nights for years before that. You must take care of yourself. Even immortal, you can damage your body and die from this behavior." Grandpa's brows were furrowed, and he hovered over his friend as close as possible, considering his blistering heat. He was clearly distraught and grieving over the suffering Adelram was experiencing.

"Excellent, then I'll double my efforts. Why would I want to continue in this fucked up world? I can't quiet the voices and the ghosts of other people's past lives. I can't escape their torment and pain. All those lost in the war...the gore, the death. Beheadings, torture, missing loved ones. I see all of it. In the middle of the night, I cry out names of people I've never met and wear the excruciating pain of losing them like a second skin I can't slough away."

Grandpa placed a glass of water next to him, but he ignored it.

"I've betrayed my people by taking their identity. My daughter and Ilus are dead because I fucking failed them. I'm reduced to servitude by tyrants who want this galaxy destroyed in a land of people who hate me and my kin. I have nothing to live for, Amrel. Why can't you just let me waste away and die?"

The absolute torment and desperation searing through his wide eyes had my breath locked in my lungs. This felt like the first time I was truly getting insight into what made Adelram the wretch he was, and none of it was his fault. He was a man in pain.

Grandpa bunched his hands and slightly shook them, his voice filled with passion and love. "Ad, my dear friend, you are so wrong there. I told you long ago that you have a great destiny. You have one of the greatest parts to play in this story."

Adelram scoffed and waved his gray hand in Grandpa's direction. "I don't want it! Haven't I given enough? Haven't I already played my part? I'm ready for my story to end. It's been long and painful, and I'm not sure how much longer I can endure the humiliation of the Guardians and the Solians. My people live without a true leader."

Adelram was in full tears on his knees, begging Amrel with his hands twined together tight. "Please. I beg of you. I ask of you now not as my best friend but as The Creator speaking to one of his subjects. Just let me go...*please*."

Amrel's own eyes began to glisten, and his lip quivered.

"I know. I know your load has been unfair, and I am truly sorry. You have no idea how much it pains me to witness someone so dear to my heart in this much pain. It hurts me even more that I cannot grant you your wish. I need you to keep going, for your destiny is not yet done. The time is fast approaching when you will need to retrieve Cyra and bring her home. I need you to keep an eye on her."

"You ask me to go back to Earth, the place I despise worse than Solis, and then serve another Solian! You ask too much!" Adelram was yelling now, his eyes wild with disbelief. But Grandpa was calm and still, his voice quiet.

"Yes, I do. And I'm afraid it must be done. I'm so sorry, my friend."

Adelram put his hands flat on the bed, bunching the sheets on all fours, and bent his head, shaking in anger, frustration, and desperation. He slowly got out and stood with tears still falling down his face, flooding his moonlit eyes, looking right into Amrel's golden light. The pair of them was like witnessing the moment day and night met in the sky.

"Then it will be done." It was barely a whisper, as if it was all he was capable of doing. "Just don't pass judgment on me when I have to eradicate my mind into oblivion as often as possible just to survive the day."

Amrel nodded, blinking so slowly, plagued with sadness for his friend.

"Then I'll see you in the Pog in a week, as usual." Adelram slowly crept back into the black silk sheets, laid face down, and passed out again.

I awoke and sat up in bed, tears already in my eyes. Why was I having more visions of Adelram? Was there a clue in there somewhere?

Exhaustion made my thoughts too muddy to consider, so I fell back to sleep until late the next morning. The fact that nobody woke me to attend training pissed me off, but I had nobody to blame by myself. It was my job to ensure I was properly skilled, so I promised myself I'd make a point to get some lessons in later.

I rushed to get ready since I didn't want to miss breakfast, and even though it was the day of the wedding, I dressed in my fighting leathers so I could sneak in training whenever I had time. My aching legs hobbled downstairs as quickly as possible, and everyone was just finishing their meal.

Choosing my usual seat, I sat and looked for Brugan, but he seemed to be gone. Right before I was about to go and serve myself, Vjera stood, made me a plate, and set it down before me. Kane, Merick, and Kal all quickly put their utensils down and gaped.

"Okay, what the bloody fuck is going on?" The color from Merick's face had lightened as if he was genuinely concerned.

"Mind your business," Vjera snapped, hiding a grin.

I could sense Kane's eyes on me but couldn't feel anything between our bond. He was still taking this *repulsion* seriously.

Fine. I wasn't about to be the first to break.

I ate my breakfast quietly but was disturbed by the silence between us. There was no buzzing, no humming, or magnetic pull. Nothing was connecting us at all, and it terrified me. Did he officially reject the bond? Were we over?

Cyra. You have the power to decide our fate.

My fork fell from my hand and loudly clanked onto my plate before my cup tipped, spilling my water all over the table. What the hell? Why were the Buruj still in my head? Why weren't they pestering Kane, the king of their planet?

"What's wrong?" Merick asked as Kal stood.

My eyes darted toward Kane, and he whispered to himself in shock. "I didn't feel anything." He didn't feel my panic and fear—what did he think would happen in a state of *repulsion*?

To avoid any public tears, I stormed from the room, forgetting about my breakfast.

"I'll meet you at training in five since you slacked off this morning!" Kal yelled after me.

Training was exactly what I needed. I've come to rely on fighting as a means of escape—I gave all my resolve into my training, determined to be a better warrior, and right now—it was all I had.

As I approached the training camp, someone was standing in our usual practice area, unmoving, with a sword in his hand, stabbed into the dirt. His head was bowed as if in quiet meditation or reflection, and when he heard me approach, he slowly raised his head to glare at me.

I recognized him from our trip to the villages—his hut was the most run-down and damaged of everyone in Varjutus, and here he was—an equally terrifying threat to that of Kalmali.

It was Ondour of the *Curadh*.

I looked around, but Kal was nowhere to be seen yet. Migor and Garwein approached, looking pale, terrified of Ondour and what he might do to me.

"Since you saw fit to invade my privacy, I thought I'd return the favor." His voice was deep and calm as he glared at me with hatred through his dull blue-gray eyes. Most of the Varjun's eyes had a hint of a glow in them, bright and vibrant, but Ondour's eyes, just like his skin, was inert like a bit of his life force had been snuffed from him.

But none of this dulled his ferocity, and I was trying as hard as I could to hide how scared of him I actually was. I was used to threatening Varjun men with attitude, but with Adelram, there was always a sense of safety, some feeling that he'd never hurt me. There was no such sense with Ondour.

He was not unattractive but wasn't a traditional beauty by Varjun standards. His long multicolored black and gray hair fell to his upper back, and his facial features were sharp, strong, and proud. I didn't know why I had offended him with my attempt to help, but it was clear that I had.

"I'm sorry I disturbed you. I was only trying to help."

"Well, perhaps you'll allow me to reciprocate by sparring with you and teaching you your place." Ondour growled through his teeth, his canines unusually long. I was less than eager to enter a fighting ring with this massive being whose rage was directed at me, but I supposed I'd dealt with Kal and Kane before and survived—and their *Curadh* rank surpassed his.

"Ondour, stop. She's a *colt*. *She's* not ready to fight you," Migor pleaded. *Colt* must have been their term for a trainee—A.K.A. someone who would get their ass handed to them by the likes of him. But what terrified me was that Migor was no bleeding heart. His concern at Ondour's threat only intensified my anxiety.

His hands were still gripped tightly on his sword plunged into the earth, and he slowly turned his head toward Migor with that unnervingly calm voice. "Nonsense. From what I hear, she's bested two other *Curadh* at least once. She's ready."

"That was hardly the same…"

"Silence!" Ondour belted through the grounds. To my shock and horror, both Migor and Garwein bowed to him and backed away.

Needing to protect myself, I ran and grabbed a sword, officially accepting his challenge. I looked around one more time, but Kal was nowhere to be seen. It wasn't like him to be late, and it only added to my anxiety.

Ondour disappeared without warning, and I looked around for him but became distracted by Garwein's hand over his mouth. From behind, I felt a boot pummel into my back, sending me flying forward to the ground in unimaginable pain. He had driven behind me, and I wasn't prepared.

"Didn't Kal teach you the most basic rule of fighting? It's helpful when you *pay attention.*" His words echoed through me as if he said them in my mind. Was he a telepath? Could he see into my thoughts?

The wind had been violently knocked out of me, and I could barely breathe, but I willed myself up and attempted to mimic his move, driving behind him. But he anticipated me—he was already facing me when I reappeared, and he grabbed my throat and picked me up off the ground until I began to turn blue.

My panic was all that was left, and all rational thought was gone—my legs thrashed, and I could hear Migor and Garwein screaming in the background. Everything started to go quiet within me, and I had visions of Brendon and me laughing under our favorite rainbow eucalyptus tree, where we pretended we could absorb magic from its depths. We spent countless hours under it on the soft grass staring at the leaves flowing in the wind, whispering our dreams for our futures—the endless possibilities of life ahead of us. One of my happiest memories—and near death, my mind went to this memory of my best friend.

With my lips completely blue, I finally opened my eyes, which lit into flame, and my hands followed suit. Ondour yelled in pain and dropped me to the ground. He looked surprised I could penetrate shields, and an arrogant smile grew on my lips. Wasting no time, I turned around to kick his ankles, causing him to fall to the ground with me. I jumped on top of him with my thigh dagger at his throat, eyes still on fire so I could see their eerie sight reflected in his.

Finally, I heard Kal scream in the distance, exiting the castle and running at full speed toward us. Ondour used all his strength, kicked me off him, and threw a massive blow into my face, so I hit the dirt and went still for a moment. I disregarded the pain and blood and turned to my back, but Ondour kicked my ankle, making me scream out in agony. He had most certainly fractured it.

Through the immense pain, I forced myself up and hobbled backward, putting all my focus on my next move to drive behind him, and grinned to myself with blood freely falling down my face and into my mouth. I spit the blood onto the ground before I disappeared into the space in between but held the drive and reappeared in the same spot—and sure enough, Ondour had his back turned, anticipating the internal thought I had of driving behind him. I rammed the backside of my sword into his neck, and when he fell, I started pommeling him.

"Cyra! Get away from him!" Kal's voice was desperate and deep, and his legs moved so fast they were almost a blur.

Ondour grabbed my hands, and I lit them on fire, but this time he wasn't surprised by it—he gritted through the pain of the burn and kept his hold with the foulest grin I'd ever seen as if he relished it. My eyes bulged at his pain tolerance as I burned away his flesh, and he used my shock against me. He pinned me to the ground and started mercilessly beating me until everything started to fade—but before I passed out, I was back under the rainbow eucalyptus with Brendon hearing him whisper, *This is just the beginning of our story together, and we'll always have each other, until the very end.*

I was in and out of consciousness as Kal drove me to Kane, who screamed angrily. And even through my brain fog, I could feel powerful bursts of energy shooting from him. Eventually, I awoke again to the deep melodic sound of his voice with a crowd of people.

"Do you know how creepy it is to sleep amongst a room full of people?" I asked out loud. Everyone stood, and Kal and Vish came up and grabbed my hands.

"I'm going to fucking murder that asshole," Vish spat.

"You'd die before you even lifted your sword." Kal side-eyed him, his voice bored and annoyed.

"I'm going to heal you." As Meili worked, healing everything but my pride, I looked up to a red-glowing Kane pacing back and forth, shaking in a rage at a distance, unable to get close to me. His hands were covered in ice, and I was glowing red when I looked down at myself.

"What's with the red?" Garwein asked as I noticed he and Migor were here too.

"Don't worry about it." Kane snapped at them with a brutal

263

growl, causing them to flinch in surprise. He was never this agitated, like a lion trapped in a cage, raging to escape.

"He's resisting the bond. We're in a state of *repulsion*. I bet he can't even come closer to me if he tried because of the energy force," I said quietly.

"Is this true?" Kal's head jerked to Kane, his eyes wide and looking at him with disappointment.

"Kane, what the hell?" Merick responded.

"It's nobody's business but mine and Cyra's," he said through his teeth.

"Cyra—is this what you want?" Merick asked in shock.

Kane started to ice further, causing the room to drop in temperature. Everyone immediately stopped asking questions.

"I've never seen anything like that, Cyra," Garwein said, changing the subject. "You gave him a damn good run for his money—I will never in my life forget the look of shock on his face." He shook his head in disbelief and chuckled, looking at Migor, who nodded in agreement.

"Well, I'm thoroughly pissed. It feels like my tutors have been taking it easy on me if that's how a *Curadh* really fights." My ego was bruised at how badly my ass was handed to me, and it reinforced the fact that even though I was significantly improving, I wasn't where I needed to be. But I was brought out of my self-chiding when Kane cursed, and his power surge cracked and shattered the glass window. Meili was the only one brave enough to move, walking to the window to fix it.

After a moment, Kal jerked to his feet, his nostrils flaring. "Ondour has a tendency of fighting dirty, and he was fighting with a vendetta. He was trying to punish you, which is an utter disgrace to the *Curadh*. Our duty is to train and prepare you for what is to come, Cyra. Not to pulverize you to within inches of death. He got into my mind and sent me on a fake errand that I thought was requested by the king. He intentionally kept me from the fight so that I couldn't help you."

Kane belted in anger, and wind circled the room. The temperature dropped even more, and darkness started creeping in around us.

For heaven's sake.

"Everyone out—now!"

Garwein and Migor didn't need to be told twice, running for the exit while Vish and Meili looked at me with longing.

"Come, cherub—Cyra will help him." I was grateful that Merick rushed her out of the room.

"Vish, you need to go now."

Kal looked at me, not budging an inch.

"Kal—please take Vish and go. I've got this."

He softened even though his face was overwhelmed with worry. He bowed his head and grabbed Vish by the arm, dragging him out.

"Kane, please calm down. He's an ass, but he wouldn't have killed me." My heart almost broke when he looked at me with wild, raging eyes, and I almost didn't recognize him. I couldn't help but start crying.

He was my soul mate—and he was forcing me away. I inched to the edge of the bed and slowly toward Kane, but this time, his wind cut me. His *repulsion* had made me no longer impervious to his magic. He had cast me out, and I was no longer a part of him.

Frost began to line my skin from the intense cold, and shivers overtook my body, but I held my ground. It was the second time in a matter of a few hours that I was turning blue.

"Kane, please! Please don't shut me out. What happened to soul mates? What happened to you telling me you waited your whole life for this? What has changed? Please tell me what I did so I can fix it!"

Kane looked at me and fell to his knees, covering his face. I couldn't understand what was happening to him, especially since I couldn't sense his feelings anymore. I walked toward him and pressed as hard as possible against the magnetic push, but it wouldn't budge. The harder I pushed with Kane not giving in, the bigger the *repulsion* became, and it was impossible to get to him.

Cyra...you're almost out of time. Fix it now.

I screamed in frustration. Frustration that I had so much on my shoulders. Anger that I felt so useless yet again, and anger at Kane for appearing to give up on us. I closed my eyes, cleared my mind, and saw the only thing that was clear in my mess of a life. The answer was clear when I wasn't fighting all the thoughts in my head and the circumstances around me.

You're still fighting it. You're still not accepting who you are, and if you work without the king, all is lost.

The Buruj was right. I wasn't sure if I could ever fully accept the faith people had in me as a "savior," but it was time to stop fighting myself. Kane's behavior hurt me, but he needed me just as much as I needed him. He was in pain, and my job as his Star Mate was to swallow my pride and do whatever he needed to save him. I stood and spoke the only thing that was inside of me.

"Kane...I love you."

His head jerked up, and the ice and wind melted away, but he held a look of utter terror. I was just relieved he was in control again. I stepped toward him, arm outstretched, but he crawled away from me and whispered, "You don't understand." Not a second later, he was gone.

Hours later, Meili knocked on my door, informing me it was time to depart for the wedding. I looked down, surprised that I was completely dressed and ready. Had Meili come and dressed me? Did I dress myself? I couldn't even remember the last few hours after I told Kane I loved him, and his answer was instant disappearance.

You don't understand…

What didn't I understand? Kane's memory of the dead woman returned, and I knew it had to be related.

A shiver crept up my spine. It was unfathomable how empty and alone I felt. The loss of his presence within me was more devastating than I could have imagined, as if a piece of my soul was dead.

Meili repeated her words, urging me to come with her. To a wedding of all things. Sometimes I really did think the universe was trying to fuck with me in cruel and unusual ways. I guess one saving grace was that my Kometa gave me some small training on how to momentarily erase the gaping pit inside myself to survive an immediate task at hand. Despite my overwhelming grief, I still had a responsibility to fill, which was a thousand times worse than any near-death beating Ondour could give me.

I stood up and smiled at Meili's angelic face, giving her no sign of my internal hellfire. "I'm ready." I limped toward her, almost falling, forgetting my ankle was broken. Meili didn't let me leave until she repaired it.

When we exited the castle, Vjera was there with her arms crossed, leaning against the wall.

"It's about damned time. I've been told to escort the Solian to the wedding. We'll meet you there."

Meili squinted her eyes, clearly suspicious of Vjera, but agreed and disappeared.

"Nobody in their right mind would ask you to escort me anywhere," I said, looking at Vjera with my eyebrow raised.

"Hell no, but I wanted her to go away."

This time I folded my arms.

"Did you seriously give the great and mighty Ondour that black eye and third-degree burns?"

"He had it coming."

"Damn! You crazy bitch. You do realize that was incredibly stupid?"

"So?" It occurred to me that I might be assimilating to Varjun culture, becoming more aloof and arrogant.

A sideways smirk formed on her lips. "I like it."

"Not going to lie…it felt good. He did almost kill me, though. I'm not entirely sure if he would have kept me alive."

"I'm sure that was the point. He's a prick and a half, and he was establishing himself as alpha dog since you pissed on his lawn. But you fought back. He didn't kill you. That's also a lesson."

"Sure, a lesson that next time I'm taking a bigger piss."

"Are you *trying* to get me to like you?" Vjera's brows raised. Her smirk still firmly in place.

I shook my head and shrugged. "Where would the fun be in that?"

"Shit, we're going to be late. Jonsi will cut my balls off. We don't want to miss the *sacred event* of holy indentured servitude," she said with as much sarcasm as she could muster.

I couldn't stop the small laugh that escaped.

When we arrived in the forest by the sacred pond, Vjera scoffed and sauntered off to become invisible, but I stood stuck in place by the beauty of our surroundings. Moss and vines hung by the trees, creating a canopy all around us that held tiny twinkling lights and lavender-colored flowers and leaves falling over the glowing pond spread throughout. Jonsi stood front and center on a dais with the groom, who had a bright, endearing smile, waiting for the ceremony to begin. The villagers were standing on two sides, making a walkway covered in lavender leaves and petals that I assumed were for the bride.

Right on cue, she appeared at the end of the long path and began her journey to her betrothed. Resources were scarce, so she wore a plain, white cotton-like dress, but her hair was splendid in a loose, messy braid with small greens and Noctis flowers placed throughout. I wondered if Meili brought some back from the private lands, and it made me happy that the bride had them for her special day.

She carried braided ribbons with more Noctis flowers and various trinkets fastened to it. Her smile was radiant as she locked eyes with her *vordne,* and he bent over in joy, laughing until he looked up at her again, starting to tear up. He brought his hands in front of himself, revealing his own ribbons, braided with more trinkets. When she reached the platform, Jonsi took her hand and helped her step up next to her future spouse.

My whole world stopped, and my heart sputtered as Kane appeared on the platform, looking stunning in a royal blue tunic and his shining King's Chain. He didn't have the usual gleam in his eye when he was with his people. He appeared subdued...distant —like his light was snuffed out.

"Welcome, friends, to this joyous event!" Jonsi exclaimed. His voice carried through the large crowd so everyone could hear, and the Varjun people cheered. "Are we ready for the king to begin?" The crowd cheered again in response.

The King? Jonsi has been the officiant of all their events so far, so it surprised me that Kane was leading this wedding. He stepped forward in between the couple and lowered his head in silence. There wasn't a sound to be heard anywhere as the Varjun eagerly awaited their king to speak. He was quiet for a few seconds as if contemplating what to say. The fact that I couldn't feel what he was feeling was so jarring that it nearly brought tears to my eyes.

"It has been quite a long time since Varjutus has seen a wedding. Something has been happening to our people that our great ancestors never could have foreseen. Our once immense numbers that spread throughout the globe are now reduced to the size of one small, impoverished village. Our larger colonies are a thing of the past. Our old professions and expert talents are long gone. Our magic is a mere sputtering hum that dies a little more every day along with our beloved planet. Our skies stay dark, and our lands have not known natural water in an age. Our lush, sacred forests and waterfalls are mere scars in the ground while the elders are aging and feeling the passing of time without the luxury of our time moving."

He paused momentarily, studying the people he served, and they were glued to him in return, connecting in a way I might never understand.

"We are still. Locked in a continuous state of decay. There is no doubt that we are suffering. Yes, it has been a long time since Varjutus has seen a wedding. But there is something we haven't lost and will never lose that keeps us alive and filled with hope. Our community, customs, way of life, family, health—and love. The Varjun value the love of all these things, so we still stand united in the face of these harsh, terrifying times."

Some gentle nods and responses of agreement sounded around me, and many in the crowd were clasping the hands of the person next to them, making my heart skip at the hope these people created.

"Our enemies are powerful and the most dangerous threat we ever could have imagined, but we are not broken. They cannot take our identity and our passion. Our numbers are few, and our births are far between, but we will *never* stop our drive to live and celebrate who we are. We will never stop uniting with peace and joy in our hearts. And that is why we're here today. We Varjun will pause from the chaos and celebrate the love that our people create. Tess and Niko declare this in front of us so that we might share in the blessed event of our people uniting as one."

"We are one!" the crowd yelled.

Kane took Tess and Niko's hands and pulled them closer together. He then secured both ribbons around their hands, binding them together as they stared into each other's eyes with pure infatuation.

"Tess and Niko, I, Kaanan Distira, King of Varjutus, bind and bless your marriage so that you are one with each other and will never be parted from this day forth until you join the energy of the universe. May your union be blessed with beautiful children and a life of respect and companionship."

The ribbons glowed and slowly began to dissipate into their skins. Their bodies seemed to absorb the union until the ribbons completely disappeared. They stood in silence for a moment as if a story was unfolding before them, and I wondered if there was something in the ribbons that only they could see. They began crying in happiness, still holding each other in a private moment before the people of Varjutus.

"Niko and Tess, you are now bound in marriage from this day forward," Kane said with a subdued smile.

They grabbed each other and kissed. It was clear that they'd been waiting years for this day. The crowd cheered, and Jonsi yelled, "Let's party!"

Through my tears, I laughed at Jonsi's spectacle of jumping off the podium for his banjo. A few other Varjun joined him, sitting on top of the dais to start playing lively music. I immediately moved to the music, unable to stop giving myself over to the sheer joy of the tunes. I had no partner, but I didn't care.

Jerky movement caught my eye, only to find Caelan dragging Kane away to dance, so I turned away to avoid the show.

Oliver ran up to me with joy on his face. "This is the best planet ever! I've never had this much fun on Solis!"

I laughed at his enthusiasm. "Enjoy, little man."

"I even bet it's time to play hide-and-seek soon." He looked off into the distance as if imagining the most fantastic dream. What was this boy's infatuation with hide-and-seek? He shook his head and spoke to his friend.

"Come on, Lorcan! This way!" Oliver said, running at full speed toward whatever had caught his attention. Lorcan looked at me and rolled his eyes, clearly drained following Oliver's boundless energy. He sauntered after his new friend, enjoying every minute of it.

With a smile still on my face, I turned and saw Kal brooding on a stump in the distance, just like the last event, and ran toward him.

"Oh no, you don't!"

"What?" he asked with his lip raised in a sneer.

"Come." I took his arm and pulled. It didn't even come close to budging him.

"Uh, not a chance in hell."

"Come on! Even *Curadh* warriors need to let loose and forget themselves."

"Cyra—I'm the dispeller of darkness. I don't dance."

I tilted my head back in laughter. My insides were still full of devastation and turmoil, but I was determined to have a moment of release, to disconnect from the prophesized girl.

"Kal, you don't want me to make your life a living hell, do you? Do I need to use the Daughter of Our Creator card?"

He rolled his eyes but stood up and followed me.

I was floored when he actually began moving to the music, and his body was fluid grace, moving to the beat. Turned out the dispeller of darkness might not dance...but he sure as hell was *great* at it.

He was like sex and grace transformed into movement, and I was baffled as to why he didn't have a woman. It would be all too easy to be swept up in his elegance and strength.

After a few minutes, he cracked a smile and joined in my laughter. We moved together perfectly since we knew each other's cadence from our frequent combat. It felt like fighting and dancing were not all that different. They were both intimate, a show of bodily precision and poise. It made sense that Kal was such a beautiful dancer, given how skilled he was with a sword.

My eyes accidentally locked with Kane's, and his jaw dropped in utter surprise at seeing us. I imagined even his friends had never seen his dancing talents before.

The music slowed to a beautiful, melodic song, and Kal nodded his goodbyes. I felt a tap from behind me and turned to see Vish's smiling face. "May I have this dance?"

"It'd be my pleasure."

He put his hands gently around my waist, and I wrapped mine around his shoulders. His dirty blonde hair was slightly tousled, as usual, and his deep brown eyes were filled with happiness for the first time in a long time. I'd never noticed it before, but he smelled like soap and spring lilacs, sending a pang of sadness through me since it reminded me so much of Solis.

"I see you and Meili successfully brought the food from Solis."

"Yes—it was a good haul this time too. I think we'll be quite full for the next week. We also tended to the garden in the private lands. It's coming on quite nicely."

"Thank you so much for your help, Vish. I can't tell you how much I appreciate you being here with me on Varjutus."

"Well, you're all I have left, Cyra."

I looked up into his endearing brown eyes, and they held years of heartache within them. Vish's past broke my heart, and his last friend, who was like family to him, betrayed him by turning on us all.

"You will always have me—as long as I live."

Vish was about to speak but stopped as a red glow enveloped me. I looked around me, and Kane was off to my side, standing quite a distance away from me, unable to get too close. The red was way more vibrant than it had been in the past, and I could feel it stronger than ever despite the considerable distance between us. We were, without a doubt, toward the end of the *repulsion* cycle, and I doubted we'd make it to tomorrow without our fate being sealed in permanent *repulsion*. It made my heart flutter with devastation.

"Can I speak to you for a moment?" he asked.

I turned to Vish. "I'm so sorry. Can we pick this back up later?"

"Sure."

Kane motioned for me to follow him away from the crowd. When we were at a safe distance, he stopped, and the magnetic push forced me to stop as well.

My arms folded defensively, waiting for him to turn and face me. I waited for him to explain after he could eloquently speak about the importance of love to his people. When he turned, his eyes were slightly red, matching his aura.

I inhaled deeply, saturating my lungs while losing all patience. "Kane—what do I not understand?"

"I..."

He stopped again.

"Kane, you are my Star Mate! I deserve an explanation for this *repulsion*! We're almost at the point of no return. Don't you understand that? Don't you love me?"

"I love you more than my own life!" he finally blurted.

A small part of me relaxed at hearing those words, even though I was still pissed. "Then...you're right. I don't understand."

"I killed someone, Cyra. Actually, two people...that I deeply cared for. I was young, still growing into my powers and trying to understand them. Nobody else has powers like mine, so it was incredibly difficult learning about them. The first time I killed was when I was four years old. My powers were so intense that nobody could help me control them. One day I played with my six-year-old cousin, who took my toy. A force spewed out of me in my anger and instantly killed him."

My eyes widened in shock. I knew this man before me. He would never kill unless forced to, and I knew the guilt would eat away at his soul. "Oh, Kane..." I whispered.

He blinked away the water in his eyes and continued.

"I didn't summon any magic. It just erupted from my body. My family was never able to look his parents in the face again. I was kept at home most of my childhood to keep the other children safe. Only some kind of abomination would be able to kill so easily at so young an age. It was a long time before I was trusted to be a member of society."

Instinctively I attempted to run to him, but the red force kept me at a distance. Even though I couldn't feel him through our bond, I felt his pain like a second skin.

"Eventually, I caught the eye of a young female I was interested in. When we started to get intimate, my power became uncontrollable again. Amid our passion, I stopped her heart cold with that lethal energy eternally bound to me. Again, it was something that just spewed out of me without me knowing how or why. I was lost in a dark place for *years*, unable to be around anyone for fear of killing them by merely standing in their vicinity. My father desperately tried to help me but didn't understand my magic. It took hundreds of years for me to master control, and while I have been with some women, I could never let myself get close to anyone. To do so would be to ensure their death."

His muscles were bunched so tightly that he looked to be in physical pain, trying to remain in control.

"The only way to keep people safe was to retain a safe distance with an iron-clad shell around my emotions. It's why I teach magically gifted children now. I hope no other child has to endure the horror of dangerous, uncontrollable power. I feared for Oliver and spent as much time tutoring him as possible—I see a lot of myself in him, except he already has better control than I ever did."

His eyes locked with mine, and genuine fear emanated from them.

"Cyra—I'm terrified of this *imana* bond. I yearn for you body and soul, but what if I harm you once I completely open myself to you? When you got a firsthand look at my dark power and cowered in fear from it, it brought everything back with a vengeance. When we were alone, I wanted nothing more than to claim you as mine. But I felt that toxic energy releasing, and it's when the reality of what I could do to you hit me. You using my energy, sent me over the edge. You are light, life, and goodness— you shouldn't be subjected to my darkness, Cyra. It's why I never considered myself the king of the prophecy. How could someone so pure be destined for someone who embodied death?"

I walked to him but was still pushed back. "Kane, that's not how this works. Let me come to you, mate."

When he locked eyes with me, the fear in them broke my heart.

"There cannot be light without darkness. There cannot be life without death. And there can no longer be me without you." I pushed and was finally able to inch a bit closer. "We are one, *imana*. The *only* way you could ever hurt me is if you reject me. Let me come to you."

The force between us quivered until the red repulsion finally shattered and dissipated. I ran to him as fast as possible and held him against me. This was the side of the King of Varjutus the world would never see. This vulnerability would only be shared with me, his *imana,* and soul mate. I lifted his head and looked into his stunning evergreen eyes, which were filled with hope. My whole body shivered at his sheer beauty.

"Promise me that nothing will ever come between us again," I pleaded.

I searched his face, and it was as if a burden was somewhat lightened from him. "I promise, my beautiful *imana*. We will walk through this life together, and if we die in this fight against the Guardians, then we die together. Either way, we are united until the end."

"The girl and the King," I whispered to him and felt relief swamp me. But it wasn't only my relief. The Buruj spoke softly into my mind.

The girl and the King have our thanks.

K ane walked me back to the celebration, and we were
hand in hand this time. I was never letting go. Kal,
Merick, and Meili were standing together talking, no
doubt about our whereabouts. When they noticed us approaching,
they looked relieved and ran toward us.

"You're bonded again! Thank Amrel." Meili exclaimed. Merick
and Kal both tapped Kane on the shoulder in congratulations. The
music slowed, and Kane looked down at me and pulled me close as
Merick did the same to Meili. Kal went back to his stump to brood.
We needed to find a woman who could hold her own with the
dispeller of darkness.

Kane gently held my face in his hand, causing my heart to race
and fireworks to explode in my gut at his touch. I'd missed him so
fucking much.

But when he smiled, it made my heart completely stop. When
this man was filled with joy, it was the most beautiful thing I'd ever
seen. "I forgot to tell you. You look stunning tonight." I looked
down because I couldn't even recall what I wore. "And that's quite
a bit of cleavage there—anyone you're trying to impress?"

"Well, as an official suitor, a woman's job is never done. I had to step up my game."

"Ah, I *definitely* like what I see. In fact, I'd be willing to see more." The seductive purr in his voice instantly made me wet. He ran his hand gently down my arm, and a small breath escaped me as I shivered and wished we were back in my bedroom so I could finally do foul things to this man.

His eyes widened, and the green in his irises flashed with light as his pupils dilated. "Cyra, I cannot control myself if you keep reacting this way. You smell fucking incredible, and I want to kneel before you and taste what your mouthwatering pussy is offering me right now."

"Oh god," I whispered, clenching my thighs together, but the magic was gone as quickly as it came.

"Where did you get that necklace?" Kane asked, tone changing.

Goddamnit. Fuck the necklace. We were in the middle of something far more important. But I answered him anyway. "Oh…uh, you missed a little while you were busy pushing me away."

"That looks like a Nebula Diamond. It's near impossible to find. That's the most valued crystal in all of Eredet and is said to be found only in Varjutus millions of years ago. Cyra, something like that is utterly priceless. Where did you get it?"

"I promise to tell you everything, but can we just have a few moments together with no worries on our minds? I feel like I just got you back. I want to enjoy you in my arms."

Kane beamed at my words, seeming to have accepted my terms. "'Till later then."

"Right answer, Candy Kane."

He chuckled and pulled me tighter as we listened to the music and swayed in each other's arms. I leaned against his solid chest and breathed in his pine scent. I was at utter peace for just a moment, and I let it consume me.

He lifted my head again, and his eyes were heavy with longing.

He lowered his head closer to me until we were nose to nose. I nuzzled him, and his look pierced my soul. I was so happy to feel his buzzing connection to me again—and it was filled with passion.

"I love you, Cyra," he whispered as he inched closer. I closed the gap and grazed my lips to his, feeling the softness of his skin and shivering at our first real kiss. He ran his fingertips down my arm again and interlocked his hand with mine as the other held my face. Unable to stand it any longer, I tasted him, and it was near euphoric.

Our heads tilted, and our tongues danced, exploring each other while our bodies begged for more. There was nothing and nobody in the world except Kane and me, and I felt his growing need. Through the bond, the lust was heightened to a new level since we felt each other's desire. Kane's breaths were deep and labored as he looked at me like he might take me back to my room.

Freaking finally. Through our connection, I begged him to, and he laughed.

He put his forehead to mine. "I promise, *imana.* You will have all of me soon enough."

I groaned my frustration, dying to continue this exploration *now.*

"Do you two need to get a room?"

We both looked up in shock, forgetting there was a crowd of people and that we were in the midst of a celebration. The music had also stopped. I looked back at Jonsi with a horrified look, unsure of how much people had witnessed. I also didn't notice that both of us were glowing.

"Thank Amrel, you two made up. I was worried I would have to lock you in a dungeon somewhere for the sake of the galaxy. Now! Let's begin the *fire husk!*" Everyone cheered and began to circle what looked to be an empty fire pit. "Cyra, since we're a little low on resources, I'm hoping you'll help us out a little?" Jonsi said, nodding his head to the pit.

"Oh, of course!" I extended my hands and shot flames into the firepit until a massive bonfire roared.

Half of the Varjun went home for the night while the ones who stayed behind started to sit on the ground and cross their legs, so I followed suit. Most of the Solian refugees also stayed, curious about the Varjun traditions.

"I always lay on the grass and look up at the sky during a *fire husk*. Join me?" Kane asked with a smirk.

"Like I could say no to that face."

"Intriguing. I'll definitely remember that."

I rolled my eyes. "What's a *fire husk*?"

"An old Varjun tradition. It's a regaling of stories, histories, and legends throughout the ages. It's a large part of how we pass information to our children and keep our culture alive. We started doing them even more frequently after losing many of our memories."

Kane lowered his voice so only I could hear. "I suspect that Jonsi still has all his memories intact. I think my father didn't have it in him to take our Elder's history from him."

"I hope that's true."

Various people took turns telling family stories, funny jokes, and memories of their Varjun community. I lay in awe and absorbed their memories, hopes, dreams, and traditions. Every day that passed, I fell more in love with the Varjun people and could see why Grandpa seemed to hold a special place for them in his heart.

"Usually, the people begin, and the Elder concludes with his own stories," Kane explained. Sure enough, Jonsi spoke when it seemed the people were finished.

"We'll start today by reviewing some Varjun history we have not discussed in quite a long time to avoid unnecessary danger. But with new guests with us, I think it is important to remember where we come from."

The excitement in Jonsi's face was intoxicating, and I was eager to hear whatever stories he had for us.

"You all probably remember the name Vangelis Distira. He was the first King of Varjutus since written history, which started in the second age. He was extremely beloved and ruled for eighty thousand wonderous years, the longest of any Varjun King or Queen to date. This is not to say that it was without some intrigue. The King never married, which is highly unusual for the Varjun, but he still sired a son who was passed over as the next King once Vangelis died. It is unknown who the boy's mother was or why they didn't trust him as their second ruler, but it was to be Leik Rueul, The Dark King. The people chose Leik over all other Varjun because he had come into some new abilities. He discovered dark arts and was able to help the Varjun in a way they had never seen before. The people were entranced by his talents."

My eyes quickly darted to everyone around us, and they had various displays of concern on their faces, clearly unsure what he would say next.

"Now, Leik started his rule well enough, but once his beloved vordne, Marlena, was brutally murdered, he was never the same again. He disappeared for a few years, leaving his council in charge, and when he returned, his knowledge of the dark arts had grown exponentially. He started to use it to the disadvantage of the race, and the people didn't trust him to lead them anymore. Some of his spells caused various pieces of land to die or made people ill from the effects. Livestock began to die off, and the planet's energy flow changed."

Jonsi used his hands to speak, doing his best to display his story vividly.

"Leik's real purpose for mastering the dark arts was to cast a spell for himself and his Marlena. He dug up her body, animated her corpse, and performed magic that would allow Marlena and himself to be reincarnated in the future simultaneously so they could be reunited."

The story sounded so bogus that I wondered if it was true, but the hairs on my neck raised as if the universe was giving me some silent warning. Instinctively I looked to the side and saw Kal, who visibly shivered like he was just as affected as I was.

"The people rebelled and arranged to have him executed since Leik wouldn't step down. Leik learned of the people's betrayal and escaped before they could capture him. He raised an army of the dead, and Varjutus had its first and only civil war—The Dead War. After a few grueling months of fighting, Leik was captured by Jesrick Mystra, a leader the people looked to after Leik's betrayal. But he had a few more tricks up his sleeve before his death. He created the Curse of Leik, which would curse the Mystra family line if they ever ruled over Varjutus. He knew Jesrick was next to be chosen to rule and wanted to ensure it would never happen. Jesrick was smart enough not to accept the nomination as the third King of Varjutus. Instead, Vangelis's shunned bastard, Oryn Distira, was voted to become the next King.

"Over the years, the people forgot about the curse and, in the Fourth Age, a Mystra was sworn in as King again. There were three Mystra Kings in the Fourth Age, and every one of them tragically lost their *vordne*'s. King Adonis Mystra lost his Queen Aesira. King Torryn Mystra lost his Queen Maldana, and we all remember the history of King Varog & Queen Dessa Mystra."

I glanced over to Vjera, and her back straightened, listening intently.

"Rule of Varjutus passed back to the Distira line after that. I don't think a Mystra will ever pick up the mantle again. Leik also promised to wreak havoc on the people of Varjutus again once he was reincarnated."

When Jonsi stopped, there was utter silence among the crowd. I could tell that none of the Varjun knew or remembered this history. They were stunned.

"I knew Jonsi had his memories intact," Kane whispered to me. I looked over to Vjera. She was a mess, shaking and fighting off tears. Clearly, she didn't know about the Curse of Leik affecting the Mystra line.

Jonsi quickly continued with his next story. "Let's talk about the Nebula Diamond."

I quickly shot to look at Kane, and his eyes widened in surprise. Jonsi must have seen me wearing it tonight and known precisely what it was.

"It's said that Amrel The Creator, trapped a portion of a nebula emission inside a crystal to harness its unique power. It's unknown the extent of abilities the Nebula Diamond can wield, but we think there is no trinket more powerful in the cosmos. It's believed that there are only three Nebula Diamonds in all of Eredet galaxy and that receiving one as a gift is the most precious bequest that can be given."

Many Varjun were intrigued by that story, none the wiser that I was wearing one at that moment.

"Has anyone heard of the legend of the Buruj?"

"Are you kidding me?" I whispered in disbelief.

"What?" Kane asked.

"It has to do with the Nebula Diamond. I'll explain later. How does Jonsi know so much?"

"His knowledge of secrets baffles me," Kane said, shaking his head.

The crowd had mixed responses to Jonsi's question.

"It's a bedtime story I told my kids," a Varjun female said, a few others agreeing.

"Well, the stories tell that the Buruj were spirits of the night and custodians of Varjun magic. It's said that they are almost pure magic themselves and capable of wondrous and terrible things. They ruled and roamed free in the dark during the First Age—the time before our history starts—and the Varjun may be distant descendants from them.

Some of the Varjun chuckled at his story. I didn't know if his details were true, but the Buruj were one hundred percent real. Something told me that Jonsi's facts were not a thing of fairytale.

"I'm going to end the *fire husk* tonight by remembering the prophecy of the girl and the King."

I looked up in shock, and unsurprisingly everyone in the crowd looked over at me and Kane.

"It's said that the girl with the mark of balance and a King of Eredet will return it to the galaxy. Amrel The Creator never doubted that this was more than a fortune telling. He saw it as undeniable truth. Seeing recent events unfold the way they have also left me in no doubt that the *virsune* is closing in upon us and that we will have the peace we have been waiting for."

"Those are lovely fuzzy stories, but I have one of my own."

Kane jerked his head in the direction of the voice. It was Ondour.

"Kane—don't." He looked at me with unfathomable rage for the man who had almost killed me hours earlier. "Just let it go."

Kane was vibrating with raging energy, and I felt his over-whelming desire to destroy him. He showed amazing restraint by lying beside me and folding his fingers through mine.

"You'll all love this one—it's a doozy. Since I know you're all overly concerned for my welfare, I'm confident your bleeding hearts will quiver."

Kane sat up and glared at Ondour, clearly not about to lay back down, so I joined him.

"Once upon a time, eight hundred years ago, a valiant warrior was taken from his home in the dead of night by the wicked and resourceful Bellum. They were paid in lavish riches beyond their wildest dreams for their handsome bounty of a legendary Varjun *Curadh* warrior. They received ships, supplies, and food. They were even awarded items of power that gave them use of small magicks, and would you believe that some of those powerful items once belonged to the beloved Varog and Dessa Mystra, infamous Moon Mate couple and fierce rulers of Varjutus."

Vjera emerged from the shadows crossing her arms and looking more subdued than I'd ever seen her.

"It was uncovered then that the savage raid and murder of King Varog and Queen Dessa by the Bellum was nothing more than a directive by the Guardians, who had just started becoming friendly with Dokoran the Demon Reina. This was the first act that established the Guardians as a threat, even though the galaxy thought it was merely a Bellum attack. And that raid gave the Guardians the unlimited amount of power they needed to become the greatest and most terrible force ever known to history—so much so that Amrel the Creator himself could not defeat them."

Ondour paused for effect, his smile gruesome, making goosebumps trail throughout my body.

"Hidden in the King and Queen's home was the Siphoning Stone, which enabled them to be the only ones other than Our Creator who could harness our energy. The Guardians laughed at the tale the Bellum relayed. They captured the King but found that the Queen was holding the stone inside her body by magic, and the Bellum couldn't simply take it. It needed to be given. They took turns cutting the limbs of the King, then did the same to the Queen as coercion to hand over the stone. Queen Dessa protected the stone so fiercely that they endured the torture of watching each other ripped apart little by little while feeling their lovers' excruciating pain. The Queen didn't let go of that stone until their last breaths were snuffed out simultaneously. The Guardians delighted in the story but chided the Bellum that they should have brought such strong individuals to them so they could find a greater purpose for those with such unbreakable wills."

I looked over to Vjera, and instead of her usual explosive rage, she was uncontrollably crying.

"It was only discovered later that there was a girl shrouded in the room, blinded by a magical shield so she couldn't witness her parents' torture and murder, but still able to hear their screams. She would have joined her parents in the final sleep if they had known she was there."

I nearly stood to slap Ondour in the face for his cruelty, going on when Vjera was suffering so much, but Kane squeezed my hand in a silent plea to stay where I was. Ondour continued his morbid story.

"We circle back to the *Curadh* warrior, who learned all this information because he was kept captive by the Guardians for *two hundred years*, tortured and mutilated in an attempt to swap his soul with that of another's. It was thought the heart of a *Curadh* was more resilient to the extreme torture of the process, but to their disappointment, their efforts were fruitless. They tried to wipe his memories, but didn't know that he had some...mental...abilities, so he was unaffected by their memory wipe. What they also didn't know was that they were right. The heart of a *Curadh* warrior is strong enough to endure...strong enough that he rejected their soul transfer, and he was positive that with a lesser man, they would have succeeded.

"Now, that is not to say that the *Curadh* warrior was not suffering and in desperate need of help. He called...and he called... and he called for the help of his king. King Adelram Distira. Only to find out later that he was face first on the ground of the Pog in a drunken heap, unable to hear his call."

Whispers of shock erupted all around, and Vjera disappeared from sight. Kane shot up from the ground in an all-compassing rage.

"You *asshole*. The Guardians disarmed his King's Call. None of his people could summon him, and it destroyed him. He was stripped of everything that made him who he was!"

Ondour raised his head and glared back at Kane with threat in his eyes. "And so was I."

Kane's steps boomed on the ground as he stormed with lethal intent. He outstretched his hand to wrap it around Ondour's throat but vanished right when contact was made.

Jonsi stood and clapped his hands together. "Okay, I think that's enough *fire husk* for tonight. Congratulations again to the happy couple, and get to making babies. We sure need some fresh blood around here."

I turned to Kane. "I assume Varog and Dessa were Vjera's parents?"

"Yes. She has nothing left of them but the rubble of their family home. It's why she is the way she is."

Merick and Kal approached Kane.

"Can we speak to you, King?"

"Um, I'll meet you back at the castle, Kane."

He touched my cheek and leaned down to give me a soft kiss. Merick and Kal, unused to Kane being romantic, were looking everywhere else but us.

"I won't be long, *imana*," he whispered back.

CHAPTER
TWENTY-EIGHT

I drove back to the castle and found Brugan after searching in six different locations. His brows lifted in surprise that I would seek him on my own.

"Can you show me where Vjera's home used to be?"

"It's nothing but ruins now, Reina," he said respectfully.

"I understand. I'd still like to see it. Can you take me?"

"Of course."

He drove me to a dark wasteland part of the planet where the second moon shone in the sky, indicating we were far from Kane's castle. There were desiccated, black mountains in the distance and dry, caked pits of land that I assumed used to be full of water.

There were thousands of remains of dead trees...what was once sacred to the Varjun, now painful reminders of what was lost. I could see that the Varjun had given up hope of this side of the planet long ago and focused their efforts on saving the land near the castle where the last of the Varjun people dwelled together, holding onto their bottomless hope that their planet, their people, and their culture will be saved. On the other side of the caverns of inert ground was a massive pile of rubble that could have been its own castle, and, sure enough, there sat Vjera amongst the debris.

"Thank you, Brugan. That'll be all." He bowed and disappeared. I made my way over and sat next to Vjera, who was a vacant display of despair.

"I deserve to be a miserable piece of shit. I deserve to spend my days in solitude on The Void until the black hole swallows me into oblivion. Ondour's a bastard, but he was right. I was there, listening like a petrified little princess, frozen in terror and unable to move. I was eighteen, old enough to do *something*. Anything! I stood there, immobilized, while my selfless parents were literally—torn—apart. I—"

Vjera started hyperventilating, unable to speak. I put my hand on her back and listened to what she had to say.

"I hear their screams every single day of my disgusting excuse for an existence. I hear the laughs of the Bellum, *enjoying* what they did to them. I hear their celebration when they got what they came for. I still don't know how mortal Bellum could constrain such powerful Varjun."

"The Bellum have a meige on their side. We don't know how or why, but we believe it's how they do a lot of the things we can't explain."

Vjera nodded. "That makes sense. I heard a hum of magic. At the time, I assumed it was my parents trying to fight back. But it was a sound I had never heard before. All these years, I've been searching for the Bellum's dwelling to eradicate their blight on history. I need my revenge—my chance to redeem myself for my inaction."

"Vjera, I didn't know your parents, but I've heard them spoken of as beloved by everyone who knew them. I am *certain* their only wish was for you to survive that attack and go on living. You are their legacy, and you would only dishonor their memory by continuing to hold on to this self-torture. We get vengeance for them by ending the Guardians and restoring the balance, and you can help us do that."

"I don't deserve Kane's constant attempts to take me into his family circle."

"Vjera. There are some things Amrel the Creator told me himself that I think you could benefit from hearing."

She looked up in shock and stayed quiet, waiting for me to speak. I knew then that I had the chance to get through to her.

"One of his repeated teachings was that *we often feel we're right because our pain tells us so, but pain is a biased and disloyal friend who will stab us in the back.* You can't keep listening to what your pain is whispering to you. It's festering and changing you, and it's not how we'll come through this to the other side. He also told me *not to close off your heart in grief as it is your biggest asset and will show you the truest path.* When your heart is closed, a part of you is turned off, and you could lose sight of what's important."

"I'm afraid it's too late for me, Cyra. When a seed of hate is planted into your heart, the infestation of vines that emerge is almost impossible to stop until it consumes you completely. It takes a great amount of effort to chip away at the vines, revealing the damaged heart beneath. What's left is a weakened, shriveled mess so fragile a soft wind could destroy it. So tell me what is better? The thorny vines of protection or the vulnerability of a withered heart?" Vjera asked, her forehead creased in genuine confusion and pain.

I took her hand, and to my surprise, she let me. "Fortunately, the heart is a muscle that can be strengthened again with practice."

She put her hand over her mouth and continued to weep. I sat with her in silence on top of a pile of broken memories of a beautiful life destroyed long ago.

After about ten minutes, I started to feel something pulling my focus. I stood in the rubble and began to walk toward the force.

"Where are you going?" Vjera asked, her voice straining from her grief.

"I feel something calling to me. Do you feel anything?

Vjera shook her head but stood in interest.

There was an incredible amount of debris since the house looked to have been either a mansion or a small castle. I finally reached the area where I felt the presence and started digging beneath the rubble. Vjera helped me pick up the larger, heavier pieces.

"There! Do you see that?" I asked.

She shook her head. "I don't see anything."

I picked up a small, ordinary-looking object that almost looked like a key. "It's emitting light and powerful energy. You don't see it?"

Vjera shook her head.

"I don't know what it is, but this item is important. I'll bring it back to the castle, and we'll try to figure out what it is."

Vjera seemed content to go home, so we drove back to the castle, where Kane, Merick, Kal, and Meili stood outside the front doors talking to each other. Vjera turned to Kane and said, "Don't ever let her go," and disappeared.

Everyone looked shocked, including Kane, but he whispered, "I won't."

After we said our goodnights, Kane led me upstairs, and I ran to my bed and flopped onto it.

"Well, that was quite a day, wasn't it?"

"You can say that." I scooted up to my pillow and lay on it, facing him at the edge of my bed. His gaze penetrated me from my head to my toes.

"Are you going to invite me in, *imana*?" he said in his low, seductive voice.

"As far as I'm concerned, this is our bed from now on."

"Is that so?" Kane asked, voice raised. He slowly climbed onto the bed, a predator coming for his prey and thoroughly enjoying it.

My body was immobilized as his powerful body crept closer to me. I bit my lip in anticipation and watched as each muscle contracted and moved in a dance of beauty, displaying a work of art. I had been fighting my physical urges for him since the first moment he stood before me on Solis, and now, my body shook in eager need and acceptance for him to utterly claim me.

He finally climbed on top of me until his face was right over mine, and I felt dizzy from his blinding beauty. This man was mind-blowingly gorgeous, strong, talented, and *powerful,* yet here he was, looking at me like I was the only person in the world.

"Are you quite alright, Star? You seem unable to catch your breath, and I feel heat radiating from all over you. Here..." he trailed his hand from my collarbone, over the swell of my breasts, down my torso, over my womb, and stopped right above my pelvis, "and especially here. A lot is happening here..."

I moaned at his actions. He wasn't even touching me, but I could feel his static buzzing energy as if his hands were actually on me right down to the spot I was desperate for him to touch, and it drove me *insane.* If it felt this divine with no contact, I was frantic for more.

"That is interesting. I think having an *imana* bond will be immeasurably fun."

"Kane...please..."

"You want more?"

"*Yes*...God yes..."

He jumped off and lay in the spot next to me, leaving my electric desire unanswered. I shot up and glared at him in disbelief, still breathing heavily. Kane bellowed in laughter at my reaction.

"While you will never know the exquisite pleasure I get from watching how much you want me, you promised me answers. And I want to know what secret dealings you've had without me. Besides, didn't I promise you that you'd know when I'm teasing you and that you'd beg for more? I haven't even *begun* to try. You haven't seen anything yet."

"Ugh!" I grunted and slammed back down on the bed. Kane laughed again, grabbing my hand and locking it with his. Knowing I wasn't going to win in this, I gave in and turned to face him, clenching my legs together. Kane noticed and gave me a devilish smile.

Goddamn him.

"Kane, the Buruj…they're *real*. They called to me after your *repulsion* started and gave me a vision of where to find them. I was able to share the vision with my Kometa, and she took me right to the cave. Vjera followed me, thinking I was working with the Guardians, so she was just as shocked as I was to see them. They told me to do everything I could to fix things with you before gifting me the Nebula Diamond, although they just said it was a sacred crystal to bring me luck. They told me about a sword forged by Grandpa and said he wanted me to find it. They claimed it could become invaluable for what's to come."

"The Sword of Istina?" Kane said, sitting up in the bed. "Could it be true?"

"You've heard of it?"

"Of course I have. The whole universe has. Look at any art of Amrel The Creator—he's holding the Sword of Istina. It was *his personal sword*. It's unknown what it was even forged of, but it's said that it makes whoever looks upon it go mad and can extract any truth only when it wants you to see it. It's incredibly dangerous."

"The Buruj warned me of that. She said it could only be wielded by one with the mark of the Sunya Reina."

"Again, with the mark of the Sunya Reina. It was the same thing written about the *sild gates*."

"Exactly."

"Do you know what a Sunya Reina is?"

"I feel some attachment to that word when I hear it like I must have known what it was in a previous life. I bet it's one of the memories that were taken from me, but right now, I have no idea what it means."

"We know what a Reina is. Meili said she could feel that I was part Sunya. Maybe that's all it means?" I offered.

"Maybe. But how do we find the Sword of Istina?"

"The Buruj said to go to the Schools of the Seas."

Kane let out a sigh. "The last thing I want to do is go back to Solis. It's incredibly dangerous after angering the Guardians and Theo's betrayal."

"I agree, but what else can we do? I don't know why, but I trust the Buruj. I have a feeling that it won't just be handy but that we will *need* it to succeed."

"I think I'll be making a trip to visit these Buruj. And tomorrow, we'll meet with Merick and Kal and discuss the next steps."

"Okay. What do you think about Ondour's story?"

"I think he's a thorn in my side, and I'm incredibly suspicious about how he was able to simply leave the Guardian's captivity."

"Do you think he's working for them?"

Kane was silent for a moment. "I don't want to pass judgment on my people without knowing all the facts. For now, I'm only suspicious and don't necessarily trust him, but I want to be a fair and just king. Despite my doubt, I can't help but feel profound pity about his capture. I know the pain of being tortured by the Guardians. What it feels like for them to attempt to suck out your soul. It's the most excruciating experience imaginable. And I was only there for five years—I cannot fathom being stuck there for two hundred."

I squeezed his hand that was still in mine. "Honestly, it's amazing that he's in one piece at all. I still have constant nightmares about being experimented on. They cut open my torso and did internal examinations to study my organs without any pain support. They'd take samples of everything in my body as I watched...." Kane's lips turned downward as if growing nauseous at the memory.

"Being immortal and hard to kill can be a horrific curse. I'm not one to beg for my life, but I begged that they just kill me and take what they needed. I was near madness at the constant torture, the hunger and thirst...and watching other victims suffer the same thing while I could do nothing to help them. It probably hurt worse than my own pain."

"I'm sure there was no bargaining with Orphlam."

He shook his head. "The Guardians never spoke to me once. They ignored my pleas like they weren't even aware I was alive. The machine they had that tried to capture my soul felt like a dull machete, slowly slicing my body in half from my head to my toes for hours on end. Eventually, my vocal cords stopped working from all the screaming. I lay in my dark cell for days on end, in my own waste and the constant vomit from the pain, trying to drown out the screams of the other victims. Amrel help anyone if they are ever successful in taking their soul. Having your identity and existence in limbo must be a fate worse than death."

My body was shaking with rage. I couldn't imagine my Kane— my *imana* trapped in that putrid hell hole being tortured like that. I lit into flame all over my body and struggled to breathe.

"It's okay, Cyra. It's long over now. I'm here—I'm okay. I have you, and you have me."

He held me until I could snuff out my rage, impervious to my fire. He repaired the areas I had burned without saying a word. From the sheer exhaustion and emotional turmoil of the day, we fell asleep in each other's arms—together all night.

The following day when I woke, I thought I was dreaming. For the past few years, I was stuck in a cycle of waking from nightmares and from a burning pit in my chest I couldn't explain. The act of waking up had been torturous for so long that I had to make sure I wasn't dreaming when I saw the precious sight of Kaanan Distira, King of Varjutus, lying beside me, peacefully asleep.

His lids slowly opened to reveal his bright green eyes that resembled a forest in full bloom. He took my hand and put it to his lips, causing me to grin like a love-drunk girl.

"Good morning, my love," he whispered.

"Can we just stay like this forever?" I begged him.

"When we set things right, we'll have as many days like this as we want," he promised. "But for now, come here." He pulled me close, and I burrowed into his mountainous chest and full arms, which were glorious without a shirt. Wrapped into his rock-solid body, I felt no harm could ever reach me. We lay there in blissful quiet until Merick's call sign glowed on his arm.

"It was nice while it lasted," I said, looking up at him and sighing.

He smiled and leaned down to kiss me, making me weak.

"To be continued, my Star."

I got up and pulled my fighting leathers out of my closet, and Kane froze, realizing I was about to undress.

"You don't want to be late to your summons, do you, King?" My voice oozed devilish sarcasm, which he ate up.

"Screw it. I'll change later. It's infinitely more important that *you* get changed. And right now."

I smiled and made a slow, tantalizing show of dressing but not showing him anything important. I giggled, never seeing him more alert and focused on anything—and his eyes weren't the only thing on full alert. I could only imagine just how substantial he was based on the size of the bulge in his pants. In fact, I couldn't help but think…

"See anything you like?"

I snapped out of the fantasy that I obviously didn't hide well and dropped my pants so that all I wore was a white shirt that barely covered anything. Kane leaned forward, his elbows on his knees. He closed his eyes and breathed deeply.

"That's it. I've waited long enough." He was so fast that he was a blur of movement, and before I knew it, he had me pinned against the wall, my arms above my head locked with some sort of shield so I couldn't move. My legs wrapped around his waist as he held my ass. Holy shit had I learned the true meaning of being manhandled.

His voice was low and heady, and his eyes glared into mine with a promise of something debauched coming my way. "You are not leaving this room until I've finally gotten a taste of you."

"But what about—"

He held one finger over my mouth as he somehow managed to hold me with one arm against the wall. "Not another word will escape your lips unless it's you screaming my name. Do you understand?"

Again I asked, *who the hell was I to refuse the king?* I eagerly nodded with my lips sealed tight.

He leaned down and gently touched his lips to mine, so featherlight that it had me quivering for more. My mouth opened to him, and he held my face as his tongue caressed mine. We kissed like we'd been starved for each other, and the first bite was fucking euphoric.

While still holding me with one arm and my hands bound above me, he reached his free hand below my shirt, causing me to cry out with relief, joy, bliss, satisfaction—all the emotions when he *finally* touched my pussy which was utterly saturated for him. He groaned with delight when he felt how slick I was, and his finger plunged inside of me as my head bent forward on his shoulder, overcome with a small portion of him filling me.

He withdrew and brought his finger to his lips and into his mouth, sucking it dry, and his eyes fluttered shut with a deep growl rumbling in his chest. "Holy shit, Cyra. I know without a shadow of a doubt that nothing will ever cross my lips again that will satisfy me the way your sweet essence has. You have ruined me."

Oh fuck. A girl could get used to this.

He swiftly lowered to his knees, causing me to slide lower down the wall. But his power still had my arms locked above me, so I was entirely at his mercy. With him kneeling before me, he had my legs over his shoulders, and he closed in, putting his tongue to my clit. Nothing could have stopped the moaning cry that escaped me. Holy shit, that felt *amazing*. The moment he touched me sounded muted and my skin singed with blistering heat. His tongue began swirling around it with a speed and accuracy that blew my mind and I wasn't going to last long at all. Lazy stroke, after lazy stroke, caused my breath to become faulty, and my nails dug into his shoulders to keep from bursting at the seams.

He hummed a feral sound of approval, the vibrations, and hot breath making me pulse against him with urgency.

But when he slipped a finger inside me, my world stopped. Lights burst under my eyelids as he kept thrusting. I thoroughly came apart, unable to keep it together as I came with record timing, calling out for him.

"Kane!"

"Mmm, that's it, my Star. Scream my name so the universe knows that you're *mine*."

"Oh God."

"That'll do too."

I attempted to laugh but screeched when I felt a strange sensation.

"What the hell was that?"

His eyes slowly slid up to mine with a devious, arrogant grin. "Oh, you mean this?"

He put his finger to my clit again, and I felt an intense, bursting, warm vibration that had me almost seeing freaking stars. My breath was still labored, and I could barely get my words out as I writhed on his shoulders.

"What. Is. That?"

"Didn't I tell you, *imana*, that you hadn't even begun to experience my talents yet? Well, I'm a master at manipulating energy, and what is energy but various forms of vibrations? You are mine now, and I will make it my life's mission to blow your mind at every turn with pleasure and joy."

Mission. Fucking. Accomplished. My mate a walking freaking vibrator. How the hell did I get so lucky? "Now stop squirming around, or the vibrations stop."

Damn, he was so bossy when he was pleasuring me into oblivion. I did my best to stay as still as possible, and he slipped two fingers inside me this time while his other hand increased the vibration, making fireworks erupt and electric shocks of pleasure course through me. I could never have fathomed that anything could feel so euphoric, and the way Kane worshipped my body with care and enthusiasm had me singing his praises.

"Come for me again, *imana,* and do not hold back. I will not be satisfied until I know you've gone to heaven and back."

Needless to say, I barely lasted a few seconds before I actually did see stars and shattered apart into a mind-blowing orgasm. He had sent me through an epic journey of utter bliss, and the reprieve from the seriousness of our lives was everything.

Kane looked up at me with a smug grin and took mercy on me, noticing I was spent. And when he released the shield on my wrists, they fell to my sides like jelly. He lifted me into his arms and helped me onto my feet, but I still felt like I was not of this universe.

"I don't know what you just did to me."

"I gave you a small teaser of what it will be like to be mine."

Oh lord. *A small teaser?* I had no idea what I had gotten myself into. I looked down, and he was still hard as a rock, and my mouth watered at the thought of reciprocating. My hand wrapped around his erection through his pants, and I moaned at how wonderful he felt, but Merick's call sign glowed twice as if warning Kane to move his ass, so he bent down and kissed me. "Another time, Star."

I nodded, but if I didn't know better, I swore I could see a slight hint of relief on his face like he was still afraid to hurt me with this power of death.

We walked into Kane's study and were greeted by Kal, Merick, Meili, Vish, Vjera, and Urien. Merick grinned and was the first to speak.

"Hey, nice outfit you haven't changed from. Walk of shame, eh?"

Meili gasped. "They've sealed the bond!"

"What does she mean?" I asked, looking at Kane.

"No, everyone, relax. I just haven't had a chance to change yet."

Kane avoided my gaze, and Meili's words festered until they really bothered me. Weren't we already bonded when the *repulsion* ended?

It was also nearly impossible to concentrate. Kane had unleashed a feral beast within me, and I couldn't stop eying how shapely his ass was in his fitted black pants. Or how well he filled out his tunic. I wanted to skip this meeting and continue where we left off, running my hands down each defined line of his body, tasting his skin, and watching him lose his mind the way he had done to me. I wanted to munch on him like the tasty snack he was.

Bad! Bad, Cyra. What has he done to me?

Kane's commanding voice brought me out of my completely inappropriate fantasy, and he continued to speak.

"Now, let's get to business. Merick, what progress have you made on The Void?" Kane sat at the oval table, and everyone else followed suit.

"I've seen a lot of extra activity with Bellum out in the open, traveling in packs. I follow them, but I can never seem to stay locked to their trail. I think their meige uses distraction magic where we cannot see their true activity or where they're dwelling. There's also been an unusual amount of Voidlings wandering alone. I think since the Bellum have the *mikla*, they're more focused on unlocking the real power, plus they've officially made enemies with the Guardians, so they have nobody to sell them to."

"I noticed there are no Voidlings on Varjutus," I said to Kane. Kal and Merick hissed in disgust.

"I will never condone the use of slaves, no matter how far gone they are," Kane said.

"It's foul," Merick agreed.

"Is there anything we can do for these Voidlings?"

Merick's lips tightened into a thin line. "I'm sorry, Cyra. I wish I could help them, but there's very little we can do. They're usually transferred by spacecraft since they would never survive an interplanetary drive. We only have access to one tiny ship, and it would take an immense amount of time and resources with countless trips back and forth just to take back a few. They just don't live long enough for us to justify risking our people."

I nodded and looked down, expecting his answer, but it didn't hurt any less. Kane took my hand and squeezed.

"So, we still have nothing to go on regarding The Void. We'll just have to keep up our recon until we get something usable," Kane answered.

Merick bowed his head to Kane. "Jaike has decided to take in Lorcan and give him a home. He still feels the loss of his woman and unborn child, and he believes his *vordne* would have wanted him to help himself by aiding a child in need."

"That's excellent. I think that will be a great match. What news from Solis?" Kane asked, looking toward Urien.

"Theo has not been seen since he returned to Solis. I think he's still recovering from whatever injuries Meili gave him."

She looked down as her cheeks reddened. It might be kinder to tell her about my vision of her wings.

"The Guardians have not been in their temple for weeks. I was able to get into *Mikla Island* once undetected but almost got discovered. They have it *very* heavily guarded now with extra magical defenses. I saw the Guardians enter their underground graveyard once and haven't caught sight of them since. They're up to something nasty—I can feel it."

Everyone shifted in their seats, becoming uncomfortable about what horrors Orphlam had in store for us. Luckily Urien continued his debrief, so my imagination didn't get too creative.

"Three nobles have disappeared, and now they don't leave their houses. As far as we know, this is the first time the nobles have been in danger. All their Voidlings have perished, and their estates are falling to shit without new shipments. There's very little life left for Solis, and the people still remain in hiding, trying to stay invisible to the Guardians—but I fear how long they have before the Guardians find them all. I've convinced Eleri to evacuate the temple with anyone hiding there since Theo knows of the location. We're not sure what he will do now."

I scratched at my brow, my anxiety at an all-time high. "Please speak to Blaze and Bad and see if we can organize another round of refugees to come to Solis."

Kane nodded his approval. "I think that's wise. Kal, I want any Varjun who wants to fight to start training as often as possible. I know we hold regular community training sessions, but I want it amped up to a few times a week. Have tonight's first training session ready and recruit as many as possible."

"Understood, my King."

"Cyra and I need to discuss a trip to the Schools of the Seas, but before that, what other open business do we have?"

"Oh! I forgot I did have something, but I left it in my room. I'll be right back." I stood, and Kane looked at me with surprise. He'd recently granted me access to drive, so I quickly went to my room and returned with the item I was looking for.

"I found this in the rubble in Vjera's parents' home. I was drawn to it and saw a glow emitting from it with strong magical energy. I think it's important, but I don't know what it is." I handed it to Merick, and he observed it and passed it around the table.

"I've never seen this before, and I don't see anything extraordinary about it," Merick explained. Nobody else seemed to either until Meili took it.

"Wait a minute. I think I've read about something like this before. It looks like a failsafe key."

"Failsafe to what?" Kane asked.

"There's no way for us to know. A failsafe key works only for the one thing it's meant to nullify. The fact that it was in King Varog and Queen Dessa's home—I have no doubt it's very valuable. I bet

Jonsi would know more," Meili concluded. Merick beamed at her contribution.

"Those were my thoughts exactly, Meili. Cyra, you hold onto this. Since you can see its energies, I think you were meant to be its guardian. We'll visit Jonsi when we're able to find out more," Kane said.

Putting it safely back in my pocket, I nodded my agreement.

"There's one last piece of news to discuss. Cyra received intel that the Sword of Istina is in the Schools of the Seas and that she is to retrieve it."

Kal stood from his seat, gripping the table until his knuckles whitened. "The Sword of Our Creator? I will come with you to retrieve it no matter the danger."

Kane laughed, crossing his arms. "I would like to validate this information in a few moments, then venture out to the Schools soon after."

"Who gave this information? Can we trust them if they knew such valuable intel and merely handed it over? Why not take it for themselves?" Merick asked.

Kane looked at me to answer.

"It was the Buruj. They told me Grandpa intended for me to have it and that it would become invaluable to our future."

No one spoke for a moment.

"You've got to be shitting me." Of course, it was Merick who answered with disbelief.

"What are Buruj?" Vish asked, clearly having left before Jonsi's story.

"Legend," Kal responded, half-laughing.

"Well, I intend to validate it now. We'll meet you back at the castle in a bit."

"Oh, I'm definitely coming with you," Merick said, standing up.

"No." Everyone stopped to look at me with surprise. "They're incredibly private. They won't see us if too many people invade their sanctuary."

"Cyra and I go alone. I will call you if necessary."

Nobody looked pleased to be ordered behind—anyone would want to witness the magic of the Buruj if they were real, but I didn't want to ruin the chance of them accepting our visit. If anyone deserved to see them with their own eyes, it was the King of Varjutus.

We said our goodbyes and the group departed.

"Well, my Star, it looks like you will have to drive me to our destination this time."

"Me? Oh...I hadn't thought of that. What do I do?" I had only just started driving successfully on my own. How was I going to cart a two-hundred-pound Varjun male with me?

"Just imagine driving as you normally would, but this time imagine carrying me in your arms as you travel."

I looked him up and down and his six-foot-five-inch body. "Kane, you don't exactly look like *anyone* could carry you, much less me."

He laughed and took my hands. "If you believe you can't, then you won't. Here, look inside me."

With my hands in his, Kane opened his power source to me so I could search within him. Just like the last time we trained with Jonsi, I saw a well of darkness and patches of violet energy at my disposal. Kane drove out of the room and back in with me, and I could see his process as he did it. I felt how he used his power with ease, like it was a normal part of his life, a stark contrast to how I usually struggled. I carried that feeling with me as I focused on the cave dwelling of the Buruj, and we began the drive.

It was immensely more difficult while carrying someone, like gravity was pushing me backward as we traveled, but there was no way I would break the connection and lose Kane along the way. To my utter relief, when I opened my eyes, we were standing before the cave, and Kane was still with me, looking down on me with love and appreciation as I shook like I had just lifted a thousand pounds and sweat dripped down my forehead.

"I had no doubt you'd be able to master that with ease."

"You call that easy? I'm sweating with effort! I was terrified I was going to drop you!"

"Cyra, it takes most people a hundred years to be able to drive with someone else with them."

I folded my arms and shifted my weight to my leg. "Why the hell didn't you warn me of that!"

"I didn't want to scare you because I knew you could do it. I've seen what incredible feats you've mastered in such a short time and the tremendous amount of power you have. I have complete trust in you."

My mouth opened, fully prepared to yell at him more about fully educating me on the dangers of magic, when a familiar other-worldly voice entered my mind.

The girl and the King. Please come in.

"Did you hear that?" I asked in a whisper.

"I... I did." Kane's eyes were wide with astonishment.

He took my hand in his, and we entered the dark cave.

"It's unnaturally dark in here. Even I cannot see much. Can you use your flame?"

"No. They don't like it."

"Thank you for respecting our wishes," a voice echoed as a soft light approached us. The female and male I had seen before appeared, and I forgot how spectacular they were with their dark shimmery skin and glowing constellation marks.

"I can't believe it," Kane whispered in awe.

"I have waited for you a long time, King of Eredet."

From the soft glow of the Buruj, I could see Kane tilt his head in confusion. "Me? Why? What could I be to the Buruj?"

"Everything."

306

"What do you mean?" An overwhelming desire to protect my Star Mate ran through me to the point where it was almost irrational. He squeezed my hand back, no doubt feeling it from me.

"The King is very precious and dear to us. Have you not noticed his unusual gifts?"

Kane straightened, unfolding his arms and taking a step closer to them. "What...what am I?" There was a desperation I had never heard from him before. It was as if someone had just handed him Pandora's box, and he was helpless to open it and find out what was hidden within it all this time.

"What a strange question to ask," the female said. "You are Kaanan Distira, King of Varjutus."

"You know what I mean," he said in frustration, attempting to quell a small growl.

The female approached closer and began to circle Kane, studying him. "You are the legacy of our beginning and the embodiment of the future. The Distira line has always carried a dormant piece of ancient magic long lost. It began to awaken in your father, Adelram Distira, with his gift of the mind and has erupted alive in you. You have only begun to brush the surface of this magic."

"That's...impossible. It took me two thousand years to be able to control the magic I do have. I don't want any more." My heart ached at the pain and fear he felt.

"It is irrelevant what your wishes are, only what is true. Your fear has closed off the majority of your ability so that you haven't even begun to unlock your potential. And your potential is, indeed, immeasurable, as is Cyra's. If you ever overcome your fears and combine your magic, there is no end to what you could accomplish."

Kane looked away, clearly distraught.

"Why do your gifts disgust you? It is as natural as breathing air and beautiful as the cosmos."

"I would hardly consider draining the essence of life out of someone beautiful."

The female stood before Kane and looked up into his eyes with compassion.

"Sometimes the kindest thing you can do for a life is to end it."

She looked at me this time as if sending me a message. It was the second time she'd said those words, and I started fearing what they could mean.

She twirled her hand, her movements hypnotic and fluid. "Take another look at that Voidling, Mylo. There are many things that can be accomplished when life and death are combined, such as reversing a fate worse than death."

My mouth shot open in shock at what she was implying, and Kane looked to me, mimicking my surprise. It was the first small glimmer of hope that we might be able to do something to help him. The woman took a step closer to Kane and touched a finger to his forehead, leaving an imprint of a glow on his skin before it disappeared.

He rubbed at his face as if it itched him. "What did you just do?"

"Remove some energy blockages from your mind that will help ease the flow of some of your gifts."

Kane backed away, clearly not happy by it.

"You have no right to mess with any guards I put up for others' protection."

"Your guards had a purpose when you were little, but they hinder your progress now. Go and find the sword, as was Our Creator's wish."

"Now that we've accepted the bond, have we sealed the fate of the prophecy?" I asked.

Her head tilted in that ethereal way of hers. "You have not yet accepted the bond. You merely ended the *repulsion*. It is not yet concluded whether you will succeed in fulfilling the prophecy or not. It is your choices that will define that."

"How can we choose the right path if we don't know what that is?" I asked anxiously.

"I believe Our Creator has already given you that answer. Search within yourself."

Kane and I looked at each other, completely baffled.

The Buruj started to disappear, not answering any of our questions. But before they did, the woman said one riddle. "There is one thing that I do see as a certainty. Whether the prophecy comes to pass or not, you, Cyra Fenix and Kaanan Distira, will bring upon the end of all ages in Eredet."

CHAPTER
THIRTY

"**W**hat the *hell!*" My confusion and frustration were at an all-time high when we returned to the castle. "I am more confused now than ever before. How is that their version of useful information?"

Kane was staring off into the distance, bracing himself against a wall. "Do we really bring upon the end of Eredet? Regardless of if we succeed?"

It was definitely a hard pill to swallow. Were we doomed regardless of all our efforts? I walked to him and held him in my arms. "I won't lie. Those words are going to haunt me every single day. But if we focus on them, it could drive us mad, wondering what they mean. I think the best thing we can do is focus on what grandpa Amrel tasked us with—how to release the power in the *mikla* and destroy the Guardians. That can never be the wrong answer."

"You know, for one so painfully young you, you're incredibly wise."

"I did have one incredible teacher," I whispered, smiling at the memory of my grandfather's loving face. "As soon as we're back from the Schools of the Seas, I want to see if we can do anything to help Mylo."

Kane nodded but was clearly disturbed by all the crazy revelations from the Buruj cave. He was already known as the most powerful being in the galaxy after the Guardians. What did it mean that he hadn't reached his true potential?

"I guess I better finally get dressed. Come with me?"

I smiled and followed him to his bedroom. He retrieved his standard garb from Solis—a leather vest and cuffs. It was an effort not to salivate as I watched every muscle in his naked torso move in a fluid dance as he dressed. Something from the corner of my eye distracted me, and my heart dropped when I realized what it was. I went over and picked up Poopsie, the teddy bear knight I had given Adelram the day he died.

"I couldn't bear to part with it," Kane said, running his hands down my arms.

"Kane...twice people have insinuated that we are not officially bonded Star Mates. Is that true?"

He sighed as if anticipating my questions. "You're an official mate to me."

"That means we're not. I thought getting rid of the *repulsion* meant we had accepted the bond."

Kane led me to his bed, and he sat on the edge of it, pulling me toward him between his legs. I tried not to get riled up by our position, but the saturation of his scent from being in his room, the memory of what he had done to me earlier, made me weak at the knees. He took my hands in his.

"I heard the stories, but I already confirmed it with Jonsi. An *imana* bond is not officially accepted until it is...consummated. We won't feel the full effect of the bond until we have sex."

My mouth formed an "O," and he laughed with joy in his eyes. He put his hand on my cheek, and I leaned into it, closing my eyes.

"I didn't tell you because there is no rush to make that happen.

311

To me, you are already my bonded mate. I made that choice when the *repulsion* ended. But I am still terrified about controlling myself with you. I've never completely given myself over to someone—power, energy, and my whole soul exposed, so I have no idea if I can control what spews out of me. But when the time is right, I'm willing to try—with you."

I climbed into his lap and wrapped my legs around him, smiling at the small groan that escaped him. "I am a little disappointed to learn it's not real yet."

"I told you it *is* real."

"No, we could still reject the bond at any time."

"I promise I won't do that to you again."

"Well, I'm willing to seal the deal now. That is, of course, unless you don't want to..." I bent down to softly kiss his gray neck, teasing him, running the tip of my tongue against his beautiful, shadowed skin, kissing to his pointed ear, and whispering, "If you check, you'll find that I am more than ready for you."

Kane let out more of a growl than a groan. "Amrel, help me." He hoisted me up higher, grabbing my behind until my breasts were right before his face. He burrowed into them and breathed in, slowly kissing my chest and working his way up to my neck. He lowered me back to his lap right over his throbbing cock, and I tilted my head back in desire.

"I think you're ready too."

He buried his hands in my hair and pulled me in for an intense kiss. It wasn't the sweet, innocent one we'd had before. It was full of lust and longing—a savage claiming. I bit on his bottom lip, begging for more of him which only made him more feral. With both of his hands on my face, I pushed him down to the bed, pinning him beneath me so he would have no choice but to give in to me.

"You are mine, Kane Distira."

His eyes slowly blinked as if savoring the most beautiful sound he'd ever heard. "I am yours, forever. And you are mine."

My fingers began to undo the fastening to his vest, and his eyes radiated green light. I smiled and touched him with featherlight fingers from his chest, down his arms, over his stomach, and down to the very defined vee above his pant line. Eagerly leaning down, I kissed every inch I had just touched with my hands, feeling his soft skin with my lips, tasting his glorious body. It was not enough, I needed more of him—all of him, and I delighted in the moans escaping him. I leaned against his stiff cock still in his pants and pressed in, making contact in just the right spot and beginning to moan myself, imagining how thoroughly he would fill me.

"Kane...."

He growled again, a primal sound that sent shivers throughout me. He sat up quickly and placed me so I could feel him right at my entrance. I ran my hands through his smooth onyx hair and grabbed hold as I kissed him. This bonding was going to happen now. Kaanan Distira, King of Varjutus, was mine for the claiming... until I noticed a glow that made me open my eyes.

"Are you kidding me?" I asked, thoroughly frustrated.

"Ugh," Kane groaned.

I whimpered in unanswered need, still feeling Kane stiff beneath me.

"Don't worry, my love. It will happen. Unfortunately, we have the weight of the galaxy on our shoulders, and too many things are demanding our attention. Like my annoying, sarcastic advisor, for instance." Did Merick have some kind of kink radar that went off when we were about to fuck?

Kane's smile disappeared when he saw my mood had shifted. "What is it, Star?"

"I just...nothing. It's silly."

"Tell me."

"I just want to accept the bond. I want you all to myself with no room for doubt."

"And you have me." He looked down at me with a devious smile. "We'll have to be careful with timing because once those floodgates open and I've buried my cock as far within you as possible, I will likely never want to leave this room again. And I've tasted your divine pussy. I know I will be insatiable when I claim your body and soul."

"Must you torment me…"

"Oh, Cyra, I have only begun. I will delight in your sexual torment for as long as we live."

Good lord, help me.

We begrudgingly met everyone back in Kane's study.

"It's about time," Merick said with his head in his hand and elbow on the table. "Kal is so eager to see this sword he's about to eat Vish as a snack just to get his mind off it."

Kal rolled his eyes, but I knew there was a hint of truth in there. "Do we have a plan for finding the sword?" he asked.

"Not really," I answered. "We didn't get any specific information on how or where to find it, but I assume we'll have to use the Paela to avoid detection as long as possible. They might be able to give us more information, Laine knows a lot of secrets, and she knew grandpa Amrel."

"It's baffling to me that Our Creator was friends with sea dragons but never showed his face to us." Merick sounded as if he was genuinely upset by Grandpa's absence.

"Maybe we weren't worthy," Kal offered with a shrug. Merick raised then lowered his brows in a fury of emotions.

"Grandpa had a reason for everything he did. I doubt offending anyone had anything to do with it," I said.

"I think we'll have just to go and see what we can find," Kane said. "We'll venture to the Island of the Creator and summon our Paela. Let's hope they can take all of us on one trip."

The door burst open, and Vjera walked in with her usual dramatic flair and dual swords strapped to her back. "Did I miss the meeting invite?"

"You've never wanted to be involved before," Merick said with a dismissive shrug.

"Wherever you're going, I'm going too."

Kane looked at me, and I nodded. Vjera needed to be a part of this fight. He smiled appreciatively at my approval.

"Fine. Let's not waste any more time," Kane said.

Before we left, I sent a bird to Urien to tell him of our plan, figuring he could warn us of any danger he might suspect on Solis.

We drove to the Island of the Creator, and much to my dismay, Eleri stood outside the temple. She wasted no time marching toward us when she saw us daring to stand on her island.

"Where the hell have you been!"

My fingers pinched the bridge of my nose. "What are you talking about, and why are you here? I thought you had evacuated," I said, trying not to sound annoyed.

"We missed our sanctuary." With her yelling, the temple doors opened, and my heart sank to find Solian citizens watching the scene. "You have left us here for the Guardians to pick us off one by one, and you've done irrevocable damage to Theo." Well, I couldn't exactly argue with her on the last point.

"That's enough!" Kane bellowed, causing everyone to go silent. I looked at the faces of the terrified people of Solis and couldn't blame them for their feeling of betrayal. They were here without a ruler, hope, or knowledge of our plans. They were left in the dark, and to them, they were merely biding their time, waiting to die. I marched for the temple and entered as the people made way for me. My crew followed, and for the first time, the people of Varjutus entered the Solian Temple of Our Creator. I gave them a moment to take in the splendor of the sanctuary and the art of Amrel. The Varjun were in awe, and I could have sworn I even saw a tear threatening to fall from Kal's eye.

They walked to the statue of grandpa Amrel and knelt before it in prayer. Vjera looked extremely uncomfortable and not pleased to be around so many Solians, but she joined them, kneeling before Our Creator. Kane stayed by my side as a temple full of frightened souls watched me.

"I know you are all afraid, and I'm sorry you have felt the absence of your Reina."

"Reina, have you been captured? What happened to you?" a Solian asked, noticing my extensive injuries from training.

"No, I have not. I have been training daily in preparation for the fight to come so that I will be ready when we face the Bellum and the Guardians."

"Do you think getting yourself beaten senselessly will protect us against this threat?" Eleri said, walking toward me. The people in the temple held on to every one of her words as their *Silta*, and I was getting sick of her shit.

Kal stormed over, followed by Merick and Meili. "Show some respect!" Kal boomed. "You are speaking to the daughter of Our Creator."

Hushed whispers erupted throughout the temple, and I had to try not to erupt in flame for him revealing my secret. I didn't want these people to think I was more than I seemed. I still had no idea what I was doing or how to keep them safe, and I didn't want them to have blind faith just because of what Siare said about my genetics.

Another Solian spoke out. "Look! That's her in the tapestry! The girl and the King! It's true!"

Everyone started kneeling before us, including Merick, Meili, Kal, and even Vjera. Eleri stood in absolute shock and disgust, and I couldn't fight the burning in my face. Kane could feel my overwhelming embarrassment, and he squeezed my hand and nodded as if to say *this is what they need. They need this hope.*

We left the temple after answering some questions, listening to their concerns, and advising them to hide elsewhere.

To everyone's surprise, Laine and Josko were there already waiting for us. The Solians from the temple gasped in shock. Probably the first time they'd ever seen a Paela.

"They're *Paeladoned* Warriors! There is hope!"

God, I hoped so.

"We are ready to take the girl and the King to the Schools of the Seas," Laine said.

"You already know what we're after, don't you?"

"You seek the sword of Amrel the Creator."

"How does everyone seem to know more about my life and destiny than I do?"

"It is your journey to walk and your future to wield, but Amrel ensured there would be lights to guide your way."

"So far, none of these lights have been very illuminating."

"Perhaps you must open your eyes to see it more clearly."

Why did everyone accuse me of not seeing what was before me? What was I missing?

"Okay, Laine. Let's go."

The two Paela were able to bring all of us over in one ride, and we approached the chain of islands Theo once took me to. When we were on the shore of the main island, I started to have trouble breathing as the fear of being so close to Theo was somehow a thousand times scarier to me than the Guardians. It took me a moment to realize it was because I cared about him. I had a soft spot for him, and knowing myself, I'd still want to try to help him until the very end. And that was dangerous for me. I would have to steel my heart and lose my empathy if I were to face him again. Laine bent her massive neck and nuzzled against me, feeling my internal turmoil.

"Do not change who you are for others."

"Are you sure about that?"

"You know, as high and mighty as the *Paeladoned* warriors are supposed to be, they sure look utterly ridiculous standing around in silence with weird looks on their faces," Merick blurted.

"They're talking to their Paela, you ass," Vish responded. "Cyra, are you alright?"

"Yes, I've just been here before with Theo. I'm feeling the loss of who he was."

Vish rubbed my back in comfort, and Kane straightened at the sight of it. I swore I could hear one of his characteristic growls in my mind.

"Where are we supposed to start?" Meili asked. "There are so many islands."

"I think we should split up to cover more ground," Vjera suggested.

"We need to be quick. We don't know what methods the Guardians use to sense us. No using magic and no driving. We know they can sense that. We travel by Paela. Merick and Meili, start here, take the main island, and work your way down. Cyra will travel to the furthest island with someone, and I will travel to the center," Kane said.

"I'm going with Cyra," Vish responded. I tried not to laugh because I could feel Kane seething through our bond.

"Fine. Cyra must also take a Varjun so we can all call each other if needed," Kane insisted.

"I'll make sure the Solian keeps his hands to himself," Vjera volunteered. Vish huffed, his hatred for Vjera no small thing, but to his credit, he didn't utter a word.

"Let's ride. Be careful."

Vish, Vjera, and I hopped onto Laine and made our way to the far end of the Schools of the Seas. They were full of empty, abandoned buildings and rubble, a ghost of a previous era that I could picture bustling with the excitement of young and educated individuals. It looked like part of the Great War took place here and nobody could bear repairing it or cleaning the debris. It was the same with Vjera's parents' home. Nobody had used the rubble as resources for their crumbling community. They were shrines—reminders of what was lost since there were so few memories left.

The three of us spread out and searched the remains of the schools. I entered a massive library that didn't have a single book on its half-rotted shelves. It was painful to wonder at all the millennia of knowledge that was destroyed for petty gain.

The next building was a small temple that held cracked statues of beings with wings. The largest of them I knew instantly to be grandpa Amrel, and Kane was right. In this depiction, he was holding a large, blue flaming sword with a stunning hilt in the shape of wings. To his right was a fierce, intimidating-looking individual with flaming hair. I reached out to touch him, unwittingly trying to soften his rage. It was my dear Xenos, and his tablet read, *Xenos, Commander, and Protector of the Sunya Rei—ruler of the Sunya people.* I went back to Grandpa's tablet to read what was written about him, but it was destroyed. What was required of Xenos in the billion years he existed? Was his life hard? Did he really never experience a friendly touch in all those years?

There were five other statues, but most of them were destroyed. I could see one with a tablet that read *Siare, High Oracle of the Sunya Rei—ruler of the Sunya people.*

Next to her statue, there was a male face and pieces of dark wings appearing as if they were black. It surprised me that this particular Sunya Rei was different than all the others. His tablet was badly damaged, but I saw the word "fallen" etched on it.

There were more empty bookshelves and I figured this was a

place of religious study. With everything else destroyed and no sign of the sword, I continued on.

"Have you found anything, Vish?"

"Just a lot of rubbish."

"Same here," Vjera responded. "What baffles me is that this place doesn't seem secure. Why would the Sword of Istina be hidden here?"

We walked to the next island since it was shallow water. I listened to the blistering wind, which was unlike anywhere else I'd been on Solis. The wind was eerily cold like it held the trauma of what was lost here. Who had died on these islands? There was a faint echo of death in the winds and it made my stomach clench into knots.

The next building we came across looked to be for the study of defensive magic. I walked inside and it didn't seem as decayed as the previous buildings.

"Hey guys, come in here!"

Vish ran toward me and crashed right into an invisible wall, and fell backward.

"What just happened?" I asked.

Vjera laughed delightfully and stepped over Vish to try to enter the building, but she too, couldn't get in.

"It must be shielded," she said.

An overwhelming presence behind me caused me to slowly turn around but there was nothing but a bare-looking wall.

"Guys, I think there's something behind here. We should call Kane." There was an unmistakable feeling of vitality and warmth that was eerily similar to what I felt in Grandpa's presence and it astounded me that it was clear to me now, but I had never noticed it before. His essence had a signature, a distinctive imprint that I immediately recognized, and that's how I knew the sword was here.

Vjera didn't hesitate to touch a mark on her arm. A few minutes later, Kane and Kal ran toward us.

"Did you find it?" Kal asked.

"The building is shielded," Vjera said.

Both Kane and Kal tried to enter but were unsuccessful.

"What do we do now?"' Vish asked

"Kane, I think the Sword is shrouded in the wall somewhere, but I can't see it. We need to find a way to get you in."

"Use the Star Mate bond," Vjera said, not looking us in the eye. She knew more about high-level bonds than any of us since her parents were bonded. "You should be able to borrow Cyra's ability to penetrate the shield even though you're not fully bonded."

I nodded to Kane and opened my mind. I felt him immediately seep into it, probing for the answer. I felt it the moment he found it. He used my power as if it was his own and walked through the door.

"There it is! I see it here!"

I ran over to where he said it was and reached through the shroud, gasping at what I found.

"What is it? Are you hurt?"

"Oh no, oh no, oh no," I whined out loud. I took out the sword. In two pieces. "The Sword of Istina is broken."

"No." Kane's shoulders slumped slightly in devastation.

"No, it can't be…." I heard Kal lament from outside.

"What's that sound?" The panic in Vjera's voice caught my attention, and Kane and I rushed toward the door.

"I hear it too," Vish chimed in.

When we exited the building we started to feel a vibration in the earth.

"What the hell…." Kane said.

"This can't be good," Kal whispered.

"Cyra! Run!" Laine screamed in my head.

"Run to the Paela!" Kane said, mimicking what Josko had probably told him.

On every side of us, I saw rabid-looking vicious animals charging toward us. They appeared utterly unnatural, like magic was involved in warping their bodies. In fact, I could hear and feel the sickening hum of dark magic radiating off them in waves. They were oozing some unknown neon green liquid from various orifices on their bodies, and they screeched an unnatural sound, making us cringe and cover our ears. I quickly secured the two pieces of the sword into my belt as we ran at full speed toward the Paela, but we didn't make it halfway until we were surrounded. Flames burst from my hands at the same time Kane released ice into the wave of demonic animals.

"That didn't slow them down at all!" Vish screamed. Vjera used lightning which singed their skin and damaged them, but they kept on coming like pain had no effect on them. There was nowhere we could escape, and they stampeded over us in a wave of fury. Vjera screamed out as an ancient and terrible-looking beast, reminiscent of a massive warthog, sank its tusks into her shoulder. Green liquid oozed out of its mouth and ears and she writhed in pain at the spots it touched her skin. I didn't get to see what happened to her next as a different monster pinned me down, and I screamed at a searing pain in my ankle, but I realized it wasn't my pain—it was Kane's. The protective urge rushed through me knowing he was in danger was instinctive and visceral. I managed to get my Varjun dagger, and I stabbed the monster in the eye, but the green fluid gushed out all over me, causing me to vomit at the vile feel and stench. It was that same corrupted feeling I had when I was overcome by the power bracelet on Solis and it made me incredibly ill.

The weight of it as it fell on top of me was so great I almost couldn't get free, but the sound of Kane's cry as he was cut again made me reach into something inside of me that propelled it away with unnatural force. Kane jumped up and cut the head off three of the demon-like monsters in a matter of seconds. A yelp escaped me at the sight of one of them knocking him down from behind, ripping into his shoulder. I ran to him and stabbed the beast in the neck.

Vish picked up one of the massive beasts from Vjera and threw it across the field. My jaw dropped, realizing he hadn't been kidding when he said he had physical strength.

Kal was using his double swords to create a vortex of fury, taking out an impressive amount of the beasts in his fluid, effortless movements.

I looked around at the few hundred of them coming for us and realized we wouldn't *make it out alive.*

"Yes, you are," I heard Laine whisper in my head as I was knocked down and gashed in the arm.

"You will suffer for that!" Laine screamed with her mouth unmoving, but Josko was the first to attack. His mouth opened and sprayed some type of fluid over the animals around us, and by some magic, my crew was unaffected. It was apparent that Josko's fluid was acid, and the beasts were melting away in a heap of gore. Laine attacked as well, and her fluid was like molten lava. They eradicated the beasts in a matter of moments.

There was only a moment of relief before I realized who we were missing. "Meili!" I screamed

"Josko, we have to get to Merick and Meili now!" Kane screamed.

We jumped onto the Paela and swam to the main island at full speed to retrieve our friends. We probably could have driven at that point, but it was still safer to err on the side of caution. When we reached the main island, Josko and Laine obliterated the hundreds of beasts infesting it. Urien was there fighting like hell with his power of camouflage. It appeared that the beasts couldn't see him, and he could attack them without retaliation.

When the Paela destroyed the remaining beasts, I panicked when I couldn't see Merick and Meili anywhere.

"Meili!" I screamed. "Merick!"

"There!" Kane yelled under a slight arch. I didn't see anything until Merick dissolved his shroud. He was lying on top of Meili, protecting her with gashes all over his back, blood everywhere. We ran to them, and Kane had to pry Merick away from Meili. And when he did, Merick fell to the ground, shaking.

"He's lost too much blood," Kane said with worry.

Meili ran to him and kneeled. "He saved my life. He pinned me down and wouldn't let me move. I have you, my love. I will heal you."

Merick was unconscious, and Meili's glowing hands slowly started mending his severe wounds. When they all looked to be closed, Meili turned Merick around and held him in her arms.

"Wake up, my love." She shook him gently, trying to stir him from unconsciousness. "Please...please wake up. I need you. You promised I'd never be alone again," she whimpered, starting to cry.

"You know I can't bear the sight of your tears. That would stir me from any grave," Merick said, smiling and touching her face. Meili sobbed even harder, pulling him closer.

"I thought I lost you. I knew those monsters were ripping you apart, and I thought I had lost you," she cried.

"They'll have to try harder than that to take me from you." He sat up and kissed her gently, lost to the gore around them. Laine's voice entered my mind.

"We must return to the temple, now!"

I looked up, and another wave of hundreds of aberrant beasts were stampeding toward us at supernatural speed right over a sea of carcasses, burying them into the wet ground. The sight of them sent fear rippling through me as the green ooze and remains of the dead beasts saturated their bodies. Their skin was sizzling away from excess acid and lava on the ground, and it didn't phase them in the slightest—their only focus was on us and ripping us to shreds.

We jumped onto Josko and Laine as they rushed us back to the Temple of Our Creator, and we dismounted, relief flooding me that there didn't seem to be any beasts or Guardians in sight.

The Paela disappeared back into the depths of the ocean, and we were preparing for the interplanetary drive back to Varjutus, but when I turned around, I was stopped dead in my tracks with my heart dropping to the floor. Sound seemed to disappear, and there was nothing but this moment. Before me was Theo, and half of his body was still covered in black burns from where Meili had nearly decimated him.

"Well, you've been busy." His voice was barely a whisper, strained and raspy as if his vocal cords had also been burned. Those once stunning turquoise eyes were still red and utterly filled with rage and regret. "What, no get-well card or well wishes? I'm disappointed, truly. Not even an attempt to come and kill me off. Really, I expected more from you, my darling Cyra."

Unable to speak, I slowly turned to see that Theo had blocked off everyone behind a shield. Kane was the only one making any progress, pushing against it as it slightly yielded more and more with each attempt.

"I supposed you've been too busy enjoying yourself and fucking your *true love*."

My fists bunched together until they lit into flame. He could call me whatever disgusting, vile thing he could think of, but he would not insult my mate to my face.

"And there it is. You care enough to kill me over *him*."

My eyes came to life with flame, and I blasted fire toward him, which he could barely fight off, and I rejoiced that there was a tinge of fear in his eye after what he'd suffered at Meili's hand.

"Enough!" His voice invaded my mind, and I was immediately powerless, floating on a cloud, unable to control my own body. This new power of his was extreme, and it scared the shit out of me not to be able to block him out at all. Was he somehow alerting Orphlam that we were here? Was it all over for us?

"You want to know what Orphlam is up to. Don't worry. He's been very busy elsewhere. I know you just met his new friends. There are thousands more where they came from. Plus, some other new surprises."

At that moment, Eleri came running out of the temple, screaming for Theo as many other Solians followed her. Theo was so shocked that he released me from his mental grip.

"Eleri, no! Run and take everyone out of here!"

But it was too late. Theo was overcome and raised his hands, blasting a mammoth force of energy toward the temple. Not everybody escaped before it completely crumbled to the ground.

T heo had disappeared. He had spent all his energy and needed to recover. My crew was now free, and Urien had arrived, sensing trouble. Eleri managed to survive and finally took the threat seriously enough to assist Urien in transferring the remaining Solians into hiding.

When they had all gone, I stared at the few stubborn, bent, and crooked flowers peering from the rubble of the garden of the lost ones, refusing to let the memories of those souls be forgotten. A tear fell down my cheek at this tremendous loss, a place of refuge that the people of Solis collectively powered with their dwindling energy where they could worship and grieve without fear. The beautiful effigies of Grandpa and his stained-glass art were all gone.

All this senseless loss made me fume with anger and disbelief. Kane put his arm around me and spoke softly. "Come, we must go now. It's too dangerous to stay." I nodded as we all drove back to Kane's castle on Varjutus.

"He didn't even realize I was there," Vish spoke quietly, visibly shaking.

"This galaxy is fucked," Vjera said from the ground, her hands over her head.

"The Sword of Istina…" Kal said in horror, looking at the broken pieces on my belt.

"Yeah, we are fucked," Merick responded, agreeing with Vjera.

Meili started making her rounds healing us, and I only let her heal the bare minimum of what I needed to survive. My body was becoming a tapestry of my struggle. Like the abandoned buildings and rubble in Eredet—wounds of their communities, I wanted my wounds to remind me of what was at stake. And it was clear the stakes were incredibly high.

"Kal, please make sure the community training is ready for tonight. It's more imperative than ever since there's no telling when those beasts will make it to our home."

Merick looked up, the color draining from his face. "Do…you think the Guardians could send them here? We'd stand no chance, especially without the Paela."

Kane looked down. I felt his heart breaking for his beloved people through our *imana* bond, and I damn near doubled over in grief from it. He grabbed his King's Chain, and I knew his burden was almost too heavy to endure. I wished my mate didn't have to reign during the darkest time in Varjun history, but I also knew nobody was more suited for the challenge.

"I think we have no choice but to prepare for the worst. It is mandatory for every *Curadh* Warrior to attend the community training and lead a group of *colts*. Merick, please spread the word throughout the villages so all those who volunteer are ready. The rest of us will go to Jonsi and see if he has any information about these beasts," Kane concluded.

I also hoped Jonsi knew how to repair the sword. Kal and Merick went to carry out their King's orders. The rest of us drove to Jonsi's hut.

"What has happened?" Jonsi asked seriously as he let us in. He knew something was wrong before he even saw us.

"We were attacked on Solis," Vjera answered.

"And *why*, pray tell, would anything compel you to go within spitting distance of the Guardians?" Jonsi asked, clearly annoyed.

"To get this," I said, bringing out the broken sword.

Jonsi's eyes bulged as he gasped. "Well, I'll be damned."

"Can you fix it?" I asked in desperation.

"I'm afraid the only one I know who could fix it is Our High Creator."

I grunted in frustration.

"Who gave you the intel on where to find that?" Jonsi asked, intrigued.

Kane and I looked at each other, still sore about our last visit with them.

"The...Buruj," Kane said quietly.

Jonsi nodded, not looking at all surprised.

"Jonsi, what aren't you telling us? Why am I not surprised that you know that they're real?" Kane asked.

Jonsi rolled his eyes. "Son, how often do I have to tell you that I know almost everything because I'm older than dirt."

Kane wasn't convinced.

"Even with that being the case...there's still a lot we don't know about the Buruj because they reigned free before we kept history. I am a living keeper of our ancestor's knowledge, but I can't keep what even they did not know. What was passed onto me was the information that the majority of them died out millennia ago for some unknown reason. They've stayed hidden, and nobody has seen one since then, which is why the Varjun think they're a legend. That said, if they told you this sword was important to the future, then I would keep it close."

"Much use that'll do in two pieces," Vjera said in defeat.

"There were hundreds of beasts with oozing green liquid

coming from their bodies. They had multiple tusks, glowing horns, and sharp armor-like scales hidden throughout their fur. They were unaffected by pain. Does any of that sound familiar? I thought most of the animals of Eredet, except for livestock, died out from the curse. I've never seen wild animals in such great numbers before," Kane asked.

"While I'd be happy for our wildlife to return in numbers, it can't be good news. What you're describing sounds like the *Deabru*, but they've been extinct since the Second Age. They were way too vicious and destructive to survive as a species. The fluid and the intolerance for pain sound like an experiment of the Guardians. If they were able to bring back an extinct species of animals and fortify them like that, I fear for what else they're planning."

"I was afraid you'd say that," Vish said.

"I have Kal and Merick organizing additional trainings for the villagers," Kane said, running his hand through his hair.

"I think that's the best course to take right now," Jonsi said softly. "I'll prepare extra healing remedies and defensive poultices."

We all looked at each other in sadness, knowing what was being unsaid. We were preparing for an inevitable invasion.

"Jonsi, there's something else I wanted to ask you about. I found this among the ruins of King Varog and Queen Dessa's home. It called to me, and I think it's important. Meili mentioned it might be a failsafe key."

Jonsi took it and looked it over. "I don't believe it. You've done well, my dear. Very well."

"What, Jonsi? What is it?" Kane asked. Vjera walked closer, intrigued by what Jonsi had to say.

"Meili is correct. It is a failsafe key."

"For what, exactly?" Vish asked.

"It is the failsafe key to the Siphoning Stone. It is the only way to deactivate the draining of our power and render the stone void unless the Guardians decided to end it themselves. Once the fail-safe key is used, the Siphoning Stone can never be activated again."

"I had no idea there was a way to stop part of the draining of our energy! I thought opening the *mikla* would unleash all of our power," I said, astonished.

"That will release the part that the Guardians cannot access, but it won't stop the source of power they're using right now. It's how they currently control us all. Use this failsafe key against the Guardians, and you will even the playing field in this war."

"This is great news!" Kane straightened and rubbed at the stubble on his jaw.

"It's about time we had some," Vjera agreed.

"It won't stop all of their power, and they could still have substantial stores saved, but yes, it would definitely make it more of a fair fight, plus it will help save our sun," Jonsi said with a smile. "Keep that safe, Cyra."

"Oh, rest assured, I will."

CHAPTER
THIRTY-TWO

We had set a time to regroup after a day of rest so that we could attempt to help Mylo. I relayed everything the Buruj had told us, and Jonsi looked excited and eager to help. We all met at the magic pond—a place that held great significance, ceremony, and magic for the Varjun people. It was our hope that the location could only help us.

Kane brought Mylo to the pond, and I gasped when I saw what bad shape he was in. He laid him on the ground since it appeared he was unable to stand on his own.

I rushed to his side and bent in close, trying not to gag at the putrid odor his decaying body was emitting. "We're going to do everything we can to help you. I believe we can." It felt like I was giving myself a pep talk, trying to convince myself. He locked eyes with me, and all he could do was slowly blink in response.

Sitting on the ground with my legs folded, Kane joined me. Vjera, Meili, and Vish watched as Jonsi stood behind us. Kane grabbed my hands, interlocking his fingers with mine, and he nodded in reassurance. This would be the first true test of our Star Mate bond's effectiveness.

We shut our eyes and concentrated, quickly gaining access to each other.

Jonsi spoke softly but firmly. "This creature is stuck in a state of limbo—a state of living death as he rots before our very eyes. You must tune into these energies, cut the cords of death attached to him by a curse, and nurture him with the energy of life. Neither of you can do this on your own. You will only succeed if you are one with each other—in true harmony and acceptance of your bond."

Kane and I both probed the essence within Mylo, feeling the energies tied to him. A gasp escaped me when I felt the smallest amount of life force energy I had ever felt in a being. He was so close to death that I knew if we didn't succeed in this session, he would die by the end of the day. The clutch of death energy was overwhelmingly strong, and it's something I wouldn't normally feel on my own without Kane's gifts.

"Do you feel his death?" Kane asked.

"Yes, it's overwhelming. It's everywhere, suffocating him."

Kane nodded. "I'm going to begin by trying to untangle some of these unnatural ties of death, which might break the bonds of the curse." I watched on with our second sight, and he weaved through the delicate threads of energy, successfully dissipating one at a time. After thirty minutes, we both began to grow tired. I lent him more of my energy so that he could keep picking apart the ties of death from his curse.

Vish's voice sounded many feet away through muffled water. "Look! Mylo is gaining some natural color, and he doesn't look as sickly." I smiled but didn't disconnect from our plane of energy. It took quite a while longer until Kane stopped, and I could tell he was covered in sweat. His speech was slow, as if he was overly fatigued. "I think that's all I can do without more lifeforce energy."

I was worried I wouldn't be able to hold up my end of this because of the debilitating fatigue I also felt, but I wouldn't give up until I had no magic left.

I always held a decent well of energy within myself, but I knew I would have to borrow from other sources for this. I started with what was available and filled Mylo with a golden healing life force energy that I could immediately feel make a difference. Still, I was astounded by how much he would need to combat the remaining effects of the curse.

I recalled when I had transferred energy to Bad when he was depleted, and it was a tiny spec of power compared to this daunting task before me. It was clear that I would be giving nearly all of myself, plus some I shouldn't, to save him. Energy flowed through me as if I were a conduit, and Mylo greedily absorbed more and more into his body.

Meili yelled in surprise, but I could barely hear her over the rushing wind and energy vortex I had created. "He looks nearly restored to life! It's working! Cyra, you're doing it!"

The waning energy in the galaxy had never been more apparent to me than it was now when I was grasping for it, but not enough was coming and not fast enough. My body started to slump a little, but Kane spoke into my mind, giving me more of himself in the process.

"You're almost done, my mate. Hold on a little longer. You amaze me with your light as bright and powerful as the sun, and what is the sun, after all, but a life-giving Star? Just a little longer, *imana*."

He gave one more forceful push of what he had left to give, and Vjera spoke off in the distance. "Jonsi! They have to stop. The trees and bits of the forest are rotting away!"

"They're almost done! Just one more moment, and I will have them stop."

A last burst of light rushed out of me, and we nearly fell over from the unfathomable fatigue, but we stayed awake to witness the awe of what we had done. Mylo was glowing in the air, lighting up the usual darkness of Varjutus.

"He's a Sunya Rei!" Meili shouted, her hand over her mouth in shock.

His wings were massive, just as Xenos and Grandpa's had been, and he was filled with vitality and strength. Some of his light dimmed a bit as if he were trying to absorb the energy required of a being of his magnitude, but it simply wasn't available.

It made sense why Mylo had survived so long after the curse was triggered. He was a Sunya Rei, just as I was sure Meili was, but they were unable to come into power because of the state of our galaxy.

With tears in his eyes, Jonsi handed Kane and me tonics to drink.

"Quick, drink this. It'll restore your strength and keep you from passing out."

It immediately revitalized me, and I stood to take in the glory of Mylo, but within his ethereal beauty, I saw terror and pain in his features. He was only there for a moment longer, locking eyes with me before he disappeared.

We loitered for a bit, discussing what happened and where he might have disappeared, but we decided to give him some time to adjust and heal. He would have a lot of unpacking to do with the amount of suffering he had gone through.

Even with Jonsi's tonic, he insisted Kane and I rest for the remainder of the day before our community training the following day. As we began to leave, Jonsi stopped me.

"Cyra, one more word before you go, please."

He took my hand in his and smiled. "I know you're worried about that sword, but I know Amrel well. I am almost certain that the answer to how to heal this sword is already within you. You just have to find it."

CHAPTER
THIRTY-THREE

Kane and I readied for the community training the following day as we talked more about Mylo.

"I never could have believed that my power of death could be used for good."

I wrapped one arm around his and held his face, which was rough with stubble. "I don't know how you could ever think otherwise because you are filled with goodness. We are what we manifest, and you cultivate family and community every day you draw breath."

He held me tight and pulled me to him, breathing deeply as if he were capturing my scent. "You are utterly stunning, and I'm the luckiest man alive to have you."

He reluctantly released me and walked to his official *Curadh* battle armor on display left by Brugan. He painstakingly secured every piece, and I watched in awe as his fearsome presence made me unable to look away.

His armor was all pearlescent black and reached a downward point on every edge. He wore a black tunic underneath, so where any skin would have shown was covered in darkness. The torso of

336

the armor reached down to his upper thighs, and it was paired with black pants and black leather knee-high boots with armor covering his shins.

He explained that since he wasn't on the battlefield, there would be no helmet, and instead, he had a sleek black hood with armor covering the forehead portion, and he held a forest green face mask that looked to cover his mouth and nose.

He looked like death incarnate.

"I'm proud of you for this initiative of training your villagers. I look back at my time on Solis and how, with their bracelets of power, they were still so powerless. They would be easily eradicated if war came to them, and I'm positive that's exactly what the Guardians want."

Kane smiled at me sadly. Clearly, something bothering him. "My father forced me to train for hundreds of years, and I hated him for it. The endless grueling pain and focus on killing, I despised him for so long that I didn't think I would ever forgive him for it. I had already unintentionally killed others, destroying a part of who I was, and then Adelram forced me to become even more lethal."

He rubbed at his stubble, shaking his head at the memory.

"Our training was brutal. We learned how to survive in captivity and how to deal the most damage to our opponents. When it came time for the test to become one of the *Curadh* in the *Warriors Sanna*, I failed intentionally. It was the only time I'd seen shame in my father's eyes. Only later did I realize how childish that was and that my father was only trying to do everything he could to keep me safe, to prepare me for this fight and what was to come. To make me a worthy king who could protect his people, and now I couldn't be more appreciative that I have the skills to keep you and my people safe as long as possible. I would do anything to look my father in the eyes and say thank you for making me the best man I could be."

"I understand your hesitation. When I came here, I was just a naïve girl who didn't know more beyond her own small, insignificant life. I never would have dreamed of a day I'd be fighting for anything, but now I want nothing more. I suppose sometimes we must fight to earn our peace." As I thought through my words, one thing became clear that genuinely shocked me. "Kane, I want to take the *Warrior's Sanna*. I want to be one of the *Curadh*."

His brows lifted briefly, but a small grin replaced it as he took my hands. "Then I will do whatever I can to help you get there. But you will need more training. I have seen into your heart and know you have the strength it takes. You have the heart of a warrior."

"For the sake of Eredet, I hope that is true."

"You must learn to have faith in yourself, my love. To see yourself the way I do. The way we all do."

Maybe that was part of the answer everyone kept telling me to find.

After eating something quick that Brugan had brought to Kane's room, I hid the Sword of Istina in my quarters, and we drove to the training camps. I was taken aback by the number of people who showed up–nearly all the Varjun left alive. The determination and community of this Varjun race were something to admire.

A small boy started to run toward me.

"Cyra! Look, I brought Fela. She said she could help me become a *Curadh* too."

"Joven...uh, hi. You're here to train, too, huh?"

"Of course! I will fight for our home," he said, running off with my small D&D character.

I looked at Kane in surprise. "You guys aren't going to let him train here, are you?"

"No Varjun who wishes to fight is turned away, not even children. When our enemies come for us, they won't be sparing our young. They have just as much a right to have a fighting chance as our full-grown."

I was at a loss for words—because I couldn't develop a valid argument. Kane gave me one last strained smile before he raised his mask and joined the other *Curadh* in the center of the training camp. They all stood in line, side by side, with two swords strapped to their backs and their arms folded behind them.

With their hoods, masks, and armor all covered in black, they looked like harbingers of death, and I understood why people took it seriously when they spoke of the most fearsome warriors in the Galaxy.

Ondour's cloth mask had the face of a skeleton nose and mouth on it, and I didn't want to admit that it made me quiver just looking at him. Migor's mask had a mouth with fangs open in a roar. Kal's mask was plain black, fitting for the dispeller of darkness, but there was one more *Curadh* I couldn't identify. I had completely forgotten that I hadn't met the fifth member—Erek. His mask looked to have metal in the middle and cloth at the sides. I wondered how on earth he was able to breathe.

They stood a few feet apart, legs spread and hands behind their back so their arms formed a triangle. Kane yelled a command, and they all grabbed the double swords behind their back and criss-crossed them over their head and across their body until they pointed them to the ground with their feet together. Their sword overlapped with the sword of *Curadh* next to them. They moved as one unit like they were connected, and it only increased my excitement for the possibility of becoming one of them.

Oliver and Lorcan approached me in utter awe, and it was the first time I'd seen some life in Lorcan's face since his father had passed.

"I want to be a *Curadh*," Lorcan whispered.

"Me too," Oliver mimicked.

"And so do I," I replied, as they both looked at me questioningly. Their doubt made me want it even more. I looked over and saw Vjera with her arms crossed, looking bored and I walked over to her.

"I'm surprised you're not one of the *Curadh*. You've got the most lethal spirit of anyone I've ever met."

"Please. I could hand any of their asses to them any time. I don't need to prance around in a fancy suit to prove it."

It was more of her punishing herself, convincing herself she wasn't worthy.

"Besides, why would I want to be stuck in an all-boys club? I'm confident in my abilities without the attention of eyes staring at my ass."

"I'm sure you are, but what about the other women of Varjutus? Look around—hardly any women at all showed up. Maybe they need another woman to show them it's possible," I whispered.

She looked around as if noticing the crowd for the first time. "Well, shit."

"I think you and I should take a trip through the villages tomorrow and see if any women want to join the fight," I said.

"Yeah, sure. Sounds like a plan. And if you're so keen to strut around in black, why don't you take the *Warrior's Sanna?*"

"I have every intention of doing just that."

She looked at me like I had two heads but fought a side smirk and nodded her head. "Give them hell."

It was also very disappointing not to see a single Solian, so I'd also visit their camps.

Kane stood forward from the middle of the formation and addressed his people while the other four *Curadh* stayed unmoving. He never moved his mask as he spoke, but his voice wasn't muffled by it as it boomed throughout the crowd so everyone could hear.

"As I stand here before you, I am filled with pride. I'm proud of the fight within my people and how we can set aside our fear to protect our right to live. We stand here at the brink of war, and we've never faced enemies so powerful, and the cost has never been so great in the history of Eredet. We don't fight for territory, riches, pride, or equality. We fight for the most basic of rights for the children of Amrel—the right to *survive*. We fight in Amrel's name to protect all his wondrous creations."

Flames from torches flickered all around us, providing a little more light than usual since so many would need to pay close attention, and I could see the looks of pride and determination on their faces.

"We fight to restore Varjutus, and *all* of Eredet, to what it once was. Our galaxy is known as the Creation Galaxy because we were the first lifeforms of the cosmos. We should be an example of celebrating life and what it has to offer, not succumbing to death and destruction. And although our interplanetary relations have failed to live up to that honored status, we have the chance to change it and recreate this galaxy in the image we want it to be. We Varjun are peaceful, yet here we are, united in arms, preparing to defend what we have left. Here we are, ready to die to give Varjutus a chance at tomorrow."

Everyone was silent. There were no cheers or applause—it wasn't the time for that. We all stood in silent reflection at the seriousness of Kane's words, but our hearts were swollen with fortitude and pride.

Being here in more frequent training meant Kane was preparing us to fight to the death, and for many of us, it would probably come to that.

Kane split us into groups, and I was happy I was put into Erek's instruction. I learned something new and valuable from each new instructor, and I was interested to see Erek's fighting style.

He spent hours teaching us basic defensive and offensive moves, and I was slightly bored since I had been through it many times, just not so formally. With Kane and Kal, my training was more 'trial by fire.' Either fight or die. And I found it immensely more effective. But there were a lot of different ability ranges in his group, and he had to cover all his bases.

The crowd dispersed when we finished the first day's training, and Erek stopped me from leaving.

"Going so soon? I thought you'd want a little one-on-one training," he said in a rough, deep voice. He still wore his hood and mask, so I could only see his glowing hazel eyes with blue, gray, green, and amber flecks. They reminded me a little of my immortal eyes, except less blue and gray and without the reflective specs of light.

"I'd love that." I wouldn't dismiss any offer to help me achieve my new goal.

"If you want to be one of the *Curadh*, you're going to have to be training around the clock," he said simply.

"How do you know that? I only just told Kane before we got to the field, and he hasn't spoken to anyone else since then."

"I pay attention to my surroundings. That is the most important lesson you still need to learn."

"You've seen me fight? I've never seen you at the grounds before."

"And that is exactly my point."

I merely blinked at him, baffled.

"Jonsi is my best friend, and he has quite the mouth on him. And Amrel visited me once, asking me to share my specific knowledge of fighting with you when our paths crossed. He thought it would be the most crucial part of you understanding your power."

"What does my power have to do with my fighting?"

Erek began to circle me with his hands behind his back, his presence fierce and menacing behind his armor. "Everything. A true warrior uses all the resources at their disposal, including your power. You still haven't tapped into your power when you fight, which means you're not using your instincts."

"I burned Ondour. I've been using my power."

"I'm not talking about your petty tricks. I'm talking about your well of impressive energy that lets you see beyond our physical world. You can see the construct of our universe, so you should be able to fight a whole army even if you were blind and had no weapons."

I thought back to Mikla Island when I was able to sense the essence of the soldiers. I easily took them down when my friends were threatened. And the training on Solis when I could sense Kane up in the tree and pinned him down without...*seeing*.

Erek started nodding. "You know exactly what I'm referring to. You will never become a *Curadh* unless you unlock this ability at will and use it to fight because that is the heart of who you are."

"I...I don't see it that often."

"Because you're fighting yourself. Your training with me will differ entirely from that of Kal or Ondour's. You won't be limping home in a pool of blood and bruises. It will be all slow and deliberate movements and enemy anticipation, and it will all be blindfolded."

Well, wouldn't you know, I went back to my room not two hours later with a black eye and a fresh gash on my arm.

CHAPTER THIRTY-FOUR

I t was disappointing that Kane wasn't in my bed when I got back to my room, and I was getting increasingly impatient about when we would complete our Star Mate bond. I imagined that was why he went to his room and not mine. Despite how badly he wanted me, he was still deathly afraid of hurting me. But just because there was so much happening in our lives and so many people to worry about, that didn't lessen my desire for him. Every day that went by made my need for him almost unbearable. I even fantasized about tying him down or handcuffing him so he couldn't escape to another emergency.

Real nice, Cyra.

I was interrupted from mentally yelling at myself for my selfishness by a knock at the door, and, to my delight, it was Meili.

"Come in! What do we have here?"

"I invented something new for you."

"Invented?"

"Yes! I started worrying about all these essential items you're carrying now. I think it's important to have the failsafe key and your *syn* with you at all times, so I created a 'bottomless pocket,'" she said with a smile. "Here, put on these pants."

I did what I was told, and she instructed me to put those two items in my pocket, and when I did, I found I could push my whole arm into empty space.

"What the hell...?"

Meili laughed. "Now you'll be able to carry lots of valuable items without a bulging, heavy pocket."

"Meili...how did you do this? This seems like very complicated magic." Reaffirming my suspicions again that she was actually a Sunya Rei that couldn't come into her power.

She simply laughed again. "I'm Sunya. We're able to easily... make things."

"Come, join me. I've missed you terribly." I jumped into bed and patted the spot next to me. She joined me, giggling and radiating her usual light. I thought of the two women in my life. They couldn't be more night and day. Vjera was a fiery vortex of rage, passion, and aggression but with a well of loyalty beneath her surface, and Meili was a pure, angelic creature of grace and kindness. She thought of everybody but herself.

"Vjera and I are going to the villages tomorrow to encourage more women to learn to fight. Will you join us?"

Her smile faded. I knew she couldn't bear the thought of war and more bloodshed. Honestly, I couldn't bear the thought of her in the thick of it. But I knew she wouldn't want the women of Varjutus to be ill-prepared.

"I would love to."

"Great." My hands went to my shoulders, attempting to battle my constant itch, which had come out of nowhere. "Would you mind?" I asked, pointing to my back pleadingly.

"Of course."

I turned, and Meili blissfully eased the incessant itching I couldn't shake.

"There must be something in the atmosphere here because I've been all itchy too."

When I was blissfully satisfied, we changed positions, and I scratched her back as well.

We had both fallen asleep after talking for hours and the next morning, I awoke to find Meili already gone. I got up and took off my night dress and froze when I heard the door open behind me. I turned and pulled the dress to my chest to cover me. Kane crossed his arms and gave a devilish grin.

"My timing is impeccable."

"So it is. Have you finally come to give me what I want?"

His voice was as lighted and playful as my own. "And what is that, my love? Jewels? New dresses?"

"You know I care little for those things."

Kane walked closer to me, intrigued, but he didn't give me the answer that I wanted. "We have time for that, *imana*. Don't you want it to be more special than ten hurried minutes before your morning training?"

"I do, but time is not something we're guaranteed, and I'll take anything I can get at this point."

Kane laughed. "It pleases me to no end how eager you are, my little Star. But I'm not willing to settle. When I take you for the first time, I want hours to do so."

"Oh. What a shame. Oh well." I dropped my night dress to the floor, so I didn't have an ounce of clothing on.

Kane straightened quickly, and his eyes bulged. "Amrel, help me."

Walking to the closet with my back to him, I bent over for a fake item I didn't need, ensuring he had a full view of *everything*. A feral growl erupted behind me, validating it had the desired effect. I could feel his eyes all over me, and I dreamt it was his hands instead. I stayed there, enjoying myself, my legs spread apart. He rushed up behind me and squeezed my ass. Then gripped my hips hard and possessively.

"You know, for one who wants to be a *Curadh*, you do not fight fair."

I waved him off with my hand. "I need to get dressed. You're the one who's in my room."

He touched my arms and brushed my hair across my shoulder when I stood straight. He kissed my neck, and I bent to the side, inviting him in, praying that this was the moment. Our moment. He put his hands at the top of my waist and ran them down my curves to my hips before bringing them forward, and I mentally begged him to reach all the way around and touch me more. I turned to face him, and my breasts were against his soft leather. He looked down, moaning, and leaned down to kiss me. I jumped up and wrapped my arms and legs around him, and he easily pinned me against the cabinet.

"Kane, I want you now. Please don't make me wait anymore—I need you."

His eyes flashed with intensity, his voice deep and gravelly. "No more waiting. I will make you mine until the entire galaxy can scent it off of you." He started to walk to the bed with me still in his arms, and I ran my hands through his soft onyx hair. We were both panting in need and glowing with light, the bond between us buzzing at an unbearable level, ready to be solidified.

A loud bang on the door had us stop, still panting and never more annoyed.

"Cyra! You're late! Get your behind to the camp now—you'll have an extra hour of training for your insolence!" Kal yelled.

My jaw dropped in utter disbelief. "Really!"

Kane groaned in frustration before laughing, sitting on the bed with me on top of him.

I was *livid* and more sexually frustrated than I ever thought a person could possibly be. "Doesn't he realize my behind is currently in your hands? I'm beginning to think the universe doesn't want us to bond. Or at least just your council."

"I am going to be dreaming of you naked *all day*. Amrel, help me. You are a goddess." He leaned down and kissed me, and I didn't think I'd be able to leave him.

"After this war is over, we're taking a *very long* vacation where nobody can find us," Kane said. "But until then, I'm taking a souvenir I desperately need."

"What do you…"

While looking deep into my eyes, he lowered his hands and lightly touched me between my legs, feeling my wetness. I gasped in surprise, then moaned, wanting more with my heart beating out of my chest.

"You weren't kidding, my love," he whispered softly in my ear, making me quiver. "You are quite ready. I *love* that you respond to me that way. You feel incredible."

"I think you should check again." I felt no shame about the desperation in my voice.

"I'm shaking right now, trying to control myself. You feel heavenly, my Star." He picked me up and gently placed me on the ground before he stood, rock hard and tense. I wondered how many times I'd have to look at him in that state and be unable to do anything about it.

"You are going to drive me crazy all day with your scent on me," he whispered.

"Well, I'm glad you'll have something to remember me by since I don't know when I'll see you again. I have a more intensive training schedule than ever, and I'll be going to the villages later with Vjera and Meili to try to convince more women to join the fight. Then I have my second training with Erek. I won't see you until tonight."

"How did I get so lucky to have you as my Star Mate and future Queen?"

My heart stopped for a moment at those words. How easily he accepted that I would be at his side in every aspect of his life.

"Everything you're doing for my people. How hard you're working...I love you so much."

"I love you too, Candy Kane." He always smiled when I called him that, despite how ridiculous it was, and he kissed me. Before I knew what was happening, he dug one hand into my burgundy hair possessively while lowering his other hand. His finger took a long slow swipe in my slick wetness before plunging it deep within me. I cried out in shock, convulsing at the bliss of his touch. Anytime this man filled me, it made my mind short-circuit. I could only imagine how blissful it would be to feel his cock. When I opened my eyes, he had already disappeared before I could beg for more.

Goddamn him! That man had an effortless talent to drive me absolutely insane. The absence of his touch was a new form of torture I never needed.

I dressed as quickly as I could and bolted for the training camps. Kal's look of displeasure was quite frightening, and he took it out on me in our training. I tried to incorporate Erek's suggestion of using my magical instincts to fight, but I was too distracted by Kane. It wasn't just what was left undone that was driving me crazy. I was beginning to think that delaying the bond made our separations much more unbearable. The force behind the Star Mate bond was acting as a catalyst for us to make it official. Concentrating on anything was immensely difficult, and the static in my head was intolerable.

Kal knew I wanted to take the *Warriors Sanna*, so he had been extra difficult during our session. With that and the fact that I couldn't concentrate, I walked away with countless bruises, gashes, and bloodstains. Kal was even more pissed at me by the end of the training than when we started.

"Get your head out of the clouds, Fenix! Our lives are at stake!

And I thought you wanted to be a *Curadh*! My ass." Kal huffed and stormed away, shaking his head.

"Hey, Cyra!" I turned slowly and saw Garwein and his sweet smiling face. "Oh, man, you don't look too good."

"Yeah, I was late to class."

"That'll do it. Kal doesn't wait for anyone."

I laughed and flinched at the pain in my ribs.

"Obviously, not today, but I was wondering if you'd like to train with me sometime. I'm also training for the Warrior's Sanna, so I thought it could only be beneficial."

"You are? That's great! Yes, I'd love to train with you. Maybe tomorrow would be good?"

"Sure thing. I've taken the *Warrior's Sanna* three times and failed, but I'm not one to give up that easily."

My heart sank. Garwein was a decent fighter. In fact, he was better than me. If he failed three times, what did that mean for my chances?

"Well, then plan on me drilling you for details of the test," I said, laughing.

"We're sworn to magical secrecy. I literally couldn't tell you about the test if I wanted to. But I can show you some fighting techniques that might help. You're already an amazing fighter, but every little bit counts."

He was such a sweetheart. I wondered why he wanted to be a warrior at all. Sadly, he reminded me of a Varjun version of Brendon. "You're very kind, Garwein, but I have too much to learn, so I will gladly accept your help. Come find me when you're ready to train."

"Will do, Cyra. See you then."

I limped back to my room to wash and dress.

Meili was waiting for me, and she gave me a look that said *not again*. She helped me clean and dress and quickly, healing the spot where I was bleeding while I wasn't looking so I couldn't protest. I shot her a look that made her raise her palms in defeat. Vjera barged in a few moments later and stopped when she saw us.

"Oh hell, I'm not into braiding hair and crying into our desserts."

I rolled my eyes at her, and Meili looked nervous like she felt like she was intruding. She still had the mentality of a handmaid, but she was so much more than that. Maybe it was time to tell her soon.

"I asked Meili to accompany us. I thought three women would be better than two."

"Oh, so the *cherub* is fighting now?"

"She's just helping us recruit," I said, but I could tell Meili was uncomfortable.

"Are we going to get this over with or what?" Vjera asked.

We drove to the first village, and my head was buzzing out of control from the great distance from Kane. I stumbled a little, and Meili steadied me.

"Are you alright?"

"Honestly, I can barely think straight. I think the *imana* bond is messing with me. I have a crazy humming in my head that I can't get rid of, and it's worse today than it's ever been. I don't know how much longer I can deal with it."

"It's because you haven't accepted the bond yet. The force is urging you to complete it," Vjera said.

"Cyra, still? You really need to get on that!" Meili said uncharacteristically. Vjera and I both turned our heads to her in shock and burst out laughing.

"Who knew the cherub could be so saucy! But seriously, I thought you'd be at it like rabbits by now," Vjera said, shaking her head. Meili blushed but smiled.

"Cyra, what is holding you back? I know the way you feel about each other. I see it when you look at one another," Meili asked innocently.

"There seems to always be some obligation getting in the way, but it hasn't been just that. Kane has been…hesitant. He says there is no rush, but hell…we could die tomorrow."

"Kane does not easily open up to people. I'm not surprised. But I have seen what he's like around you. He's never loved anyone as he loves you. Don't worry. The bond won't let him prude out on you forever. He won't be able to. My mother tried to resist my dad, and you heard how ironclad her will was. She made it a grand total of three days before they accepted the bond. My brother was born nine months after that."

"I didn't know you had a brother," I said.

"He died when he was young."

"I'm sorry," Meili said, her hand on her chest.

"I never met him. It was long before I was born."

We came to the first house and knocked. It was the newlyweds, Tess and Niko. "It's so great to see you again!" Tess greeted us. "Would you like to come in?"

"No, that's okay, thank you. We just wanted to make rounds to invite the women of the villages to the community training to learn how to fight." I spoke with too much enthusiasm, and it felt like I was selling her a new state-of-the-art vacuum. *Tone it back there, Cyra.*

"Oh, I would love to, but I suppose you can be the first to find out. I'm pregnant!"

"Oh, how wonderful, congratulations!" Meili beamed with her hands clapped together.

"Hot damn, that was fast," Vjera replied in shock.

"We are blessed by Amrel. We thought it could take a hundred years, but we couldn't have been luckier."

"Well, congratulations," I said as we left. This wasn't off to a great start, but there were plenty more women in the villages. We noticed a group of women standing together, so we headed for them, and I became nauseous when I saw who was with them. Fucking Caelan.

I repeated my pitch, and Caelan was the first to answer, laughing and sneering at me. "If it's a requirement to look like you after training, I'm inclined to pass."

Vjera immediately tensed up, and I knew it wouldn't end well. "Then maybe you can join as target practice, and Cyra can show you her skill by ripping your ass through your mouth. On second thought, you're right. You'd be better suited screaming like a little girl when our enemies arrive, leading them away from us so we have a better chance. We're delighted you volunteered as useless bait. Gives the rest of us a greater chance at survival."

My hand flew to my mouth, trying as hard as possible not to crack up. Damn, Vjera was really becoming a favorite of mine.

Caelan's eyes bulged out of her head.

"You're telling me the Sunya is going to fight?" another Varjun female asked.

I began to respond on Meili's behalf, but she cut me off.

"Yes. I am going to start training to learn the basics. I don't want to be completely defenseless when the time comes." She stood straighter in defiance, even if her voice shook with doubt. Little did she know what a powerhouse she was.

Vjera did a double take at her, then clapped her on the back. Meili winced and rubbed her shoulder.

It took us a few hours to get through the three villages, and we didn't get any confirmed yeses.

"I just don't get it. The Varjun women seem just as tough as the men. I'm surprised more don't want to fight."

"Varjun are all about tradition, and getting them to break it is almost impossible. There have been plenty of fierce female warriors in our history, but with our population becoming so scarce, we've encouraged the women to step back and stay safe, so we had a chance to increase our numbers."

"Well, now I feel like an asshole," I said. It never even occurred to me to think of that.

"You're not an asshole. You're just an idiot. You did the right thing, they have just as much chance of dying as the men, and our enemies don't give a shit about population count. You're an idiot because you second-guess yourself."

"I always appreciate one of your encouraging pep talks, Vjera."

"It's what makes me so special and likable. I'm a people person. I aim to please."

We all laughed as we headed our separate ways.

I ate quickly in my room, redressed in my fighting leathers, and massaged my aching arms. Training around the clock was doing a number on my body, and as I looked at my arms, that thought was validated. I had barely been able to pick up a five-pound weight my whole life, but now there was definition in my arms out of nowhere. A smile spread onto my lips in surprise, feeling my own strength, and it motivated me to see how far I could take this.

Ignoring the incessant buzzing in my head, I left to find Erek at the training camp in full *Curadh* armor. Without saying a word, he handed me a blindfold, and I took it without question, but Erek's training scared me more than anyone else's so far. Fighting blind sent my anxiety into overdrive, and I couldn't stop my hands from shaking trying to anticipate Erek's moves. With the blindfold secured, I tried to calm my mind and listen. But I didn't hear a thing as Erek pointed a knife at my back, and I flinched and jumped away.

"It's even worse than I thought. You have completely closed off a part of yourself. Seeing your surroundings should come as naturally as breathing. No wonder Jonsi drugged you. He knew the same thing and was proved right when you didn't think twice about using your gifts when you were unburdened. You will never be a *Curadh* until you accept this."

It was getting really old hearing people who didn't know me telling me what I was and what I wasn't. I was doing the best I could to merely survive. With everything that's been thrown at me so quickly, what did everyone expect of me? As if reading my mind, Erek answered.

"Cyra, you don't have the luxury of time to find yourself and come into your own. You don't have years to go through life and learn as you go. I'm sorry this destiny has been thrust upon you, but we must find a way to overcome this challenge with the hand we're dealt. Now *anticipate my attack!*" Erek boomed.

Eventually, he lost his patience, threw his weapons to the ground, and resorted to pushing, kicking, and hitting, which was more personal. After the tenth time being knocked to the ground, I screamed in anger and jumped to my feet, and the matrix of energy I'd seen before bloomed alive within me like a veil being ripped away from my eyes. The light of Erek's yellow essence glimmered like a beacon, and I tracked the outline of his lifeforce tiptoeing back to me from my left. My body stayed utterly still, feigning continued ineptitude with the soft, frayed fabric of the blindfold covering my eyes. He continued to circle me like a predator preparing for the kill so quietly that I would never have known his presence without this power of mine. When he raised his fist to strike me in the face yet again, I took his arm, bent it behind his back, and pinned him to the ground, nearly growling in primal fury.

"Finally!" Erek yelled. I felt a tingling of pride from a great distance, and I stood, turning my head to follow it to find a massively abundant and flaming violet energy of light, and I knew it was Kane watching. I also felt his surprise that I was looking directly at him with no sight. My triumph was short-lived as Erek pummeled me to the ground, causing my magical vision to sputter out.

"Lesson one for today, *pay attention* and never get distracted during a fight. Lesson two, you're going to have to hold onto your power longer than sixty seconds if you want to survive."

CHAPTER
THIRTY-FIVE

Sleep was a sure and sweet thing for only the first half of that night, as I was utterly exhausted from my intensive training. It eventually became disruptive as a vision seeped into my subconscious.

I was in a place I had never seen before, and it was mind-blowing that it was even more beautiful than Solis. It was radiantly bright, the vibrating waves of the sun a visible thing, like blistering sound waves of light. Beings with white wings flew swiftly and freely in the sky to destinations I couldn't imagine. I was sure it was the Sunya Rei, out in the open like it was a normal day. There were large, peachy-orange maagaline birds everywhere and pristine, glistening waters. My energy was absolutely booming with overabundant power being this close to the sun, and I had never felt this level of calm and serenity.

Light percussive music echoed in the streets from performers with magical instruments playing transcendent melodies on clean, light cobblestone streets. What was truly shocking was the considerable and diverse *crowds* of people, laughing and going about their day with no hint of the desperation of a crumbling galaxy. These people were living normal lives–happy, healthy, and full of power. The plant life, flowers, and trees were stunning, with an array of color, vibrance, and biodiversity. My heart ached looking at this abundance of *life* and joy.

I did a double take when I saw a familiar face passing me, and it took me a moment to realize it was Urien, about twenty years younger and without the scruff, dark bags under his eyes, and inexplicable pain in his eyes. He held hands with a stunning woman with honey-brown hair streaked with blond, glowing highlights and light brown eyes. Our distance from each other continued to grow, so I hurried after them in hopes of learning something important. They entered a sizeable mountain-style home with multiple beautiful pointed peaks on the roof and a welcoming wrap-around balcony where I pictured them sitting together on many calm, quiet nights. It overlooked the glistening water, and I could picture living in such a stunning house. I followed them inside as if I was actually a part of their world.

"Have you brought the rest of your belongings from Solis?" the woman asked with joy in her eyes. "Saniya, your people are creators. I'm sure you could conjure up anything I forgot." Urien shrugged, waiving it off like he couldn't care less about any ties of possessions.

"Sure, I may be Sunya, but I can't replicate your memories." She gently put her finger to his temple and tapped. "I don't want you to regret leaving your home. Please bring everything important to you."

He chuckled and shook his head. "Everything important to me is right here." He took her hands in his, gently putting his forehead to hers, and my breath hitched at the genuine, blissful smile I'd never seen on him before. "I can't wait to marry you in a few days, and I will *never* regret that. Wherever you are is where I want to be, always. Looma is my home now." His head tilted, lowered, and kissed her gently, and she giggled joyfully. He picked her up, spinning her around as they laughed, lost in the moment before they fell over.

They lay there for a moment, looking at each other with complete infatuation. I began fidgeting and averting my eyes, feeling like I was intruding on something intimate and special. Saniya got up quickly, and Urien and I followed her into a room filled with flowers and vegetation. My chest expanded as far as possible, taking in the wonderful fragrances.

"I've been preparing for the wedding. It's tradition for a Sunya couple to grow their most treasured plant life to present to their betrothed. I know you don't have the power to cultivate, so I've prepared extra, representing both of us. The *Indarra Fern* represents strength, protection, and fortitude, and I thought that was the perfect representation of who you are. The *Aareton* flower symbolizes eternity and undying love. And these *Lotira* blossoms represent family and fertility," Saniya concluded. Urien cleared his throat, full of emotion.

"You are the most beautiful soul I have ever met, and I can't wait to start a family with you, so make sure there's a ton of those *Lotira* flowers."

Saniya blushed and looked down.

"I knew of the Sunya tradition, and I'm sorry I cannot grow for you. But I do have something I would like to contribute."

Urien went to a box and pulled out a round object the same color as his skin. "This is the Masked Stone. It's only found on Solis, and it's very rare. I carried it around for fifty years in my pocket for luck, hoping I would find an element it was destined for one day. The stone camouflages itself to its surroundings, never really having its own identity until it finds another element it's attracted to, and it will bond with it to morph into something completely new and beautiful. One day I felt it tugging in my pocket and found this dull, lackluster rock that it was trying to connect with! I couldn't believe it had found its other half after fifty years. I imagined it could take thousands of years—if ever—to come across that one perfect stone that it was meant to link with. I kept them both, waiting for the right moment to join them together, and now is the time. I thought it was the perfect representation of us."

He put the stone next to what looked like plain ore. They snapped together and started to seep into each other, changing shape. I watched in utter fascination for a few moments as it slowly became a beautiful golden, semi-translucent sparkling crystal.

The same crystal he always touched and wore around his neck.

Saniya gasped. "Urien, that is so beautiful. It is absolutely perfect."

A massive trembling through the earth stopped their conversation, and he quickly pocketed the crystal. They ran outside, and hundreds of petrified Sunya were in the streets investigating the source of the shaking ground. I thought it was an earthquake, but it was far worse than I ever could have imagined, even knowing the fate of this planet. Off in the sky, the sun was disappearing behind something black and terrible. The blackness grew, and a maelstrom of violent wind began destroying the buildings and plant life.

"Urien, what is happening!" Saniya screamed.

"I don't know. Stay close," he said, grabbing his large dagger and pulling her to him.

The ground began to crack and split as the citizens of Looma screamed and dispersed in chaos. Trees were violently ripped from the ground before they flew up into the atmosphere toward the growing black hole. There were more screams as people pointed to the sky, where glowing winged beings beamed some sort of light energy toward the black hole.

Front and center, I recognized grandpa Amrel and Xenos fighting the force that was destroying Looma. Four of the Sunya Rei fell from the sky from injuries, and I couldn't see where they landed, but Grandpa and Xenos continued to battle the black hole.

Eventually, they seemed to freeze the expansion of it and hold it at bay, but that couldn't prevent what happened next.

The remaining trees and plant life started to shrivel, crack and break down, and the Sunya screamed as their beloved planet decayed before their eyes. Their screams only worsened as their light—their grace—slowly dimmed.

Saniya was shaking in fear at the realization of what was happening to her, and she looked to Urien in desperation.

"Saniya, No! Come, I've got you. I'm taking you to Solis," he said, trembling at his beloved, shriveling before his eyes.

"Urien, you must go now. It's too late. I feel it."

"Like hell! I'm not going anywhere without you."

Saniya looked down in horror as her radiant glow sputtered out until she was dull and gray. Her once dewy, satiny skin began to bruise over, wrinkle, and dry out as her beauty and essence were stripped slowly from her being. In her panic, she used the last of her magic before it was gone forever.

Her voice was a dry, raspy whisper. "I will always love you, no matter where my spirit has gone. You will always be the greatest fragment of my heart, the other piece to your Masked Stone. Our love has already transformed into something beautiful that cannot be broken." She raised her hands and emitted a force toward Urien, and he screamed as he started disappearing. I heard his screams vanish with him.

"Saniya, please *don't!*"

When he was gone, Saniya fell to the ground and writhed in unimaginable pain beside her people, who did the same. The beautiful, effervescent, and peaceful Sunya were being drained of their lifeforce—and within a matter of minutes, I saw the birth of the Voidlings and the fall of Looma to be known from that day forward as The Void. Saniya crawled with every bit of determination she had left as she reached another female on the ground screaming in pain. She grabbed the woman's hand to comfort her, and they didn't let go until their suffering was ended. Children were crying in the streets for their parents, who couldn't help them. Those children would be forced to live without their families and be made to procreate to continue this vicious cycle until they suffered the same fate as their parents. I looked back to Saniya and Urien's destroyed home, and her *Aareton* flowers—the flowers for eternity and undying love—were flying into the dust and debris to rest among the Voidlings on the ground.

My equilibrium was disrupted when the deafening noise suddenly disappeared, and I realized I was back on Solis, where Urien was screaming in anger. He tried to drive back to Looma, but Saniya's remaining power had blocked his drive. He was rolling around in tears, and a clank on the ground made him stop and take out the source of the noise from his pocket. It was the golden crystal made from the Masked Stone, the gift for his Saniya for their wedding that would never happen.

"No!" Urien couldn't get up from the ground, even when a dark figure entered his home and stalked toward him. It was Adelram, and his eyes were cold and empty.

"Trust me. This is for the best. Rest easy. I'm here to take away the pain," he whispered as he took Urien's torment from him by removing his memories. He waved his hand, and Urien fell asleep, finally still and quiet. As Adelram turned to leave, he had to brace himself, tears running down his face as he struggled to breathe. I knew how taking memories affected him and that Urien's painful experiences would plague him. He grabbed his chest and straightened up, leaving a broken Urien asleep on the floor.

"No!" I screamed, shooting up in bed, looking into the dark of my room in the Varjutus castle. Sweat poured down my face as I panicked, and I couldn't catch my breath as I broke down in tears. My hands shot to my temples, and I pressed firmly, trying to rid myself of the horror of what I witnessed.

Kane sat up and held me. I didn't even realize he had come to my bed.

"What is it, Cyra? Are you okay?"

"I...I saw the downfall of Looma." I explained what had happened between Urien and Saniya.

"This was different from the visions I'd had before—I was *there*. I felt the planet tremble beneath my feet and smelled the foul stench of their decaying bodies. The dust in the air made tiny cuts in my skin, and I felt the energy dissipate in the air of their destroyed planet. I felt a supreme amount of power within me before the planet died and witnessed the formation of the black hole with Grandpa and Xenos freezing it in place." I couldn't finish talking since I was utterly devastated.

"Cyra, I'm so sorry you had to see that. I can't even imagine..."

"What do I do? Do I tell Urien of his lost memories?"

"I don't know, Cyra...it might not be a good idea, but you have time to consider it. For now, let's get you back to sleep."

"I don't know how I can ever sleep again after living through that nightmare. And the worst part is....it was real. Reality is more horrifying than my nightmares could ever fathom."

But Kane gently led me down and held me tight, and his soothing pine and wood scent and his strong, protective arms wrapped around me eased my mind as I finally fell back to sleep.

CHAPTER THIRTY-SIX

When I woke the next morning, Kane was already gone. There were no more visions or dreams, so I slept soundly and felt much better. He had left a note on the bed, so I grabbed it and read his words.

Sorry I had to leave early. I didn't want to wake you after the little sleep you got. I had to force myself not to touch you, and it's getting infinitely harder by the day. The buzzing in my head is unbearable, and I'm haunted by your addicting taste and need more soon. Kal hasn't been pleased with how I've been acting lately, and eventually, he's going to have my ass.

I love you,
Your Candy Kane.

Just reading the letter made my mate bond come to life tenfold, causing me to groan in frustration, but Kal's unhappy voice yelling from down the hall doused the fire within.

"Don't make me wait for you again!" Kane wasn't the only one whose ass would be handed to them by Kal.

"Ugh." Kane was right. Training for the *Warrior's Sanna* was more challenging than I could have imagined. I checked to make sure the Sword of Istina and Grandpa's box were still in hiding for peace of mind and then made for camp.

We only got in thirty minutes of training time, but it was brutal and effective. Kal had to end training early that day, so I figured it was the perfect opportunity to train with Garwein. My legs were light and relatively pain-free since it was a short session, and I whistled to myself as I headed to the smaller camp where he and Migor trained with other Varjun males. Their resources were limited, so it wasn't much more than an open space with weapons strewn across the dirt off to one side.

"Hey, Cyra! What brings you to our neck of the camps?" Garwein smiled.

"I'm done early. Care to spar?"

His eyes lit up like I had offered him free tickets to his favorite sporting event. "You're on."

He followed me back to the main training area with his usual broadsword, so when we entered, I grabbed the same weapon from the weapons table and stalked toward him. The broadsword I could now use effectively with two hands was still somewhat cumbersome for me but not nearly as painful as it once was.

"Ready?" Garwein smiled and wiggled his eyebrows at me. I laughed and ran for him. With Kal, Migor, Ondour, Kane, and even Erek, it always felt like a fight to the death.

Kill or be killed.

But it was a joy to spar with Garwein. It felt more like a dance, an example of artistry. It was *fun*. While I still received some knicks and bruises, I wouldn't leave the camp today in a near crawl. That's not to say he wasn't skilled…Garwein had tremendous expertise, and I learned new tricks through his maneuvers, but I again wondered why he wanted to be a *Curadh* warrior. I supposed it was about the honor of serving his planet as an elite fighter.

"Cyra, you've grown by leaps and bounds. I've got some sweat glistening on my brow. Not so good for my ruggedly handsome warrior façade."

"You look just as deadly with a bit of sweat…perhaps even more so."

"Why don't we try something new? Have you ever thrown knives? Something tells me you'd be excellent at it, and it's a great distance tool since you're still working on your magical ability."

I immediately lit up in excitement at his words. Why hadn't we tried that yet?

"No! Kal has not trained me in throwing knives. I'd love to try." We walked to the weapons table, and Garwein handed me a faded, worn twelve-count knife holster to strap to my thigh. I had my doubts that the scratched, shredded leather wouldn't stretch out and break off while wearing it, but I wasn't about to complain. My hands slowly reached out with reverence as if I had just received the greatest treasure, and I was certain my eyes were glowing.

"Yes…I think I will enjoy these immensely." I was practically salivating as I strapped the holster to my thigh over my pants while Garwein set up a target.

He showed me the proper stance and throwing techniques, demonstrating himself as he spoke. Garwein explained the appropriate rotation of the knives based on distance. I started relatively close, holding the knife blade first. The moment I released it, there was some kind of intrinsic skill within me, and I knew it would make contact.

"Wow…impressive! Double your distance and try again." Practically skipping there, I did as Garwein suggested and hit the target right in the bullseye. Without waiting, I ran to the furthest point of the training camp and used all my strength and a little energetic magic to propel the next knife the great distance to the target and again hit the bullseye. It could have been my excitement that enabled some magic to guide me, lowering my inhibitions and doubt. Or it could have been beginner's luck. I wasn't going to dwell too much on it, just appreciate my fortune.

"You're a natural!" Garwein yelled from across the field.

My hips swayed as I approached him with a swagger that should have made me blush at my own arrogance, but I didn't care. I was happy to finally be excellent at *something*. "Do you think you could get me my own set of these? And don't tell Kal about it...I don't want him to know."

"Your secret is safe with me," he winked. "I've got to run, so let's end here for today."

My fingers went to my temple, and I gave him a small salute as I walked away, still strutting, remembering Kane's words as a devilish smile took over my face. *The element of surprise is a weapon in itself.*

The next time I fought Kal, I had the throwing knives hidden. When he least expected it, I turned my back to him, grabbed a throwing knife, twirled to face him, and threw it directly into his thigh. Kal's eyes bulged in shock, and he fell to his knees without a sound. The bulging veins and muscles in his neck did all the screaming for him.

He kneeled on the ground for a few seconds, unsure what to say, until he mumbled, "Ow..." Kal looked at me in a different light from that moment forward, and I had legitimately bested the greatest warrior in the galaxy for the first time.

A few weeks went by in a similar pattern of training and preparing, the monotony and routine giving me something to cling to–something to keep my mind occupied and my body primed like a well-oiled machine. Kane and I were so busy around the clock that we barely saw each other, which only made my ever-present lust grow to an exasperating level. My training was really improving, and I had even managed to get a few hits in during my blindfolded sessions with Erek—although if you asked him, he still wasn't satisfied with my level of performance. I was pleased that more women continued to show little by little for every community training session, including some of the Solians. I think half of the reason for their appearance was fear of Vjera, and half were convinced by Meili joining the training. Either way, I was glad they were preparing themselves for the inevitable.

When Kane and I finally had a moment to be together, we headed to his study, but before we could enter, the light on his shoulder tattoo lit up.

A weighted pressure formed on my chest at that innocent-looking glow, instantly knowing it wasn't good. "I've never seen your King's Mark light up before."

"It's the people—they're in danger." The true panic in his voice made my gut wrench into knots. He grabbed me quickly and drove to the site of the call, which was Baum village.

There was mass hysteria everywhere, with villagers being attacked and screams echoing in the darkness. It appeared to be the Bellum, raiding and attacking the Varjun people. Kane quickly touched a double-crossed sword tattoo I hadn't seen him use before, plus Merick's call sign.

The *Curadh* appeared in their full garb only a moment later, and Merick yelled angrily, prepared to attack. Kane magically transformed his clothing into Curadh armor to match his brethren.

"Kal, Ondour—go to Riva village. Migor and Erek—to Leht. Merick—get me eyes on the enemy and shield as many people as you can. Cyra, you're with me."

Although my hands shook, I nodded without hesitation, ready to join the fray to keep the villagers safe.

Kane held out his hands as he concentrated, and a plethora of weapons appeared before us, and I ignored the fact that even though they were well cared for, they were old and well-used. Thankfully I was always wearing fighting leathers these days, so I was prepared with my dagger and throwing knives, and I grabbed a familiar sword I knew I was skilled with. I hesitated momentarily, my breath increasing and my heart racing, realizing this was the first real battle I was witnessing, and it scared me senseless. Combat training was *vastly* different from standing amid screaming men and women, blood and gore spewing into the air—people who have become dear to me dying right before my eyes. Quickly returning to my senses, I shook the tremors away and sprang into action.

I ran to the closest hut to find a Varjun already dead while a Bellum was scavenging their belongings, especially the food, stuffing things into various dust-covered bags he had on his person. He locked eyes with me with no hint of surprise, thoroughly prepared for a fight, and ran at me screaming, but I easily struck him down.

Days.

Weeks.

Months.

I had worked my ass off endlessly, training to become a seasoned warrior, and this kill with a sword took nothing but seconds. Blood pooled around him, and while I had killed some attackers on Solis with magic, this felt personal and real. This was a mortal man fighting for his own survival.

Looking down at the poor Varjun, who was gone, I only spared one more moment of remorse before running to the next hut to find a Bellum man pinning down a woman with his hand around her throat. It was then that I realized I didn't care what dire conditions they suffered on The Void, they had no right to pillage in this way, and it sent me into a burning rage, screaming with extended arms shooting flame from them until he was completely incinerated. My endless training paid off as I was able to control my power, and he was the only thing that caught fire. I handed the woman an extra dagger I had and ran out to the crowd.

A Bellum with a full bushy beard and missing teeth was running at full speed toward Celestine, the Solian noble I had once bought a black dress what seemed like a lifetime ago. Her body was visibly quaking, and my body went numb, knowing I was too far to reach her even as I ran.

Right before the Bellum man raised his blunt weapon to strike her, she stilled as she saw a sword beside her. Something snapped into place in that moment, and it appeared as if she had woken from an eons-long trance. Her foot kicked the helm of the sword, causing it to lift into the air deftly. She grabbed hold of it with a rage and certainty I had never seen on her before. Her body circled three hundred and sixty degrees as she swirled her sword with her, decapitating the Bellum with a seasoned warrior's skill, precision, and mastery.

Nobleseru.

Blaze had told me that the nobles of Solis were once Nobleseru, heroes of the Empire of Knights of Solis. While her memories were taken from her, some survival instinct must have kicked into overdrive, and her body knew what to do.

When I reached her, her eyes were open wide with utter disbelief. I didn't have time to explain, so I patted her on the shoulder and said, "Welcome back."

Off in the distance, Kane was fighting a few Bellum men at once. They all had enormous cloth bags filled with the livelihood of the Varjun, and the air around him seemed to be drained of the small light that was available on Varjutus. Five more Bellum ran toward him only to end up blind in his darkness. But, oddly enough, I could see beneath it—another thing our bond shared. Kane ran away from them while growing black energy in his hands. I'd seen him use this move before—all the Bellum before him were ripped apart in two halves. Gore and sinew spilled everywhere in their vicinity, and I quickly had to bite down the bile rising in my throat. Everyone knew war was vile and cruel, but experiencing the reality of it, smelling the metallic tang of blood and death, and hearing the screams and clash of weapons were beyond imagining.

Through our bond, I was able to feel the dark energy magic Kane had used, and while he experienced a moment of intense grief and guilt, he swallowed it down to save his people.

Before I could find my next target, I was blasted back by a flaming boulder that had fallen before me. Looking up, I saw about fifty more of them falling to the ground, causing the earth to quake and people to falter on their feet. I closed my eyes and searched for that magical construct of sight, and I found one being shining more brilliantly than the others.

Their meige was here, and he was using his magic against us.

This mayhem needed to stop. The pathetically weak huts were crushed and destroyed by the gigantic stones. The Varjun people were fighting as best they could, but I could see the fear and fatigue on their faces. My course of action was abundantly clear. I ran as fast as I could for the meige and would destroy him.

"Cyra, wait!" Kane yelled from behind, but I didn't slow down.

The meige looked down at me from the hill he was standing on, and a wicked grin emerged on his thin, hollow face. He held a long staff with a glowing crystal at the top, and it flickered at his command as if that was his energy source. His robes billowed around his tall thin frame as he shot a force at me that sent me flying backward countless feet.

My ears rang as my head hit the earth, and when I rolled to my side to stand, my vision was doubled and blurry. The meige appeared weak and almost sickly, but the great power he was able to use was undeniable. Kane's cries for me were muffled as I regained my bearings, and he knelt beside me to help me up.

"I'm fine!" I shot back up, brushing off the pain. Without thinking, I shot out my hands and emitted my flame toward him in anger. He bellowed in laughter and snuffed it out with a wave of his hand. Not knowing what a meige was, I didn't know his weakness or how to defeat him, but I had distracted him from using more destructive boulders.

Kane started to grow his energy ball again, and the meige reached out his hand and used a force that seemed to interfere with Kane's ability to use it. Kane fell to his knees and was experiencing extreme pain from whatever the meige was doing.

It sent me into a rage.

My second sight immediately burst to life, and I saw an energy throbbing around me as if begging to be used, flowing directly from the meige. My jaw clenched to the point of pain while I sucked in all that energy, then blasted it from my hands and knocked the meige backward thirty feet. Kane looked up at me in shock but smiled.

"Let's go," he ordered, dismissing his lingering pain.

We passed rows of tiny destroyed homes and scattered wooden debris. I envisioned that every treasured little shard and splinter once held together large dreams and memories of a special and unique community. It fueled my fire even more as we ran to where another group was fighting, and I was elated that the Varjun community was holding their own, which was clearly a shock for the Bellum. The Varjun had some injuries and deaths but managed to slay most intruders and keep them from stealing their essentials. Kane and I assisted in taking down the rest.

Jonsi emerged with a sheen on his brow, panting and fatigued with a blood-soaked sword. "Is Baum safe? I'll start treating the wounded."

"Yes, I think we've driven them out and managed to save some of the resources."

Needing to make sure, I closed my eyes and searched around me.

"Cyra? What is it?" Jonsi asked, putting his arm on my shoulder.

I opened my eyes but was still seeing with my other sight. "I'm searching for the meige. There! He's in Riva Village."

"Cyra, your eyes!" Kane exclaimed. "They're swirling silver with no pupils."

I came out of my sight and looked at him with confusion.

"She's doing exactly what she needs to be doing," Jonsi said with pride.

Kane nodded, shrugging it off. "If the meige is in Riva, then that's where we're going. Jonsi, see to the people."

Out of habit, Kane pulled me close, and we appeared in the run-down village of Riva. I gasped at the complete decimation. There were raging fires everywhere, barely any huts left standing, and bodies scattered throughout the village that I couldn't yet discern whether they were Varjun or Bellum.

A Bellum man crept up beside Kane and cut his arm, but I sighed with relief that it was a small scratch. Kane stuck his sword through him with ease. I stopped dead when I heard the voice of the meige inside my head, and I saw him off in the distance smiling at me.

"So, you're the one all this big fuss is about? You're just a frightened girl with no significant abilities of her own. Your parlor tricks and semi-skilled fighting ability are surprisingly small."

A group of more Bellum ran for us, and Kane was forced to turn his attention away from me and fight the onslaught as I zeroed in on the meige.

What surprised me most was that he looked like a mortal man. He spoke while looking almost amused. "We're doing nothing but working on how to open the *mikla*—and when we do, this will no longer be your galaxy."

"All this time, you've had the *mikla,* and you have no idea how to open it. I think you run your mouth a little too much without being able to deliver. Typical self-absorbed asshole if I ever heard one."

I reached inward for my second sight and saw his red energy growing, preparing for an attack. At that moment, I knew exactly what to do.

"Kane! Follow me!"

He took down the Bellum he was fighting and ran after me without question. Approaching the meige at full speed, I waited for him to throw his magical attack and saw the moment it released through him. I grabbed tremendous energy from all directions and shot a reflective force toward the meige that pinned him to the ground, trapped in a bubble of my magic he couldn't escape. Kane and I reached him, and he was screaming and thrashing inside, trying to escape.

"You see, meige...I don't waste my energy on useless talk and unfounded self-glorification. I prefer action, and it makes your astonishment all the more sweet," I said, finally returning my own smile.

"And you know what I'm excited about?" Kane asked.

"What's that, darling?"

"I have this fancy new power where I can share my mate's gifts. Like penetrating shields." Kane raised his dagger and drove it through the meige's heart as he screamed for mercy.

"Enjoy hell, asshole." Kane sneered at him.

We looked around, and even though the poor villagers' homes were destroyed, they cheered, and the sound resonated through me as I sighed with relief. Merick and Kal appeared before us, and I could already see Meili healing the wounded. I had taken the meige's staff, interested in studying it to see what it could do.

"Thank Amrel for the extra training. Our people were a force to be reckoned with. There are minimal casualties," Kal said. "The other *Curadh* are helping the villagers."

"I returned twice with intel, but you were in the middle of a fight with the meige. Nice work, by the way," Merick said to Kane and me.

"Let's wash up. Then we'll address the people and their destroyed houses. If you return before me, start assessing the situation and seeing to the people's needs," Kane said, looking at Kal and Merick.

Kane pulled me close, and we appeared in his bedroom, but he didn't let me go when we arrived. "You were amazing."

I blushed and stared into his green eyes. "We did it together."

Kane walked me to his bathroom, lowered his mask and hood, and started to remove his armor. I got a wet cloth and began wiping away the dirt, blood, and sweat as he watched me intently, letting me erase the signs of battle. He continued taking off his armor, but he started to cough and bent over, appearing to be in pain.

"What is it?" I asked, my worry starting to grow.

"Not sure. I feel...off." His coughing intensified, and he hunched over, unable to breathe.

I felt a tickle at my throat as well, like I couldn't swallow, and a burning began to rise in my forearm—only it wasn't my pain I was feeling. It was Kane's.

"Your arm!" I ripped off the protective armor near the wound, and the tiny scratch the Bellum had given him had turned black and purple, with his veins darkening near the site of impact.

He looked up at me with utter shock on his face.

"Kane, what is it? I'm going to get Meili."

His head lowered as he stared into a void, utterly speechless for a moment. His look of defeat had me nearly jumping out of my skin. His voice was so soft that it was a struggle to hear. "It's too late for Meili. The poison has already spread too far. I was struck by a Varjun dagger."

My heart fluttered in my chest, struggling to pump my blood because it felt like he was crushing it. "No...no. That can't be. How would a Bellum get a Varjun dagger? I'm going to get Meili!"

The desperation in his voice immediately made me pause. "No, please...please don't leave me. Based on this wound, I don't have long left and don't want to die without you with me." Kane's breath was already labored and wheezy, and I felt his excruciating pain and inability to air his lungs.

His blood felt acidic and putrid, eating away at his cells and tissue. He slowly melted away from the inside out, and a single tear escaped his eye.

I was overcome with panic, crying, and struggling to breathe with full body shakes. I was confused between his physical pain and my mental pain, but I was in a full-blown anxiety attack. Kane started to slump to the floor, and I steadied him down and held him in my arms.

"Kane! You can't do this to me. I can't live without you. If not for me, then for Eredet. We need you for what's to come. Please... my love. This isn't happening."

His skin was pasty and pale, and his wheezing slowed to a dangerous pattern. "I've waited for you for almost two thousand years, and the wait was well worth it. You bring light where there is darkness and hope to all around you. The fire and passion in you are awe-inspiring. It takes my breath away how much you care about people. I see you, Cyra, and you are filled with love. You are what I never could have even dreamed of for myself, the best thing to ever come into my life. Thank you for that."

My head shook violently as tears fell from my cheeks. "Stop. Stop talking like that."

He gave a small smile in an attempt to calm me down. "Do not worry, my Star Mate. I can die in peace, finally knowing love and true happiness. "He inhaled deeply and struggled with his last words. "I came *alive* when I met you."

Kane's eyes began to flutter and close, and another tear rolled down his face. His breath was so faint I couldn't hear it. My screams for help went unanswered.

It wasn't possible that this was the end of our story. We were just beginning, and he helped me to understand the precious beauty and joy life could bring despite our dying worlds. Every precious moment we had together flashed through my mind in rapid succession, and I refused to let this happen.

I held his wound in a panic, and my second sight returned without trying to summon it. I looked down at Kane and saw the black infestation of the poison like his skin was translucent—and it was almost at his heart. Without thinking or feeling, I transcended to something else—or somewhere else. It was the same feeling I had when I stepped into the gate at the bottom of the ocean and was connected to something higher and divine. And even though I didn't understand how I could access this plane of energy and existence, I instinctively knew what to do.

My hand hovered over the wound, and I slowly and carefully drained the poison from his body. I blocked out his shallow, labored breathing that would have normally shut me down in a panic and focused on what I needed to do. The world around me was gone except for the task at hand. When every last drop of poison was extracted, I eradicated it, so it was unmade.

My hand drifted back down to his wound, and it glowed as a white healing energy repaired his veins, damaged tissue, blood loss, and skin. When it was done, I came out of my trance and started to breathe again. I didn't know how I'd just managed that or where it came from, but I gently shook Kane and tried to wake him.

"Kane, are you okay? Did it work?" He was unresponsive and limp in my arms, so I held him closer to me and cried into him. I held him to my chest and put his hand in mine. I wouldn't let him go, even if I were unsuccessful. I couldn't be parted from this man.

A small moan escaped him, and I screeched with joy.

"What happened...how am I alive right now?" His voice was strained as if he'd just undergone the fight of his life, which he had.

I leaned back to look at him, an absolute mess crying tears of joy. "Oh, thank God!"

"Cyra—did you...*heal me?*"

"Yes," I whispered.

His eyes squinted as he shook his head in disbelief. "That is a wound even the most gifted healers would not have been able to save me from."

"I don't know how I did it. I just knew I needed to. I would move the stars in the sky if it would keep you with me."

His eyes softened as his hand touched my chin. "I don't doubt you could do it with your power."

He sat up and held me, and I climbed onto his lap as he laid his head on my shoulder. I ran my hands through his silky hair and let him regain his strength.

"I felt the bond slip away. It was one of the scariest moments of my life," I said, looking him in the eyes. He looked back at me with sadness.

"I *never* want to face death again without knowing you're my mate in body and soul. I don't want another moment to pass where we are not bonded," Kane said, his eyes glowing with intensity.

"Never again," I whispered.

Kane held my face with both hands and slowly inched closer as our breaths intertwined. "I am ready," he whispered, and the static grew as that magnetic force pulled our bodies together.

How long had I waited for him to say those words? The mere utterance of them nearly drove me over the edge and made me moan in lust. Without conscious thought, my hand immediately went to touch myself, and I blushed at my lack of restraint. His smile was knowing and proud, and his eyes glowed in fierce antici-pation. I needed this man, and I needed him *now*.

Well, after a quick wash.

We undressed and cleansed away the effects of the battle, knowing that our friends were caring for the citizens and assessing the situation. We had this moment. The people were safe, and we weren't leaving until we were one.

After we dried off, a soft glow emitted from our bodies, and I kissed him with greater longing than I'd ever felt before. It wasn't with a delicate sweetness but with a strong, all-consuming need.

Lost in this blinding passion, he moaned as he touched my breast, full and aching with anticipation. Kane stood back and closed his eyes, moaning and trying to compose himself. It nearly brought a tear to my eye, knowing that this divinely beautiful man inside and out could so thoroughly worship someone like me.

In one fluid movement, he grabbed my ass, hoisting me up so I could wrap my legs around him, and he carried me to the bed, gently letting me down to stand near the edge. He took his hands and tantalizingly touched from my collarbone down my bare breasts making me inhale sharply, down my torso before he knelt before me. I had to brace myself on the bed to keep standing straight. My breathing intensified as he slipped his finger through my slickness, and he groaned with approval.

"You are so perfect, my Star Mate. I love how you are always ready and willing to take me."

It was an immediate, intense desire coursing through my body. Each soft touch was like explosives bursting through every inch of me. I was already near orgasm, his gentle touch like nothing I'd ever experienced.

It wasn't simply the touch of a man but one of an indestructible soul mate crafted from the cosmos just for me. He found my nub and circled his finger slowly. Kane gently emitted a slight vibration that made me wild, and the weakness of it made me pulse against him, begging for more. He chuckled, delighting in my sexual torment.

He was a drug. A stimulant I would *never* be able to get enough of, and with only three or four strokes of his hand on me, I came... *hard.* How could he make me climax by barely doing anything to me?

He chuckled, keeping his finger where it was and slipping a finger deep inside me. I was so wet and needy for him that there was no resistance whatsoever.

I shivered, standing in place for a near minute...convulsing again, his finger thrusting in and out of me. My God, Kane barely needed to do anything to make my whole world explode. I was saturated for him, my need soaring by the second, the two orgasms clearly not enough.

No, it wasn't. Because he wasn't inside of me, and that's what I needed more than anything. My desperation made me dangerously close to erupting in flames because of my connection to this man.

As I caught my breath, utterly astonished at what just happened, he stood and looked into my eyes. "You are so magnificent."

He should take a look in the mirror. Kane was beyond perfection. He was the one that should be worshiped.

His towel was still tight around his hips, so I released it. I was finally rewarded by witnessing the full breathtaking view of Kaanan Distira. And it indeed took me a second to inhale again. "Wow. I don't think I'll ever see anything more wonderful again in my life."

He smiled at me, and this time I noticed a little pink flush on his cheeks. He picked me up again, holding me by my bottom with my legs wrapped around him tightly. He raised his head and smelled the air, and let out a feral growl, attuned to the state of me.

"Fuck, Cyra. Your desire for me will forever be my favorite scent."

He slipped a finger into me again, and I screamed out in bliss. His dominance was put to good use while he was in utter control of my body, and I was not about to complain. I stayed limp in his arms, letting him have his way with me. He kissed me slowly and deeply, and I could feel his rising desperation through our connection. It sent me over the edge, whimpering for more.

"Cyra, you have no idea how crazy your moans make me, and I'm nowhere near finished with you."

Oh lord. If his mere touch could drive me to ecstasy, I couldn't imagine what would happen when I could experience the bliss of him deep within me.

He seemed to read my thoughts, throwing me onto the bed, so I laid before him, bare and open…inviting him in with everything I had. It took all my resolve to avoid touching myself again because I couldn't bear one more moment without him in me.

"I feel your acceptance, Star. I feel your desire, your need, and your *lust*," he said as he crawled over me with his cock trailing over my body as I arched my back, relishing the sensation.

I sighed with a mix of hunger and agony, the mating bond tugging at our souls and emotions to complete this act. It made it so I didn't just need his body inside of me. I needed his essence.

My eyes lit with fire, and Kane smiled with a smug satisfaction. He savored how I reacted to him, and I had no control over it. I didn't want the control. I was fully invested in the primal lust of it all.

He reached down to my neck, gently kissing and teasing his tongue over my skin before he lowered and held both of my breasts, taking one in his mouth, tasting and exploring me. While I was still in his mouth, he lowered his hand, teasing me again near where I was begging for him to touch me. But instead, he touched every inch around it.

"Kane, please."

"What is it, my love?"

"I've had enough. I need you inside me, now."

"But I have barely begun with you. I have so much left to explore."

"If you don't fuck me now—"

"As you wish."

He lowered his face right above mine and never took his eyes off me as he tantalizingly put himself at my entrance. He waited for just a moment or two as I became even more saturated for him, and then he entered me so painstakingly slowly.

Kane paused for a moment and let out a moan of his own—we both felt each other's pleasure, and it was an overload of emotion.

He inched further into me, with his hand on my cheek and his eyes so bright that I saw a gentle green light around them. His lips locked with mine again, and I couldn't get enough of his intoxicating taste.

In a land of perpetual darkness, he was a true beacon of light of life shining through to my soul. And when his entire length was finally in me, we moaned simultaneously, hands intertwined and dizzy from this unparalleled bliss. Relief rushed through me as I tightened around his body within mine.

He kissed me and began long, slow strokes in and out, and I grabbed him to push him in further. With every stroke Kane made, I could feel something tightening within us. Something I didn't know was loose and frail to begin with. We could both feel the coils of our bond strengthening, hardening, and growing more precious by the second. I had never felt so close to another being, and I knew I never would again. Kane was my beginning and my end. He was my everything for as long as we were lucky enough to have one another–the ultimate beauty of life. He was the piece of me that I always felt was missing, and now that he was in me, I felt a completeness I never could have imagined.

His movements slowed as he realized his power was flowing from him, and there was an immediate panic in the tenseness of his body, but I turned his face so his eyes were locked on mine. Yes, death energy permeated the room so powerfully and abundant it would have killed anyone else. But I was fully open to him, and my power released from me to meet his, so they bonded together to create a beautiful balance.

"See, there is nothing you can do to hurt me. I was made for you, and you for me."

Utter relief washed through him, and we both got lost in his thrusts as they quickened and became more desperate, more filled with need to see what was waiting for us on the other side. I felt our inner light brighten and spin around us in a vortex, binding us together in a cocoon as we prepared to jump into a new life together.

Kane moved faster within me, and we knew we were almost there. As we began to climax at the same time, Kane released his essence within me, and we screamed out in pleasure.

Something within us snapped and sealed securely as we both came again, feeling a new level of connection as Kane filled me some more. When he was utterly spent, he gently laid down on top of me and gazed into my eyes with wonder. With him still strong inside me, he whispered, "I have never experienced anything more astounding before in my life."

"Neither have I. I feel all of you like you're a part of me. I felt it to a small degree before, but nothing like I do now. We are one, Kane." I kissed him, and he held my face.

"I feel whole," he said. "For the first time in my life, I feel...right."

"I couldn't agree more. That part of me that I always felt was missing was you. It was you, Kane."

He gave me the biggest, brightest smile I'd ever seen on him, and it damn near melted my heart again. We took a moment to catch our breath and come back to this plane of existence.

"It's quiet," he said.

"The buzzing...it's gone." I opened my palm to him, and he placed his against mine. There was no snap, no electric shock. We were bonded, two halves that were once being coerced together by forces unknown didn't have to fight anymore. We were transformed into something new, just like the Masked Stone.

He nodded, fighting a tear, and put his forehead to mine. He lifted me up in one fluid movement, never breaking our connection until I was on his lap again.

"How are you still hard after coming twice?"

"Oh, Cyra. That was just my appetizer. I've got hours of fun left in me."

I smiled and raised myself up his long, thick shaft as he moaned out again before slowly lowering down.

"You feel fucking incredible. I could live in you all day long."

"I'm ready to test that," I said with a grin.

He groaned, but this time it wasn't in pleasure. "I must see my people. I feel bad as it is that I haven't joined them yet. I know Jonsi and my team are caring for everyone, but I need to be there."

"I know. I'm sorry. We should go."

"Yes. We should. But since I'm already in you, it would be a shame to waste it without one more quick round." He grabbed my ass and began moving me up and down on him, and I laughed in delight as I took over. We made it all of sixty seconds before we climaxed again…twice.

I cleaned up as quickly as possible, but it took longer than I thought, considering how much fun we'd just had. When we finished dressing, we wasted no time driving to Baum village. I felt like a new woman. Like I'd just beaten the end boss and got a bonus level up of ten levels.

I felt stronger, surer, and more confident. That constant voice of doubt and confusion in my head was muted for the moment. Again —I felt whole. And when I looked at Kane, I could see a change in him as well. Although our lives would never be the same because of what we just did together, our reality was unchanged, and we had to face the consequences of our recent attack.

"What happened?" Merick asked, looking at us. "We all felt a force blast from the castle. We thought it was another attack."

Kane and I looked at each other in slight embarrassment and tried not to give ourselves away.

"I was struck with a Varjun dagger."

"What!" Kal boomed.

"What can we do?" Merick matched Kal's panic.

"No…" Meili was truly afraid. As a healer, she knew what that meant with the amount of time the poison was in his body.

"That can't be." Vjera was beside herself, trying not to shake.

"Cyra healed me, and now there's no sign of the injury." He raised his forearm to show everyone.

"That's impossible. That poison was in your system for far too long, nobody could heal a cut from a Varjun dagger." Merick shook his head in disbelief.

"Nobody except the daughter of Our Creator," Kal said quietly. It seemed to end the issue, but Meili looked at me with awe and smiled. Vjera crossed her arms and tilted her head in puzzlement.

I was thankful when Kane moved on. "What's the damage report?"

"Riva is completely wiped out. There's extensive damage in Baum village from the fire boulders but I think we can repair most of it. Leht has barely any damage but faced the biggest theft of food. We were able to take back about fifty percent of what the Bellum tried to steal, but that's still too much—the people will go hungry until our next delivery of food. There were three casualties and Jonsi and Meili have been seeing to the wounded," Kal reported.

"The Bellum must be getting desperate, I'm sure their supply of food has stopped," I said.

Kane nodded in agreement. "And desperate men are dangerous."

"I will write to Urien and Bad and see if they can get us any resources to help rebuild," I offered.

"Thanks, my love. In the meantime, we will open the castle grounds to the people for shelter and protection and we'll house as many as we can in our available rooms."

· · ·

F or the next few days, we cleaned through the debris, took anything useful, then made camps on the castle grounds for the Varjun people without homes. Urien and Bad both came through for us in our time of need and were able to secure enough wood to repair most of the damage in Riva. The Varjun of every village worked together to rebuild, knowing that we could be attacked again at any time. I marveled at these people and their resolve. The way they came together in crisis gave me hope at Kane's words. Maybe love was enough to save us.

We made the community training a daily occurrence, and most Varjun showed up, including a surrendering Caelan. She couldn't make eye contact with me, but I didn't care. It was enough that she was ready to take our threat seriously.

After multiple attempts, the Solians took part in them as well, and many of them were able to reactivate their past Empire of Knights training.

The *Curadh* introduced hand-to-hand combat into the mix of the training. Kane had explained that there could come a time when weapons were scarce, and we'd have nothing to use but our own bodies to protect us. Kal gave me extra on this training since he said my sword skills were significantly improved. Hand-to-hand was vital, but it wasn't going to be my strong suit.

I used magic a few times against Kal but he forced me to stop. His training was physical ability, while Erek's was focused on magic. They were making sure I was proficient at all aspects of fighting, and I couldn't have been more grateful for their help. I had never felt stronger or more agile in my life, and my confidence level was greatly increased for any surprise attacks to come.

During my first session with Erek after the Bellum attack, he handed me my blindfold and I told him I didn't need it. He gave me a devilish grin and said, "Then let's dance." My eyes instantly became that swirling mist of silver—no doubts or hesitation. "That look alone will strike terror into your opponent."

I didn't know what had changed in me. If it was the sealed connection I had made with Kane, making me feel whole or the attack on the people that had come to feel like family, but I didn't struggle with my internal sight nearly as much anymore. It wasn't perfect all of the time, but I had improved by leaps and bounds. It finally felt like I was using an extension of myself rather than fighting to use a power I wasn't sure was mine.

When sparring with Erek I held my own, it even shocked me that his magical ability was no match for my own. He finally took off his mask and hood for the first time so I could see his face, and I was beyond surprised—Erek looked to be in his late fifties, and for the Varjun, I knew that meant he was *very* old. I remembered he said he was great friends with Jonsi—maybe they grew up together.

"Hey, Cyra!" Erek and I turned, and Garwein was standing with a terrifying-looking Morningstar flail. "Since you're so advanced now, want to try something new?" He wiggled his eyebrows, and I couldn't help but laugh.

Erek chuckled under his breath and walked away. "Good luck with that one!"

Migor arrived to watch, his hands crossed in front of him and his feet far apart. After observing the weapons I decided to grab a shield and a short sword.

"Only pansies without magic would use a shield!" Migor heck-led. I rolled my eyes, but when I saw Garwein shrug and nod, I threw the items back on the table and walked to Garwein bare-handed. More onlookers gathered around in interest, excited to watch a match with the small, skinny Solian girl with a massive, armed Varjun warrior.

My arrogance was probably premature with my level of skill but I went with it. "Alright then, Garwein. Give it your best shot."

My smile grew feral as my eyes glazed over in the silver swirly mist with no pupils, and Garwein yelped and stepped backward. The crowd was boisterous with laughter, and I was pleased to see that Erek was right. I did strike fear in my opponent. My *experienced* opponent.

I put my hands behind my back and Garwein charged at me, swinging his chained Morningstar around a few times to gain momentum until he went for the kill, releasing the force straight for my head. I deftly dodged the attack and twisted out of the way, and stood facing him, unfazed and waiting for more.

For the first time fighting me, Garwein was enraged. Although it surprised me, I didn't let it distract me. Using my second sight, time seemed to move in a state of slow motion, and it was very easy to anticipate his movements. I could see the energy move in his muscle tissue, and I could follow the trajectory of that movement to see the impending attack before he even made it. His next swing was a fake-out. He threw the Morningstar to the ground next to me then immediately dragged it across the earth to trip me.

When I jumped over it, he brought it up diagonally to try to disorient me and make contact, but I was able to flip backward out of the way and the crowd gasped in shock. Nobody was more in shock than Garwein, and it fueled his anger. He continued to swing the Morningstar overhead. He almost confused me into missing his attack, but I realized the outcome and twisted out of the way with a three-hundred-sixty-degree turn. I kicked the spiked ball with my heavy-duty boots back toward him so it punched him in the gut, forcing him to fall to the ground.

I lifted my arms in victory, and the crowd was mad with cheers. Not one person in that large crowd would have suspected that I would be the victor in this fight—no weapons and no shield. And although I could tell I had hurt Garwein's feelings, I was incredibly proud of myself.

I walked to Garwein and held out my hand to help him up. His reddish-brown eyes flashed a glow of anger but then he softened and reached for me, allowing me to help him. I hugged him and thanked him for the incredible lesson.

"I doubt I did much help there. You handed me my ass."

"I hope you're not angry with me. I'd love to continue our lunches and our training sessions together."

Garwein smiled at me. "Of course, Cyra. We're in this together. Actually, I've been meaning to give you this." He brought out a small silver object.

"It's a warrior's pin you can put on your holsters or leathers. It's meant for good luck. It's a replica of the Noctis flower. I'd recommend putting it on your throwing knives holster since you always have it on," he said, smiling. He had given me those knives himself.

I was so touched. "Garwein, that's amazing. Thank you so much!" I took it and immediately put it on my holster, and went in for a hug.

"With you on our side, the Varjun already have better luck. Now a Varjun is giving some back to you."

After about another month of brutal training, Erek and Kal took me to see Kane and Jonsi.

"We believe Cyra is ready for the *Warrior's Sanna.*"

Jonsi gave a look of pride and wasn't at all surprised. Kane tried to hide his shock, giving a pathetic smile, but I could feel his fear which I had never really felt from him to this degree before. That was saying a lot since I'd seen him fight the Guardians and the Bellum before. It took me off guard, but I realized it was fear for my safety. He knew I was experiencing his genuine emotion, so he quickly spoke, trying to mask his anxiety.

"It normally takes a warrior years to be recommended for the *Warrior's Sanna,* and many fail multiple times. Some are never able to complete the challenge."

Kane walked to me and took my hands in his. "But you are not most people. You are truly remarkable, and I cannot tell you what it means to me that you want to undertake this serious Varjun rite. The ultimate test that marks the best and strongest Varjutus has to offer. I have no doubts in your abilities, and Kal and Erek have *never* recommended anyone that they didn't feel worthy. I would be honored if you took the test, and once you're a *Curadh*, you would officially become recognized as one of the Varjun people. The test will commence one week from today."

Kal and Erek bowed before me and Kane, then left Jonsi's hut. One part of Kane's speech gave me an incredible amount of hope and excitement. To officially be considered as one of the Varjun was something I wanted more than anything, not only because I wanted them to approve of my match with Kane but because I also genuinely loved them as a people.

It was strange that I'd never felt that same connection to Solis except for some of the people I grew close with. Varjutus had become my home and even if we brought peace back to Eredet when it was all over, I'd want to spend my days here—with Kane. I smiled at that beautiful vision of a future, and it filled me with such hope and longing that it brought a tear to my eye. It's exactly what I was fighting so hard for. The chance at life.

Jonsi brought me out of my daydream. "I'm so proud of you, my dear, and Amrel would be too."

"Well, I haven't passed anything yet." I let out a self-conscious laugh, becoming nervous now that the stakes were so high for me, and failing would mean failing Kane and his people. "I don't know what this test entails, but I'll give it everything I have."

"It certainly won't be easy. There are five parts to the *Warrior's Sanna*. The strength of fist, the strength of will, the strength of courage, the strength of mind, and the strength of steel. How long it takes depends entirely on you, but most find it takes at least one full day."

It took effort for my eyes not to bulge out of my head, but apparently, I was unsuccessful. Jonsi and Kane laughed.

"I won't tell you not to worry because one should never think they're immune to any battle, but I will tell you that Kane's words are true. It shows wisdom to never underestimate your opponent. We all have the ultimate faith in you, and we all hope our real enemies do end up underestimating you. I am fairly certain that they'll never see you coming."

CHAPTER
THIRTY-NINE

K ane and I headed back to the castle and saw to the needs of the people still camped on the grounds. Erek gave me that night to rest and regroup, and Kane said he wanted to spend the night alone together. It's what I'd wanted since I learned we were Star Mates. He took me to the sacred pond in the forest and started to undress.

"What are you doing!" I whispered, looking around us in a panic.

Kane laughed, and his usual commanding and fierce gaze softened as he looked at me, making me swoon. "Why are you whispering? There's nobody here. Everyone is locked away in their homes or on the castle grounds. We won't be disturbed." Kane didn't stop until the full glory of his body was revealed, and he looked like a god of the night. It felt like I was under a spell as I approached him and ran my fingers over the shadowy skin of his arms. He stood and watched me as I explored his body and relished feeling his strength.

For just a moment, I looked up at the stars and couldn't fathom that of all the people of the galaxy—of the universe—this perfection before me was all mine.

My hands went to his chest, and my fingers trailed down the divots of his torso. I wrapped my arms around him and moved them up to feel his back and shoulders, determined to have every inch of him ingrained into my memory. I was only taken out of my trance when he moved and started to circle me. From behind, with his cock against me, he whispered in my ear.

"Undress." It was a command, not a request. I smiled to myself and took off one article of clothing at a time until I was naked with him. He kept circling, inspecting every inch of me, and I enjoyed every minute of his tantalizing display, not knowing what he would do next. He stopped behind me again and started rubbing my shoulders, causing me to moan in delight. My body was so tense, and his large, calloused hands felt divine against the softness of my skin. He then felt from my shoulders down to my waist and wrapped his hands around me. He grabbed my breasts while he kissed my neck. My breathing was heavy from his touch, and the feel of his hardness pushed against me, begging for more. He stopped, picked me up into his arms like I weighed nothing, and started walking for the pond.

He stepped into it, still holding me, and my heart fluttered at the beauty still to be seen in this dying land. The glow of the pond, the bioluminescent lavender-colored leaves, and the moon above were incredibly romantic, and I looked into Kane's green eyes and saw overwhelming love. I felt him squeeze the coils of our mated bond, and I squeezed back.

"I know some see immortality as the greatest gift, but they don't realize how great of a burden and torment it can be. It was the ultimate pain spending two thousand years alone and in constant fear of my powers. I had to harden my heart and close myself off to the world, and I was certain love would never be an option for me.

After the loss of half of my family and the years in the Guardian's dungeon, I had never felt so alone."

The water gently ripped from the movement of our bodies, and it caused the moonlight to glisten on his face, illuminating the pain and gratitude both held there.

"It was all made worse by the fact that Varjutus was dying and at the mercy of Solis. I had lost all hope—and I began evaluating if my suffering was even worth it. That first time I saw you on Solis, sitting in that nightdress playing that beautiful music, was the first time the light of hope was ignited within me in millennia. There was a part of my soul that was saving itself for you, and now that you've filled it, I can finally treasure the gift of immortality—the promise of a beautiful future with you. You are my salvation, Cyra. You were the distant light I was treading through hell for all these years."

The water echoed in the silence as I put my hand to his face. "You never have to be alone again. We're in this together. Always."

Without warning, he pushed into me forcefully, and I moaned out, feeling the bliss of his body in mine. And joined as one, he looked at me with reverence as if I was the greatest gift life could bestow him.

He took my hands and kissed them gently as he pulsed slowly, causing my eyes to flutter shut for a moment. When they opened, I brushed his hair away, getting it wet, and I couldn't help but smile at his beauty.

We swirled in the glowing water under the stars, the only two souls in the universe. It was exquisite torture feeling him hard within me but not moving at all. My breath was labored from the euphoric feeling, and I couldn't imagine that there could be anything in life better than this. This moment with my mate, alone and in love, just enjoying the feeling of each other with an unbreakable bond. The intimacy of it was so overwhelming I thought I would climax without him ever moving an inch. He felt my pleasure and smiled at me.

"I could stay like this forever," I whispered.

Kane leaned down and kissed me, and after a few minutes of being still, I couldn't tolerate it anymore, and I moved my hips in a rhythm.

"So eager, my love?" His voice was a heady whisper that sent a shiver up my spine.

"Yes. Please," I answered, unable to get anything else out.

"I told you, when I teased you, you would beg for more," Kane said in my ear. He slowly inched out of me, and my lip pursed into a pout. But then he thrust himself back in, and I had to try not to yell in relief. He made long, slow, and powerful movements, so I felt every bit of him. He took me to the edge of the pond, and I braced myself against it as he took my breast in his mouth. My head fell back in pleasure, and when I opened my eyes, the stars were blinking above me.

With my body bare to a vast world and him worshiping me, I felt like a goddess. Free—unencumbered and divine. I succumbed to the oblivion he was offering me, and I climaxed and saw colors of energy around me as if we had created our own light.

"I'm not finished with you yet," Kane purred.

I was positive I couldn't stand any more intensity, but Kane didn't stop his thrusting. His pounding quickened and strengthened with water splashing around us, and just like that, I couldn't get enough. I grabbed his ass and encouraged his movements deeper within me, causing him to chuckle.

"I am here to serve you," Kane whispered. He used his incredible strength and energy to increase his pace and found an angle where there was no part of him that wasn't connected to me, and I felt him so deep and full within me that it was the most incredible heaven.

His muscles danced in a beautiful rhythm, and just when I

thought I was spent, he released inside me, and we both had the longest orgasm I had ever experienced. Our ecstasy lasted the same length of time, and when he finished spilling into me, I slumped onto his shoulder in sheer exhaustion.

Kane was breathing heavily, and I savored the sound of his breath and the strength of his body as it gently caressed me. In the comfort of his arms, I felt nothing could ever harm me. And even though I knew it wasn't true, I allowed myself to give in to the feeling.

"Are you quite alright, Cyra? You seem to be unable to move."

Smugness personified. He was thoroughly amused that he could utterly destroy me.

"This was the most romantic night of my life, and I've never had so many orgasms at one time. In fact, I didn't think that was possible. No, I cannot move."

"Don't worry, my Star. You don't need to. I will carry you home."

Home. Our home. In the arms of the love of my life. I might just pass out from joy.

Kane drove us to his room, still naked. He got a towel and put it on the bed, and gently laid me on top of it. With another towel, he dried off my body and then his own.

He climbed into bed behind me and raised my leg. I still wasn't in control of my body, so he had full command of me. He angled me so that he could easily slide inside me again, and I gasped. I still wasn't used to how large he was and how incredible it felt, filling me until it was almost too much.

"I love how saturated you are even after cleaning you up," Kane said in my ear, holding my breast.

"That's all you," I responded lazily.

"It's not just me. It's both of us." He wrapped his body around me, and I clenched tight on him, causing him to moan. God, he felt *so good*. Would I ever be able to get my fill of Kane? Wasn't I just thoroughly spent?

Apparently not. I started to move up and down, trying to get him to thrust, but he placed his hand over my pelvis and stopped me.

"Oh no you don't."

"I can't just lie here. It's too much."

"No. Patience, Cyra."

"How can you stand it! And good lord, how can you stay hard for so long?"

He laughed but kissed my neck and ran his hand down my curves. For minutes he didn't budge, and with him wrapped around me like a cocoon of protection, his intoxicating scent and the exhausting bliss of the night, we fell asleep, still joined together as one.

The next morning, I woke up and my body was sore all over, and it wasn't just from my training. Kane was still in bed with me, and I turned to see his peaceful, sleeping face.

I smiled and quietly got up, not wanting to be late for my training. It was more important now than ever since I would be taking the *Warrior's Sanna* in just a few short days.

In dire need of a bath, I filled the tub and soaked in its warmth. When I opened my eyes, Kane was leaning against the doorway with his arms folded, completely naked.

"This is a sight I could wake up to for the rest of my life." I smiled, thinking the same thing about him. "Last night was incredible," he said.

"Yes, it certainly was. I'm still recovering from it. That spent me more than any of my training," I said in shock.

Kane bellowed with laughter and pure joy in his eyes. "Don't forget that was only a taste of what I have to offer. If it wasn't for the obligation we have to our people, there'd be no escape from me for at least a week."

"Oh my," I squeaked with a blush, and he laughed again, still leaning on the frame, watching me.

I leaned back in the tub and emptied my mind, simply enjoying the quiet, but after a few moments, a pit formed in my stomach, and I started feeling guilty at how blissful I was. How many things had truly changed. What day was it now on Earth? What year? How many birthdays had passed, and how many Christmases? God, how I truly missed Christmas with my family, and I would have loved to bring Kane and introduce him to everyone.

"What is it?"

"I was actually just thinking about my family at Christmas. It was our favorite time of the year to share together. Grandpa Amrel would always do something wild and bizarre, and there was never a dull moment. He truly made the holiday special, and it hurts not knowing how many Christmases have passed since I left that my parents had to endure alone." My head shook, trying to erase the pain. "I don't know why that came up."

Kane had his hand to his chin as if deep in thought. He approached and kissed me before heading back to the door. "Try to come back to our room early tonight. I have something to show you."

"Okay." I stepped out of the tub and began drying myself off.

"By the way, I arranged for some of your clothes to be brought here." Kane opened his closet and opened it to reveal a bunch of women's clothing next to his own. "I asked Meili to provide a variety of clothing for my chambers, particularly for an occasion such as this."

I looked at Kane and smiled, touched that he was so easily sharing his space with me. "As you said, as far as I'm concerned, this is *our* room now." The man made me swoon with almost every sentence he spoke to me.

I dressed in my fighting leathers, kissed him goodbye, knowing I wouldn't see him for hours, and made my way to the training camps, finding Kal in his *Curadh* armor.

The sight of the fearsome warrior looking even more deadly took me aback. I had fought Kal countless times, but the armor really was intimidating.

"Now, daughter of Our Creator—show me if you're worthy of the name *Curadh*. Give me everything you've got."

I knew what he was saying. He wanted me to finally use my full power to fight, not just my sword. And when my eyes silvered over, he smiled and ran for me.

We fought with no weapons, he knew it was where I would be the weakest even with being able to control my magical sight. It was exciting that I was now able to anticipate most of his attacks as if he was moving slower than I was.

Kal told me he didn't have any magical ability since the curse, but I saw the dormant energy within him, begging to get out. It was unsettling to see like a part of him was locked away and inaccessible, but there was still a decent amount of power that was available to him. His fighting ability was enough to compensate for the lack of magic, but I still wondered why he didn't use the power he did have left.

The more I used my gifts, the easier and more instinctive it became. What I was able to see and anticipate grew every time I practiced and there was always something new to learn. I noticed that I could even feel the small energies of Kal's muscle movements so I could be there before his attack. While this all helped me in my fight—in fact, I pinned him down more times than he did to me—he was still simply physically stronger than I was. When we ended the fight, I felt triumphant, but I didn't walk away without multiple cuts and bruises.

It was one of the few times Kal was working to catch his breath. "That was very impressive." There was a look on his face I'd never seen before. Maybe it was surprise?

The first time I'd ever fought him he'd never moved from the spot he was standing, with a look of sheer boredom and hatred. Now he was working to catch his breath with a beaming look of pride.

"I must say I think you are my best work yet, Cyra," he said with a smile.

"Probably your most difficult one too."

Kal laughed and clapped my shoulder. "You're going to do just fine."

"Thank you, your confidence means a lot to me considering how worthless you thought I was when we first met."

Kal straightened and stuttered.

"Don't worry. I don't blame you. It's true that I was clueless, and I owe it all to you and the Varjun people for guiding me and making me the fighter I am today. Thank you, Kalmali."

Shockingly, a hint of pink colored his gray cheeks as he took my hand. "I did have my doubts…in the beginning. And I am still so ashamed by how I treated you, but you have proven yourself the worthiest of opponents all on your own. I've never seen anyone work as hard as you have, and it has been the greatest honor of my career to train you and fight by your side. I'll fight with you to the end."

My chin raised as I looked him in the eye. "So will I. Although I have to ask you, why did you not use any of your magic while fighting me?"

Kal looked confused by my question. "You know I don't have any power left since the curse."

I shook my head. "Some of it is inaccessible, that much is true. But there is a substantial amount waiting to be released and used, I can see it within you."

Kal looked utterly shocked, and I squeezed his hand gently.

"In your darkest hour, look inward, not to your sword, and you'll find it there waiting for you."

I was eager to return to the castle that night, wondering what Kane wanted to show me but also because I was mentally and physically exhausted. The extra efforts going into the protection of Varjutus and my *Curadh* training was taking their toll on me. The only thing keeping me sane and light on my feet was my mate.

Groaning with aches and pains, I opened the door to his—our—bedroom and stopped dead in my tracks when I saw the scene before me.

What in the actual fuck?

The room was its standard dark, gothic décor, but it was fully decorated in various colored twinkling lights hanging from the ceiling in addition to gold and silver shimmering pine cones which were a little worse for wear. The windowsills, cabinets, and corners had a fluffy substance scattered throughout which was painted white, and on closer inspection, it was random brush and debris from the forests made to look like snow.

There was a poor, suffering evergreen tree which was more brown than green, but standing in a massive pot of dirt, likely so it could be replanted back into the forest. It was adorned with more colorful pine cones and fairy lights and beneath it was that goddamn Lucky Pecker as if it was the most precious offering in the world.

But the piece de resistance was Kane himself, completely naked with two life-sized candy cane replicas facing each other so they made the shape of a heart, covering his family jewels at the bottom. He stood beneath a browning berry plant hanging from the ceiling, made to look like mistletoe with a deadpan expression as if he had no idea how I was going to react.

It was the most pathetic display of Christmas ever and yet the most *wonderful* thing I had ever seen in my life. After my initial shock, I burst out laughing, unable to stop and a smile crept onto Kane's mouth, relieved that I thought it was funny.

"I don't want you missing out on your treasured traditions and you deserve all the respite you can get. Hopefully, this provides the shock value you're accustomed to."

He had listened when I told him the story of Grandpa providing shock value every year at Christmas, and seeing this god-like warrior naked with a heart of candy canes was the best gift I could have ever been given. My love language was laughter, joy, and silliness—and he had thoroughly delivered.

My voice was a squeak, trying not to laugh. "My Candy Kane?"

He nodded slowly, wiggling his eyebrows at me. Another fit of laughter escaped me and he took one of the life-sized fake candy canes and hooked me with it, jerking me toward him as I continued to laugh, and he threw the other one away dramatically. He had never celebrated a Christmas in his life so it was apparent he had studied up on the holiday just to make it special for me.

"Are you pleased with your Candy Kane?"

"You have no idea."

Suddenly my lack of energy was completely gone and all I wanted to do was solidify our bond again by ravishing him all night. I took one more look at the pathetic dried snow fluff, the twinkling lights that only flickered because of the lacking energy source, and the half-rotting plant life before he lifted me and threw me to the bed, causing me to giggle at his eagerness.

My heart had never been so full.

The day before the *Warrior's Sanna*, my nerves started to get the best of me, and it showed in my training. After three hours of declining combat ability, Erek stopped me.

"Cyra, what is going on? The first hour you handed my ass to me nonstop, and now it feels like you're giving up."

"I'm not giving up—I'm just…nervous."

He looked at me incredulously. "I could be a prick and say something like your enemies don't give a shit that you're nervous; get your act together. But instead, I'll just ask why? You've proven you can take down Kalmali and myself, so what is the hesitation?"

I couldn't bring myself to answer and admit that I was terrified more than anything that I would fail and wouldn't be accepted as one of the Varjun. I wanted to earn my place among them and by Kane's side. Now that we were fully bonded, I could never live without him again. What if the people never accepted me? Would Kane have to choose another woman to be his Queen?

"Come with me. I want to show you something," Erek said, pulling me out of my thoughts. I nodded and he drove me to an area of Varjutus that had mountains worth of old debris and remnants of buildings that had been picked apart for resources. There was one thing still standing amongst the decay, a small statue of a Varjun warrior.

"This was once Rauha, our largest settlement on Varjutus before the Great War and where I lived for many years. We once held grand balls, concerts, theatrical numbers and showcased some of the galaxy's greatest artistic treasures. By any other planet's standards, it was still a small city, but the people of Varjutus always prided themselves on our tight-knit communities. This was also the location where Lydon saved the Varjun race."

Erek led me closer to the statue and I recognized the man instantly from the painting in Jonsi's hut.

"Lydon was Jonsi's partner," I said out loud.

"Yes. For many, many years. And he was the bravest and best of men. The Guardians came to Varjutus with Dokoran, Bellum, and the Empire of Knights, who still served the Demon Reina. They had every intention of eradicating the entire Varjun race, knowing we would never submit to Guardian rule, and they came very close. Many lives were lost during their attacks."

I circled the statue of the warrior Jonsi loved as I listened to his story.

"During that time, the Guardians possessed a *spejl*—an object that could mirror the effect of another magical object. Orphlam was much more dangerous then since he could go anywhere he wanted within Eredet. The *spejl* mimicked the magic of their Siphoning Stone and special magicks housed in the Guardian temple where they could control all aspects of our lives. It was well known that anyone who breaks a *spejl* while in use would suffer grave consequences, and the greater the power the *spejl* was harnessing, the graver the aftereffects."

My heart sank, knowing where he was going with this. This was the story of how Lydon died a hero.

"Lydon knew this and he gave his life destroying the *spejl* from Orphlam's neck. They have never ventured back here since then and we owe it all to Lydon's bravery. Eventually, the Guardians included Varjutus in the curse, locking our planet in place so we would have to be at their mercy, especially when they realized how useful Adelram and Kane could be to them. Lydon was the one who founded the *Curadh* and everything they stand for. He was the one who turned the Varjun into a fighting people who stood a chance against our enemies. Whenever I feel fear in my heart, I think of Lydon and his bravery. How that one man changed the course of Varjun history. And now, when I think of the hope of our future, I think of you."

I looked up in shock at Erek's words. How could he possibly compare me to the splendor of Lydon and his incredible sacrifice?

"I hope I can live up to your faith. Thank you for bringing me here and telling me this story."

He smiled and nodded. "Now get some rest and, for Amrel's sake, make sure you don't get distracted by anything."

He disappeared, leaving me alone in the great shadow of Lydon.

After looking at the statue for a while I drove back to the castle and prepared for bed. Kane was still out, and I wasn't sure if he was sleeping in his room or mine, so after I changed, I got into my bed. Meili came a moment later with weapons and clothing for the big day.

"I have some lovely new royalty-grade fighting leathers and a new double-back scabbard to hold two swords," Meili said with a smile.

"Thank you, Meili."

"Are you nervous?" she asked quietly, sitting on my bed next to me.

"No." At that moment, it was completely honest. Erek really did put things in perspective for me.

"Cyra...I—I just wanted to tell you that I'm so proud of you. And I admire what you're doing. Your parents would be so proud of you, and I am so lucky to call you a friend."

"That means so much to me. Thank you, Meili."

"Is there anything else I can get you for tomorrow? Are you hungry? Would you like me to come in the morning?"

"No, thank you, I'll manage in the morning. I think I just need to get some rest."

"Of course. Good luck, Cyra. I know you'll do great."

I laid down to try to fall asleep early, but a voice in my head made me jerk back up in surprise.

Cyra, it is time to heal the Sword of Istina.

The Buruj. I still didn't know the female's name who kept speaking to me. I'd have to ask her the next time I saw her. I went to my closet, where it was hidden, and took out the two broken pieces. I still had no idea what to do to fix this thing, yet Jonsi and the Buruj both thought I could do it.

Placing it on the bed, touching and inspecting the cold metal. Multiple curses of frustration echoed in my head, but words started to fail me as everything went quiet. The pieces of the blades in my hand grew warm and it felt like it was calling out to me, as if in need of help. I ran my hands up and down, feeling the actual life force of the sword like it was a living entity.

Heal. Jonsi and the female Buruj both used the word. I reached for that warm force of life within me that I was able to use to heal Kane. I opened my eyes and watched in wonder as the pieces slowly started to fuse together. I felt a rush of energy when it was whole like it was alive or sentient, and I knew I could command it with my will. When I held it up it erupted in blue flame, pulsating with power.

Now give them a show they will never forget.

I smiled to myself. That's precisely what I would do.

Once I fell asleep, I was plagued by unwelcome dreams. I found myself walking the streets of Rauha and was in shock by the sight of the sun shining in the sky over Varjutus, but it was still partially obstructed by smoke and ash filling the air. The burning smoke filled my lungs, causing me to cough, and the smell of blood and decay overwhelmed my senses. It was horrifying watching a school burning to the ground with children running out of it screaming in fear. Buildings were crumbling around me, and I almost doubled over in grief as I watched the Empire of Knights from Solis murdering Varjun people in cold blood and destroying their largest city. No man, woman, or child was spared, as the knights from my birth planet showed no mercy. The *Curadh* were off in the distance and I moved toward them without thinking in hopes that I could help. It took me a moment to remember that this was the past, and I was merely a phantom.

"Back to the villages, all of you!" Lydon yelled.

"But you will need backup. You cannot face the Guardians alone!" a fellow *Curadh* responded.

"Do as you're told! I have a plan."

The warriors hesitated but followed their leader's command. When Lydon turned, Orphlam and his companion stood before him, laughing behind their horrid masks.

"You know fully well that you don't have the power to defeat us, and yet you remain, knowing your fate," Orphlam sneered.

Lydon stood tall and proud, with no hint of fear plaguing him. "I have no intention of trying to kill you, only of saving my planet."

With the quickest movement I'd ever seen, he ripped the *spejl* from Orphlam's neck and used his magic to blast it apart. My smile grew wicked when I heard the vile sound of Orphlam's screams.

The Guardians immediately disappeared, and Lydon was thrown with incredible force from the destruction.

One of the *Curadh* returned to Lydon's side but left to get help when he saw the condition he was in. To my horror, Lydon's skin began slowly peeling away as he seemed to burn from the inside out. Jonsi appeared before Lydon, who was on the ground, and his screams nearly tore me apart.

"No! Lydon, what have you done? What have you done!"

"I'm sorry, my love. Please forgive me but I had no choice. Varjutus is now safe. We have a chance. The Guardians won't be able to come here for any prolonged time again. Protect our histories and pass it to the future generations."

Jonsi's eyes squeezed shut in pain as tears poured down his face. When he opened them again there was nothing but love and admiration remaining. "There is nothing to forgive. I am so very proud to be able to call you mine. I just don't know how I will ever go on without you."

Lydon was shaking, his body in full shock as it continued to burn away. His voice was strained but he kept talking. "You must. Our people need you now more than ever. You must lead them and protect them through these dark times. The worst is yet to come, and you will be their guiding light."

Jonsi broke down in tears as he held Lydon in his arms. Twelve *Curadh* warriors circled around them and said their goodbyes to the man who bested Orphlam and prevented their complete annihilation.

The scene changed and I looked around me in shock. It was my parents! And something broke within me looking at their wonderful faces. I could even smell my mother's lavender and lemon scent. My heart skipped a beat as I heard Grandpa's voice.

"Are you sure this is what you want?" he asked my parents gravely.

"They are coming for us. We have no choice. You said yourself their corrupted magic makes them immune to the sword's defenses, and they will use the Sword of Istina to get the truth from us about where you are hiding and who Cyra really is. There is no escaping it."

"We will never let those monsters get a hand on our daughter," my mother said in tears. "We bear the mark of the Sunya Reina and are more than sure this must be done."

Grandpa looked pained but responded. "I cannot touch the sword after Orphlam cursed it, but I can still summon it."

"Do it. Now before they come," my father said.

Grandpa nodded. "This is the last chance to change your mind."

"You said yourself, you and Siare saw no future where Orphlam didn't get the information from us," my mother said.

Grandpa raised his hand and summoned his sword and, without touching it, laid it down before my parents. My father picked it up and looked at my mother with tears in his eyes.

"We're doing the right thing, my love. It's for our little girl and for the future of Solis," my mother said.

"I know...I know. I just—I'm just going to miss you and Cyra so much," my father said, fully sobbing now. My mother matched his tears and took his hands, and led him down to sit on the floor with her.

"Amrel..." my mother said, looking up at him.

"You have my word. I will take care of Cyra and make sure she succeeds. I will protect her with my life." What he didn't say was that he already knew he would exchange his life for mine in the end.

"You're sure that using the sword in this way will render it useless to the Guardians?" my father asked.

"Yes. I have it programmed to shatter in such a circumstance. I will make sure it's never found by them again."

My mother and father nodded.

"Rhythen, you must do it. I don't think I have the strength or courage."

"Don't worry, my love." He placed her in his lap, and he held her tight and took his hand in hers.

"Sing me the song you sang when you proposed," my mother pleaded.

My father sang with a beautiful deep voice, and she lay against him, letting it soothe her. She held up a picture of me, and my father took one last look as he lifted the Sword of Istina. My parents never took their eyes off my photo as my father plunged the sword into their bodies, and I watched the life leave their eyes as they died together. A flash of light erupted from the sword, and it broke in two. Grandpa turned, and I saw tears in his eyes—more than I'd ever seen fall to his face. He put his hand to his mouth and closed his eyes.

"Goodbye, my dear friends. Your brave sacrifice will not be in vain," Grandpa said in sadness. He turned at a movement in his peripheral and gasped.

"Cyra! What are you doing out of bed!"

"Grandpa, what happened?"

Adelram appeared, and Grandpa spoke to him. "It is time, Adelram. Take her now."

I woke up screaming into my hands. Kane was deep asleep beside me and I debated waking him, but I didn't think he deserved to be burdened yet again with the horrifying memories of Eredet's past. I couldn't fathom what it must have been like for Adelram, living the memories of everyone he had to take from.

All this time, I believed my parents had died at the Guardians' hands but they sacrificed themselves for my chance at survival, for Eredet's future. Theo's parents might have conspired with the Guardians to murder them, but it was their own hands that did the deed with the very sword I had healed and hidden in my closet.

The blade that was broken because of my parents' self-sacrifice, stealing its power from the Guardians.

I couldn't bear the never-ending grief I witnessed in my dreams and visions, but between the selfless acts of Lydon and my parents, I no longer felt any fear of the trial in the morning.

CHAPTER
FORTY-THREE

Kane was already gone when I woke. He left me a letter wishing me luck with a promise of time alone together when it was over.

I looked through the leathers and armor Meili left me, and none felt right. I didn't want any fancy new leather. I didn't want the makeup she left me or the new boots.

My only desire was to fight today as I had since I came to Eredet, with nothing but my sheer will and determination. The only new thing I would have would be my grandfather's sword I'd healed on my own. The sword that my parents used to save my life and could help us in the fight to come. It was a symbol of hope, unity, and protection for the people in this galaxy, and I wanted them to witness that we had it in our possession in the fight against the Guardians.

I put on my everyday shabby fighting uniform and a double back scabbard with the Sword of Istina and another plain sword. Not wanting to kill anyone, I hid my Varjun dagger in Grandpa's box and replaced it with an ordinary dagger. Food was waiting for me on a tray, so I quickly ate, knowing I wouldn't be eating until bedtime. I went to the door, but someone knocked on it before I could leave.

"Well, if you would have told me that the second time I came to your room, it would be to escort you to a *Warrior's Sanna*, I would have said you're batshit crazy. But…it seems you have surprised us all, and it is not easy to win the favor of Varjun hearts. Are you ready?" Merick stood before me in a rich, deep blue blazer that complimented his eyes.

There was no hesitation, doubt, or fear. This is what I had been tirelessly working for. "Yes."

"Then let's go." He pulled me close and drove me to an open area that appeared to have every Varjun on the planet in stadium-like seating so they could watch the test. I had no idea how they managed to set this up with the little magic they possessed, but it was impressive.

And intimidating.

I remembered being told that the test was held before the people, but I never imagined the magnitude of it. Merick led me to the center of the circle, where Kane and Jonsi were already waiting. The *Curadh* were suited and waiting in a straight line behind them with their hands folded behind their backs.

Kane was dressed in his "King's business" attire and not his *Curadh* armor, which surprised me, but he did have the ability to magically change if he needed to. They smiled at me as I approached, which put me at ease.

"Hello, beautiful." Kane's soothing deep voice was music to my ears and instantly brought about a sense of calm. Here I was with my hair down and wild, no makeup, battered fighting leathers and cuts and bruises, and he looked at me like he meant every word.

"Good luck," Merick said sincerely and winked before he disappeared.

Kane spoke to his people with his voice booming in every direction so all could hear him.

"We are here today to witness the attempted growth of our elite legion in a precious rite founded by our bravest warrior in Varjun history, Lydon Urande. We continue the *Curadh* tradition and rejoice at the strength it has given us in our greatest time of need. We are at a time in our history when many of you have stepped up to learn to fight to protect our lands and lives, which speaks to your unwavering resolution. This *Warrior's Sanna* tests a fighter's courage and strength to the very ends of their limits, and since we put our lives in their hands, we would expect no less from our champions. That is why this test is so demanding. We mandate that our warriors are capable of keeping our people safe."

Kane locked eyes with me, and the corner of his lips turned upward before he spoke again.

"Who comes here today to take this challenge to become the ultimate protector of the people of Varjutus and of Eredet?" He reached out his hand, motioning for me to step forward.

"I, Cyra Fenix, am here to take this challenge." There was complete silence in the crowd, so I saw that as my opportunity to bring forth the Sword of Istina. I reached behind my back and unsheathed the sword, and it erupted in blue flame at my side, the power and energy pulsating from it truly remarkable.

The crowd finally buzzed with sound, and many of them were standing to verify if what I was holding was the Sword of Istina. Even Kane looked at me in utter shock, but Jonsi did not. He had a knowing smile on his face.

"You fixed it?" Kane asked in wonder.

I nodded my head solemnly. This sword was bittersweet—it was a living piece of my Grandpa and a symbol of hope, but its hand in my parents' death would always be a weight I carried even as it served as a reminder of their deep and unconditional love.

"Just when I think I know you completely, you continue to surprise me." Kane turned back to the audience.

"As you see, Cyra wields the Sword of Istina, the sword of Our

Creator, Amrel. Cyra Fenix, daughter of Our Creator, will take this challenge today," Kane said to his people. The crowd finally cheered in recognition, and I could see their boredom was gone, and they were ready to see what I could do.

Jonsi walked toward me and spoke to the crowd. "I will officiate the games, and the first test will be the strength of fist. No weapons will be permitted. Cyra must survive thirty minutes of fighting with each opponent without being knocked unconscious or pin her opponent to the ground ten times, whichever comes first. She must best three of the four opponents to proceed to the next round. The King will not be participating since he and Cyra are Star Mates, and they would be able to anticipate each other's attacks."

The crowd erupted in noise. This was probably the first time they'd been told that Kane and I were Star Mates—the highest level of bond in the universe. I looked around to see how the people of Varjutus felt about it, but I couldn't tell from this distance. It explained why Kane wasn't in his *Curadh* armor. I had assumed I was going to be facing him today.

"Migor is the first opponent. Your time starts now," Jonsi boomed.

Slightly stunned at the random start, I watched as the *Curadh* warrior with the fanged mask approached me quickly. I hated that the strength of fist was the first test since it was my weakest area. If I made it to the next round, I would be severely compromised and fatigued.

My eyes silvered as I finally crouched down, preparing for battle, when Migor was instantly before me. His arm was pulled back, about to attack, but he stopped, completely shocked by the foreign sight of me. It had been a while since we'd fought together —before I could use my magic while fighting. I used that opportunity to strike him and jumped on top of him, pinning him to the ground.

Nine more to go.

He threw me off with incredible strength, and I lithely rolled when I hit the ground and jumped back up. Migor stalked toward me slowly, and I saw no magic within him. None at all. I wondered if it had disappeared since the curse or if he was born without any.

He started attacking me with a fury of movements, and he was so fast that eventually, he knocked me to the ground, and I saw stars bursting around me. His melee skills were incredible. They had to be since he had no magic.

As he jumped in the air to land a blow to knock me unconscious, I rolled away, and his fist hit the ground inches from where I was, causing him to grunt in pain. I swiveled my leg to trip him, causing him to land on the ground, which I used as another opportunity to pin him quickly. He knocked me off him, and I landed on my back and grew dizzy from the force of my head hitting the ground.

It had only been two minutes of my first opponent, and I panicked that it was going to be a *long* grueling test. I managed to pick myself up, but since I was still dizzy, Migor punched me as hard as he could, and I heard my nose crack as blood fell down my face. He pinned me down three more times, and I refused to go down this early in the test. I put some distance between Migor and myself, closed my eyes, and took a deep breath.

Migor didn't have high energy levels within him from magical forces, but I could still see the tiny energetic movements of his body. I needed to focus on that to anticipate his attacks. It was clear that Migor was much stronger than me, so I changed my strategy from trying to get my ten pins to attempting to tire him out until the thirty minutes were over, and it was much more effective. It was music to my ears when Jonsi called time.

Thirty minutes of hand-to-hand combat had felt like an hour. I was just thankful to make it to the next opponent. Migor walked over to me, and I flinched.

"Relax, darling. The fight is over. You did a remarkable job," Migor said with a chipped, toothy smile, extending his hand to me.

My shoulders dropped in relief as I shook his palm. The change from bloodthirsty warrior to friend took me aback, but I shouldn't have been surprised since I knew none of these fighters would take it easy on me. I didn't want them to. I wanted to be a true warrior that survived by her own skill and determination.

I healed my nose and prepared myself for the next fight just in time for Jonsi to speak. There was no rest or downtime whatsoever.

"Erek will be the next champion to face Cyra. Your time begins now!"

The lack of rest and extreme pace was a blow, but I wouldn't let it rattle me. Frantically, I searched for Kane and locked eyes with him, trying to ground myself. It was almost impossible not to feel Kane's worry throughout the last fight because Erek was right. I couldn't afford the distraction.

Having a Star Mate was the ultimate distraction since I couldn't help but be highly attuned to his changing emotions. He looked back at me and tightened the coils within us, giving me the strength to face Erek, who was already racing toward me at full speed.

My eyes silvered again, and I witnessed Erek's magic scattered through the air around us. Panic overtook me since I didn't know what he was doing, I had never seen someone spread unused energy like that before, and I couldn't anticipate what he was going to do. He was trying to throw me off my game and had probably intentionally never used this move during our training, so I would have to overcome it in this trial. I was so disoriented that Erek sent me flying backward from his first attack.

Unbelievable—my nose was broken again. I spit out blood, and the energy saturation around me made me dizzy even though Erek was using none of it on me. It wouldn't stop oozing out of him.

And as I stood again, I felt like I was suffocating from some kind of poison.

It's the same way I felt when Orphlam was in my presence.

I fell to my knees and held my throat, looking up at Erek, who refused to give me respite. There was no mercy in his eyes, none of his usual nurturing demeanor. He picked me up by the neck, and I thrashed in pain. My magical sight failed, and I saw nothing but destruction in his eyes. Using all my strength, I elbowed his arms to get him to drop me, but he did not come close to yielding.

Kane's overwhelming fear and anger were invading my mind, and I could have sworn I heard the word "fight," but I had to force it away to concentrate with the few precious seconds I had left before I fell unconscious from lack of air.

With no options left, I studied the lime-green energy Erek had emitted, and in my desperation, I absorbed it. The feeling of it within me made me violently ill, shaking and sweating from every inch of my body. Unable to contain it, it blasted from me in all directions causing Erek to fly fifty feet away.

I rolled in pain on the ground and threw up from the apparent poison. Jonsi ran to Erek's side as Kane came for me, but I erupted in an inferno of fire that spread thirty feet beyond my body. The citizens stood and watched in confusion as the sickness slowly melted away and transformed into unfathomable strength and power combined with a sense of unburdened confidence and freedom that was euphoric.

Kane was moving his mouth forcefully as if he were yelling, but I could barely hear his words. "Cyra, I can't penetrate your magic! What has happened?"

Only two thoughts were coursing through me.

Rage and hatred.

It was the same feeling I had when I wore the power bracelet on Solis, and I was ready to annihilate every one of the *Curadh* until I was the last victor standing. Jonsi ran closer, and I lifted my arms and let my flames rise in the air.

"Cyra! This is a part of your test of will! You must choose to overcome the dark magic within you! Release it and return to us!" Jonsi screamed through the flames.

My lip curled at him. *Idiot.* Why would I let go of this power when I could end this war right now? I knew without a shadow of a doubt I could kill every Bellum and become impervious to Guardian attacks. I considered leaving this ridiculous spectacle and doing just that. This could all end with me right now.

A forceful invisible tug yanked at me, and I turned toward the direction it was leading me.

Kane.

His eyes showed a wild desperation, but I felt no emotional connection to him. It was for the best. Connection to people only brought pain and heartache. There had been far too much of that recently. I looked at all the meaningless faces in the crowd and could end them all with a thought. What did it matter anyway?

Kane took another step toward me, but Jonsi stopped him.

"You cannot interfere. This is her challenge."

Doubt.

He doubted I could pass this thing, which was ludicrous since he knew what kind of power I had now.

I laughed at them both again. "I can smell your panic, and you *should* be afraid." I lifted Jonsi in the air without touching him. He clutched his throat, and my hand was held out like his throat was actually in my hands.

"Cyra, don't!" Kane screamed in horror. But Jonsi looked at me with kindness in his eyes, making nausea roll within me. Anger was still overwhelming my every thought, and it resonated from me through the matrix of energy I was connected to. The ground beneath us started to shake, and the Varjun people screamed in fear.

"Cyra, this is your last chance," Jonsi choked out with kindness. "Look into your *imana*'s eyes and see your truth."

Why was he submitting to me when I was ready to kill him? I looked at Kane, and his eyes were filled with tears. For a brief moment, even at this great distance, I could see a reflection of myself, and I inhaled sharply in surprise.

When Jonsi fell to the ground, the earth stopped trembling. *The test of will.* This wasn't who I was. What was I doing? Yes, I was tired of fighting, and the fear and doubt plaguing me every moment of every day was draining my soul. But giving up wasn't what I truly wanted. I didn't want to cause others pain, even if it meant my own suffering.

I got lost in Kane's eyes, feeling more of his presence returning to me. I started to panic, finally returning to my senses with the realization of my actions. My eyes silvered over, and I looked down within me and saw massive amounts of that lime green energy, and I was able to create more of it on my own, so it had grown beyond the quantity that Erek released.

Thoroughly disgusted, I immediately expelled it from me with vehemence, instinctively dispersing the energy into the atmosphere. My knees buckled. I hit the ground, throwing up again, shaking from the poison of that energy.

Kane and Jonsi ran to me, and I couldn't bear to look them in the eyes. Dark magic acted like a deadly drug for me—the high and release were extremely dangerous, and it was so painful to admit that I wanted to feel it again. The guilt and shame I had to face now was unbearable.

"You did it, Cyra. You did it." Why the hell did he have wonder in his voice, like he was impressed by the evil that had so easily overcome me? And that I found it addicting after overcoming the initial sickness?

"What are you talking about?" I asked in horror. "I almost killed everyone and very nearly killed you."

"It was a test. We gave you a large pure dose of the dark energy the Guardians use. Amrel said if you could overcome the effect of that energy, you could overcome anything." My head turned away from him, unable to look at that innocent smile.

"You drugged her again?" Kane asked with anger.

He held up his palms and spoke calmly. "It was Amrel's wish that she be tested."

It made me incredibly self-conscious that Grandpa had specifically wanted to test me with this dark magic. Did he know how hard it would be for me to reject it? Did he worry I was too similar to Orphlam and might end up like him?

"And what if I couldn't have resisted it? What would you have done if I'd destroyed the planet?"

Kane looked at me, his brows raised, and lips parted. He probably didn't realize how close I'd come to just giving up.

"Our thoughts and intentions do not measure who we are. Only what we have acted on defines our true character." My thoughts quickly jumped to Theo before he continued. "You resisted as I knew you would. You proved your internal strength."

No matter what he said, it felt like I had failed by letting it take hold of me so easily and truly loving the feeling of being free. Jonsi stood and addressed the crowd.

"Do not be alarmed, my dear people. This was part of Cyra's test. She was given the poisoning energy of the Guardians, and she was able to resist its corruption. She has proven her strength of will. Erek was knocked unconscious, so we will commence with the next opponent, Ondour."

Oh lord. I was about to have the fight of my life.

CHAPTER
FORTY-FOUR

Kane and Jonsi disappeared from the circle, and Ondour walked toward me with his skull mask, but I could tell he had a vicious grin beneath it.

I was still incredibly sick and weak from the poisoned energy that had just left me, but there was no choice but to get up and fight. Ondour anticipated my attempt to escape on his right and kicked me so hard I heard a crack in my rib.

A scream erupted from me as Ondour picked me up and held me over his head. I quickly cleared my mind and let it go blank so he couldn't anticipate my next move. And as he started throwing me, I disappeared, driving behind him and knocking him to the ground until he was pinned beneath me.

"You bitch." His words were quiet and cold, and I flinched when he immediately disappeared. I jumped up and started to circle to anticipate where he would appear, but I didn't expect him directly above me.

He fell from the air and restrained me to the ground, punching my face mercilessly. With my arms covering my head to protect myself, I was inwardly begging to disappear, and it took me a moment to realize that I did. I was standing next to him, but it was clear that he couldn't see me. Did I really have the power of invisibility like Merick? I walked closer to Ondour and whispered in his ear.

"Are you afraid?"

He jumped up and backed away from me. Oh, I could get used to this power. A smile crept onto my lips as I tiptoed around and kicked him to the ground. Unfortunately, the shroud quickly dissipated, and I was unable to use it again. We fought for what felt like an eternity, and just when Jonsi called time, Ondour pinned me to the ground for the tenth time.

"Looks like you lost, princess."

"You pinned me after Jonsi called time."

"Tell yourself whatever you need to so you don't feel like a failure."

"That was nine pins by Ondour, so Cyra has already qualified for the next round but must still fight every member. Kalmali is the final *Curadh* to face Cyra with the strength of fist. Your time starts now."

One fight after another after another. The lack of rest was ruthless.

Kal was so fast and lethal that I had to use every ounce of my attention to try and anticipate his attacks. There was the slight advantage that I had fought Kal so many times that I knew his fighting style very well. I managed to finish thirty minutes of fighting him with only a broken arm, a large welt on my leg, a few cuts and bruises, and nine pins.

The crowd cheered when Jonsi called time, and I fought every urge to fall to the ground and grimace in the fetal position. My rib was still in searing agony even though I had healed it.

"Cyra has passed the test of fist, plus the first round of the test of will. We will now move onto the second portion of the strength of will." Jonsi raised his hands, and a massive maze appeared behind us. I sighed in desperation. If part one of strength of will was any indication of what the second part would entail, I did not want to enter that maze.

"You will have as much time as you need to get to the other end of the maze, but you must do it alone. You may begin."

I looked back at Kane, and he smiled sadly at me. It was comforting to know that he would be there waiting for me at the end of this ordeal, whether I passed or failed. Without hesitating another moment, I entered the maze, and it became eerily dark. Varjutus was covered in eternal darkness, but there were always small sources of light from the moon, the Varjun people, or some bioluminescence to help keep it from being *this* dark.

I lit my hand on fire to see where I was going, but it didn't help enough. Along with the pitch black between the leaves of the maze was utter silence. It was as if I was in a pocket of space separate from existence, and that alone was more terrifying than what could be in this trap.

When I turned the first corner, I screamed and backed up to the solid leafy wall behind me. I tried to leave the way I came, but the wall was now closed off. There was nowhere for me to go but forward, and in the way stood Orphlam. He started laughing, and the sound was so piercing that I had to cover my ears.

"Look at you. Your healed wounds don't fool anyone, you barely made it through the first round, and your body is severely battered and bruised. You're almost exhausted to the point of giving up. You're so tragically weak. You don't really think you'll come away from this alive, do you?"

The polished gold of his mask glistened in the light of my fire as it tilted to the side. There was something so terrifying to me about being alone in his presence as if I was looking into a reflection of my possible future.

"You heard the Buruj yourself. No matter what outcome the future holds you will bring about the end of all ages in Eredet. Why even bother to continue to fight me? You should spend what little time you have left to enjoy your Star Mate before I rip you both apart piece by piece, just like I did with Varog and Dessa. It's the most grueling death you could ever experience, and it's the only thing that's waiting for you, unless you give in to me now. I will spare you and your people the ruthless death that awaits them, if you yield to me."

Orphlam quietly chuckled with mock pity as he looked down at me. "I can see you are considering it. And why should you not? The constant painful visions you see of the destruction of your galaxy's people...you could make that all go away. It could be *that* simple. Give in to me. The pain is only going to get much more unbearable."

"You'll have to drag me to hell with you before I stop trying to destroy you."

"As you wish," Orphlam said with a smile behind his hideous gold mask. He snapped his fingers, and I was somewhere else entirely–back in the putrid dark caves on Solis where the Guardians kept all their secrets.

It took me a moment to realize I was naked, strapped to a table, but it wasn't my body. This...was Kane's memory. My hands immediately began to shake because I knew what was about to happen, and I used all the strength in me to try to break free.

Orphlam was right, I was weak. I didn't have the strength to watch Kane's years of torture.

"I want to know why he's special. I want to know how he has so much power and why it's so different from his race. Test his pain levels and see if there's anything different in his anatomy. I think he is the strength we've been looking for to be able to make the transfer. Our people are waiting on us to find the answer to immortality. We will be able to decide who lives and who dies. Nothing commands greater loyalty than the sheer will to survive," Orphlam said.

"But our *tolk* has informed you that we need the full energy of Amrel unleashed to sustain the immortality."

"I am well aware of that. I have no doubt that in time we will open the *mikla* and finish draining all the energy of the galaxy to bring home."

Orphlam turned toward Kane and slapped my face. "Now wake up. I don't want you to miss a thing." He motioned for a Bellum to start his work, and he inched closer to me with a sharp knife before cutting into my stomach while I watched in horror. I screamed in anguish, begging for it to stop, unable to peel my eyes from the freely flowing blood.

"His anatomy looks unremarkable on the inside, sir. I don't see anything in here that suggests exceptional ability," the Bellum said.

Despite my sheer will not to give Orphlam the satisfaction, I couldn't stop wailing, and I tried to break the restraints as he moved around organs as if I wasn't even there, awake.

This isn't real. This isn't real. This isn't real. But I couldn't break free and the pain was absolutely real.

"Sometimes things are hidden beneath the obvious. Take samples of everything and run some tests."

The next moment I passed out from the horror and agony.

I was forced awake again as Orphlam's mask hovered over my face. "Time to step it up a notch."

This time I was suspended in the air, hanging by my arms, and judging by how numb they were I assumed I was up here for a long time.

"You are a mystery, Kaanan. But I think I'm about to crack you," Orphlam said. "This is Masym." A long breath escaped me when I saw a small innocent boy.

My (Kane's) voice was barely a whisper, raspy and dry to the point of pain. "No, please don't. I beg you...just leave him alone."

"You alone have the power to save this little boy."

I—Kane—looked at the boy who was crying. I felt his heart breaking for the child who was surely going to die. He made up his mind that he would not yield to the Guardians' experiments, and he couldn't give in to the boy's soul.

"Now let's see what you decide," Orphlam said.

My screams began again as I felt searing pain as if my body was being torn into two pieces inch by inch. The poor boy cried on the ground and then went still, as I could feel his essence attempting to invade my body.

I knew Kane's decision. He fought like hell pushing out any chance for the boy's soul to meld with his. After about an hour of torture, Orphlam finally stopped, and the boy who was lying in his own urine from fear ceased to exist, and I dared not think what happened to his soul.

My body slumped over in pain, and I blacked out. When I awoke, Orphlam was at it again and again and again. It felt like days' worth of torture until I finally screamed, "ENOUGH!" and everything went dark and quiet again.

Thank God I was back in the unending pit of the maze. My legs began to move, running as fast as I could, but there seemed to be no end and no beginning. I couldn't tell how long I had been here since it had felt like I had been in the Guardian's torture chamber for days. Could the Varjun crowd see me now? Did they know where I had just gone? Did they see Kane's broken and tortured body?

After my legs simply couldn't carry me anymore, I fell to the ground, feeling lost and defeated, and thoroughly mentally drained.

"That's it," Orphlam said, appearing before me again. "Give in to your despair. It will help you make the right choice."

"Leave me alone!" The sight of him made me want to vomit and I was consumed with hatred.

"I can give you back your bracelet. The ultimate power. You know it felt good to give in to that rage, to feel no pain—only power. The power to decide your fate, make your own rules, and see the outcomes you choose for *yourself* materialize. You can do anything, including kill me. You almost killed the Varjun Elder and your precious mate. Remember how little you cared about it? I can help you erase all your pain." He walked toward me with that putrid energy, and I backed away anxiously. That dark magic was now one of my greatest fears. "You fear it because you desire it," he whispered slowly in my ear.

I looked away, with tears running down my face—ashamed. Because it was absolutely true. I wanted to forget all this pain and misery. It *did* feel good to be free. How glorious it would be to feel unrestricted with no more burden on my shoulders? No more worries about prophecies or destinies.

But at what cost? I looked down at my bruised body and remembered why we feel pain, why it was absolutely vital. I was tired of fighting, and I was tempted by Orphlam's offer more than I ever thought possible, but I would never be able to disappoint grandpa Amrel, and I would die before I gave up the fight.

My voice was shaky and dry as I spoke. "I'll tell you again, go to hell."

"Still haven't had enough of it? If you insist."

Random visions appeared of the recent nightmares I'd had of the fall of Looma and the decaying Sunya race. Adelram screaming in torment, alone in his room in a drunken mess, unable to function from the horrors in his mind. Kane being tortured and thrown into a stinking cell next to a rotting corpse.

"Stop!" I screamed, humiliated that I couldn't stop crying.

"You know you cannot defeat me, and it is not your fault. You… are just a girl," Orphlam said.

His words had the opposite effect of what he intended. *You are just a girl.*

The girl and the King. That's where those words of prophecy stemmed from.

I thought of Kane and how he was once utterly broken down in body and spirit and yet he prevailed and became the protective, loving man I knew now. I thought of Lydon, dying for his planet without a moment's hesitation, even at the cost of leaving the love of his life. I thought of my parent's sacrifice to save my life so that I could protect the people of Eredet. I saw Grandpa's golden eyes, like little beacons of sunlight, and he, too, chose to live a mortal life and die so that I might be safe.

These people sacrificed so willingly and bravely, and it gave me the strength I needed. I stood from my whimpering mess on the ground and glared at Orphlam.

The finality in my voice was all the strength I had left. "I will *never* give in to you. Go ahead and do your worst. I will never stop fighting, and neither will Kane."

Orphlam screamed and vanished into a cloud of smoke, and the exit of the maze finally appeared. Sheer exhaustion overcame me as I walked to the soft, glowing eternal night of Varjutus. Jonsi was there, his brows pinched together, waiting for me with a vial in his hand.

"Well done, Cyra. You made it."

"How long has it been?" I whispered.

"It has been eight hours since the start of the test."

Jonsi addressed the crowd, not appearing concerned by the state of me, but perhaps he was trying to help me by making this go by as quickly as possible. "Cyra has passed the second trial of will and will now endure the test of courage, mind, and weapon in succession."

He turned to me and handed me the vial. "The end is near, Cyra. You can do this. Kane and I both believe in you. You must drink the contents of this vial, then jump into the hole."

Jonsi pointed to a hole in the ground that seemed to have no end.

"What is at the bottom?"

"It is different for everyone. Have courage, Cyra, and you will find your way. And remember, no matter how lost you find yourself, there will always be a part of your mind no outside force can touch. You are special, Cyra. Remember that. Your time starts now."

Tilting my head back, I took the vial and drank it without question, just wanting the test to be over. My feet inched to the edge of the hole, about to dive in, but I hesitated. I looked into its depths again but couldn't see the bottom.

After only a few seconds, I breathed in deeply and jumped in with no fear. The fall went on for many seconds until I landed on top of someone, and we both groaned in pain.

"Careful, Cyra! I know you're my best friend, but you can't use me as a parachute!"

"Bre...Brendon?"

"Who else did you think it was?" he asked with a smile.

I burst into tears. "Oh god, Brendon. I've missed you *so* much it hurts." I grabbed him and pulled him close and cried onto his shoulder.

"Don't cry. You're almost at the end. You should be so proud of yourself. I know I am. Just imagine—you're living the life of the games we've played together all our lives. A warrior princess fighting to save her people. However, I'm not at all surprised. I always knew what was in your heart, even if I couldn't see the full extent of it. I am just a mortal human, after all."

"Brendon, you're one of the most important people in my life and you always will be. I swear, when I have the chance, I am coming for you."

"You don't need me. Look at all the power you have."

"I don't care about power! I care about having the strength to help my people. I care about my family and friends."

His familiar smile beamed on his sweet face as he squeezed my shoulder. "And that is why you will win. We must always believe love will triumph over evil."

"Do you really believe that?" I asked in a desperate whisper. I valued Brendon's opinion and I hated to admit I really had my brief moments of doubt.

He took my hands in his and I couldn't stop the tears from falling.

"I know it," he said. "Now it's time for your test of courage," Brendon said, holding up a dagger.

"What's that for?"

"You have to finally put me in your past to succeed in your future."

I was horrified by what he was insinuating. "What? No, I don't. You will never be simply a part of my past. You are a piece of my heart, always."

"You must do this to get to the next round, Cyra. You have to finish this test."

"I'm not stabbing you, Brendon. I know you're not real, but I'm not doing it."

"Why would you say I'm not real? Kane's torture was real. The fall of Looma was real. Adelram's nightmares were real."

"That's different. Those were visions…memories."

"This trial is very real, Cyra. And to get to the next round you must stab me."

He placed the dagger in my hands and led me to the ground so he could lay in my lap, and I couldn't stop the tears from falling.

"I know you went back to the rainbow eucalyptus with me when you almost died. I'm happy it's a time in your life when you felt safe and free." He waved his hand, and I was there again, still holding him, and we both looked up at the swaying leaves.

"Why did you take me here?" I asked.

"Because you will feel peace," he whispered. "You must do it now, Cyra. The end of this round is closing."

My hand twirled through his loose curls, listening to the leaves sway and enjoying this moment with him.

But I had a job to do. I slowly raised my dagger, and he closed his eyes, accepting his fate. My hand shook on the blade as I began to feel dizzy.

Memories came flooding to my mind and I saw Brendon's sweet smile the first day we met, and he gave me his lunch so I would feel welcome in a crowd of kids I didn't know. I saw his gentleness when he comforted me when I was sad. I saw the look of love in his eyes when we bared our souls to each other with secrets only the two of us would ever know. This man was the embodiment of human goodness, and even though we had not seen each other in a long time, he would always be a soulmate of another kind. The dagger, still shaking in my hand, started to slip from my clammy hands.

"Screw this," I said and threw the blade.

"Cyra, you will never be a *Curadh* and the Varjun people will never accept you as their Queen. That's everything you want right now."

I stood and touched the tree that looked like a surreal painting and remembered all the childhood dreams Brendon and I hid within it.

"No, that's not all I want right now. I want to do what Grandpa sent me here to do. I want to restore the balance. Yes, I want the Varjun people to recognize me as one of them and I want to be accepted at Kane's side, but I won't do it at the cost of being a monster. I still have to live with myself when this test is over, and if the Varjun think me weak, so be it. I won't stab you, Brendon. I won't kill someone I love for the sake of proving something within me. I guess I'll never be a *Curadh,* and if this is the price, then I can live with that."

He stood and walked to my side, also looking at the beautiful tree and running a hand over its multicolored bark. "As grandpa Am said, you always know the right thing to do. You didn't let your irrepressible fear of failure change who you are, no matter the cost. Goodbye, Cyra."

The scene before me changed and I was back in the center of the people of Varjutus. Had I never left it? Were the past hours all in my head? Was I still in the test, or did I dream up the whole thing?

The ground beneath me felt like it was moving, and I couldn't see straight. I shook my head and tried to get my bearings, but it was ineffective. Jonsi approached me and when he spoke to the crowd the sound sputtered in and out.

"This is the final test for both mind and sword. Migor will be your first opponent. You have fifteen minutes to pin your opponent five times or last until time runs out, whichever comes first. Your time starts now."

Drugged. The vial Jonsi gave me was some sort of toxin. I now had to fight the fiercest warriors in Eredet without being able to think clearly and I had to best all of them. This was the moment I had been waiting for, and I couldn't concentrate.

My hand clumsily reached behind me to unsheathe the Sword of Istina, and it glowed in blue flame. The people stood and watched with eager anticipation.

My magical sight came into view and Migor wasted no time in landing a ruthless attack that made me stumble backward. I was increasingly off balance, and I didn't know how I was supposed to fight in this state but when I picked up my sword I saw something move in the blade. I squinted to look again, and time seemed to stop around me.

Migor was mid-step in a run and stuck in place and the people who circled us were mid-cheer. I looked back into the blade and saw the poison living in my brain. I touched the blade and knew I could heal myself, so I concentrated and slowly began to untangle the toxin from my mind. When I finally had some clarity, I continued to see images flashing in the blade and it contained visions of what had not yet happened. In fear, I pulled my eyes away before I saw the outcome of the *Warrior's Sanna*.

The Sword of Truth. Is that what I was seeing in the smooth blade? Truth? Possibilities? Or lies? Once I removed my eyes from the blade, time continued to move at normal speed. I blocked Migor's attack, and he stumbled in surprise. I stood tall and raised my hand with the blue flaming sword, and the crowd around me erupted with excitement.

With my second sight, I saw every movement of my opponent before they struck, and it felt like a dance in combat. When I fought against Ondour, his ability to read my mind was disabled by the sword and I was shamefully delighted by how much it threw him off. I destroyed him by pinning him down five times before the fifteen minutes were over.

"Your trick won't keep you safe. Eventually, you'll need real skill to defeat your enemies."

"Tell yourself whatever you need to so you don't feel like a failure," I said coolly, smirking at him.

He sneered and gave a contemptuous smile before he walked away.

The dispeller of darkness walked toward me in his black mask, looking every bit the embodiment of his nickname. He stopped and bowed before me, and the crowd went wild at the show of respect from the most fearsome *Curadh* warrior.

My throat was painfully dry from lack of water, and I was hungry and nauseous at the same time. My body was battered, bruised and still suffering intense pain from the parts of my body that had been broken. My mind was ferociously shaken by how I had reacted to the dark magic and the visions I had seen in the maze. I was sick to my stomach from how I seriously wanted to give in to Orphlam and just let go of everything. I missed my friend Brendon more than ever and I was weak and spent.

Kal was the last challenge before me to be able to call myself a *Curadh* warrior and he was the most challenging opponent I'd ever faced. Fifteen minutes. I only had to make it...fifteen... more...minutes.

"Your time starts now!" Jonsi bellowed, and Kal immediately attacked. I had sparred with him countless times since I came to Varjutus, but every time his speed and agility took my breath away. It forced me to up my game and move faster than I ever thought I could to protect myself against his attacks. He was the one who made me into the fighter I was today, and I wanted to show him the gift he had given me by giving him hell.

It turned out Erek wasn't the only one who kept tricks up his sleeves. Kal started using moves that I had never seen him use in our training, and it broke a bit of my confidence. I remembered Kane's words on Solis.

The element of surprise is a weapon in itself.

I was constantly learning from the cleverness and depth of the Varjun, and I had to adapt and respond with speed. Kal pinned me three times and I was panicked that we still had five minutes left of the trial. He could easily pin me five more times in that span.

There was no other option but to think fast and find a way to shock him. I looked at the dark sky and searched for the sun's presence in the distance with my second sight, and although nobody else could see it I felt the sun's energy calling out to me like a warm embrace. I let it seep into my body, and a euphoric calm washed over me, and it was the antithesis of the dark magic that corrupted me earlier.

This felt like an energy that was always a part of me, and with it, I could do anything. Before Kal was able to attack again, I burst the golden light energy from me and lit up a small piece of the sky above us as if I were a small star. The whole crowd screamed in shock as they went utterly still.

I realized then that it might have been a cruel choice of distraction since these poor people haven't seen a bright sky in millennia. Even the dispeller of darkness himself couldn't help but stop in awe of the light illuminating their beloved land for the first time in too long.

I pinned him down, threw his weapons away, and held his hand back. He eventually got me off of him and I could see that the light bothered his sight as he was used to fighting in the dark, so I kept the light in the sky and brightened it as much as I could so all the Varjun were squinting and adjusting their sight.

"Time!" Jonsi yelled. He and Kane ran onto the field toward me. Kal took off his mask and smiled.

"I'd be much obliged if you dimmed that light, please," he said with a smile.

"Oh, right, sorry!"

I held out my sword and started to sheath it but stopped when Kal looked at it with admiration. But his look quickly changed to horror as he stumbled and fell back to the ground.

"Kal..." He disappeared, and I didn't get to think about it further as Kane scooped me up into my arms and twirled me around.

"You did it, my love," he whispered. The triumphant happiness, pride, and love I felt from Kane melted all my worries away and I leaned into his arms.

"Cyra Fenix has successfully completed the *Warrior's Sanna*. She is the newest member of the *Curadh*!" Jonsi beamed, clapping with pride. The cheers of the crowd were nearly deafening and I let out a breath of relief and utter exhaustion. My reality hadn't quite caught up to me yet, because I couldn't believe I had done it. I was no longer a young woman with no job, living with her parents playing video games.

I was now a warrior.

Kane bent down to embrace me and speak into my ear. "Well done, my Star."

"Thank you. If it's alright, I'd like to go home."

"I thought you'd never ask." Leaving the noise and crowds behind, he drove me to my room and was able to catch me before I fell unconscious to the ground.

CHAPTER
FORTY-FIVE

Mercifully, I slept like the dead and had no dreams that night. I woke up the following day with Kane holding me, and it was the best feeling in the world. My body attempted to turn to face him, but I groaned in unimaginable pain. Kane chuckled from behind me.

"I had to sleep with one eye open, lying next to a *Curadh* warrior all night."

"Yes, how terrifying. If we're lucky, in five minutes I might be able to roll all the way over to face you. You're in grave danger."

"I'm in grave danger of never leaving this bed since you are in it. But you are in pain, so we shall."

Kane got up and to my delight, he was deliciously naked. I would never get enough of seeing his exposed muscular body, and it was all mine.

"I'm glad I can make you smile," he said deviously.

"The sight of you naked will always put a smile on my face."

"Nothing makes me happier than being able to please you," he said, picking me up quickly. He walked me to the bathroom and stepped into the tub, and sat with me in his lap. The hot water was glorious, and my muscles were already letting go of the debilitating tension. I slumped back onto Kane's chest, and he started to wash me.

"I don't know what you put in here, but I already feel so much better."

"Choku salts. A favorite of our warriors and the only way we can recover and do what is required of us day after day. We've all thought you were crazy fighting so hard every day with no pain relief."

"It got me where I needed to be. And I'm thankful I fought through the pain, or I never would have made it through yesterday."

"You were incredible. I won't lie, it was hard watching you suffer. Seeing my brothers fight you while I couldn't be there to protect you tested my resolve. I know you can handle yourself, but I will never want to stand aside while you are in pain."

"I had to put aside our connection so I could concentrate on the trial. I felt flashes of your fear and anger, and I started worrying about your well-being in turn." My head turned back to look into his loving green eyes. "The *Warrior's Sanna* was the hardest thing I've ever done, and there were a few times where I really didn't think I was going to be able to finish. I faced some things about myself that completely terrified me. When I came to Solis, I had no idea who I was after my world was turned upside down and my memories were returned to me. I found out that my family and friends, whom I lived with all my life, were never mine to keep. I had to learn a whole new way of life with people I didn't know and a destiny I had no choice in accepting."

My body moved closer to him and melted into his wall of protection, causing the water to slosh around us.

"It wasn't until I came to Varjutus and started to learn to fight with the support of my Star Mate that I felt like I was getting a grasp on who I was and what I was meant to do. But this trial has opened a whole world of doubt. I almost killed Jonsi and…I felt infinite power coursing through me. The incredible magnitude of destruction I could have caused, and…I didn't care. Orphlam offered me an escape, an end to all of this, and I'm so ashamed that I wanted to accept. One thing that was always a constant in my life on Earth, Solis, and Varjutus, was that I stood by my convictions no matter what, and now…who am I?"

Kane turned me around so I faced him, and my legs were over his. "Cyra, you are the same person you've always been. We all face self-doubts from time to time, but our choices define the kind of person we are. The fact that you passed the test tells me that you *chose* not to give in to Orphlam. You *chose* to stay true to yourself and reject the dark magic even though Amrel said it was the most difficult thing he'd ever experienced in his life, and he was Our Creator! You were tired and under great physical and emotional stress, so, of course, you considered giving in. But you did not. You fought, just like I knew you would. That is who you are, Cyra."

He held my face, and I touched my forehead against his.

"We never have to walk through this life alone again. I will be there in your times of doubt. And you will be here for my times of need. I have no doubt of who you are because I feel it here." He took my hand and held it to his chest. "I feel it in our bond."

I nodded and put my hands on his arms. "It's how I broke free of the dark magic. I looked into your eyes and saw myself there. I couldn't feel our connection, but I was still tied to you. I saw how you saw the evil within me, and it instantly pulled me away. You are my salvation because I know even if I doubt myself, I will never doubt you."

"That love will carry us through whatever life throws at us."

"Kane, there's something else." I started shaking and crying, just recalling the experience. He picked me up and put me on his lap so I was closer to him, and he wrapped his arms around me.

"In the maze, I endured some of your torture during your time as captive by the Guardians."

His eyes widened before they shot down in shock. "I am so sorry." His voice was quiet and full of remorse.

"It was not my own pain, which was the worst part. It was having to see the level of detail by which you were tortured. I felt every bit of it as if I were you. I watched as Orphlam tried to put a boy's soul into your body, and his dead body was tossed aside like a piece of garbage."

Kane put a hand over his mouth, and my heart broke at his haunted look.

"I hope you don't think less of me for my decision."

"You were in a no-win situation, Kane. We all would have been worse off if the Guardians got what they wanted from you. I'm so sorry you had to go through that for so many years. I can't even imagine."

"There were many, many more Masyms. I remember every single one of their little faces and I started ending their suffering before it began so they didn't have to endure that excruciating experience. I cherish children. I never, in my wildest dreams, believed I could be the cause of their end. It was one of the darkest times in my life."

The Buruj's words that seemed strange to me when she said them were ringing in my head now. *Sometimes the kindest thing you can do is end a life.*

"You were not the cause. The Guardians were. How were you able to go through such traumatic experiences and still be the loving and caring man I know now? How could you come through it and still have so much strength?"

He smiled sadly and held my hands. "I did not come through it unscathed. I can never be the same innocent young boy I once was. It was taken from me the first time I accidentally killed my cousin. My life has only gotten infinitely more difficult since then, and there are parts of my mind I have to bury in a deep dark place, or I wouldn't be able to breathe. The way I see it, we all have two choices in life. We can let our pain break us down until we are an empty shell. We can choose to let it kill us or we can choose life. We can learn from our pain and let it build us into a new, stronger person. Or we can choose the slow festering decline to a grave. I chose life, and I'm so glad I did because my bliss was waiting for me at the other end of the darkness. My reward for not giving up was you."

Kane leaned down and pressed his lips to mine. I felt a wide range of emotions churning within him, and my own mimicked his. We kissed in each other's arms, knowing we were never promised a tomorrow. Today, this moment, was all we had, and we savored every precious ticking second. I slid slowly onto him so we were joined together, and we expressed our love and gratitude through our bodies during this time of cruelty. Afterward, he helped me out of the tub, and we laid naked together in bed and allowed ourselves a little while to enjoy each other in quiet peace.

The girl and the King. Come and see us.

"Did you hear that?" Kane asked.

A sigh escaped me, knowing our special moment was over. "Yes."

"I knew we couldn't lie here forever, even though I wanted to try." Kane chuckled.

"I guess we'd better go. I do want to speak with them."

"So do I. Later we celebrate to recognize you as a *Curadh*, and you will be presented with your official armor. The King chooses it for the new warrior, so I had the pleasure of designing it myself. I used some fabric of my sister's old clothing plus some old metal weapons that belonged to my father that I had been unable to part with. "

My heart skipped a beat. This moment already meant the world to me, but Kane had literally taken a piece of his past and molded it into something new for me. His future. "I've become so used to you taking my clothes off it'll be an interesting change watching you present me with clothing."

Kane laughed. "Don't tempt me, or we'll never leave this room."

I groaned, wanting to let him trap me here for a few months, but I was very eager to hear what the Buruj had to say. "Unfortunately, we have to. Let's see what they want."

We dressed quickly, drove to the cave, and entered the familiar darkness. They were already there, waiting for us.

"I haven't yet made you out, Cyra."

"What do you mean? And what are your names?"

"I am called Nexia. I am the first of my kind and *Gyam* of my race—their leader. This is Einri. He is also from the first days of the Buruj. I cannot understand why you choose to ignore what is plainly before you."

"I still don't know what you're talking about."

"You absorbed that dark magic."

"I was about to fall unconscious. I had no choice but to try to use that against my opponent."

"Oh, but you did have another option." She pointed to the Nebula Diamond around my neck, and it started to glow. "I gave you that gift to protect you, and you ignored its call. You chose instead to give into the darkness."

"I...I didn't hear any call."

"Did you not? I know you've become vastly adept at lying to yourself, but you cannot lie to me. The Nebula Diamond can significantly decrease the effects of unnatural magicks, and yet you didn't use it."

I looked down in shock, remembering a pulsing around my neck, but I had assumed it was Erek and his hold on me. Again, I was terrified that I had more darkness in me than I wanted to admit. Did I give in to it?

"You emerged a victor, so it is of no consequence. I am merely surprised by your choice."

"What would Jonsi have done if I gave in to the dark magic?"

"You repeated the words this morning. You know what would have been required. Sometimes the kindest thing you can do…"

Is end a life, I said in my head, the blood draining from my face. He knew going in that he might have been required to kill me, but he had every faith I would succeed.

"What am I?" I asked in a whisper.

"The answer is plain before you, and you will not see it. That is a realization you must make on your own."

She turned with her eerie eyes and looked at Kane. "And you mimic her question. It constantly plagues your mind."

"Yes," Kane said quietly.

"You are very special to us, Kaanan. The first King of Varjutus, King Vangelis Distira, fell in love with a Buruj woman."

"The first King of Varjutus and a Buruj?" Kane repeated in surprise.

"Yes. He was much beloved and had the longest reign of any Varjun King since his time. But they did not approve of his love for a Buruj woman, even though they were *imana*."

We both looked at each other in shock.

"I'm sure you can imagine the heartbreaking loss of your *imana* and what it would feel like to wander through life without them by your side."

"How horrible," I whispered.

"Why?" Kane asked.

"As I said, the people did not approve of their love. They wanted the King to choose a Varjun Queen, but they couldn't stay away from each other. Magnets will always find a way to get to their other half. The Buruj woman fell pregnant with the King's son, and they hid the pregnancy from everyone, the woman staying in hiding until the birth. When the people realized what had happened, they started persecuting the Buruj and demanded their seclusion from their own society and wouldn't accept the son, Oryn, as a leader until the fall of Leik and the Dead War."

She stepped closer to Kane, looking at him with a kind of familiarity reserved for family.

"You look so like him, Kaanan. For one hundred and eighty thousand years and four ages, the Buruj magic lay dormant in the Distira line until now."

"Amrel, help me," Kane whispered, attempting to swallow.

"Amrel knew what you were. He knew you were a true son of the Buruj and that your magic would be unparalleled to any in Eredet except your Star Mate, Cyra Fenix. You, Kane, are our kin and look so like my son, Oryn." Nexia finished. Einri walked to Kane and touched his King's Mark on his shoulder, and Kane's eyes shot to Nexia. She merely nodded, acknowledging that she was the Star Mate of Vagellis Distira and he was her very distant grandson.

"We are honored to know you and we pray for your and Cyra's success in restoring peace. You are our last chance for a new life," Einri said.

"How could I not know any of this?" Kane asked in shock.

"Your father did not know of this. Even the Varjun Elder does not know. We took this memory of the Buruj-Varjun pairing from the first Elder so he could not pass down the knowledge. We never wanted to relive that history again, so we could be safe in our seclusion. But the time has come for us to move on. Either this is the end of us all, or when it is all over and the Guardians are defeated, you must promise us that we can live our lives in freedom."

"You have my word," Kane replied with conviction.

"And Cyra?" Nexia asked.

"Of course, you have my word as well, although I think I have little influence over your future."

"You have the greatest influence over us all."

They stood and simply observed Kane for a while and I couldn't fathom how painful her long life was, being separated from her *imana* and her descendants. We turned to leave, and Nexia stopped us.

"Oh, and Kaanan?"

"Yes?"

She walked up to him and put her hand in his, and whispered something to him before disappearing with Einri.

"What was that all about?" I asked.

"I'll tell you later," he responded, clearing his throat.

CHAPTER
FORTY-SIX

We drove back to my room and Kane told me he had some business to take care of. I wondered if he just wanted some time alone after what we'd heard, but I didn't question him.

Having some time on my own, I decided to find Kal to make sure he was okay after his reaction to looking into the Sword of Istina.

First, I attempted to find a guard to tell me where to find him but I realized that I had the ability to find him myself. I used my second sight and looked through the structure of the castle to find Kal's energy signature. It was on the floor under mine, so I made my way down and knocked on his door.

"Oh…hi, Cyra," Kal said in surprise.

"I'm sorry to bother you. I just wanted to make sure you were okay. You saw something in the sword. What did you see?" I asked.

He cleared his throat and looked down, clearly thrown by my question. "My entire life, I would have done anything to get a glimpse of the Sword of Istina in person…and now I would give anything to have never seen it. I'm not sure I'll ever be okay again."

That really surprised me. "What was it, Kal?"

He looked away, scratching the back of his head. "I am not ready to speak of it."

"Okay, I understand—just one more thing. When we first met, I was a pathetic excuse for a champion of Eredet. You had told me that I was useless, slow, and weak, and you were absolutely right."

"Cyra, please don't repeat the cruel things I said—"

"They were true, Kal. I took the words you said to heart, and they reverberated in my head every day because I couldn't stand being a disappointment."

Kal looked down, his white hair and tiny braids falling forward.

"You also said that you do not train cowards. I hope I was able to make you proud and prove that the tireless training you've given me made me a better person. I wanted to thank you for not giving up on that inadequate girl and for helping me to become a warrior who could try to defend all people of Eredet. Thank you for putting me one step closer to fulfilling my grandfather's sincerest wishes. Without you, I never would have gotten here. I know I have lots more to learn, but you gave me a fighting chance." I took his hands in mine and looked seriously into his dark eyes. "Thank you."

"Cyra, you do not possess a cowardly bone in your body. I've watched in utter awe at your fortitude and strength and the incredible speed at which you've excelled. I'm sorry for my ignorance and premature judgment. You have far surpassed my wildest dreams and for the first time in a few thousand years, I have hope for our future. You have bestowed on me the highest honor of my life to have been able to have played a small part in the training of the daughter of Our Creator."

"It was no small part, Kal. It was everything."

He put his hand to his mouth, and I was astonished that he was trying to fight back tears in his midnight-blue eyes.

"Please excuse me," he said and closed the door.

What had he seen in that sword to make the dispeller of darkness afraid?

"Cyra! I was just coming to see you." I turned and it was Meili's bright, smiling face. "I have a lovely dress for tonight. I can't wait to see you in it."

"Meili, you don't have to make me dresses anymore. I told you you're not my *criada*."

"Yes, I am free. I am free to choose to never stop serving you. I will always be here for your needs, Cyra."

I put my arm around her. "Have I told you lately that I love you?"

She smiled and put her arm around me as well. "I could never hear it enough. And I love you, too." We walked into my room and Vjera was already sitting on my bed.

"Have you ever heard of a thing called privacy?" I asked.

"Yeah? And? Have you ever heard of me following the rules?"

"She's got a point," Meili said.

"That looks pretty skimpy, Meili," I said, looking at the dress when she laid it out next to Vjera on the bed.

"Looks like a lot of fabric to me," Vjera commented.

"Well, I've worn nothing but fighting leathers for the past few months, so it'll be weird to wear a dress again."

"Which is exactly why you need to wear something like this," Meili said.

"What was the *Warrior's Sanna* like?" Vjera asked. Meili stopped what she was doing and looked at me, too, no doubt curious herself.

"It was the most grueling thing I've ever experienced. I'm just so glad it's over."

"From our angle, it looked like you were running around in circles for ten hours."

"Seriously?" I asked.

"It's true. I had no idea what you were doing in there when it wasn't one of the combat rounds," Meili said.

"It nearly broke me."

"But it didn't. That's why you're now a *Curadh* warrior," Vjera said. "Finally, it's not such a meat fest."

"You can still take the test so I'm not the only woman."

"Eh, maybe one day when I'm bored enough."

"I can't believe you and Kane are Star Mates and both *Curadh*," Meili said with a smile.

"And *Paeladoned* warriors," Vjera offered.

"He's my soulmate. I guess it makes sense we have so much in common."

"You're on equal ground. You're lucky," Vjera said. "Most of us will never find that kind of connection."

"I believe there's a perfect connection for everyone," I responded.

"Then you're naïve. But you're young. You'll grow out of it," Vjera said, looking at her nails.

"Come, Cyra. Let's get you changed," Meili said.

The dress was baby blue with crisscross straps that only covered my breasts, so there was a diamond cutout with only beaded lace covering my torso. The skirt was a double split thigh cut that was opened at the sparkling jeweled belt all the way to the floor. There was beaded lace underneath that fell to my upper thigh, so there was a lot of bare skin. It was stunning, but I couldn't hide my thigh daggers.

Vjera saw my concern. "I think you'll be okay one night without your daggers. Besides, you're a *Curadh*. You're supposed to be able to survive with a rock as your weapon."

I rolled my eyes but supposed she was right. The door opened and Kane walked in.

"Oh, apologies, I didn't realize I was intruding."

Meili stood uncomfortably and Vjera didn't even look up.

"You're not intruding," I said, smiling at him.

"I'll see you soon, Cyra," Meili said and tip-toed out of the room.

"Man, she spooks easily. It's just Kane. What's there to be scared of?" Vjera murmured.

"Gee, thanks," Kane said, smiling.

"He is a teddy bear–or should I say a Candy Kane?" I winked at him. "She's just used to keeping a low profile. I supposed it'll take a while for her to come out of that shell."

He stepped closer to me, and his chest expanded as if swelling with pride, making butterflies erupt within me. "Are you ready, Cyra?"

Vjera winked at me and disappeared.

I had some unexpected nerves, but I was ready for this moment. "Let's do it."

Kane took me to the forest and the people of Varjutus were already there. The first people to run to me were Oliver, Lorcan, and Joven.

"Cyra, you are awesome!" Lorcan exclaimed.

"I can't believe you're a *Curadh* now!" Joven said excitedly.

"I've known her for years," Oliver said competitively, puffing out his chest.

I couldn't help but laugh at these little boys that I'd come to love.

"Can you teach me to fight?" Joven asked.

"Me too!" Lorcan said.

"Yes, we can spar at the community training. Maybe you guys can teach me something. I'm always ready to learn."

They looked at each other in awe, and Kane led me away to the platform I'd seen so many times before, but I was standing with him this time.

Kane's eyes shone with enthusiasm, and when he spoke, he used his hands, which was unusual. The way he came alive for an event honoring me made me all gooey inside. "This is an important moment since we are gaining a new ally in the fight to save our people, and in that, we gain a new citizen of Varjutus."

When the people cheered, I breathed a small sigh of relief.

"Cyra has already proven her dedication to our people by providing us with food, water and her tireless efforts in training to protect our people as well. She has now made the ultimate declaration by taking the *Warrior's Sanna* and becoming a *Curadh* warrior. It is my honor to present her with her fighting armor."

Jonsi held a large burlap bag and passed it to Kane. As Kane handed me the bag the people cheered, and music started playing around us.

The ceremony was shockingly short, and the people dispersed and started dancing and celebrating. Kane faced me and took out the mask. It was black with very slight crimson, blue, and violet notes in the threads. You had to inspect it closely to see it. There were also faint minuscule specs of silver that glittered in the light. My first thought was annoyance that Kane felt he had to "bedazzle" my mask because I was a female, but then he explained.

"You are a beacon of light that shines on everyone around you, but I want you to never forget that you found yourself and your home amidst the darkness of the night sky."

Why was everything he said always so wonderful? "It's absolutely perfect. Thank you." He leaned down and kissed me slowly and I almost melted to the ground.

"It suits you very well," Jonsi said with a smile.

I looked up in surprise. Then ran to him and took his hands, trying to fight my tears.

"Jonsi, I'm so sorry for what I did to you. I'll never forgive myself."

He shushed me kindly, comforting me in a way only he could. "Don't say another word about it. I'm sorry we had to do that to you. Amrel told us that dark magic is one of your greatest weaknesses. It's like a poison to your magic. It was not your fault."

"I don't understand."

"You don't have to right now. Tonight, we celebrate." Jonsi departed before I could ask him any more questions.

"He's right." Kane touched a tiny mark on his arm and Brugan appeared. "Please bring this back to Cyra's room."

"Yes, sir," Brugan bowed.

Kane took my hand and dragged me away. "Now you're dancing with me until we're both dizzy."

I laughed at his infectious enthusiasm, and I watched in shock as he jumped around at the music. I was mesmerized by this dark god-like warrior of a King frolicking with abandon. I laughed until my side hurt.

"Stop laughing at me and join me!" he said with a smile. We made fools of ourselves, jumping, running, kicking, twirling, and moving to the beats. People started to circle around us, clapping and cheering us on. We continued for about an hour until the music slowed, and he jerked me close to his body.

"You know my grandfather used to say *music is the language of our souls while dancing is the embarrassment of them.*"

"I have no idea what you're talking about. I'm an amazing dancer," he said, stifling a laugh.

I looked around and to my pleasant surprise, I saw Vish dancing with a Varjun woman. Vjera and Kal were sitting together talking and Merick and Meili were dancing, looking deeply in love. The three boys were pretending to fight with wooden swords and Jonsi was playing his banjo. There was plenty of food and water on the tables and there was laughter all around. Everything was simply perfect.

"Come with me," Kane said, taking my hand. He led me away from the crowd. "Something Nexia said stirred me. She advised me not to make the same mistake as her and King Vangelis since *imana* separation is unbearable. She said a *Curadh* recognition celebration is the perfect chance for the people to accept the true worth of a ruler. I know we have not been together long, but it feels as if I've known you all my life. We are bonded for eternity by an indestructible force, and I could never again be parted from you. There is no doubt in my heart that I want you by my side, always, as Queen of Varjutus."

Kane held my hand and slid a ring onto it. "Cyra, will you marry me?"

I looked up into his eyes in utter surprise and was slightly dizzy from the strength of emotions coming from him. His love, his sincerity, and his slight nervousness made me smile.

I had always been so unsure about everything. I have never felt true belonging anywhere I've lived in my life. I've also felt incomplete and confused.

But this man before me, my Star Mate, was beyond reason and sense. It was beyond a typical relationship of love and lust. We were two halves of the same soul, already bonded...there was never any going back, and I would never want to. The moment we bonded, I had given myself to Kane. We were branded—imprinted in each other's hearts and minds.

We were destiny.

This wasn't a choice. We were already essentially married. There would never again be anyone else and it just made sense.

"I have never been so sure of anything in my life. Yes, I will!"

He picked me up in his arms and kissed me. "You've given me more happiness than I ever could have conceived possible. Tonight, I will ask the people of Varjutus for their blessing," Kane said.

Dread washed over me, snuffing out my excitement.

"Don't worry. The people love you."

"After the story Nexia told us today, I'm more afraid than ever."

"I am not. I have the ultimate faith."

I looked down at the ring and it was an emerald cut stone.

When I inspected it closely, I swore the brilliant colors within it changed as it sparkled in the glow of the night. How was it able to sparkle in the darkness? It's as if there was light trapped within the diamond. It shimmered in a spectrum of color as it moved, but it was almost as if whatever light was trapped in there was from its own source of energy.

"My father told me this is called a Destiny Diamond and that this is the only known one in existence. He couldn't tell me much more about it than that but said it was incredibly precious. Apparently, Amrel had gifted it to me at my birth. I had it engraved." He took it off my finger and handed it to me.

We Are One was engraved on the inside.

"It's absolutely beautiful. There's something about it that feels…familiar."

"Have you seen it before?" Kane asked.

"No, never. It's more like I feel…connected to it in some way. It feels like home."

"Then it's the perfect ring for you," Kane said, smiling.

"Yes," I said breathlessly.

"Come. I will speak to our people."

Our people.

We walked back to the grounds and Kane touched his King's Mark. There weren't many Varjun that weren't at the ceremony, but the ones who weren't appeared at his call. The music stopped and the people congregated before the platform. My heart started pounding out of my chest and Kane squeezed my hand to calm my nerves.

"I'd like to call a spontaneous *Valik* Ceremony."

The people looked surprised, but Jonsi had a dopey smile on his face and joined us on the stage.

"Cyra has become instrumental in our lives on Varjutus, but even more than that, she's become everything to me. You all know now that she is my Star Mate and we have officially accepted the bond. I could never live without her by my side, and I firmly believe she will help bring our planet back to the beautiful home it once was. She is not just my future, but all of ours. I ask you, my family, for your blessing of my marriage to Cyra. I ask you to accept her as the next Queen of Varjutus."

I held my breath throughout his speech and watched the expressions of the Varjun people. I shook from head to toe, never so nervous for a response in my life, and the silence went on for an eternity.

"*Sove!*"

"She's the daughter of Amrel!"

"She is already our Queen!"

I finally let out my breath and was utterly relieved and touched by their acceptance. Not only did I have a special, unique bond with Kane, he would now be the family I was so desperate to be a part of.

Jonsi stepped up to speak while the people applauded in unity. "My King, I have spoken to all the members of Varjutus, and they have already given their approval. Cyra Fenix will rule by Kane's side as the next Queen of Varjutus!"

The people yelled in celebration and approbation and were overwhelmed with delight. I looked into the crowd and Meili was a blubbering mess of tears. Vjera and Kal were happily clapping, and Merick was whistling and dancing like a fool, making me laugh.

But I was surprised when I saw Vish. He stood still in silence. It couldn't be helped. Even if Theo didn't make the choice he did, I would have no choice but to be by Kane's side for the rest of my existence. I would have to talk to him later and make sure he understood.

Kane picked me up in his arms and twirled me around, and jumped off the stage.

"The wedding will take place in three days!"

Oliver ran to us, excited. "Finally!"

"You knew all along, didn't you? You knew that Kane and I would be together and that you would live in the castle with us."

"I saw it, yes," he said with a smile.

"What other things do you see?" I asked.

"That it's time to play hide and seek soon," he responded, his smile vanishing. "I'm just glad you're getting married now. It's the right thing to do. I feel something really, really bad coming soon, and we need you together to survive it."

Oliver went to go play with Lorcan and Joven like he didn't just drop a bomb on us, and Kane and I silently looked at each other with dread. We knew how advanced his abilities were, and anything he said was not to be taken lightly.

Kane sighed. "Let us think about that tomorrow. We have a lot of struggle and heartache in our future, which we cannot avoid. For now, let us celebrate the love that will help us fight it."

I nodded, and he held me close. I breathed him in and let myself feel at peace. We danced for hours, and even though it was pure darkness, I could feel it when it was morning. Kane and I walked back to the castle hand-in-hand. Our home and the place where I held all my future hopes and dreams.

CHAPTER
FORTY-SEVEN

With Oliver's words echoing in my head, I spent the next few days training tirelessly. I even kept my word and taught Oliver, Joven, and Lorcan some basic defensive techniques and offensive moves. We also scoped out places of hiding for the children in case of attack. I did everything I could to make sure they had a fighting chance in case we were invaded by the Bellum again.

I tried to get Oliver to elaborate on what he felt was coming, but he was reluctant to say anything, and I didn't want to keep pressing him—he seemed really afraid, which filled me with dread. Oliver was never scared.

My time was also spent running a few errands in the villages, refilling water, and making sure food was stocked. Vish and Meili had done an excellent job with the crops in the Fenix private lands on Solis, and it helped tremendously in supplementing the food we received from Bad.

Also, in hopes of fostering more unity and goodwill, I spent time with the villagers and Solian refugees preparing for the wedding. Many people were involved, discussing menus and decor we could manage with the resources we had.

Not wanting to leave anyone out, I enlisted some help to try to find Mylo, but nobody had seen any hint of him. I could only hope that he was taking the time he needed to recoup and come to terms with what had happened to him, and I secretly hoped he would make a surprise appearance.

While preparing for the wedding festivities I recalled something grandpa Amrel mentioned to me and sought help from the people in making it happen. I also prepared for the *siduma* ceremony for the wedding. Kane told me it was traditional Varjun wedding practice to bind the marriage together with ribbons containing trinkets of the couples' happiest memories so their partner could magically share in their joy.

It sounded like a beautiful tradition, and crafting Kane's ribbons was right up my alley. He told me all I had to do was magically transfer my memories into a trinket and when Jonsi officiated the *siduma,* he'd be able to harness them.

Two nights before the wedding, I sat alone and thought about what parts of my history I wanted to share with him. It was much harder than I thought it would be to think of special moments in my life that I wanted him to experience for our wedding.

Kane was there for the moments when I grew more strength and confidence. He was here for my new life in Eredet. I wanted him to see how I began and my love for Earth. My love for my grandpa. My bracelet charms gifted from Brendon were the perfect representation of my life and the story of who I was. I asked if Meili was able to duplicate them, and she did it for me that morning.

The sun charm was exactly where I wanted to start. I gripped it tightly and held it to my heart, thinking of my dear grandfather. After practicing a few times I was able to transfer my thoughts of our mornings watching the sun rise and the magic made it seem like I was reliving the memories in real-time. I laughed, recalling the endless times we pranked my parents with fake rodents, surprise Nerf fights, fake electronic malfunctions, lost items, and random scare tactics.

We spent hours over the years laughing at my poor parents, but in their defense, their retaliations were brutal and we paid for our antics quite a bit.

I included memories of Grandpa wiping my tears and holding me tight when I was sad, as well as times we camped under the stars while he taught me the constellations and told stories of what we thought was out there in the vast universe. Turned out he had the upper hand in that game.

I showed his terrible dancing skills in his favorite t-shirt, *If Grandpa Can't Fix It, We're All Screwed*. Most importantly, I included the memory of his infectious laugh, his incredible smile, and the way his eyes glowed like golden amber. I gave him the gift of knowing The High Creator as simply a loving man like nobody else could.

Next, I took the holding hands charm and instantly thought of Brendon and me running through my parent's grounds as children pretending we were magicians that could command the world around us.

I showed us under the wondrous rainbow eucalyptus tree, Brendon writing down some secrets he shared with me, like wanting super-human strength, riches beyond his wildest dreams, and magical prowess. Some secrets he wouldn't share with me, and we hid them under pieces of bark.

My childhood wishes included finding my true love, the power of invisibility, and seeing the future. I pictured walking hand in hand with my parents as we went on hikes in the mountains. I made sure to include the many movies Brendon, my friends, and my parents saw in theaters, plus my silly BBC Masterpiece Classic Series and how Xenos would lie in my lap glued to every word.

With the game controller charm, I focused on my parents'

arcade, where I spent most of my time growing up around customers who knew me so well they all felt like friends. I remembered the days the misfit crew spent playing D&D and how I was mercilessly laughed at for my Drow character. I showed him how Bart felt like an adorable yet annoying little brother that I teased and played with for a few years before I knew him as Oliver.

My cello charm was infused with the years I learned to play and how much joy I felt doing it. My mind ran through the look of pride in my parents' eyes as they watched my talent grow and how I played my grandpa's favorite song at his funeral. But my favorite cello memory was now of Kane the first night I saw him while I was playing and how overcome I'd felt by him in my presence.

Finally, I took a small drawing I did of Kane's face and included memories of him and the overwhelming love I felt. I thought of how I tried not to be angry when I walked back to Eluroom Castle half-naked after Kane kicked my ass in our training. The time he took me flying on his Kometa and how I might have fallen fully in love with him then.

I infused the memory of him holding the crying and vulnerable Oliver and how my heart pounded with the sight of him with a small child, followed by how full of respect and pride I felt when Kane kneeled before his people and was sworn in as King. I thought of the first time we made love and sealed our Star Mate bond and how there would be few moments that would be able to compare with it for the rest of my life. I poured as much love as I could into the drawing and hoped it would translate in the *siduma* ceremony so that he could feel the intensity of my memories and love.

This whole exercise made me miss him terribly, made worse by the fact that Kane and I decided to sleep in our own rooms until the wedding, and it was infinitely harder than I thought it would be. Three days without him felt like three months, especially because I could feel his presence all day through our connection, and it made me want him desperately.

Regardless, the days flew by and the night of the wedding, Meili and Vjera stayed with me in my room.

"It's a Varjun tradition. You know, so you keep your purity," Vjera said.

"Excuse me?" I asked.

Meili blushed and gave a look that seemed to say, "Uh oh."

"Yeah, obviously the entire planet knows that ship has sailed, but we Varjun like our traditions anyway."

Meili burst out laughing and I tossed her a look of fake indignation as I joined in the laughter.

"Who the hell would have ever thought a Solian would become a Varjun Queen? Even crazier, I'm not trying to kill you for it," Vjera said, shaking her head.

"Vjera, could you actually...like me?" My head tilted to the side and I put my fingers to my chin with pursed lips.

"Don't be a smart ass, or I'll perfume your dress in licorice. Kane despises licorice."

"You'll have to answer to me if you ruin that beautiful dress," Meili said.

"What could the cherub do to scare me?"

We all went quiet as we heard a noise like leaves rustling. Thorny vines started to quickly grab Vjera and tie her to the ground, binding her legs and arms and covering her mouth so she couldn't scream. Before I could even stand, she was in a cocoon of foliage.

My eyes darted to Meili in utter shock as she sat perfectly still, concentrating on Vjera. She finally looked at me and shrugged with a smile, and the thorny vines started to retract and dissipate. She healed Vjera's wounds from the thorns.

Vjera gasped, stood, and backed away from us quickly. "Holy shit. I promise to never piss you off again," Vjera said in shock.

"Who knew you had that in you."

Meili shrugged dismissively. "I've been practicing."

"Well, I'm going to sleep easier knowing the blonde can suffocate and stab my enemies with a tiny shot glass of a plant that's half dead," she said, pointing to the tiny fern I had in my room. I seconded her thought.

"We should get some sleep," I said. When I got into bed, I felt the coils of the Star Mate bond tighten within me. Kane was letting me know he was thinking of me, and I tightened back. I fell asleep feeling his love as a living entity inside of me.

"Are you lost, dear?" Grandpa asked in his fierce presence, blinding as the sun. The lady he was speaking to flinched in surprise then her face gaped at the sight of him.

"Aren't you… Amrel, Our Creator?" she asked in awe.

"I am."

"Nobody has seen you in millennia. Why do you appear before me?"

He clasped his hands behind his back and smiled. "You intrigue me."

"How could that be? I'm just sitting next to the water, watching the sun rise. I'm nobody special," she said.

"I think you are. You puzzle me since I cannot see any of your futures or even into your soul. I can see all things and yet I cannot see beyond what your face shows me now," Grandpa said, tilting his head in wonder.

"Is that abnormal?"

He chuckled with delight. "Very. How wonderfully refreshing. What is your name?"

"Polaris."

He stilled, straightening his back and lowering his brows. "Interesting."

"How so?" she asked, confused.

"I've had a vision that I encouraged a man to name a star Polaris on a mortal planet since it was very dear to me, but the vision didn't explain why."

"That is odd. I've never heard the name Polaris before except for myself."

"Precisely. May I sit and join you, Polaris?"

"Of course! How could anyone say no to Our Creator?"

He chuckled, and his eyes shined with amusement. "Please, just call me Amrel."

She smiled and blushed, moving to the edge of the bench, giving him room.

"Are you fond of the sunrise?" Grandpa asked.

"Sunrise and sunset. I just love watching the sun's movements. I feel a strange connection to it, more than the normal person, since we all love the sunshine. Your heat feels very similar to it, actually."

"That is because I am a part of the sun. It's where I draw my energy and how I create life."

"How wonderful," she said, reaching out her hand toward him.

"No! You must not!" Amrel was arched away from her, true fear in his wide eyes.

"I'm sorry. Forgive me, sir. I didn't mean to be impudent."

"No, my dear, you misunderstand me. Just as you cannot touch the sun, you cannot touch me. It would either burn off your hand or kill you instantly. It affects people differently."

"Oh, I see," she said sadly.

"It is for the best if I keep my distance." The sadness in his voice broke my heart since I knew how much he truly loved to be around people.

Polaris tucked her beautiful deep brown hair behind her ear and turned to face him on the bench. "How terribly lonely."

His voice broke for a moment when he responded. "Yes. Yes, it is crushingly lonely."

"Well, I come here most days. You may join me any time."

Amrel smiled at the true hope shining in her eyes. I watched as days and months passed and grandpa Amrel visited Polaris by the water and watched the sun. He opened up to her like he had never opened up to anyone. He poured out his heart about his loneliness and his tremendously complicated responsibility as The Creator. He laughed with her and the light in his eyes danced just a bit more joyously. She shared every moment of her life with him and explained everything that was in her heart since Amrel still could not read her at all. Until one day, after a year of experiencing joy, Grandpa ended it.

"I think this should be the last time I visit you."

"Why? Please don't stop coming to see me," she begged.

"I am ashamed of myself for having let it go on this long. It is utterly selfish of me."

"How could that possibly be so? I love your company...and you know that to be true."

"Yes, and that is why it is selfish of me. Why do you not bring a *vordne* here instead of me?"

"I do not want another."

"My sweet one, I cannot give you a life. I cannot give you children and you can't even touch me. I have nothing to offer you but painful loneliness."

"With you here, I am not lonely. I don't need to have children to be happy. I have grown to love you, Amrel."

"You don't know what you're saying, Polaris. Not once in my existence have I ever romantically loved a woman before you, and I don't know if I could bear it. I couldn't endure watching you and not being able to take part in your life. I must stop seeing you for your sake."

"No, please..."

He disappeared and didn't show up for days after that. She called out for him daily and he cried in lonely desperation. After pacing for a long while, he took a clear emerald-cut crystal and held it near his heart. When he closed his eyes, light poured from his chest into the stone, and it sparkled and shone in a stunning array of colors. The next day when he knew Polaris was at their spot alone, he appeared to her.

"Oh, Amrel, I didn't think I'd ever see you again. Thank you. Thank you for coming back."

"It is not forever, my love. I just couldn't keep watching your grief. I've come to give you a gift—a...piece of me." Without touching it, he sent the ring over to Polaris and she took it.

"I can never caress your beautiful face, your wonderful curves, or kiss your inviting lips. I cannot give you little sons and daughters that will have your eyes and your laugh. I can't be your companion who you sleep next to every night and confide all your troubles that a spouse could relate to."

He opened his mouth to speak and struggled to speak the words as if it was the most painful admission he'd ever made in his life—the deepest wish of his soul.

"I am not a part of life. I am merely a creator of it. It is the greatest gift and greatest torture that could ever coexist. I cannot be a part of what I create and must pretend it doesn't break my heart. I can guide my people and provide support and advice. I can monitor and keep them safe. But to *live* a life...would be the greatest joy. What I can give you freely is a piece of my soul to keep with you always. With that ring, I hope you always feel my presence and know that I'm thinking of you every single day. It will be the closest you can ever come to touching me. If you are ever in trouble or need anything, it can help you. If you take it off, it will return to me, and I'll know you no longer need it. If it ends up in anyone else's hands, it will return to me as well."

Tears were running down Polaris's face as her lower lip quivered. "I don't know how I'll get on without you."

"You will," he whispered. He stepped as close as he could to her without burning her. "I love you, Polaris, and I will until my existence ends. I'm sorry I couldn't be more for you, but you will find someone who can be."

For a few thousand years, Grandpa watched her from afar as she went about her life and never married or had children. He scorned his selfish action for ever having interfered at all because his greatest wish wasn't realized. He wanted her to live the full life that he never could, and his meddling ensured that she didn't.

His weakness brought about the unhappiness of the one woman he ever loved, and was forced to endure her succumbing to the curse of Looma. He had spent every bit of his energy and had to watch in horror as his beloved Polaris decayed before his eyes. He had never in his existence been so powerless and he almost damned the consequences and warnings of Siare to attempt to rid the universe of the plague of the Guardians. If it was not for the fact that he had to reserve the last of his power for Cyra's survival, he might have given up entirely.

After he successfully held the black hole at bay, he found Polaris and fell beside her in horror at her state. He made it just in time before she perished.

"I have always loved you, and I always will," she said brokenly. Since she was already near death, he grabbed her in his arms and put his face to hers and she had a serene smile on her face as she faded away to dust. The ring never hit the ground before it returned to his hand.

He roared to the skies with his wings outstretched, looking around at his beloved race of people that writhed on the ground in pain, and he felt broken and weary. He cried and sat with her ashes in his hands, unable to move until Xenos appeared before him.

"Come, my friend. We must go."

"My only comfort is that soon I will be able to join her in death. I will burn to ash as well and welcome it gladly."

"Amrel, we've talked about this. I know we only have enough power to keep one of us immortal, but you cannot be the one. You are Our Creator! Let me be the one to sacrifice. It would be my honor."

"No. My time is over. I suppose I'll destroy this," he said, holding the glimmering ring.

"Amrel, that is a piece of your soul."

"My soul is damaged now anyway."

"It's invaluable, you cannot. There's no telling what would happen if it was unleashed."

"Fine. I will ensure my dear Cyra receives it as long as she chooses true love."

I jolted awake and cried out at Grandpa's pain. My view of him would never be the same—I had no idea he had loved and how incredibly lonely he was.

Vjera jumped up with a dagger in her hand without hesitation. "What is it? Is there someone here?"

"Are you alright?" Meili asked beside me in the bed.

"I'm sorry, it was just a dream."

They both laid back down and went to sleep. I looked down at my ring and couldn't believe it was a piece of Grandpa's soul.

The Destiny Diamond.

I thought of the time Grandpa and I had our first camp overnight on our grounds, just the two of us. He pointed to the night sky.

"That bright sparkling light is the north star, Polaris. No matter what time of the year, you can look up at the night sky and always find it watching over us. Other stars come and go with the seasons, but Polaris never wavers in her constancy. She is always there to guide our way."

CHAPTER
FORTY-EIGHT

Meili dressed me the next day as Vjera sat useless on my bed and watched, bouncing her leg. The moving sparkle of my grandfather's ring entranced me, especially the fact that it held a piece of his soul. It explained why I felt some connection to it. My soul spoke to his soul, and Kane and I would celebrate our love in the way he would have wanted.

My dress was white, as I'd requested, with a sweetheart neckline and off-the-shoulder lace beaded straps. The whole dress was hand beaded with pearls and crystals Meili had brought from Solis and permeated down the small train. Loose curls bounced down my back as I turned to take a hair comb Meili was handing me.

"This was your mother's. It has the symbol of each planet in Eredet. She believed in peace and justice for everyone in our galaxy and did her part in trying to make that happen. She would be so proud of your efforts for making her vision come true. She would have been beside herself with happiness with how the people are joining together."

"Oh, it's beautiful, Meili, thank you. I'm so happy to have something of my mother's on my wedding day."

474

"And this…is from your mother, Sarah. She gave it to Adelram, and he immediately gave it to me, not wanting responsibility for it."

It was a small oval locket, and inside was a picture of my parents and me together. I started to cry.

"I'm so sorry they can't be here today, Cyra. But I can sew this onto your belt, so you have it with you all day," Meili said.

"Thank you," was all I could manage to say.

Vjera walked over to me and gave me a hug which astonished me, but I didn't say a word about it and Meili pretended not to look. I now had representation from each set of parents I loved, even though none of them could be here. My birth parents of Solis. My Earth parents and Amrel, Our Creator. I felt the love from all of them within me.

Meili attached the locket and put some flowers in my hair. My hand bouquet was Kane's favorite Noctis flowers from the Fenix private lands and the long lavender-colored branches from over the sacred pond.

"Are you ready?" Meili asked with a huge smile.

"Yes." And I really was. I wanted to be by Kane's side again.

We drove to our normal spot by the sacred pond and my heart stopped as I saw Kane waiting for me at the end of the walkway lined with Noctis petals.

Tears instantly filled my eyes looking at that dark, beautiful, powerful, and loving man—and he wanted to spend the rest of his immortal life with me. The coils of our bond were on fire within us, and we were both overwhelmed with emotion, causing my heart to flutter and butterflies to bloom in my gut.

My senses were on overdrive. The intoxicating smell of the Noctis flowers, which were similar to hyacinths, made me slightly dizzy.

The bouquet was wrapped with the braided ribbons and charms I'd prepared for the *siduma* ceremony, and Kane's ring fastened to it. It felt as if my breath was magnified in my head while the sound around me was muted and distant, but quickly returned when Kane smiled.

In an uncharacteristic public display of emotion, Kane put his hand over his mouth and tried to keep his composure as I could feel tears forming in him. I couldn't stop grinning like a fool as I felt him mentally touching every inch of me with his fierce glowing green eyes.

I had never felt such overwhelming joy, love, and bliss, and it was hard to fathom that we were in the middle of an apocalyptic war. Kane gave me a reprieve from the horrors Grandpa needed me to face, and I didn't have to do it alone. He was my lover, my teacher, my *imana*, the King of my prophecy, and soon, my husband.

Each step forward I took felt like one more step toward destiny, and nothing had ever felt more perfect. The Varjun people on each side of me were filled with acceptance and support, and their king before me was waiting as I walked to him and accepted this place at his side as my new home.

When I stepped onto the platform and felt the warmth of his love, I knew I would never be without family again. He took my hands and I nearly swooned at his gentle touch. I would never get enough of the way he looked at me like I was the rarest gem in the universe. I never dreamed that I was able to love like this, and it made me feel stronger. It made me want to fight harder.

Jonsi spoke and I attempted to come out of my haze of emotion to listen. "Most of you know what a long time feels like. We're immortal beings, and sometimes we can feel the fatigue of age. We even have a term for it—it's called *tenhador*—the lonely pain. I've felt it myself these past long years since my Lydon passed, but it's said if you are lucky enough to have found true love, you can never fall into the throes of *tenhador*. Love makes you feel tenacious and alive. It gives you a reason to celebrate every moment of the existence Our Creator has gifted us. Amrel gave us not only the gift of life but a *reason* to live it. Imagine how difficult it must be to never know the feeling of love, to be able to touch another being and feel that connection, either paternal or romantic."

My heart wrenched thinking of Grandpa and Xenos and how much they suffered through never-ending *tenhador*.

"It gives us hope, power, strength, and it gives us family. Kane and Cyra will now burn the Plodan Flower that Meili was so good as to grow for us."

I looked at Meili and I swore she was squealing with delight. "What is the Plodan Flower?" I whispered to Kane.

"It's...uh...a fertility flower," Kane responded.

Kane laughed at my sudden look of utter shock and terror. He took my hand and we both burned the white flower, and I followed his lead, bending over to inhale the smoke.

"May their union be blessed with love, happiness, and children. Present your rings and put them on your *vordne's* hands."

I untied the ring for Kane from the ribbon and slid it on his finger and he did the same for me.

"I made this ring myself with Varjun gold that the first King, King Vangelis, gave to his *imana*," Kane said with a smile. I looked at it and it looked handmade, which I absolutely loved. The Varjun gold looked similar to rose gold.

It was incredibly special that he used the same gold that his ancestor gifted his Buruj mate, Nexia—Kane's other descendant who gave him his special gifts. "It's so beautiful, thank you. Your ring was given to me by grandpa Amrel the day he died. He told me to wait and give it to someone very special and that I'd know when that time was, and he was right. I had the inside engraved to match the one you gave me."

His eyes twinkled with green light. "Thank you for choosing me," he whispered.

Jonsi took our ribbons and wrapped them around our hands in

a tight knot. When he was done, he put his hands on top of them until light started to glow, and the ribbons disappeared and seeped into our skin. I was alarmed when I started seeing visions of Kane's past as if I were living through them.

His stunning mother was the first thing I saw, and she held him tight as a little boy and rocked him to sleep.

The scene changed and Kane's reflection in a mirror made my heart skip at the sight of the beautiful little boy. The next vision was of his father sitting with him in his lap, teaching him lessons with passion as Kane's answers made Adelram beam with pride, no sign of the internal struggles he'd had when I knew him.

The memories changed quickly, making me somewhat sad I didn't have more time to spend with them. But I was awed when I saw the castle covered in Noctis flowers under a bright shining sky and a massive waterfall behind it. The sheer beauty of Varjutus before the curse was something to behold.

I watched as Kane and his sister, Luna, played in the bright blue waters and caught strange-looking fish before the scene changed, and Kane sat with a beautiful wolf-like creature with a sleek, long head and chrome-colored fur. It had beautiful golden designs through the fur that made me wonder if it was painted on. A creature I realized must now be extinct.

Kane had infused a memory of him learning to ride a Kometa and I was pleased to know he wasn't born confident and talented. He showed me massive Varjun gatherings with fire husks, dancing, games, merchant stores, and hundreds of thriving cities.

He danced with his mother and sister as Adelram watched from afar and laughed with a joy in his eyes I had never seen before. This Adelram was a whole person very early in his reign as King.

A younger, unwilling Kane dragged his feet with Lydon, who was training him—but much of their time was spent with Lydon merely sitting with Kane and letting him express his feelings.

I saw the birth of his sister and how Kane held his baby sister in his hands with wonder and excitement, and his father watched with tears of pride and joy.

My own tears began to form, watching his memories because every happiness he had known was destroyed until his newer events appeared.

He shared the same memory I had given him of the first time we met while I was playing the cello, except I saw it from his point of view and his feelings of love that he couldn't explain. He showed me the memory of me blabbering about him smelling like Christmas magic and I laughed out loud when I heard the words Candy Kane.

I saw him looking down on me after we bonded.

When the memories stopped, he felt my heart breaking for him, and he held my face and said, "I have you now. I have new happy memories to make, and I'm the luckiest man in the universe for it."

His unwavering strength was truly remarkable, making me want to be better than I was—for him.

"You are now bound together not only in marriage but with the unbreakable bond of *imana*. You will now be bound together as King and Queen to the people." A Varjun woman stepped forward with a massive tie with trinkets offered by the people. Jonsi wrapped it around us, and just like before, the ties and trinkets disappeared into our skin.

"The fastening is complete. You may kiss."

Kane picked me up so I was at eye level with him, and he kissed me like it was the best day of both of our lives. I wrapped my arms around him and barely heard the screams and clapping in the background.

"Cyra will now kneel before the people," Jonsi said.

I raised the skirt of my dress and knelt on my bare knees just as Kane had done almost a year ago. Kane stepped forward and stood beside me with his hand on my left shoulder. One by one, the people walked up and presented an item before me and touched my right shoulder.

The majority of the people presented me with small glasses of water or a tiny bit of food like one grape or a berry. Some gave me small trinkets from their homes they valued and drawings of the Varjutus they hoped I could restore for them.

I realized that they didn't have the long history and connection with me that they did with Kane, so these were the things they associated with me. I tried not to cry as Joven placed one of his warriors before me, and Lorcan offered a dried flower his father gave his mother.

Oliver walked up before us and asked, "Can I offer something to Cyra?"

"Of course," Kane answered.

Oliver placed an ARCADE-ON game coin on the pile of offerings, and I nearly broke down in tears, but mercifully, I could fight them off, so I didn't make a spectacle of myself. He touched my right shoulder and whispered, "You're going to do great things for us all, not just Varjutus."

How could such a young boy say such extraordinary things?

When everyone had presented an item, Jonsi raised them into the air, emitting light as they transformed into two small chains that clasped around my ankles. Kane looked at me in surprise and I wondered why.

"Cyra Fenix Distira, you now walk with the weight of our people with every step you take and bear the mark of the Varjun Queen." An interconnected knot tattoo matching Kane's appeared on my right shoulder when Jonsi removed his hand.

"Rise and Rejoice! For our Queen, Cyra Fenix Distira!"

Cyra Distira. In the midst of these wild few days, it hadn't even occurred to me that my name would change. I felt like I was in constant evolution as I discovered more about myself and who I was. Cyra Fela. Cyra Fenix. Cyra Distira. Was this my final destination?

A quiet whisper of voices began to enter my mind, followed by flashes of memories. Crying, laughing, babies wailing, celebration. It was the voices of the Varjun people running through me from their offerings and from the trinkets. I looked at them all—their hopes and fears showing through their cheers. Kane and I were all they had left to help lead them through the evil and survive to see the future.

Kane took my hand and kissed it. "Are you okay, my Queen?"

I looked at him and smiled. "Yes...I'm just taking everything in."

"I know it's a lot. But I'll be right by your side."

"I know."

Kane led me off the podium and I nearly fell off of it. "What the..."

"Oh, I probably should have mentioned that. The King and Queens's Chains carry weight with them, especially in times of crisis. The more our people suffer, the heavier the burden. Sometimes I feel like my chain is going to crush my chest and my heart with it. Adelram was the only other Varjun ruler to have ankle chains so I was surprised when they chose you. He said it felt like wearing shackles, and some days he could barely walk, but he only had one."

Just when I thought I had enough trials in my life. "Oh boy."

"Come, I'm going to dance with my wife," Kane said.

"Wife?" I asked, smiling.

"That's what you call it, right? I want it to have meaning to you."

He had a knack for taking my breath away.

"Yes, husband," I whispered. I wrapped my hands around him and kissed him. "Can we request only slow songs tonight? I think I'm going to have to relearn how to walk."

"When it gets too heavy to bear, I will be here to carry you."

"And I'll be here to protect your heart when it's in danger of being crushed."

"You have no idea how long I've been waiting to hear someone say that."

I leaned my head down on his chest and breathed him in.

"Do you know what this ring is?" I asked him, raising my grandfather's ring.

"The Destiny Diamond? I don't know what it's capable of."

"I don't either, but Grandpa sent me a memory last night. He was once in love with a Sunya woman, and she loved him too. They couldn't be together because of who Grandpa was—he could never touch her or give her children.

When Jonsi mentioned living in *tenhador*, I knew that's exactly what grandpa Amrel had experienced. He was such a loving person, and I could feel his overwhelming heartbreak watching her from afar, not being able to be with her. He gave her this ring to keep a piece of himself close to her. It's the closest they could ever come to touching. This ring contains a piece of his soul, and he wanted me to receive it if I had chosen to accept true love."

He looked down in shock. "That has a piece of Our Creator's soul? No wonder it's so beautiful. It explains why you felt a connection to it too."

"This ring is the embodiment of true love."

"Then it is certainly the perfect one for you, Cyra."

CHAPTER
FORTY-NINE

We danced for hours, and I had the time of my life surrounded by the people I'd sworn to serve. Kane and I separated to mingle with everyone, and I watched him alive and in his element. Caelan approached him looking defeated and I tried really hard not to gloat. They started dancing and I smiled at Vish, who approached me.

"Care to dance?" he asked.

"I'd love to."

"Congratulations. You look breathtaking."

"Thank you, Vish. It means a lot to me that you're here. You've become part of my family and I have a lack of that here, so thanks."

"Yeah, you know I'd do anything for you, Cyra."

What a bore.

My head jerked around to find the source of the voice, and saw Kane looking at Vish. Did I imagine that?

I turned back to Vish. "And I'd do the same for you. Have you acclimated any since coming to Varjutus? How have you been feeling?"

"I'm dealing. It's no Solis, but I'm alive and you're alive. That's all that matters. I'm enjoying the time nurturing the crops in the Fenix lands."

"I'm glad. I should give those history books another stab so we can finally get a better picture of our past."

Doesn't she know he's in love with her?

What the fuck? I looked back at Kane and he was staring directly at me and smiled innocently when we made eye contact.

"Uh, I'm sorry, Vish, I have to…"

"Yeah, no problem."

I walked over to Kane. "Do you mind if I borrow him?" Caelan rolled her eyes and walked away.

"What's going on?" I whispered to him.

"What do you mean?"

"Vish is not in love with me."

"…I didn't say that."

"Yes, you did."

"You heard my thoughts?"

"I guess?"

Can my life get any weirder?

"Your life is not weird. If you call your life weird, you're calling me weird," Kane said.

"I didn't say that out loud," I whispered.

Can you hear me?

"Yes, I can!" Kane said, his eyes bulging.

"Is it our wedding or just a delayed gift of our bond?"

No idea, but that's dangerous, Kane said

Only if you have something to hide, lover.

On the contrary, I was thinking about how you'll have to bear my thoughts of tasting you and making love to you…feeling you from the inside…

"Okay, I get the hint," I said, laughing.

"That's what you get to look forward to later."

Oh, I can't wait. I winked at him.

Kane shivered at my whisper in his head. Merick, Kal, Vjera, and Meili noticed us acting strange and wandered over.

"Gross, you two, get a room," Vjera said.

"Oh, we plan to very soon," Kane responded

"Nice," Merick said, and Kal rolled his eyes.

"You know, Cyra, I think it's time for you to get your first call sign now that you have your Queen's Mark. I want you to always be able to call me as well. It's another Varjun rite," Kane said with a smirk.

"I would love that." It was just one more thing to make me feel like a real Varjun.

"I would be honored if you received one for me as well," Kal said. "I'm here to protect you, always."

"And for me," Meili said.

Merick and Vjera looked at each other with a half sneer, and I laughed.

Vish came out of nowhere, chiming in. "You will always have me by my side. I'd be honored if you had a mark for me."

"Okay, fine. Me too," Merick replied.

"What the hell. I can always just ignore your call. No harm done," Vjera said.

I looked around at my friends. My chosen family. "Well...it seems like I'll have barely any free skin left."

"We can make them small," Kane laughed. "But if you're okay with it, I'd like to get a matching call sign for you that matches your birthmark."

"That's perfect, and I'll make my birthmark into your call sign."

"I'll get Jonsi to perform it for us," Kane said, walking away to get him.

"I'm already here! I'd be happy to do it."

"Come, let's start a *fire husk,* and I'll make your call marks.

Jonsi led us to the giant fire pit, and I lit it on fire. The villagers gathered around and started to tell family stories.

"Let's do Kane's first," Jonsi said. "You want to use your birthmark as the call sign for you both?"

"Yes," we both responded.

Jonsi took my right wrist, and his hand glowed in a golden light. I felt a warm, burning sensation, and when he removed his hand, my birthmark was a dark tattoo. Jonsi took Kane's hand and mimicked his action until he had a matching mark on his left wrist. It meant a lot to me that Kane wanted the same mark I was born with.

"Who's next?" Jonsi asked.

"Me!" Meili jumped in. She sat next to me, and I saw the excitement in her eyes. "I thought we could do a Rodina flower. It symbolizes family and friends," she said.

"That sounds perfect, except I'm going to add a twisting vine with thorns since there's power under those petals," I said with a wink.

"Where would you like it?" Jonsi asked.

"I think I'll put them all under my left arm so I can easily get to them."

Jonsi touched a spot closest to my elbow and made a beautiful flower that looked similar to a peony with a stem and a twisting thorny vine around it. He did the same to her in the same spot, and when she touched it afterward, my matching mark glowed, and I felt a beacon directing me to her. It made us both smile since it was the first time we'd felt a call sign.

"Okay, do me next," Vjera offered. "After all, I'm your cousin and don't want to be put in your armpit. That's where Merick belongs."

I laughed and nodded my agreement as Merick scowled.

Jonsi made a lightning bolt to represent Vjera, and Kal offered to go next.

"I'll go next. My sign is a full moon partially hidden by two dark clouds."

The dispeller of darkness with the power of wielding weather. Jonsi made the mark right above Vjera's bolt, which I thought was appropriate.

"Merick?" Jonsi asked.

But I interrupted before Merick's turn. "What about my mark on Kal and Vjera's arm?"

"The Varjun can use the Queen's mark on all of us to call you. You should be able to hear who's calling you when it's used," Kal answered.

My shoulders shrugged. "I guess time for the armpit," I said, laughing.

Merick hissed with mock annoyance. "Mine is unsurprisingly the symbol for invisibility. Two chains bound together, and the point where they intersect is black. That's the place where I hide."

Jonsi put his hand underneath the top part of my arm. "You know it's said that those who walk invisible belong to no single dimension."

The villagers stopped their stories and looked at Jonsi.

"That's rubbish," one of them said, laughing.

"That's what the Elders of the past have said."

"What does that even mean?" Vish asked.

"Just as it sounds."

"While I like to retain my cool and mysterious image, I have to agree with the crowd. My skin goes invisible, and then it reappears. Nothing exciting."

"If you say so…" Jonsi said with a smile.

"I'm up," Vish said. He was more eager than I'd seen him in a long time.

"I supposed we'll put you on my right arm. I've been thinking about it. What do you think about the lovely tree at your family's farmhouse with the swing?"

"That's perfect. One of my happiest memories is playing on that swing with my little brothers."

"Great."

"But if you don't mind, I'd like your mark on my arm to be a big sun. It's what I associate with you."

My eyes raised, shocked that someone thought of me the way I thought of Grandpa, but I was touched by it. "Of course."

Kane looked down away from us, still holding some silly grudge against Vish. Jonsi completed the tree where I asked, and Vish got his call sign for me on his left bicep.

"Cyra, you should probably get one of the *Curadh* as well. We all have one," Kane suggested.

"And that one needs to be large and visible," Kal said proudly.

I thought about it for a moment. "Okay, let's put it on my back, right shoulder under my Queen's mark."

I looked at Kal's *Curadh* mark, and it was two crossed swords facing upward with Noctis flowers down by the hilt. Where the swords form a "V," "Varjutus" was written next to it in black. "Curadh" was written in cursive underneath it in the same crimson color as the Noctis flowers.

"I'm surprised to see flowers with the deadly *Curadh* swords."

"Well, Noctis flowers are deadly poisonous. Part of their extract is used in our Varjun daggers," Kane responded.

"What! Then why would you have them everywhere?"

"Well, as long as you don't eat them, you're fine," Jonsi said.

"The Varjun certainly live dangerously," I said with a laugh.

"And don't you forget it," Merick responded.

I looked down at the art that told the new story of my life with the people who'd become my family. A family of my own making who had just pledged to be there for me no matter what. So much so that it was etched into my skin forever.

In a matter of a few hours, I'd gained a husband, a new civilization where I belonged, and a loyal family. I was lucky enough to realize that after three sets of parents, I couldn't be with, the people we chose to surround ourselves with could matter most to us.

After a few more hours of listening to the stories of the Varjun people, they started to go home and wished us a final congratulations. Kane held me up and drove me back to his bedroom.

"I think it's time you moved in here with me."

"If you insist, husband."

"I insist on sharing everything with you."

"I like the sound of that," I said with a smile. There was a large fireplace in the room, and I lit it with my flame. I walked over to the soothing crackling sound and started to undo my dress until I stood naked before him.

"How beautiful." Kane also undressed until he was naked, and I felt him studying me. Seeing his strong body and what it was about to do made me ache for him.

I do so love hearing your thoughts, Kane spoke silently.

I sent him an image of me touching myself, rubbing a finger on my clit before and moaning his name, and the bulging of his eyes matched his growing cock. He returned an image of him moving my finger away and replacing it with his tongue, licking and sucking on me. It felt like the vision went on forever, and when I climaxed, I wasn't sure if I did in real life as well. My breath uneven and labored as if I actually had.

It was strangely erotic, and flames erupted all over my body. Kane finally walked toward me and held me in his arms, immune to the fire. His fingers frosted over, and he started grazing me all over with his chilled touch. While I was immune to his magic, he still felt colder than usual, just as he described my fire as a pleasant warmness.

He touched my lips, and his temperature was in deep contrast to mine, and it heightened my senses since it was new and exciting. I felt the cold running down my neck, and when he touched my nipple, I cried out in shock, shivering in pleasure and surprise. My pussy clenched in burning anticipation.

He kissed my neck with his cold lips and tongue and when he breathed out, I saw his breath as if it were freezing temperatures in the room. I slowly slid down, touching his defined body, and when I was kneeling before him, I took his beautiful cock in my mouth.

"Holy fuck," he whispered.

As I worked on him, sliding the tip of his cock over my tongue while holding his base with my other hand, I sent him images of what I was doing so he could see from my point of view. He trembled, enjoying what I was doing to him.

"Holy *fuck!*" he cried, and I smiled at his reaction. I stopped when he was about to come, and he hissed with surprise.

He picked me up and threw me on the bed, his hands still cold to the touch.

"It seems you delight in teasing me," Kane whispered in my ear.

"One of my new greatest delights."

"Then let me return the favor, my love."

He lowered toward my pelvis to do what I had just done to him. His tongue was ice cold and wet, and when he slipped an icy finger into me, I clenched the sheets and yelled his name.

He chuckled as he continued his work, repaying the favor by sending me an image of him kissing all over my body while his hands were on my breasts. With the vision and what he was currently doing to me, it felt like he was doing the work of two people. Heat bloomed in my core, and I started to pulse on him, so close to coming.

He stopped everything abruptly and looked at me with a smile.

"Kane!" I gasped.

"Yes?"

I jumped up and threw him down, pinning him on the bed this time. He let me have my way with him, giving me complete control, and I slowly placed his cock in my entrance. The little growl that rumbled in his chest was such a fucking turn-on, and he watched me intently as I slid down inch by delicious inch until I was full, and we were complexly joined. I started to move on him, slowly at first.

He held my hips, his fingers digging deep into my skin. And as my pace quickened, he moaned and moved his hands up my curves. Craving control again, he grabbed my ass and began sliding me up and down on him, leaving me at his mercy. His strength and speed were on display as he slammed me down onto him repeatedly, pressure building through my body before we erupted and came apart at the seams. His cock pulsed, releasing within me, and my body quivered with a mind-blowing climax.

Unable to move, I fought to catch my breath but he didn't give me much of a reprieve before he threw me down and turned me to my belly. He raised my ass and damn near purred in delight at the sight of me bent over like that. He gave no warning before he forcefully entered me from behind, and I gasped at the fullness of him in this new position.

There was no soft build-up or tension. Instead, he thrust quickly, pounding against me hard and fast. My knuckles were white from gripping the sheets so tightly, and I screamed when he reached around to touch my bundle of nerves. The euphoric vibrations from his special little gift drew me over the edge.

He knew exactly what to do to my body and I could do nothing but whimper as I came again, at his mercy, while he simply kept going. When he finally released inside me, I came again. It seemed the simple act of him coming also made me do so. I slumped to the bed, unable to take anymore, and he mercifully laid down beside me.

"I can't believe I can have this any time I want," Kane said, panting.

"Well, not quite any time since we have so much going on right now, but often enough. I can't believe I get to call someone as beautiful as you my husband and soul mate."

"I don't know how I got so lucky," Kane whispered, touching my face.

"You deserve it, my love."

"We both do."

CHAPTER FIFTY

I fell asleep in my husband's arms and had no dreams disrupting my sleep. When we woke, I couldn't tell what time it was. Mercifully, it felt like we'd slept for ten hours since nobody had disturbed us.

I rolled over to look at Kane. "Well, this is the best wedding present ever. I needed that sleep," I said with a smile.

"Me too. It was glorious."

I burrowed into his chest, and he wrapped his arms around me. We both looked up when we heard a loud noise in the distance.

"What was that?" I asked. Kane shot up in worry.

"I don't know."

I got out of bed to look out the window but I instantly fell to the ground. I got up again and was stunned when I tried to walk.

"Oh my god. It's like walking through cement."

Kane put his hand to his chest, and it was evident that lifting it with his next breath took effort. "My chain is heavy also...the people are in trouble."

Right on cue, our King and Queen's mark lit up, followed by a burning on my back.

"The people are calling," Kane said.

"From everywhere!" I was overcome with fear, not knowing what was happening. As promised, once the *Curadh* mark was activated our armor appeared on our bodies. We drove to the castle courtyard since that was the closest call. Kane called for the *Curadh* to meet us there.

Varjun were running and screaming and there were three sickly-looking people attacking them with magic.

"Who are they? They're not Bellum," I asked.

Jonsi, Merick, Meili, Vish, Kal, and Vjera appeared. One of the invaders threw some magic in our direction and Jonsi held up his arms and blocked the attack, but the magic didn't stop at him. As Jonsi held the barrier, I saw him weaken.

"Jonsi, we need you to reserve your strength!" Kane yelled.

I used my second sight and saw about sixty of these magical beings throughout Varjutus and I gasped.

"What is it?" Kane asked.

I blasted the three invaders in the courtyard, and they were knocked back into the air.

"There's about fifty to sixty of them," I said to Kane.

"*Halogi*," Jonsi whispered in disgust.

"*Halogi*?" Vish asked.

"It means contaminated," Vjera whispered.

"They're unnatural," I said. "I feel that dark magic radiating off them at the highest levels I've ever seen. I feel queasy already." Just as I finished the statement, I ran and threw up from the poisonous energy.

I started to feel a strange pulsating and buzzing in my head. It felt like something was calling to me. The Sword of Istina! I innately knew that I would be able to summon it. It was *begging* to be united with me. I raised my hand and called out to it silently, and it materialized in my hand, glowing in its blue flame.

The *Curadh* and Garwein appeared. "All of you split up. Kal, give them direction, and Merick shroud as many villagers and houses as you can. Meili, stay as hidden as possible and heal anyone you can save. Vish, stay with Meili. Jonsi, be careful. We need you to conserve your energy."

Oliver appeared as Bart in front of me.

"Oliver, get all the children to the hiding place we discussed." He nodded and disappeared.

"Cyra, where are most of them?" Kane asked.

I used my second sight to track their energy. "Baum village."

"Let's go."

We drove there and I almost broke down at what I saw. There were lots of dead Varjun since they had no defenses against this type of magic. These former Solians looked like they had the same affliction as the beasts we saw on Solis, with ruptured skin and lime-green ooze seeping from the cracks like there was so much power within them it was bursting from their body. Merick appeared and started to shroud the villagers.

Kane, Ondour, and I began to fight the Halogi so Merick had a chance at hiding everyone.

"They have no thoughts!" Ondour screamed. "It's like they're programmed. I only hear them saying 'kill' and 'destroy'...and... 'Cyra.'"

Kane looked at him in shock.

Over my dead body, I heard from his mind.

About ten of them came running toward me and I blasted my fire toward them. Just like the beasts, they were unaffected by the pain. They were slightly singed, but they were able to deflect most of the fire. Kane tried to rip them apart with his pressure ability, but they easily deflected the energy.

"I don't think we'll be able to win with magic!" Ondour yelled as the ten *Halogi* knocked me down.

The former Solians started to rip at my skin, and I screamed in pain. The corrupting energy radiating off them made me hazy as it had in the *Warrior's Sanna*. I managed to get the Sword of Istina free, and I stabbed one of them in the gut. The thick green liquid started pouring out of its mouth and fell onto me, making me vomit. The *Halogi,* still on my sword, eerily smiled, and I could sense no life inside of him. His pupils were the same lime-green color as the substance spilling from them.

A tugging at my chest caught my attention, and I remembered the Nebula Diamond! I tried to activate it so it would absorb the dark energy around me so I could stop the sickness. I held the diamond in my hand, and it glowed a bright blue. The effects were instantaneous, clearing my mind of the sickness fog so I could function without retching.

Kane and Ondour were fighting the other *Halogi* that were running directly for me, and Merick had successfully shrouded all of Baum and disappeared to Leht. I saw Meili behind the shroud healing the wounded villagers and Vish joined us in fighting the *Halogi*.

Raising my sword, it erupted in the blue flame, and I swung and decapitated the *Halogi* I had stabbed, and it finally stopped moving. We had only killed two so far, and there were still at least fifty more of them on Varjutus.

The *Halogi* we were fighting all stopped and held out their hands and blasted us backward as if they were working as one. With my second sight, I saw the attack they were about to make, and I counteracted the effect of the blast and stood in place. They walked toward the shrouded village, and I could tell they couldn't see beyond it, but they threw magic against it and the shroud quickly started to weaken. It took everything in me to run toward them since my Queen's Chains were so heavy it felt like I was running tied to thirty-pound weights on each foot.

I decapitated two of the *Halogi*, but the remaining ones managed to destroy the shroud, and they attacked a large group of the villagers while I watched in horror as some ran screaming with their skin melting away with some kind of poison.

When Kane, Ondour, and Vish returned, we killed the remaining *Halogi*. Meili and I ran to the suffering villagers and were able to save half of them, but their skin was still damaged even after healing them. We were too late for about twenty poor souls who lay on the ground in a pool of gore. I wiped my tears and got up because there were way too many *Halogi* out there to stop now.

"Let's go to Leht," I said. I could feel that what was left of Riva was destroyed, and most of the *Halogi* were concentrated in Leht Village.

Merick had managed to shroud the people of Leht, and the *Halogi* were blindly attacking, mercifully missing most of them. Erek, Kal, Vjera, and Garwein were there with other skilled men fighting against them. The villagers who had no magic barely had any chance of survival against these monsters. Merick was decapitating them while invisible, but we were grossly outnumbered.

How are we going to beat this many of them? I asked Kane silently.

He looked back at me with the most heartbreaking look of defeat I've ever seen on him.

We go down protecting our people until the end.

I nodded. We would die together, fighting for our people.

A blast of dark energy hit us, and we flew backward. Merick screamed out as he was impaled by a dagger that was stuck in the ground. His invisibility failed and I saw the weapon stuck in his shoulder.

"Merick!" Vjera and Kane screamed.

When I looked forward, I was filled with fear as a *Halogi* appeared above me, but a sword plunged through its neck, causing nausea to roll in my gut until I saw who had come to my aid.

"Urien! Oh, thank God."

"This looks like the end…" he whispered.

I nodded. "Thanks for being here."

"I will not leave you."

He helped me up and I heard an eerie whisper in my ear.

How do you kill that which is already dead? It was Nexia of the Buruj. I looked to Kane, who had just slain another *Halogi,* and I could tell he heard it too.

You cannot win by killing one at a time. How do you kill that which is already dead?

I looked at Kane with my eyes silvered over and I saw his dark violet energy spilling over in waves, waiting to be used.

You drain it of its essence, I replied.

Yes.

"Protect us!" I yelled at the *Curadh.* I ran to Kane and held his hand.

It's dangerous. I could end up killing innocent people with the Halogi.

We have no choice. We do it together, I said silently. There was a slight tremor of fear running through him but he nodded.

He let me infiltrate his magic and we both started absorbing all that available energy he vowed he'd never use. The energy that made him fear himself and what he was capable of. It's what he hid from all his life and now, it was the answer to our prayers. We absorbed as much as possible and I gave Kane extra energy he normally would not have been able to use. The *Halogi* pushed through everyone that was attacking them and ran for me and Kane. We released the energy as one and directed it at every corrupted soul before us and I helped Kane focus the energy so we didn't harm any citizens. The *Halogi* stopped in place and started to scream and fall to the ground as we pulled the energy and what-ever life force that was keeping them "alive" out of them. I saw the torment on Kane's face, and I felt it too. It wasn't like a soldier killing an enemy. We could feel the panic, torture, and desperation of the souls before us as we killed them little by little. When they were near death, we felt a small piece of the person that was left behind, and they begged for help.

They are beyond saving now. Their minds and bodies were too corrupted, Nexia spoke in our heads.

A tear fell from my eye, and I never broke the connection, draining what was left of them.

Sometimes the kindest thing you can do…

…is end a life, I finished. *You've been preparing me for this.*

Yes. This moment and so many more to come.

I was filled with horror by her statement, and Kane's suffering nearly broke me. We felt the last bit of life and energy leave the *Halogi* until they were empty shells. Our people were safe for now, but at what cost? Many of our people died, and these *Halogi*—they were Solians that were tortured and made into something else.

"Wait—there's still one more," I said. He appeared before us and let out a force so strong everyone was knocked away…except for me.

My heart hammered in my chest and my blood ran icy cold at who stood before me. Theo was here.

Before anyone could rise and see him, he grabbed me and we appeared at the opposite end of the planet with barren, dead land as far as the eye could see. The bright cerulean moon was the only indication we were still on Varjutus.

"Theo? Please, you don't have to help the Guardians. You can still come away from this. There is still a place for you here if you stop now."

His one brow was raised as if in absolute disbelief. His eyes were still eerily red and the brightness he once exuded from his skin was now dull and lifeless.

"You really thrive in a state of denial, don't you?" He shook his head and rolled his eyes. "Come here." His finger curled toward him, motioning for me, but he was using his new power that I was unable to resist. I even tried activating the Nebula Diamond, but it seemed to do nothing. He dug his nose into my neck, holding onto it with his other hand, and breathed deeply. "You reek of him.

You've made a horrible, horrible mistake bonding with him. There was still a chance to come to your senses and save yourself, but now you're beyond help."

Through his rage and hatred, there was still a hint of hurt in his eyes. Theo was still in there somewhere.

He opened his hand to reveal a piece of paper, but I did not attempt to take it. "The Guardians have a message for you."

"What do they want?"

"You."

"Why?"

Cyra, where are you? Kane's voice echoed in my mind.

"You're what Orphlam has been waiting for these past few thousand years."

"Again, why?"

"Read and find out." His head tilted in a way so similar to Orphlam that it made me feel sick to my stomach. "How do you like his new race of beings?"

"*Halogi*…"

"If that's what you'd like to call them, I suppose it has a nice ring to it."

Every call sign on my body was lighting up. My friends tried to find me, but I ignored them.

Cyra, answer me! I cannot find you!

"You can't win this fight. There's barely any of you left on this dead planet and I can count how many of them have magic on one hand. It's over for you, give in to Orphlam's request and spare what remains. There are a thousand more of those beings waiting to take you all down should you resist, and when we're done with you, we will find the *mikla* on The Void and we will owe it all to you."

"What the hell do you mean?" I asked, my voice shaking.

"We'll see you soon."

He disappeared and I quickly ripped open the note.

My darling girl,

You may have deduced by now what I've been up to in the past quiet months. I assure you we've been tirelessly busy. And truthfully, I could not have done this without you. The moment you put on that power bracelet, I got a world of insight into your power, and it turns out you're what I've been looking for all this time. I was able to take a drop of your energy to see how you're able to wield it. Now I have an army of a thousand of the most lethal assassins in the galaxy, and I will get what I want —my sincerest thanks for your kind helpfulness.

I'm afraid I do need one final thing from you, though. I need more of your energy. To incentivize your compliance I have your friend, the cook, in my possession. Come visit me alone by morning or I will rip his throat out and feed it to my new friends. And I do mean alone.

Yours forever in necessity and destiny,

Orphlam

The letter burned away in my hand. Bile rose in my throat, and my hatred for Orphlam grew to an all-time high. He had used a part of me to use those vile creatures to kill innocent people.

I drove back to the castle grounds since I could sense Kane there.

"Cyra, what happened to you?"

I hesitated for a moment, not sure if I should tell him about what happened. "A *Halogi* took me away, but I managed to kill it. I'm fine." It was physically painful to lie to my *imana*, but I felt I had no choice. I had to keep him safe until I could process what I should do. And when I had a few moments alone, I would do just that.

Our friends were currently looking through the dead and an unexplainable feeling of dread came over me, causing me to turn in that direction. I ran to the side of the castle and lost my ability to inhale for a moment.

"No! No, no, no." I fell to the ground beside the body of a little boy, and in his hand was a small dark elf character from Earth.

"Joven, no." I picked him up in my arms and held him. "You're okay. I've got you. You're okay."

Kane ran up to me, his hand to his heart, feeling my pain before he saw what had happened. He knelt beside me and covered his mouth.

"His parents have been looking for him…. I told them he was probably in hiding."

I put my hand on his wound and my hand started to glow. Right away, I could feel no connection between his body and my healing power. I panicked and touched the flower mark on my arm.

"Cyra, thank goodness you're safe." Meili gasped when she saw Joven in my arms.

"Help me. Meili, help me. I can't heal him."

"Oh, Cyra," she said, crying at the sight of the sweet little boy. "I'm so sorry. He's gone. It's been far too long."

"Please!" I cried. "Please try!"

She nodded and knelt beside us. She put her hand on his wound and it glowed, but nothing happened. Eventually, I let her stop and I brushed the hair out of his beautiful face and picked him up against me and sobbed. This charming, innocent child didn't deserve to die.

Oliver appeared with Lorcan and I could tell they'd been crying.

"I tried to get him to come, but he wouldn't. He wouldn't listen to me," Oliver said with his bottom lip trembling. "I'm sorry, Cyra, it was my fault."

"Come here," I motioned to both of them. I held them all, and the chains on my feet felt like they were cutting into my skin.

"It's not your fault, either of you. Okay?" They nodded through their tears. "This is the Guardians' fault, and we will get justice for our people."

Joven's parents ran when they saw us, and their cries made my heart break. I gave them their son and they held him one final time. I got up and looked at the dead Varjun I celebrated with just the day before. Their cold, lifeless faces had just been smiling and full of joy. I walked away in shock, unable to think straight.

"Queen Cyra! Wait, please."

I turned to Joven's parents and waited for them to tell me I was scum for letting their sweet little boy die.

"Joven would have wanted you to have this."

They handed me the D&D character I had given Joven for his birthday since his family didn't have anything to give him.

"I couldn't possibly…"

"No, please take it. You changed his life the day you gave him that. He would want you to have it."

I took it since I was unable to argue with grieving parents, much less look them in the eye any longer. "Thank you."

It would have been better if they screamed at me.

I drove to Baum in a haze and Kane followed me, never leaving my side. Caelan's father was dead on the ground, and she was crying at his side. Most of the huts were destroyed and the people were roaming through the bodies.

A pregnant Tess held her newlywed husband shaking in shock. I went to her, and he was thankfully alive, just severely wounded.

"He's going to be okay," she said through tears.

Vjera came up behind us and she took Tess into her arms. "I've got her." I nodded my thanks.

I kept walking amongst the dead, feeling like a ghost myself, and saw Jaike's lifeless body with a villager next to him, and he explained to me what happened.

"He was looking for Lorcan. I told him the children were in hiding, but he panicked. He never recovered after the loss of his pregnant wife, and when he agreed to watch over Lorcan he couldn't stop worrying about losing him. Now I guess he has."

"I suppose I'm cursed. I can't keep any parents." I turned and saw the beautiful chrome-haired boy, Lorcan, standing there with a hollowness in his eyes.

"I know how you feel," I responded, rubbing my hand down his hair. "We will watch over you. You will stay in the castle."

A lot of good that would do. I couldn't help but feel guilt and shame. The moment I gave in to my petty weakness and put on that wretched bracelet, I'd caused a chain of events that led to the deaths of all these wonderful people. It made me shiver, thinking that I was their Queen and that I should have done better.

Varjutus was in full crisis, and most of them didn't have homes. The only thing I could do now was try to right the wrong I had caused. It felt as if I had failed these people, and I damn well would walk into the depths of hell to fix it.

CHAPTER
FIFTY-ONE

We counted sixty-seven bodies and held a service for them that night. There were two children amongst the count. I was plagued by Vish's story about his small brothers that were killed. All the grand plans of hiding couldn't save them, and it didn't save all the children of Varjutus either. There was now only Lorcan, Narla, a three-year-old girl, Tess's child on the way, and Oliver, who was Solian. Three children on this entire planet, with one on the way.

The horrifying reality pierced through me with such intensity to the point where I thought I would never recover from this disaster. This Varjun race that I'd come to love like I was born of it had a very high chance of becoming extinct. A small flash of doubt also rushed through me that I could have been the worst thing that ever happened to them. But I was sure, as was everyone else, that mine and Kane's union was right. This was not our doing. It was Orphlam's.

I helped Jonsi burn the bodies until it was as if they never existed at all. Happy and alive yesterday...mere ash today. And for what?

I saw the flames in my mind long after they were gone, and within them, I imagined those poor souls from Solis who had been tortured just as I'd experienced in Kane's memory, except they didn't get to escape. They were made into something else, and I felt their relief for death in the end.

They had begged for death.

The Voidlings begged for death.

The Guardians created a galaxy where its people could not bear the horrors of their lives, and I couldn't imagine anything more tragic to grandpa Amrel's creations. It was time. It was time for me to end this madness.

Later that night, I lay in bed and Kane tried to talk to me. I couldn't bring myself to say anything at all. I still wasn't sure what I was going to do about Orphlam's letter, and I didn't want Kane to influence my decision. Kal came to our room to check on us and I heard them talking from outside.

"How is she?" Kal asked.

"She's in shock. She won't say anything. I've never felt her this distant before. It's like she shut herself off, and even I have a hard time feeling her emotion. It's her first day as Queen. It wasn't a great start."

"Let me know if I can help."

"Thank you, Kal. Keep scouts around Varjutus. Has Jonsi created his defensive poultices?"

"Yes. They're placed around the castle, especially where the people are camped. Those who insist on staying in Baum have protection as well."

"Very good. It's precisely why we needed him to preserve his strength, nobody else has the knowledge or magic to create them, and they deplete a great deal of our resources which is why we didn't have them in place before, but now that we know the kind of enemy we're facing... I'm afraid we have no other choice. I will remain here tonight unless there's another attack. Call if you need me."

"Goodnight, sir."

"Stay safe, Kalmali."

Kane came back in and joined me in bed.

"My love, please talk to me. I'm here to share your burden."

I finally locked eyes with him and tried to force down my guilt and fear. "Just give me a bit." He nodded, softly kissed my lips, and laid down beside me, tucking me into him tightly.

An hour or two later, I looked back at my beautiful husband, naked with blankets covering little of his body. While he was asleep and unaware of my inner turmoil, I realized we were in this together. We had made a promise to each other and even though I wanted nothing more than to protect him and keep him safe, I was no longer willing to make these kinds of decisions without him. We were stronger together and never weaker than when we were apart.

My hand gently touched his face. "Kane, wake my love. I have something I have to tell you."

He was still on high alert, so he woke the second I touched him, and I explained the note I had received and how I had considered for a moment going alone. He sat up and grabbed both of my hands in his. Desperation and relief beamed in his eyes. "Thank you for telling me." He immediately touched his call signs for Merick and Kal. "We'll make a plan together."

They appeared immediately, still fully dressed with an extensive array of weapons on their body, ready for anything. Kane explained our situation and we began discussing a strategy, but after only a few moments, quick little footsteps interrupted us, and Kal had his sword drawn before we even knew who it was.

"Oliver, what are you doing here? Go back to bed." Kane's voice was stern, but his eyes were filled with concern as if he knew there was no getting rid of him now.

Oliver put his little hands on his hips and raised his eyebrows with an adorable display of attitude. "I know what's happening, and you can't do this without me."

Merick rubbed his face impatiently. "You're just a child and this is extremely dangerous. Leave us."

"They can't hurt me if it's just a vision of me." He displayed his abilities by duplicating himself. "You'll need a way for them to not pay attention to you. I'm good at that."

"I don't care. I'm not putting you in harm's way." Kane was in no mood to argue, and Oliver could see it. He waved his hand at us dismissively and walked from the room, but I was fairly certain that wasn't the end of it.

I pleaded with Kane to go in alone first so that Orphlam wouldn't immediately kill Bad, and it took a serious amount of begging for them to agree to it. I didn't trust his word and it was unlikely he would keep him alive anyway, but I was willing to do anything to at least give Bad his best shot.

This was the perfect opportunity to attempt to use the failsafe key to disable the Siphoning Stone. Then we might almost be on an even playing field with Orphlam. Kane would give me no more than ten minutes alone before the three of them showed up, ready for battle.

I gave Kane one last sweet, goodbye kiss before driving to the basement where the *sild gate* was hidden. Orphlam would know I couldn't drive between planets on my own, so we had to make it look authentic.

Once I walked through the gate, I gaped at the state of the private lands. It had been so long since I'd seen it, and Meili and Vish had done an excellent job with the crops. It was a comfort to know there would be some food for the Varjun if we did not make it out alive. I walked through the beautiful Noctis flowers and they were striking under the Solian starlight. This private land had become a living shrine of the hope of Eredet's future. Food for their survival. Beauty and knowledge of their past. Preservations of their history of what had come before to hand down to the children of the future. I wondered if they'd have the chance to read it to know how their ancestors began and the severe cost that was paid so future generations had a chance. I hoped this place would still be standing if we were lucky enough to live through this age.

You will bring upon the end of all ages in Eredet.

Those words caused a shiver through me, but I was done worrying about them. If we died, at least we died together, fighting for what we thought was right.

I made sure there was no ambush outside of the gates before leaving, and I was somewhat surprised by how easy and quiet it was, but they had the upper hand. I supposed they weren't worried about getting what they wanted. And when I arrived at the temple it was even more quiet and empty, only increasing the adrenaline and uncertainty within me. My hands started to shake in anticipation, waiting for Orphlam's horrendous mask to jump out and strike me down at any moment, even though I knew I was more valuable to him alive than dead.

It took a moment for my brain fog of fear to clear and jump back into action, running toward the doors I hadn't been through before to try to find the Siphoning Stone. Behind the soft glow of the heavy doors was a staircase leading to the level below. I descended them as quickly as possible, sweat now beading my brow, my heart racing, and my body shaking, but once I was on the bottom level I began to calm down, feeling immense amounts of magical energy coming from various objects within the first room I came to.

My jaw dropped at the foreign, magical objects that vibrated with energy so profoundly that it was speaking to me on a cellular level. The most surprising object was a massive translucent collection of moving circles in midair, taking up the majority of the room.

It looked like a magical Armillary Sphere, and in the center of it was a large red crystal orb that was similar to the one on the *mikla*.

Light from the spinning circles was directed down into the red stone and I walked closer to it in awe. It was beautiful and unlike anything I'd witnessed before, but as I got closer it filled me with dread. I was stuck in a trance-like state as I heard whispers coming from it and saw flashes of faces within the crystal stone.

Dread slowly seared through me when I realized it was the same feeling I had when I was inside that magical gate at the bottom of the Solian ocean. Was this somehow connected to the hundreds of worlds hidden away in the void shift? People frozen in a pocket of space? Was this what was keeping them trapped in that state of suspended death? My hands reached out to touch it to see if there was a way to deactivate it, but a searing pain caused me to back away. I would have to wait until I knew how to disable it.

Before I looked away, I thought I saw a wolf looking at me from within with a purple mystic-like energy emanating from it. I turned away, not wanting to get too close, and looked at the other two objects. There was a black orb on a stand that made me sick from where I stood, but the triangle-shaped object looked beautiful and felt like a familiar old lifelong friend.

I was drawn to that object, and the smell of it pierced my heart as I knew exactly what it was that it reminded me of. Grandpa Amrel. It smelled of sunlight and clean air. This was it. I didn't know what the other objects were, but this was the Siphoning Stone. This is how they drained our sun's energy.

I ran to it to use the key but dropped it when I heard a scream in the next room over. Not sure if the Guardians were there, I tiptoed as quickly as possible to investigate but was floored by what I saw.

Someone who was supposed to be dead.

Adelram, still alive, rocking back and forth and mumbling nonsense, utterly unaware of my existence.

The sight of him made my blood run cold at what this would mean to my mate. After all this time, his father was still alive. I approached carefully, speaking in a whisper. "We thought you were dead."

It took a moment for him to come out of his delirium and notice me walking toward him.

"Well, I suppose I've finally died and gone to hell."

"I'm so pleased they haven't managed to change how much of an ass you are." I needed to get back to the Siphoning Stone, but I could quickly release him and bring him back to safety with us. My hands gripped the bars to see if there was any give, but a force grabbed onto me, driving me into the cell so that I was now captive with Adelram.

"If you've come to rescue me, you've done a shit job, as usual." *Fuck Fuck. Fuck.*

"I liked you better when you were dead."

"You and me both."

I rubbed my hands over my face in frustration and defeat. It wasn't capture that had me dismayed. I knew what I was agreeing to when I came here. But the fact that I didn't use the failsafe key when I had the chance. "Don't worry. Your son is coming for us. He knows I'm here."

Sighing, I slumped to the ground as far away from Adelram as possible and I noticed him fiddling with a gold chain. His King's Chain. "Kane was sworn in as king. Will you take over again?"

He looked down at his chain, unaware he was fiddling with it, and hid it into his clothes. "Fuck no, I'm more than happy to step down. I did technically die for a moment, triggering the release of my duty as king, but Orphlam was so kind as to heal me back to life. My son can do a much better job."

After a moment or two, he began swaying again, mumbling nonsense under his breath.

"Are you okay? Have they tortured you?"

Adelram stilled and straightened his back, trying to appear sane. "They've tortured me the best way they know how–keeping me alive with not a drop of alcohol since I've been here."

It all became clear. There was no way for him to mute the raving effects of hundreds of thousands of memories in his head.

"Why—why would you come when you know it's a trap."

I shot up from the cold, dirty ground and ran to the bars. "Bad! What have they done to you?" He was bruised and bloody like he'd been beaten. "Did you think I would leave you on your own?"

"I was counting on that." Orphlam's voice was a piercing sickness to my ears. My heart sank, but I was prepared for this moment. He waved his hand, and we were all transported to the top floor. The first thing entering my line of sight was the horrid depiction of the Great War filled with death and destruction, but a rush of warm, loving energy enveloped me and I knew Kane had made it here. I couldn't see him, so he was probably hiding with Kal and Merick, waiting for their moment to attack. And sure enough, Kane's voice was a sweet song in my head. *We're here, my Star. Stay strong.*

Go and find the Siphoning Stone and bring it up here. It's down on the lower floor, the first room on the left. It's a smooth triangle stone.

He was already on the move, as he responded. *We will not fail you.*

Oh, and one more thing. Your father is alive. I could feel the profound impact those few little words had on him and how hard he was trying to keep it together. He stayed silent, focused on the task at hand.

I had to keep Orphlam's attention to give them a few moments to find it. I wasn't sure Kane would feel its presence as I did.

"I know it's too late for me, but spare Bad, Adelram, and everyone else in Eredet, and I will stay with you without a fight."

"As we said, the cook is an incentive, and we intend to keep him that way. We offered no false pretenses."

Orphlam produced a knife and threw it into Bad's gut. He screamed in pain and fell to the ground as Adelram was put into some kind of invisible shackles around his wrists, likely so he couldn't use magic.

I ran to Bad's side, but Orphlam stopped me with his magic and turned me around.

"You do as I ask, and we can make sure he's healed." He led me to a chair facing Bad, so I could watch every moment of his suffering. "Now, take a seat."

Through gritted teeth, I silently cried and sat in the chair, listening to Bad's whimpers and watching the pool of blood growing around him.

"First, we want to take some of your blood so we can open the *mikla*. We also need to take most of your energy, which will, unfortunately, render you a mortal. We'll keep you in our dungeons until we do have the box in case there's something else we require from you. Once we have everything we came here for, you'll have the highest honor of becoming one of our new creations you call the *Halogi*. You can rule with us with unlimited possibilities and nothing holding you back. You've used our magic before, and I witnessed the vast potential you have."

He spoke with such passion. It made me sick. How could anyone be this delusional?

"I've been waiting *so long* for this day and even my abundant patience was beginning to wear thin. When you put on that bracelet, I knew Amrel was dead and at first, I thought it was the end of my mission, but then I saw your energy signature and the answers in your power. My experiments had failed for thousands of years because I needed *you*. With just a drop of your power, my test subjects were able to continuously heal to accommodate the power within them so they could at least survive soul transference and magical enhancement. I have even successfully put three souls into one body for tremendous magical ability."

Oh God, I was going to be sick.

"I have over a thousand of them from just a speck of your energy. Think of what I could do with the rest of it."

"Why," I whispered. "Just tell me why. Do you think these corrupted beings and all this power will make you happy?"

"It's not about my happiness. It's about saving my people from extinction and regaining our immortality. I realized long ago the answer was in Creation, and this was the only place to get what I needed. I needed the power of The Creator."

"Do you really think those *Halogi* are going to replace your people? I'd hardly call their soul transference a success."

"Oh, you haven't seen anything yet. These are my friends, transferred into their new bodies," he said, outstretching his hands.

I gasped as I saw Meglyn, the Solian Noble, and Oliver's adoptive parents looking just as they usually did, unharmed.

"Their transference was a huge success, and now we know we can go back to our home and save our people who deserve it. We just need enough power to do it."

"You've been gone for thousands of years. Surely, if your people were near extinction, they're all gone now."

"Not so. You know about the other worlds, don't you? You know that we've frozen them into a void. The worlds that are worthy will be taken out. Those that are not will be incinerated."

My nausea was unbearable, but this time, with my Nebula Diamond, it had little to do with Orphlam's dark magic.

Cyra, are you sure it's in this room? We cannot find it.

Shit. Had Orphlam hidden it before bringing me up here? *It was. Keep looking. I'll try to distract him.*

Call for me if you're in danger. Your life is more important than disabling the Stone tonight.

Orphlam spoke again, breaking my connection to Kane.

"If you'd please," Orphlam motioned to two of the robed Guardians. For the first time since I'd arrived in Eredet, they lowered their hoods, and the sight of their faces made me nauseous.

"Oh, I see you know my two best and brightest. The other two are a façade," he said, waving his hands so the last two Guardians disappeared.

"Bastards. How could you offer your son to die?" I screamed in utter repugnance. "Do you even know what you've done to him?"

It was Maxilen and Lara Beaurdlaux, Theo's heartless parents. The ones who made him into the broken demon he was now.

My rage was boiling at an all-time high. So much so that I began to lose control, and I burst into a fiery inferno. I seethed in the flames, letting it consume me and everything in my close vicinity.

"Let it burn into your essence." Orphlam was exultant, never closer to achieving his purpose. "Allow the fire to consume you, body and soul. You have the power to convert your energy into something boundless, something more powerful. You can teach these parents a lesson and show them what power truly looks like. That's all they've ever wanted, just a taste of the real thing. The real power that you possess in abundance. I wouldn't even need your blood if you worked with me. I've said it once before, and I'll say it again. You and I could do immeasurable things together. You just need…to give…in…"

I was utterly overcome, but I had prepared for this moment. I was back in the *Warrior's Sanna*, remembering how much I desperately wanted to give in and forget my troubles.

My flames erupted even higher, and I glared at Maxilen and Lara, and they jumped back in fear. I raised my hands and blasted fire in their direction, causing them to scream and cower, but Orphlam shielded them as he laughed with abandon.

"Excellent, Cyra. I'll give you the chance to kill anyone you like, but these two have been valuable to me."

I looked into Orphlam's eye slits and snuffed out my flame, sweat dripping down my face and neck.

"I will *never* work with you. You will have to pry it from me."

Orphlam sighed, clearly disappointed. "Very well. Proceed, Lara."

She forcefully stuck the needle in my arm, and I yelped in pain. She took a few vials, and I panicked about what else they could do with my blood and magic.

"How do you sleep at night?" I whispered to her.

"You'd never understand," she said, unable to look me in the eye.

"Well, I suppose there's something we can agree on."

"Cyra...I love you." I heard Bad whisper. He was fading fast. He had lost too much blood.

"Please, help him! I'm doing what you ask, help him!"

They all ignored me, and I watched as Bad stopped moving. I started to shake with rage, and my eyes silvered over. He was very near death. Instinctively I poured my healing energy toward him and was relieved when it started effectively repairing his wounds, even with our distance.

"*Don't get up. Pretend to be dead,*" I said in his head. I didn't even know I could do that but was thankful when he didn't move.

"Fascinating! What did you just do?" Orphlam asked, his creepy mask inches from my face.

Lara came back toward me with a stone and put it to my chest. Theo appeared by my side and started running his hands through my hair.

My eyes locked with his, and I tried to reason with him through his emotional gift. "Please don't..."

I screamed as I felt my energy being ripped away and fought like hell to stop it. It slowed the draining down, but I could not completely prevent it. It felt like pieces of my soul were being ripped from my body, like my own power was trying as hard as it could not to be parted from me. I was certain tiny needles were stabbing at every tendon and tissue in my body, trying to disassemble me.

"She is strong," Maxilen said.

To my relief, Kane, Merick, and Kal appeared in the temple.

We have it.

Oliver materialized a moment later, causing Kane to squint his eyes at him disapprovingly but didn't say a word. Kane looked at his father, and his lip quivered for the briefest moment. Adelram fell to his knees, still weak and overwhelmed with seeing his son again.

"Cyra, I thought I said no guests," Orphlam said, his eyes flashing with light.

I shrugged and nodded my head toward Bad. "You don't follow the rules. Why should I?"

In the background, Oliver kept duplicating bodies until there were about twenty of him and counting. He then started to duplicate me as well, and Kane yelled for me before throwing me the Siphoning Stone.

I went invisible and ran to a safe corner, removing the failsafe key from my pocket, and once it actually touched the stone, the small opening finally revealed itself.

As quickly as possible, I inserted the key and twisted as the hum of the stone sputtered out. A piercing scream emerged from Orphlam, and the building shook as the connection to our sun's energy was broken and the stone burst into a thousand pieces, shards of it cutting my face. For a moment, I stood as utter relief washed over me, a small victory that we desperately needed, and I swore I could feel some tether that was tied to me snap and break away.

I turned to join the fight. Oliver was magically throwing

daggers into Orphlam, which appeared to be actually injuring him. Adelram was freed from his binds, and he and Kane were also attacking Orphlam. Even with the three of them, subduing him was still a struggle.

Theo's parents were dead, and Kal and Merick were fighting him.

We can't kill them, but maybe we can trap them as Oliver did to you during our lesson together on Solis.

Let's try it, he agreed.

But before we got the chance to start, a pop sounded, and the new arrival dumbfounded me. Someone I wasn't sure I would ever see again.

The Bellum Princess, Kaia Gessaine.

Theo had been knocked to the ground by Merick while invisible. She ran to Theo with a large crystal and held it to his head, causing him to go unconscious.

Adelram and Oliver were still keeping Orphlam at bay, and Kaia quickly approached us. "What are you waiting for?"

We had no time to react to her sudden appearance. The enemy of my enemy was my friend, and we were desperate to end this.

Kane and I clasped hands and joined energies through our *imana* bond. We both used my second sight to see Orphlam's energy and gasped in utter shock.

"He's already half-dead," Kane exclaimed. His life force energy was a swirling black, struggling to sustain him. A constant feed of external golden energy seemed to be the only thing keeping him alive, but I could feel that his power was much lessened now.

We threw him toward the wall so he was mid-air, and Kal took his largest sword and speared him to the wall so he was stuck in place. Even impaled and with less power, he still fought against us with everything he had.

We began to form an energetic wall around him, but it sputtered against our attempts as Orphlam's hands flew out before him, attacking our wall. Merick, Kal, and Adelram joined in our efforts, and it slowly broke through, gaining momentum. When we started to fatigue, Kaia withdrew another crystal and handed it to me. Undoubtedly another magical trinket from one of their meiges.

"Here, use this."

When I grabbed it, a massive pulse of energy rushed through me, and it was enough to secure the protective wall around Orphlam so he would be contained for a while.

Bad hobbled slowly to my side, holding his injury as if he was still in pain. He whistled, and Tulah appeared on his shoulder.

"Do me a favor, my darling, and blind that scum."

She flew over him and let out some kind of dust over the Orphlam that trickled into our translucent wall.

"Do you think you can keep me here? It's only a matter of time before I break free, even after disabling the Siphoning Stone. I have plenty more energy hidden where you won't be able to find it."

His voice turned into muffled background noise. I couldn't give less of a shit what he had to say because it was over. We had survived this night and had gained a vital advantage in this fight. Sure, the wall wouldn't keep him forever, but it would allow us to safely retreat and live to fight another day with his power greatly diminished.

I turned away from him, ready to leave, but stopped short at the sight of Kaia next to an unconscious Theo.

"My father has heard of Theo's corruption. He tasked me to come here and bring him back to The Void to try to influence him to our side while he's still in a volatile and influenceable state. He thinks he'll be a valuable and powerful ally."

"Do you think we'll just let you take him?" I folded my arms tightly before me, readying myself mentally for another fight, even though I had no idea what we would do with Theo.

"Actually, I do."

Merick and Kal stalked toward her, weapons at the ready. She was unfazed by their intensity, like fear was the last thing on her mind. "I wouldn't do that if I were you."

Kane took a step toward her, his eyes scanning her with curiosity. "And why is that?"

"Because I want to help you get the *mikla* back."

ACKNOWLEDGMENTS

A huge thank you to my family, who have supported me on this crazy journey even though I have no idea what I'm doing.

Thank you to my husband, who moves heaven and earth to ensure I have everything I need.

And thank you, dear reader, for sticking with me through this intense voyage. I appreciate you all.

ALSO BY CLARE ARCHER

The Secrets of the Sun Series

The Divine Oblivion - The Secrets of the Sun Book 1

The Divine Union - The Secrets of the Sun Book 2

Monstrous Matings Series

The Orc's Treasure - Monstrous Matings Book 1

The Dragon's Heart - Monstrous Matings Book 2 - Coming soon!

Follow my author page on Amazon for notifications on new releases!

Amazon Author Page

Milton Keynes UK
Ingram Content Group UK Ltd.
UKHW012026120124
435957UK00015B/179/J

9 798987 162835